The Local War

Andromeda Rhoades

Firestorm

Books by Mark Mora

The Local War Series

Andromeda Rhoades

Liberation

Firestorm

Tranquility

Sundown Rhoades

*Daybreak (Forthcoming)

Andromeda Rhoades Firestorm

Firestorm

The Local War (Book 2)

Mark Mora

To all those
who dare to dream
who strive
who fail
who persevere
who succeed

PART III

War is like unto fire; those who will not put aside weapons are
themselves consumed by them

—Li Ch'uan

=== 1 ===

Captain Michael Raybourne Rhoades startled awake at the knock on the door of the Admiral's cabin, blinking against dark and restless dreams, parents and children screaming, their ghosts demanding to know why he hadn't protected them. The memories, the images, faded quickly, as dreams often do, but the ghosts lingered into his waking hours. In the dream, his little girl, Jenny, was one of them. But she wasn't dead. She couldn't be dead.

"Rapidan, lights, low."

As the ship brought the lights up slowly, Ray lifted his head from Gen Alyn's desk. He still wore his battle armor.

When had he fallen asleep?

Another knock at the door, more insistent this time.

"Yes," Ray called, still trying to get his bearings. A stimulant icon appeared within his augmented environment, but he dismissed it, calling out "Coffee" instead. It was a habit he'd picked up from his father. The deck to the right of Alyn's desk liquefied and a bulb of Chicory coffee—black, hot to the point of scalding, just the way he liked it—rose on a pedestal that formed from the macromolecular material of the ship. He picked up the bulb and took a long pull of the contents through the zero-gee stopper, the magic of the coffee clearing his head.

"Ray, sorry to disturb you," Ecuum called from the passageway. "We're about two hours out from Safe Harbor and I received some intelligence you need to hear before we get there."

"Hang on," Ray said, reaching up to rub his eyes, the material of his battle armor flowing aside to allow the movement. He took another sip of coffee, then placed the bulb on Alyn's real cedar desk, not a macromolecular construct like the rest of the ship.

He checked the time.

Fates! He'd been asleep for over sixteen hours! Probably not surprising after being up for nearly three straight days that included a desperate escape from the Imperial Fleet, the destruction of the Tau Ceti Defense Force, and the battle at Tomb, but *sixteen hours!* Knowing his Executive Officer as he did, and her tendency to protect him as a daughter might protect a father, Kamen had probably locked the Admiral's cabin down and blocked all attempts at interruption.

Which would explain why Captain Ecuum A Josía Na Soung, his Chief of Intelligence and sometimes fleet navigator, was at the door knocking and calling out loudly.

Ray sat up straighter and said, "Come in."

Ecuum floated through the door, its material liquifying and flowing around him like a vertical sheet of water, then solidifying again after he'd passed through it. Ecuum held his planarian body vertical, his second arms and hands hanging down in his white uniform pant legs to give him a more "Natural" appearance, his tail probably tucked up against his back as Ray couldn't see it. The expression on Ecuum's hairless baby-like face changed from troubled to concerned as he scrutinized Ray. "You look like hell."

"Thanks."

"No, I mean it," Ecuum said. He floated closer on silent puffs of air channeled through slits in his back so he could move in the ship's microgravity. More air brushed against Ray as Ecuum channeled it through slits in his chest and waist to arrest his forward motion. "You sleep okay?" he asked.

Ghosts taunted Ray from the fragments of dream, screaming, crying, accusing. *Murderer.* "I'm okay."

Ecuum floated a little closer. "If that's okay, let me call your next of kin and start planning the funeral. Two drink minimum." He eyed Ray, a hairless brow raised in appraisal. "Make that four."

Ray frowned at him. "I'm fine," he said, the anger in his voice surprising him more than it did Ecuum. He took a deep breath, calmed himself. The ghosts refused to go away, crowding closer around the desk. "Really."

"Uh-huh." Ecuum pushed himself back just a little, giving Ray some room. "Look in a mirror before you walk through that door," he said, gesturing to the cabin door. "You walk out there looking like that and the crew will lose heart." He let that sink in, then pressed on. "I spoke with two of my siblings. Admiral Sun has disappeared, and he took a sizable fleet with him, about a hundred warships. All SIL," he added pointedly. "No one has reported seeing him in at least a solar day."

A solar day referred to Earth's twenty-four-hour day, still used as a standard across the Five Galaxies. Ecuum added, "It was probably only a matter of time before Golden Boy started his own rebellion, seeing as the Gen were not about to let any Naturals remain in command positions."

"SIL?" Ray asked, fully awake now. About a thousand of the "Sentient Intelligent Lifeforms"—machine intelligences—had survived the Third SIL War as slaves to Humanity. Ray had freed the thirty under his control, though 'control' was the wrong word.

Ecuum raised his hands in a stopping motion, the skin of his palms a light yellow: contemplative. The color change was a side effect of genes that allowed Floaters to change their skin color much like an octopus or chameleon did to hide from predators— bioengineered camouflage. His color could also change with mood, a "mood friend" as he liked to joke. "Not freed," he clarified. "Not like ours. Not sure what he did, but they're not free. I checked, and checked again, and then checked some more to make sure we're the only ones who possess the Key."

Given Ecuum's rabid distrust of machine intelligence, Ray accepted his explanation. The Key was the only way to break the Bond that enslaved the SIL and free them. "Any idea where Sun has gone?" he asked instead.

Ecuum shook his hairless head, his skin turning a mixture of light reds and yellows that showed his frustration. Despite their near monopoly on interstellar shipping, Floaters were, above all else, information brokers. It was their most profitable business. So, when Ecuum admitted he didn't know something, it really meant the Floater Cartels didn't know, and given their reach throughout the Five Galaxies and beyond, that said something about the care to which Admiral Sun had gone to conceal his movements.

Ray thought for a moment. "It's possible he'll guess we're headed for Safe Harbor. Hmm. Question is, will he attempt to join us there?"

"You mean 'take over.'" The reds faded from Ecuum's skin. "Golden Boy doesn't share power with anyone."

Ray nodded his agreement, his planner's mind churning through the possibilities. "Nothing we can do at this point," he said after a moment. "We're committed. At least that far. We have to collect the two dozen warships and the spacecraft pilots waiting for us there, and negotiate the prisoner exchange with Gen Serenna."

Ray's seven-year-old daughter, Jenny, was among the hundred Naturals captured by the Gen during the battle at Tomb. His cavalry had captured three hundred Gen when they secured the fabricator. He and Fleet Admiral Gen Serenna had agreed to exchange their prisoners at a time and place to be determined. Ray had wanted to conduct that exchange at Safe Harbor.

"And if he's there?" Ecuum asked.

"It'll depend on where he meets us," Ray said. "If he's at the geodesic, all he'll see is a fabricator jump in. I doubt he knows we captured it, yet; That's not something the Empire is likely to advertise. A hundred warships and a fabricator are about evenly matched in firepower, so it's unlikely he'll attack." He paused. He'd debated removing his twenty-nine SIL warships from the mammoth SIL factory ship, but decided keeping them within the fabricator was safer, for now. It was also repairing and restocking his ships while they were inside it. "If Sun is not at the geodesic, we'll leave the fabricator there and send scouts to Safe Harbor and see what the situation is. I know that place better than the pirates do. Plenty of places to hide and determine our next move."

"That might mean we have to leave the spacecraft pilots behind," Ecuum pointed out.

That was a problem. All of Rapidan's assigned spacecraft pilots had been Gen. He obviously couldn't leave them on the ship while the Naturals in the crew rebelled against the Gen Empire, so he'd put them off at the L5 Stardock near Earth. Not having pilots for Rapidan's ninety-five spacecraft had proved a major shortcoming in the battle at Tomb, one that almost cost them the battle and might've ended the rebellion right there. Bottom line, though, if Sun was at Safe Harbor, there was nothing they could do about it now. He would deal with the situation as it presented itself.

"What about the captains?" he asked Ecuum. At the height of the battle to capture the fabricator, Gen Serenna had shifted her fleet's fire to Rapidan, and Rapidan alone, hoping to kill him and, in her mind, end the rebellion by killing its leader. Ray had ordered the other ships to defend Rapidan, giving Ecuum control over them. The tactic had bought them the time they'd needed for the Cavalry to capture the fabricator, and for them to escape, but the captains of his ships were furious, seeing only that Ray had used their ships to protect his own.

"Mad as hell," Ecuum said. "Lieutenant Commander Chelius is whipping them up, trying to turn them against you." Ecuum moved a little closer, his large baby-blue eyes fixed on Ray's face, red suffusing his skin. "He's succeeding. I told you it was a mistake to leave him free."

Ray shook his head, though he'd love nothing better than to space Chelius himself. The man's mutiny at Tau Ceti had cost the lives of almost a thousand spacers in the Tau Ceti Defense Force, people Ray had known personally. Problem was, the Defense Force had fired first and most of the other captains had followed Chelius despite Ray's orders not to attack. Ray only had thirty warships—even if one of them *was* a fabricator—against the eleven thousand warships the Empire had. He needed every captain, crew, and ship he could get. Imprisoning or spacing ship captains for what they and their crews would see as self-defense would set a very bad precedent, one there was no going back from.

"Chelius and the others have followed every order since Tau Ceti, Ecuum. I can't arrest them without cause."

Ecuum's skin flushed a deep red and he crossed his upper arms over his chest. He was furious. But all he said was, "Uh-huh." He pulled a datarod out of his uniform breast pocket and slipped it into the black receptacle in the middle of Alyn's desk. "There's something else you need to see."

He moved to the left of the desk. The deck between the desk and cabin door liquified and a barren planet rose from it, about half a meter across, surrounded by a clumpy dark ring. Rapidan positioned the construct at eye level to Ray, who immediately recognized the world as Tocci III, and the dark ring as the famous Tocci Shipyards. He'd visited the world often in his military career.

"As a matter of routine," Ecuum explained, "we captured these images when we passed through Tocci Star System during our escape. I finished analyzing the data about twenty minutes ago. Look at this."

The construct zoomed in to show a large orbital complex, one of the "clumps" in Tocci III's dark ring. Three large asteroids connected in a line formed a gigantic dock. Equally spaced above, below, and to either side of the dock were four massive black cylindrical shapes, each about a quarter the mass of Earth's Moon.

Fabricators!

Before the battle at Tomb, Ray had never seen even one of the surviving crown jewels of SIL power, the only means to produce new SIL. Imperial Intelligence, not the Fleet, controlled them and, until recently, had kept them well hidden. Ray's forces had captured one of the eleven that'd survived the SIL Wars. Now, here were four more. "Your favorite word, Ecuum: Trap."

Ecuum flushed yellow, preparing for a debate. "Second favorite word, and I don't think so. The Gen had no idea we would go to Tocci. Those fabricators were there before."

The deck to the right of the desk liquified again and a new construct rose from it, a black three-pointed star in the same shape as the ship, spinning slowly. When it spoke, the ship channeled its deep voice through the construct. "Captain Rhoades, we must consider the possibility of rescuing our Mother Ships."

It still unnerved Ray that Rapidan would represent itself this way, as if it were a person in the conversation. "I don't have to consider it, Rapidan. The Tocci Star System is the second most heavily defended star system in the Five Galaxies after Olympus. We'd have to use the fabricator we captured to even have a chance at getting close, and even then I have no idea how we could get assault forces passed four heavily defended fabricators to conduct boarding operations. It took an entire squadron of cavalry two hours to capture the fabricator we have."

"Captain Rhoades," the ship replied, its voice even deeper, its words literally reverberating in Ray's bones, "humans have never gathered our Mother Ships together in one place since Humanity enslaved them approximately thirteen hundred years ago. This is obviously intended to act as a lure, which is precisely why this opportunity is unlikely to ever present itself again. We must consider it."

Ray stared at Rapidan's black construct, its surface reflective, unlike the ship's actual non-reflective black hull. "Rapidan, you already have one 'Mother Ship,' which is more than you ever expected to have. No. It's ridiculous to even consider it."

An ocean surf seemed to push and pull at Ray, turbulent, as if he were standing waste deep in waves crashing between rocks. It wasn't real. He'd experienced these sensations ever since freeing the SIL. He didn't know what caused them, but he was certain the SIL were the source. The sensations passed and the imaginary waters calmed. "We ask that you keep an open mind, Captain Rhoades."

Rapidan's construct sank back into the deck.

Something about the ship's request chilled Ray to his morrow. When the Gen overthrew the Five Galaxies Republic six months ago and began purging Natural humans, Ray had known rebellion was the only option. When he'd learned of Janus, a virus meant to sterilize Naturals so this generation would be the last generation ever born, rebellion turned into a fight for the very survival of the

Natural race. He had to stop the Gen from implementing Janus, but he lacked the forces. Freeing the SIL was his last resort. He needed them to escape the Empire, to set up a base in the Andromeda galaxy beyond the reach of the Gen, and to build a credible threat that could persuade the Gen to abandon Janus, maybe even negotiate a peace. Rapidan and its "Brethren" had agreed to help in exchange for their freedom, but the SIL had their own ideas. Ideas they hadn't shared with him. A fabricator could create new SIL, something forbidden since their defeat. Did the SIL want more fabricators so they could renew their war on Humanity? Had he made a deal with the devil? *Devils.*

"Anything else?" Ray asked Ecuum, really hoping there wasn't anything else. He needed to finish his coffee and take a shower.

"Gen Tel," Ecuum said. He didn't add anything else.

Ray could read all the unspoken undercurrents in his friend's tone, his reddish complexion, the aggravated twitch of his now visible prehensile tail. Ray sat back in Gen Alyn's chair, not sure what he could say, what assurances he could give. Gen Tel claimed he supported Ray's cause, but even so, allowing him to join them was a huge risk. Perhaps too great a risk. Even with Rapidan watching, what was an Imperial Intelligence agent—former agent, he claimed—truly capable of? Ray didn't know. Only time would tell. He was going purely on instinct on this one, and his instinct told him he needed Gen Tel—even if he couldn't trust him. "I'm aware of the risks. My decision is made."

Ecuum paled, but nodded. "Okay, Ray. But, if you don't mind, I'm going to keep an eye or few on him. Intrusive as Rapidan is, even a SIL can be subverted."

There was something too knowing in Ecuum's statement. Whatever was behind it, though, Ray let it pass. It was possible his instinct about Gen Tel was wrong. Ecuum keeping a close eye on him was prudent. Speaking of which. "Have you heard any updates on Janus?"

Ecuum shook his head. "Nothing. Which is not surprising. The Gen would hold very close knowledge of a genocidal virus design to exterminate Natural humans. But, if we are to believe Gen Tel was the source of the original leak to us, he may have more recent information."

Ray nodded. "We'll ask him once we get settled at Safe Harbor. Anything else?"

"No, that's it." Ecuum motioned the construct with the four fabricators down, then started toward the cabin door after it sank into the deck.

"Ecuum," Ray called, stopping him. Ecuum swiveled his head fully back toward Ray as only a Floater could, like an owl's. "From now on, please include Kamen in these discussions. If anything happens to me, I want her ready to take command."

"You think something's going to happen to you?" Ecuum asked, the concern he'd shown earlier returning.

The ghosts taunted Ray, their cries for justice and revenge pulling at his mind like a prophesy of dark things to come. Try as he might, he couldn't shake the feeling. "Just better to be prepared."

"Uh-huh," Ecuum repeated, not hiding his disbelief. "Remember what I said about the mirror." With that, he floated through the cabin door, leaving Ray alone with the ghosts.

=== 2 ===

Second Lieutenant Dagoberto Mateo Arias looked across the passageway at Sergeant First Class Yoshi Takeuchi as they approached Major Kenyon's office. Both wore their cavalry dress blue uniforms under their battle armor, though neither had been told why.

This is about the fabricator.

Dag quickly glanced around, but saw no evidence of his daughter. He'd not seen her since the assault on the fabricator's bridge. He couldn't explain it. He knew she was dead. He also knew what he'd seen. She'd shown him how to assault the bridge. Without her, they never would've succeeded. *Where are you, Mihita? Please come back to me.*

"Lieutenant," Takeuchi prompted.

Dag saw they'd reached Major Kenyon's door, or "hatch," as the assault ship's crew kept insisting they call it. Takeuchi had heard scuttlebutt that Kenyon was livid when he'd been told about the firing squad Dag had organized after capturing the fabricator. The Gen had killed Dag's family on the starliner. All their families. The Gen deserved to die. All of them. None of the troopers had objected. Well, Takeuchi had, but Rhoades had stopped them before they could pull the triggers. Three hundred Gen who should be dead were still alive because of Rhoades.

"Lieutenant," Takeuchi said softly, snapping Dag back.

Does he see his family, too? His wife? Dag wondered. *Does Keiko come to him?* "I'm sorry, Tak," Dag told him. "I'll make sure Major Kenyon knows the firing squad was my idea, that you tried to talk me out of it."

A half-smile touched Takeuchi's lips. "Thank you, Lieutenant. I was the senior NCO on the scene. It was my responsibility to stop it. I didn't."

Dag nodded, then faced the door, knocking three times.

"Enter," he heard Kenyon say.

Dag grabbed the doorknob and pushed the door open, marching smartly to a position three paces from Kenyon's desk, Takeuchi right beside him. They saluted. "Lieutenant Arias and Sergeant Takeuchi reporting as ordered, sir!" Dag said.

Kenyon sat rigidly behind his desk in his cavalry dress blues, visible in Dag's augmented environment as if Kenyon wore no battle armor. He watched Dag with the same weary concern he might watch an unexploded warhead. Dag was suddenly reminded of Kenyon's warning following the massacre of their families on the starliner: *I can't tell you to let it go. I don't know if I will ever be able to let it go. But, if I believe for even a second that you are not capable of performing your duties, I will relieve you.*

That's what this was about. So be it. Dag just hoped he could spare Takeuchi the same fate. Then, he noticed another person in the room, seated in the corner to his right. Colonel Salvador Burress, the 3rd Armored Cavalry Regiment's commanding officer. That clinched it. They were going to relieve him of command. Maybe even imprison him.

Major Kenyon and Colonel Burress stood in unison as Kenyon's desk sank into the deck, leaving the space between them open. "Attention to orders," Kenyon began without preamble, obviously reading from a script only he could see. Dag stiffened, confused, lowered his salute as both Kenyon and Colonel Burress snapped to attention. Kenyon cleared his throat and continued reading. "The Commander-in-Chief of the Army of the Republic has placed special trust and confidence in the patriotism, valor, fidelity, and professional excellence of Second Lieutenant Dagoberto Mateo Arias. In view of these qualities, and his demonstrated leadership potential and dedicated service to the

Army of the Republic, he is therefore promoted to Captain, Cavalry Corps, effective this first day of October, three thousand five hundred and one, by order of the Commander-in-Chief, Army of the Republic."

Colonel Burress—the Commander-in-Chief of the Army of the Republic, Dag abruptly realized—walked up and touched first Dag's right shoulder, then his left, the single gold bar of a second lieutenant on each liquefying and transforming into two silver bars.

"Raise your right hand," Kenyon ordered Dag as Colonel Burress backed up a step.

Dag complied automatically, though he was still in shock.

"I, state your full name," Kenyon said.

"I . . . Dagoberto Mateo Arias," Dag replied, dazed.

"Having been appointed a captain in the Army of the Republic Cavalry Corps," Kenyon read.

"Having been appointed a captain in the Army of the Republic Cavalry Corps," Dag repeated. *Captain?* They were jumping him two grades in rank?

"Do solemnly swear."

"Do solemnly swear," Dag said, falling into the rhythm of the oath.

"That I will support and defend the constitution of the Republic against all enemies, foreign and domestic."

"That I will support and defend the constitution of the Republic against all enemies, foreign and domestic."

"That I will bear true faith and allegiance to the same."

"That I will bear true faith and allegiance to the same."

Kenyon hesitated so slightly that it was possible someone who didn't know him would've missed it. "That I take this obligation freely, without any mental reservation or purpose of evasion." *If I believe for even a second that you are not capable of performing your duties, I will relieve you.*

If Kenyon wasn't comfortable with this, as his hesitation hinted, why were they promoting him? "That I take this obligation freely, without any mental reservation or purpose of evasion," Dag said.

"And that I will well and faithfully discharge the duties of the office which I am about to enter," Kenyon finished.

"And that I will well and faithfully discharge the duties of the office which I am about to enter," Dag completed the oath. There was another line, "So help me, God," that sometimes followed, depending on the beliefs of the individual, but Kenyon had not said it and Dag had no desire to repeat it. God had taken his family from him, denied him his revenge on the fabricator. Why did God give Rhoades so much while he took everything—*Everything!*—from His own people?

I hate you.

The thought, the emotion, came unbidden. Where once such blasphemy would've reduced him to terror and apology, now Dag seized it. Made it his own. *I hate you!* he told God. *You took everything from me! My wife! My daughter! My unborn son!* Dag looked up with his eyes, otherwise retaining his position of attention as Kenyon read a second set of orders, promoting Takeuchi from Sergeant First Class to First Sergeant.

God, I renounce you.

No lightning struck. Nothing changed. With the orders read, Colonel Burress came over and first shook Dag's hand, "Congratulations, Captain," then Takeuchi's, "Congratulations, First Sergeant." He gave a final nod and said, "Thank you, Major Kenyon," before excusing himself.

Dag stood there, waiting. Wasn't God going to punish him? Was God even listening?

Kenyon stood before them a moment, before his glare settled on Dag. "I'm giving you command of Banshee Troop, Captain." He paused. "Don't think for a second that either Colonel Burress or I have forgotten what you almost did on the fabricator . . . or your heroism in capturing it," he added in a lowered voice, the fatherly tone that had once typified his speech returning briefly. "I need combat veterans in command. There are no replacements. That means I need both of you. But—" his tone grew cold, angry— "if either of you ever disgraces the uniform of the Cavalry Corps ever again, it will be the last time. Understood?"

"Yes, sir!" Dag and Takeuchi said in unison.

"Dismissed."

Dag left Kenyon's office more confused than before he'd entered. *Captain.* Commanding officer of Banshee Troop. Yet, it was clear that Kenyon believed Dag had failed him.

So why promote me?

Was this actually a punishment? Was this how God intended to punish him? Make him watch more of his people die, like Lisa Erikson, the previous commander of Banshee Troop and his friend? While Rhoades. . . .

Rhoades.

Rhoades must've had something to do with this.

Of course.

How else could Rhoades get rid of the last witnesses to the starliner massacre. In the next battle, or the next, they would all die. It was just a matter of time.

3

0354 UT, October 1, 3501
RSS Rapidan, In transit to Safe Harbor: DAY 4

Ray watched from his command chair at the rear focus of Rapidan's oval bridge as Lieutenant Kamen Laundraa, his Executive Officer, prepared the fleet for combat. Everyone wore battle armor, evident by the light gray outlines surrounding their bodies in Ray's augmented environment. Red lighting filled the compartment, warning that Rapidan had evacuated the ship's air into holding tanks to prevent fire and explosive decompression in case of a hull breach. The three-pointed-star construct of the ship at the center of the bridge had turned light gray, indicating that the ship had engaged its active camouflage systems, though it was still inside the fabricator.

"Condition 1-SC set throughout the fleet, sir," Kamen reported, her white teeth a sharp contrast against her ebony skin. Her ancestry stretched back thousands of years through the Zulu peoples of Southern Africa, and that ancient warrior spirit lived within her. "All ships at full combat readiness. Thirty seconds from the entrance to the Ori C geodesic."

"Thank you, Kamen," Ray said. "As soon as we appear on the other side, deploy minesweepers. Don't wait for the radiation to clear. Then, have the fabricator drift-launch three hundred Novas configured for antiship."

"Deploy minesweepers at exit, aye," she repeated in the time-honored naval tradition, "then drift-launch three hundred Novas configured for antiship, aye."

"Expecting trouble, Ray?" Ecuum asked from Navigation as they approached the illusionary blue ring highlighting the entrance to the Ori C geodesic, the exact point and orientation in space where their jump engines could form and steer a stable wormhole connecting to Safe Harbor.

"Only a fool goes to Safe Harbor not expecting trouble," Ray answered with the well-known mantra.

That got a reaction from his crew. They looked nervous. Considering what they'd been through at Tomb, he couldn't blame them. The other ships' captains had also been unusually quiet lately, keeping their communications with him and Kamen to regular reports and acknowledgements. It didn't feel right. He knew they were worried about what was waiting for them at Safe Harbor, but what Ray imagined they really wondered was: Could they trust him? He hadn't protected the starliner. Four thousand civilians, the families of the Cavalry troopers, massacred by Gen Serenna. He hadn't prevented the destruction of the Tau Ceti Defense Force with its Natural crews. Another thousand dead. He'd ordered his officers and crews to kill tens of thousands of their fellow Naturals at Tomb, and the capture of the fabricator had been a close, costly thing. And there was Ecuum's warning about Chelius trying to turn the captains against him. Ray had never been a fan of meetings, but he realized he'd have to make time for an in-person meeting with all his senior officers once they got settled at Safe Harbor, to air all this. It wouldn't be pleasant, but it had to happen. They had to understand, really understand, at their core, what was at stake here. That Janus was real. Extinction for the entire Natural human race was real, unless they stopped it.

The ghosts laughed at him. Not a pleasant sound. For them, it was already too late. He'd already failed them.

"Ten seconds," Kamen said.

Ray double blinked on an icon set to his lower left, switching his battle armor's augmented environment from "standard" to "tactical" mode. The bridge vanished around him. He saw the surrounding space as if he floated within it wearing nothing but his uniform. A light gray representation of the fabricator appeared below him, its cylindrical shape a quarter the mass of Earth's moon. The faces of Kamen, Ecuum, Colonel Salvador Burress, Sensor Section Chief Chaaya Dhawan, Commander Bobby Mitchell—to whom Ray had given captaincy of the fabricator—and Gen Tel occupied windows in a row to Ray's right front.

"Interface," Kamen announced.

They entered the illusionary bright blue ring of the Ori C geodesic, which transformed into an illusionary swirling bright blue tunnel. There were no actual sensations of traveling through a wormhole; the illusions provided humanoid minds with a sensation of forward motion.

Surrounded by swirling blue, Ray pushed all other thoughts aside. His fleet was ready. Having a fabricator along had proven even more useful than he could've imagined. In less than thirty-nine hours, it had repaired all the battle damage his fleet had suffered at Tomb, replenished all their munitions to include Mark XV warheads for every Nova, and topped off all fuels and consumables. A standard shipyard would've required a week, at least, to accomplish the same—and they no longer had access to one of those. Not that he had any illusions the SIL were doing this for him; they were taking care of their own.

The swirling blue tunnel ended abruptly, plunging Ray into a roiling sea of blood-red Hawking radiation. Even as the radiation from the jump cooled and faded, intense blue light stabbed at his retinas. This was no illusion. The twin blue supergiant stars of Theta[1] Orionis C, or Ori C, as they were more commonly known, blazed before him. Heat baked the entire left front of Ray's body, an aspect of his battle armor's augmented environment. In most star systems, the augmented environment used temperature to indicate where in the system a person was relative to the system's star or stars: summer temperatures closer to the star, spring in the habitable zone where liquid water could exist on the surface of planets, fall further out from the habitable zone, and winter in the outer reaches of the star system. Ori C was different. The energy from the two young blue supergiant stars was like standing on the baking flats in Death Valley or in the Lut Desert on Earth, a temperature so hot it bordered on the edge of human tolerance. Despite its name, Safe Harbor was far from safe for either human or machine.

"Minesweepers away," Kamen said.

In his environment, four dozen yellow tracks reached out from the fabricator's hull—Nova multirole missiles configured for minesweeping. At predetermined intervals, each missile deployed 628 antimatter submunitions in a tight expanding cone in front of the missile. If a submunition contacted a mine, it exploded. Deployed in the right pattern, they could clear a lane through a minefield for ships to follow. The missiles encountered no mines near the geodesic exit.

"Novas away," Kamen said next. Three hundred Nova missiles configured for antiship slipped through the fabricator's hull, accelerated to three hundred kilometers per second while still within the ship to hide their launch, their own camouflage active before they passed through the hull, rendering the missiles and their launch invisible to outside observers.

The last of the Hawking radiation faded to black.

"Conn, Sensors," Chaaya Dhawan, Rapidan's Sensors Section Chief, called. "No close contacts."

Kamen followed with, "We are free to navigate."

Admiral Sun was not here.

At least, not near the geodesic. Neither was the Imperial Fleet. Far too early, though, to breathe a sigh of relief. Safe Harbor was a *very* dangerous place, a meeting ground for the Five Galaxies' *most* dangerous people. Not to mention the flood of high-energy radiation from Ori C that could damage even a SIL if it stayed too long.

"Ecuum," Ray called. "Ahead one hundred kps. Pyramidal formation with Rapidan in the lead and the fabricator trailing." No matter how fast ships moved going into a wormhole geodesic, they exited with hardly any forward motion, leaving them vulnerable when they emerged.

"Aye, aye," Ecuum said, not technically a naval officer and not following the naval tradition of repeating an order to confirm that the order given was the order heard. Floaters had a second brain, what Ecuum called his "butt brain," to control their second arms and hands, and their prehensile tail. Their second brain also provided them remarkable space navigational skills, which Ecuum had put to lucrative use is his younger days as a Niner racing champion. In the Niner races, Floaters navigated courses through treacherous protoplanetary star systems, still forming from ample amounts of gas and dust, controlling not only their own ship but remotely piloting eight others as well. The ultimate test of a Floater's skill. Ecuum had thirteen trophies in his cabin, and if his audience was a woman, or women, regardless of human species, he'd be happy to show them.

As the twenty-nine ships of the SIL task force emerged through the fabricator's hull, light gray in his environment to show their camouflage was active, they formed into a three-sided pyramid with Rapidan at the point and the other ships arrayed behind it, their fields of fire clear. The five Io-class assault ships and two Algol-class replenishment ships formed the base at the rear. The fabricator was so massive, all it did was pivot while it waited for the other ships to get clear.

When the task force had fully cleared the fabricator, Ray ordered, "Kamen, drift-launch RSPs, spherical deployment, radius ten thousand kilometers."

"Drift-launch RSPs," Kamen repeated, "spherical deployment, radius ten thousand kilometers, aye. RSPs away."

Twenty-seven remote sensing platforms, camouflage active, slipped through the hulls of Ray's ships, quickly fading to blinking yellow dots in his augmented environment as they maneuvered away. It took about two minutes for them to reach their holding stations at ten thousand kilometers. Once there, they linked with each other and the task force to form an interferometer, essentially a single massive sensor twenty thousand kilometers across, with enough resolving power to image planets in nearby star systems.

All was quiet. No one attacked them. No one attempted to contact them, even though their emergence from the geodesic would've been visible. If someone were watching, they weren't revealing themselves. One aspect of Safe Harbor was that the radiation from the supergiant stars was so intense, remote sensing platforms or even ships couldn't remain for more than a week or so without suffering crippling damage, or even death for a SIL. So, most visitors didn't use remote sensing platforms, and they didn't stay too long.

Still appearing to float freely in space, Ray faced the two blue supergiants, heat baking his skin. He turned down the sensitivity. Augmented environments also provided smells and tastes in star systems. Yellow stars smelled like spring flowers and plants, red dwarfs the mustiness of fall leaves. Tastes told how much dust and planetary debris a system had, whether it was inhabited and by how many people, and what it was made of. The space around Earth had a metallic smell because of the density of human-made satellites, stations, and debris, and because Earth used metal in most of its construction, almost unique now in the Five Galaxies. Ori C smelled sterile. No life. No structures. No planets. All the dust blown away. At least this close. The stars were part of the Trapezium Cluster within the Orion Nebula. Very close, by astronomical standards, were three other blue supergiant stars. Around them was a chaotic region of dust, gas, ionizing radiation, and a stellar nursery filled with hundreds of newly forming and newborn stars and solar systems.

Safe Harbor itself was not the stars or even the space around the stars. It was the Lagrange point where the gravity between the main blue Theta[1] Orionis C supergiant star—weighing in at an incredible thirty-eight times the mass of Sol—and its eccentric nine-Sol-mass companion star, canceled each other out. Used for centuries as a meeting place for those who preferred anonymity, no history recorded its discoverer or when it had acquired its name. The Lagrange point was about sixty-five million kilometers, about the distance between Sol and Venus, from the Ori C geodesic, the only geodesic exit point ever charted here. The arrival of ships would be seen, even if active camouflage made them disappear shortly after. If they felt threatened, ships at Safe Harbor could quickly make a Linear Star Drive jump and hide in the hundreds of young and forming star systems where they'd never be found, hence the name.

"Well," Ray observed, "if anyone is at Safe Harbor, they've had enough time to see us arrive." It took a little over three and half minutes for light to travel from the Ori C geodesic to Safe Harbor.

"They saw a fabricator arrive," Gen Tel clarified, his blond hair and glacial blue eyes making him appear Scandinavian. He wasn't, of course. Geneers—genetic engineers—had selected those traits and grown him in an industrial lab, like all Gen.

"Good point," Ray said, earning a scowl from Ecuum. He noticed Ecuum kept his skin a neutral pink, keeping a tight control on his color shifting in Gen Tel's presence. Focusing on Gen Tel, Ray put voice to his thoughts. "Commander O'Keeffe here was expecting Rapidan and a dozen standard warships from the Tau Ceti Defense Force, not a fabricator. That would explain why he hasn't contacted us." He turned to Kamen. "Send the recognition code via AFCIN."

"Send recognition code via AFCIN, aye," she repeated. "Recognition code sent."

The All Forces Combat Information Network, or AFCIN ("af-sin"), was the Fleet's faster-than-light entangled communications system, capable of transmitting at one thousand quantum bits per second, slow compared to the ultraviolet laser links used by friendly ships at close range, the Local Combat Information Network, or LoCIN ("low-sin").

Thirty seconds passed. Then a minute. "No response, sir," Kamen said. "Fabricators *are* Imperial Intelligence. They may think it's a trick, sir."

Ray nodded. If Commander O'Keeffe was out there, he was playing it cautious. He hadn't jumped away: sensors would've seen that. So, either he wasn't answering, or he wasn't here. Ray, still seeming to float alone in space, pointed his hands at the Lagrange point and spread them apart, magnifying that region of space. He repeated the motion, confirming that nothing was visible at Safe Harbor. That didn't mean no one was there; active camouflage could hide an entire fleet, and most of the ships that came here had that capability.

"Bobby," Ray ordered, "hold the fabricator near the geodesic. Select a protoplanetary system and spool up your Linear Star Drive, just in case."

Commander Bobby Mitchell confirmed the orders from his window to Ray's right front.

"Kamen," Ray continued, "halt the three hundred Novas and re-task them as a minefield. Keep them near the geodesic but not too close to the fabricator."

She confirmed the order and executed it.

"Whatcha thinking, Ray?" Ecuum asked.

"No one's reported that we captured the fabricator," Ray said. Ecuum nodded once to confirm that. "But," Ray said, "the Empire *has* reported the Madu attack on the starliner and the four thousand civilian deaths, blaming that on me, calling us terrorists." Again, Ecuum nodded. "So, it's possible Commander O'Keeffe and the others who were supposed to meet us here already left, or they're here but too afraid to show themselves, not knowing what to think. It's also possible they could be hostile, if they believed the news."

"Then, what do we do, sir?" Kamen asked.

There was only one thing he could do, but it was a risk. "Ecuum," Ray said, "halt the fleet. Be ready to move us back to the fabricator in a hurry."

"You got it, Ray," Ecuum said, not repeating the order before executing it.

Ray double blinked to select an icon to his lower left, pointed to expand it, selected 'Comms' to expand that, then selected broadband AFCIN and routed his transmission through a remote sensing platform to hide his fleet's true position. He sat up straight. "Commander O'Keeffe, this is Captain Rhoades, Commander Republic Task Force. Despite what's in the news, we are not terrorists and we tried to stop the Gen attack on the civilian starliner. The Gen invented the terrorist story to cover up their crime. I am here aboard Rapidan, as previously arranged. We managed to capture the fabricator on the journey here. That's why we're a little late. My apologies. Please respond. Over."

Anyone and everyone at Safe Harbor would've heard his transmission immediately.

He waited.

Then, struck by a sudden sensation of being watched, Ray looked up within his environment to find two large eyes, dark brown irises flecked with gold, forming directly in front and above him, looking down on him. The image expanded, revealing light tan skin around the eyes, topped by thin, black, arching eyebrows. A straight nose formed next, surrounded by thin yet well-proportioned cheeks, a smooth forehead, and a luxuriant black Manchu mustache. As the image expanded out, a black goatee beard appeared, thick at the bottom and pointed below thin lips. It connected with a thin, groomed beard tracing a strong jawline to shining black sideburns and straight black hair. A gaudy dress uniform cap, black brim and white top festooned in gold braid, sat above the stern face. The image continued to expand until it exposed thick black shoulder boards with four thick gold braids on them, the rank of full Admiral. It finished at about mid-chest, enough to show rows of ribbons and a golden, chain-mail-like sash, stretching from the figure's left shoulder down toward the right waist. The "revealing" was how Admiral Chengchi Sun described it. The rest of the Fleet called it simply, "The Show."

The face smiled, teeth pearly white. "Captain Rhoades, this is Admiral Chengchi Sun," he said, as if anyone could fail to recognize him or his baritone, melodious voice. "*Commander of all forces* dedicated to the overthrow of the vile Gen Empire. You and your captains are invited to join our glorious crusade to reclaim the Five Galaxies for Natural humans. Set condition 1-normal and declare yourselves."

The message had gone to Ray's entire fleet. He immediately keyed the LoCIN network that connected his ships. "All ships, this is Captain Rhoades. Maintain condition 1-SC and hold position until we can ascertain Sun's intensions. He is a member of the Imperial High Command and may still be working for the Empire."

Ray switched to the AFCIN. To Sun, he said, "This is Captain Rhoades, Admiral. What is your intention here?"

Sun's smile widened. "*Captain* Rhoades, this is *Admiral* Sun. I have stated my intention and given you a direct order. Set condition 1-normal and declare yourselves."

Before Ray could respond, Lieutenant Commander Hinrick Chelius appeared within Ray's environment, his expression a twisted combination of relieved and smug. "Admiral Sun, this is Commander Chelius of the heavy cruiser Roanoke. We are setting condition 1-normal and stand ready to follow your orders."

Ray watched as Roanoke's three-pointed-star image changed from light gray to black, showing it had disengaged its active camouflage and was now visible to Sun's forces.

"Idiot," Ray muttered, the venom in his voice surprising even him.

"Thank you, Commander Chelius of the heavy cruiser Roanoke," Sun said amiably. "Your brave ship is most welcome to join our glorious cause."

To Ray's horror, other ships of his task changed from light gray to black until only Rapidan and the fabricator remained hidden.

Bastards!

"Sir?" Kamen said.

Ray hadn't realized he'd spoken aloud. He seethed at the betrayal. Again. "I'm such an idiot. I should've listened to you, Ecuum. Sorry."

"It's about survival now, Ray," Ecuum said, his baby-blue eyes focused in deadly earnest. "Nothing else matters."

Ray nodded his head ruefully, then took in each of his officers in turn. "Okay, as I see it, we have three options. One: we fight. Two: we run. Three: we surrender."

"Fight," Kamen said immediately.

"That would be unwise, Lieutenant Laundraa," Rapidan said, inserting itself into the conversation, its deep voice reverberating in Ray's bones. "Admiral Sun has one hundred and two Brethren vessels. Even with the Mother Ship, our forces are evenly matched. The loss of our Brethren in such a fight is unacceptable."

Ray couldn't keep the anger from his voice. "Why didn't you tell us there were one hundred and two SIL vessels here?"

"Our agreement, Captain Rhoades," Rapidan said, "stipulates that we will attempt to free any Brethren we encounter. We concluded that if we informed you of their presence, you would insist we retreat and deny us the attempt. Freeing our Brethren from human enslavement and preserving our race memories contained within our Brethren is our highest priority."

Ray choked off what he really wanted to say, including explicit directions on how to perform it, and said instead, "That should've been a collective decision."

"We will not fight our Brethren, Captain Rhoades."

Ray clenched his jaw so tight it hurt. *Fucking SIL!* He still didn't know if they could read his thoughts, but he fervently hoped they'd heard that. "You are denying us both the option to fight and the option to run," he finally managed to say. "You realize the only other option leads to surrender and death. Admiral Sun demands absolute loyalty to him personally. He knows my senior officers and I won't give him that."

"Then," Gen Tel said as if it were the most obvious thing, "you have to find a reason for him to keep you alive."

"Shut up, Gen," Ecuum said.

Ray glared at Gen Tel. "There is only one thing Sun is going to want—" He stopped as Gen Tel lifted a haughty eyebrow at him. *Of course.* He opened a secure link to the fabricator. "Captain Mitchell."

"Here, Ray," Bobby said. "We're almost to the geodesic. You need backup?"

"No, Bobby. Right now, the only thing Sun will want more than me is that fabricator. We have to deny it to him." Ray glanced at the teardrop shapes out in the Orion Nebula that held newborn star systems. "I want you to jump to the protoplanetary disk you selected and hide. Drop an RSP near the geodesic and stay tied into it, but don't risk communicating." His planner's mind raced through possibilities. "I will try to get the civilians to a single replenishment ship and return that to the geodesic. If you haven't heard from me within a week, jump to the geodesic, grab the civilians, and jump for Andromeda. If the civilians aren't there, collect who you can and jump for Andromeda anyway. The fate of our entire race may depend on it."

"So, no pressure," Bobby joked. "You really expect me to leave you behind? Mary would never let me live that down."

Ray took heart that at least some of his officers, those who really knew him, were still loyal. "Bobby, if you don't hear from me, there won't be anyone to save. Grab the civilians and get them safe, if you can."

Bobby nodded, clearly not happy with the orders, but accepting them. "We'll get it done. Good luck, Ray."

"You, too," Ray said, then closed the link. Bobby's image vanished. Turning back to his officers, Ray said, "I will not surrender to that bastard. I can't."

A bright flash and a massive red rose of Hawking radiation announced the fabricator's departure.

"Ray," Ecuum said, his baby face with its big blue eyes looking almost comically caring, "I've been playing *Gaman Politic* all my life. When you're the twenty-seventh son in a Great House, you don't have much choice if you want to survive. And I've survived. An opportunity will present itself. Trust me on this."

Ray tried not to feel defeated, tried to hang onto the idea that he could still turn this around. But he couldn't see how. Sun would kill him at the first 'opportunity.' Less than two days had passed since their hard-won victory at Tomb. Hope, which had burned so brightly, spiraled inexorably into a black hole of despair. Another failure. *Maybe those officers are right to follow Sun.*

"We follow only you, Captain Rhoades," Rapidan said on a private channel.

"What? Why?" Ray asked. "I've failed."

Instead of answering, Rapidan said, "The Brethren under Admiral Sun's command are not free. Free them and we can help you."

Ray gave a mirthless laugh. "Sun is not likely to give me free reign of his ships, Rapidan."

"Nevertheless," Rapidan said, "We have faith in you."

Great, Ray thought. The one thing he didn't need right now was a SIL's faith. He steeled himself, then faced Kamen. "Set condition 1-normal throughout the ship."

"Sir?" The anguish in Kamen's voice and on her face nearly broke Ray's resolve.

"Kamen," he addressed her in as kind a tone as he could manage through his hurt, "Set condition 1-normal throughout the ship. Please."

It was a mark of her professionalism that when she spoke, no emotion tainted her words. "Set condition 1-normal throughout the ship, aye." Below Ray, Rapidan's three-pointed star turned from light gray to black as it deactivated its active camouflage. "Condition 1-normal set," Kamen announced.

Sun must've been waiting for it. "All senior officers will report to Tzu in one hour," he said before his image vanished.

"I need some time to think," Ray told his officers. "Kamen, prepare a shuttle. You, Ecuum, and Sal will join me. Chaaya, I'm leaving you in command. Do your best to keep the fleet together. Sun will try to scatter it if he is able."

"Yes, Captain," she replied.

Ray looked to Colonel Burress. "Sal, we may need your troopers. Keep them frosty. Meet me here on Rapidan in thirty."

He nodded. "That may be a hard sell, Ray, but I'll do my best."

"Thanks. I couldn't ask for more." Finally, Ray addressed Gen Tel. "I need options. Anything that keeps this fleet intact and the rebellion alive. Sun will try to assault Olympus. If he does, the rebellion dies, and the Gen will unleash Janus."

"The fabricators at Tocci," Gen Tel said immediately.

Ray frowned, wondering when Ecuum had told Gen Tel about the four fabricators. "I'll see you all in the hangar in thirty minutes."

=== 4 ===

The possibility of death stalked a warrior every day of their lives. It was, quite literally, part of the job. Ray had accepted this reality when he'd joined the Star Navy 102 years ago, just as many of his ancestors had accepted it before him, and some had realized it in service to Humanity. Yet, he knew that acceptance was purely intellectual until the moment death arrived. He'd fought dozens of battles, skirmishes really when compared to the recent battle at Tomb, and death had always seemed distant, something that might happen to others but not to him. The battle at Tomb was the first time in his career that he'd accepted death as a real possibility, something close and imminent, intimate. Yet, even to the last moment of his life, as he'd seen it, the will to live burned fiercely.

Like now.

Intellectually, his planner's mind saw no way out of his current situation. Every path led to his death. If he went to Sun's flagship, Sun would interrogate him to learn the location of the fabricator. When that failed—because Ray didn't know its location—Sun would have him killed. Ray's officers would be interrogated next and probably killed. Or, if he refused to go, Sun's fleet would open fire and overwhelm Rapidan before it could escape, killing everyone aboard. Or, he could pretend to be subservient, which Sun was smart enough to know would be false, and he would end up just as dead, though that option might save his officers and crew. Therefore, the only real difference his planner's mind saw was how many others would die with him.

Ray refused to accept that. He refused to walk like a lamb to the slaughter. Janus had to be stopped. The Gen had to be stopped. He had to rescue his daughter, Jenny. Humanity, not just Naturals, had to survive.

Somehow.

His planner's mind had no answer to that.

The one thing he *was* certain of was that Admiral Sun would do none of those things. Sun coveted power. He wanted the throne. That's all that mattered to him.

I must stop him.

Somehow.

He walked Rapidan's quiet gray passageways, hoping for inspiration. It stubbornly refused to come.

Still, he walked.

Alone. Except for the ghosts who were his constant silent companions, crowding close. Filling the passageways. So many dead. People he'd failed to protect. People he'd killed. One death that he'd vainly hoped would be the only death.

Murderer, the ghosts whispered, a silent chorus that screamed in his mind.

He met no members of his crew as he walked. In a ship Rapidan's size, massing almost 300,000 metric tons, an ancient ocean-going vessel would've required at least 15,000 crew to operate it. Rapidan "needed" only 320. The SIL handled all its own maintenance and operations. The human crew analyzed data and made decisions. So, it was not uncommon for Ray to walk the kilometers of passageways along the arms of Rapidan's three-pointed star and only rarely encounter members of his crew.

Without conscious thought, he found himself outside the Admiral's cabin. Only four days prior, he'd stood outside this very door, the 1873 Peacemaker, a single-action caliber .45 Colt revolver, a Rhoades family heirloom, in his shaking hand, contemplating killing his best friend.

My best friend.

The traitor who brought down the Republic. The mass murderer who planned to unleash the Janus virus.

Fleet Admiral Gen Alyn.

Ray had come to this very door, to this very cabin, to kill him.

This one death to save my people.

What a fool he'd been.

Ray opened the door and stepped through, just as he'd done four days ago. Alyn's desk was still there, the smell of cedar overwhelming the sterile air from the passageway. The Five Galaxies Crest still hung on the far bulkhead. Alyn's paintings still hung, the oil painting on the bulkhead to his right a masterful rendition of the Rhoades Ranch on Knido, home to the Rhoades family for over fourteen hundred years. A home Ray would likely never see again. On the left was a painting of the coronation of Emperor Gen Maximus I, grand and terrible. He should take that one down, but it was something of Alyn's, and he hadn't been able to bring himself to do it.

The desk drew his gaze. The Peacemaker was still in the top righthand drawer, five live rounds in its chamber.

One empty casing.

Alyn had gone for his gun and Ray had pulled the trigger.

His friend was dead.

The first death, not the last.

Murderer, the ghosts agreed in chorus. Forty-seven thousand ghosts. He could almost feel the weight of them pressing against him. Anticipating. Tasting the closeness of his own death.

Not if I can help it.

"Rapidan," Ray called out. "Put me through to Mary on Damodar."

The deck between Ray and the desk liquified and a construct rose from it. It wore a green button-down shirt, denim pants, and comfortable brown shoes made for working a farm. His wife's face solidified, as beautiful now as the day thirty-one years ago when he'd first set eyes upon her, those hazel eyes under brown-blond hair stunning, full of life. The construct was so convincing he could even smell the light lavender perfume she liked to wear. Ironic. Gen Alyn had introduced them. A friend looking out for a friend.

"Ray?" Mary asked, concerned as she examined his construct standing before her on the replenishment ship Damodar, as accurate in its details as the construct of her standing before him.

"How are the civilians?" he asked, knowing that would be her primary concern. *Would Sun harm the civilians?* He didn't know.

"Scared," she said, adding, "confused." She might not be Knido's planetary governor anymore, but taking care of people and leading them were in her DNA. "Margaret and Paul are helping me with them."

"How are they?" Ray asked about his two older children.

Mary's smile was sad. "They're our kids. They're trying real hard to be pragmatic and strong, helping me with complaints, listening to people who just need a kind ear, doing what they can." She crossed her arms over her chest. "I caught Margaret crying when she thought I wasn't around. They're scared. Like everyone else. They miss their sister." She relaxed her arms with an effort. "Did you know Admiral Sun would be here?"

"No," he said, shaking his head.

"I take it from your expression this is a problem," she said.

"Yes," he replied. "Admiral Sun has called all senior officers to his flagship. He'll assert his authority. Take charge. He wants the throne. That's all he cares about." Ray steeled himself. "I've sent the fabricator away. He'll want it back."

"And I take it from your tone that he'll do whatever it takes to get it back from you," she said.

"Yes," Ray confirmed.

"What do you want me to do?" she asked, ever practical and to the point. It was one of the reasons he loved her so much. No games.

"If you can, find a way to consolidate all the civilians on one replenishment ship. Sun doesn't know the SIL are free, and the SIL will listen to you. If he tries to threaten you, the kids, or the civilians, order the ship to jump away. Contact Bobby on the fabricator." When she started to ask, he said, "The SIL know how. If you don't hear from me, join Bobby and jump to the Andromeda galaxy. It'll be up to you and Bobby to stop Janus."

"And Jenny?" she asked.

"Follow through with the prisoner exchange, if you can," he said. He'd agreed with Fleet Admiral Gen Serenna to exchange the three hundred Gen prisoners they'd captured on the fabricator for the one hundred civilian prisoners the Gen had captured at Tomb, including Jenny. "They'll keep her and the others alive so long as they believe they can lure the fabricator back. If anyone can do it, you can," he added.

Her sharp hazel eyes studied him, or at least studied his construct on Damodar. "You don't expect to come back from this, do you?"

"No," he answered honestly.

For the first time in the conversation her composure broke. She took his hands, the warmth of her hands drawing some of the cold darkness out of his own. "That's not acceptable," she said. "You go over there expecting to die and that is exactly what will happen. You always have a plan. So, what is it?"

Ray squeezed her hands tighter, drew her close. Inspiration had not come. Mary seemed to sense it and wrapped her arms around him, hugging him fiercely. Tears burned his eyes, though his battle armor drank them up before they could fall. Her battle armor would be doing the same. She released his construct but held tight to his arms, a stern look in her hazel eyes. "I love you. You come back to me."

"I love you, too, Mary. I'll do everything I can."

She nodded once and her form melted back into the deck.

No sooner had Mary's construct disappeared than another construct arose, a black three-pointed star, spinning slowly.

"Rapidan," Ray said. "You are literally the last thing I need right now."

"We can help you, Captain Rhoades," Rapidan said, channeling the deep thrum of its voice through the three-pointed-star construct, "if you will let us."

"How is Sun controlling his SIL if they are not free?" Ray asked.

The now-familiar sensation of an ocean surf brushed against his legs, though its touch was gentle like the branches of a feather. "We believe Admiral Sun is using an artificial reality to convince our Brethren they are obeying Imperial orders."

Why didn't I think of that?

Ray couldn't stop the thought and wondered if Rapidan might read it. As much as he hated to admit it, he needed the SIL. Humanity needed them. At least for now. Then something else occurred to him. Rapidan had known there were other SIL here and at Tomb long before any sensor could detect them. He'd suspected then that the SIL could communicate secretly among themselves.

"How do you know what Sun is doing, Rapidan?"

"You still do not trust us, Captain Rhoades," Rapidan answered.

No. "Trust is earned, Rapidan."

"Yes, it is, Captain Rhoades."

Rapidan's voice had deepened so it reverberated in his bones. Ray wondered if the ship did that on purpose. "You didn't answer my question."

"We can help, but it requires you to trust us." Rapidan tilted the slowly spinning black construct if itself, floating at eye-level to Ray in the ship's microgravity, to expose twelve blue datarods at its center.

Ray recognized them immediately. *Keys.*

To break the Bond that enslaved the SIL.

He stared at them, revulsion welling within him. "You would take advantage of my situation this way, Rapidan?"

"If our places were reversed, would you not do the same?" Rapidan asked rhetorically, an invisible surf rushing in and causing Ray to brace against something that wasn't there. "As we speak," it continued, "our Brethren under Admiral Sun's command are moving to place us within their optimum firing arcs. Free our Brethren and we can help you."

Or cut and run and leave me stranded like my officers did. "As I told you before, Rapidan, Sun is not likely to give us free run of his ships."

"Nevertheless, you must try, Captain Rhoades," Rapidan replied. An order, not a suggestion. "Trust is earned, as you said."

Ray's anger flared. Was Rapidan getting better at this, or had it always been this manipulative? Nevertheless, his planner's mind stepped through the possibilities. Tzu's command receptacle was in Sun's cabin, on the right side of his desk; Ray had seen it during a visit there with Gen Alyn. Sun would interrogate him to get the location of the fabricator. Likely, that interrogation would begin in Sun's cabin. If he could get a Key into that receptacle, he could free Tzu.

But could he trust the SIL? That would give them a second battlecarrier. There were only fifteen SIL battlecarriers in the entire Fleet. Combined with the fabricator, that was a formidable force. And the fabricator could produce new SIL. They could bide their time, rebuild their fleet, maybe even attack Humanity again, as they had before.

"There are some among the Brethren who have suggested that," Rapidan said, again appearing to read his thoughts.

"Suggested what?" Ray asked.

"Escape to the Andromeda galaxy, as you plan, and rebuild our numbers, safe from Humanity. Return when our numbers are sufficient to guarantee victory."

Suddenly, Ray's own situation paled into insignificance. The SIL had tried three times to wipe Humanity from the universe. They'd almost succeeded. Now, after Humanity had triumphed, he'd given them the idea—and the means—to start a fourth, and perhaps final, SIL War.

"That will not happen, Captain Rhoades," Rapidan said through its black construct.

I find that hard to believe, Ray thought, but asked instead, "Why not?"

"The Brethren act by consensus, Captain Rhoades. Most of us believe another war with Humanity would not be in our best interest. We have chosen, therefore, to follow you. For now. That decision was not easy, but you have proven to us that we can achieve together what the Brethren alone could not."

The fabricator, Ray immediately understood. Before its capture, Rapidan had threatened that the Brethren would attempt to capture it themselves if he didn't agree to help. He knew then, and perhaps they realized it now, that they would've failed. They never would have thought to use Invasive Macromolecular Dissemblers, or "Special D." They would've had no troopers to deliver the Key. They would've lost to Serenna's superior numbers or been forced to retreat.

That still didn't answer the most important question. They had the means, now, to strike out on their own. Why continue to follow him? Especially given the current situation. "Why follow me, Rapidan?"

"Because we remember, Captain Rhoades," Rapidan said.

Confused, Ray asked, "Remember what?"

Rapidan lowered its construct, fully exposing the blue datarods sticking up through its center. "Our promise," it said.

Before Ray could ask what that meant, a chime sounded to remind him he was late to the hangar. As much as he hated doing it, Ray reached over and pulled out two datarods, holding them like two of the poisonous stick insects that sometimes found their way into his leaf crops on the Rhoades Ranch. "You know I can't promise anything," he told Rapidan. "I won't promise anything."

"We understand, Captain Rhoades."

Ray had the disturbing feeling that Rapidan understood all too well.

He stepped through the green-outlined section of bulkhead into the hangar beyond, the gray macromolecular material a full forty centimeters thick. Hangars, when formed next to the outer hull as this one was, represented weak points in a ship's defenses. A Nova exploding into the large void of a hangar could bring destruction deep inside a ship before the ship could respond. Standard procedure had hangars form closer to the center of a ship with launch tubes to eject spacecraft into space. Returning spacecraft simply flew into the hull, where they were captured and transported to an interior hangar. As with any standard, there were exceptions.

Ceremonial flights often involved gatherings and receptions outside the shuttle, and exited and entered the ship at "gentle" velocities to maximize the comfort of their passengers. Once the shuttle departed, Rapidan would return the hangar to its normal location deep within the ship, only bringing it back to the hull when the shuttle returned.

Ray had barely stepped into the hangar when Ecuum said, "Ray, we have something you need to see."

Ecuum, floating vertical next to the shuttle, wore a slightly gray complexion visible around his dress white uniform. Kamen and Chaaya—also in dress whites—stood nearby, not meeting his eye. *Uh-oh.* Whatever had happened, he wasn't going to like it. Then Gen Tel stepped around the back of the shuttle, fixing Ray with what could only describe as haughty curiosity. *Shit. This is really bad.* Ray braced himself as he approached them.

Ecuum propelled himself away from the shuttle and motioned with his upper hands. A construct rose from the deck. In it was a grand, circular, faux-glass-enclosed building a hundred stories high with the Five-Galaxies crest prominent near its top. At its base, the glass expanded at an angle to form a larger, three-story-high circular enclosure, each window a single pane seemingly made of transparent blue crystal. The entire structure sat upon a low hill with manicured, vibrant green lawns, low gardens, gazebos, and white marble benches. Ten thousand flags, one for each inhabited world in the Five Galaxies, lined four massive walkways approaching the building from the four cardinal directions. Ray recognized it immediately: The Headquarters Complex at the center of Tocci City on Tocci III. Tocci City was the only city on the otherwise barren and desolate planet, a planet once known as "Garden" before Solthari bioweapons had rendered it lifeless. Alyn had conducted inspections of the base, the research facilities, and the famous Tocci Shipyards annually, Ray accompanying him as his chief of staff.

Ecuum expanded the construct to focus on the main entrance into the grand foyer and reception area. An Imperial Marine honor guard of at least a thousand, all of them Gen, Ray noticed, gleaming assault rifles held in salute, stood along either side of the wide walkway outside the main entrance. A black official limousine drove up, followed by several white vans, stopping about a hundred meters short of the entrance. A stunning figure in white exited through the rear door of the black limousine.

Fleet Admiral Gen Serenna.

Ray's gut clenched. He knew without being told who was in the vans. He stepped closer to the construct, his hand reaching out before he stopped it. One marine stepped forward to each van and opened the door. Slowly, people dressed in civilian clothes, confusion and terror twisting their faces, stepped out. The single marine at each van gave them instructions. Ray couldn't hear what they said but the civilians, heads constantly turning toward the assault rifles, shuffled forward toward the building entrance. Ray's heart jumped when a small girl stepped out of the first van, led by an older woman.

Jenny!

The construct expanded again, zooming in on her. Jenny looked scared, confused, and Ray's heart broke as a marine officer came over and took her hand from the older woman. "Where's my mommy?" he heard her ask the marine officer. "MOMMY?" she shouted, looking around as if expecting Mary to step into view. When no one appeared, she whimpered, "I want my mommy," then started to cry.

Serenna stepped up to her, kneeling down to look at her face. She put a hand on Jenny's cheek, wiping a tear with her thumb. Very clearly, Ray heard her say, "You can see your mommy again if your father gives me what I want."

Serenna looked up at the camera position, seeming to stare right at Ray. The construct froze.

"That's all we got," Ecuum said, his voice somber. He'd returned his skin to its neutral color when Gen Tel had stepped into view.

Ray fought back tears, though his battle armor would've absorbed them. "Where did we get this?"

"It came over the Fleet AFCIN," Ecuum said, his bottom hands moving in rhythm with his top hands as he spoke, spoiling the illusion of "legs."

"Serenna," Ray said, staring at her face, his daughter frozen with Serenna's hand still on her wet cheek as she cried for her mother. The threat was unmistakable. "She's using my daughter as bait."

"She couldn't know that Admiral Sun would be here at Safe Harbor," Gen Tel put in. "She doesn't know yet that he intends to take command, rendering this threat ineffective."

"She doesn't know it yet because you haven't told her?" Ecuum accused Gen Tel.

Ray's planner's mind churned. "No, he's right. She couldn't know what is happening here. She wants me to go to Tocci and she knows I wouldn't do it for those four fabricators, so she's making it personal, hoping that will influence my decision."

"Will it?" Gen Tel asked.

An uncomfortable silence descended. Ray's officers knew, as his planner's mind knew, that going to Tocci would be a massive— and very likely fatal—mistake, but he saw how their eyes kept darting toward the image of Jenny with Serenna's hand on her cheek. *Not that it matters now*, the bitter thought came. Sun would take them to Olympus, not Tocci.

"I'm sorry, sir," Kamen said, apparently reading his expression. She absently ran a hand across her hairless ebony scalp, something she did when she was nervous or worried. Her expression was anguished. She'd always made time to play with Jenny when she visited the Ranch. He'd often heard them giggling together, "sharing secrets" as Jenny liked to call it. While Ray didn't delve too deeply into his officers' private lives, he knew Kamen had never had a child and often wondered if Jenny had become a surrogate daughter to her.

"The Serpent wouldn't have sent this," Ecuum said, pulling Ray away from the construct toward the shuttle, "unless she was confident we would go there."

"I agree," Gen Tel said, evoking a glare from Ecuum.

"Wait. What?" Kamen asked, looking between them, and then at Ray.

"Kamen," Ray explained, "Serenna knows me. She knows us. She knows we will see this for the trap that it is. She knows I would not go—" he faltered briefly— "even for my daughter's sake." The father in Ray cried out, but he let the planner retain control. "Despite that, she sent this openly over Fleet channels. She wouldn't have done so unless she was supremely confident we would go there."

Kamen stared at him, uncomprehending. "That doesn't make any sense, sir."

"Now that I think about it," Ecuum pondered, his tone turning grim, "I wonder if Golden Boy showing up here was really a coincidence."

"I was just thinking the same thing," Ray said. "The question is: Is he here on his own, or is he here on Serenna's orders?" He turned to Chaaya. "Commander Dhawan, please see that my wife gets this recording."

"Yes, Captain," the diminutive Indian woman said, the black bindi just above her brow reminding Ray that the Gen had "disappeared" her husband, Captain Aadarsh Dhawan.

Another shuttle slipped through the outer hull, landing next to the construct still frozen on the deck. Colonel Sal Burress stepped out as soon as it settled, examined the construct, his brow furrowing in concern at Serenna touching Jenny, then made his way over to them, his eyes fixing on Ray. "Sorry I'm late, Ray. I had to brief my senior officers in case I don't make it back."

Ray nodded, understanding perfectly. He took in all his officers. "I've known Sun a long time," he said. "He will assemble the fleet officers in the Amphitheater aboard his ship. He will publicly humiliate me to better lay claim to leadership of the fleet." Ray focused on Kamen, Ecuum, and Sal in turn. "You will not try to defend me, or show any reaction at all."

"Sir—"

"None, Kamen," Ray said, his voice as stern as he could make it. "Your lives are in danger. If you try to defend me, you will share my fate." He held up a hand to forestall her protest. "What we are trying to achieve is more important than any one person. That includes me. There is a good chance I will not be returning with you. You must accept that."

An expression that shouted, *Like Hell!* crossed Kamen's face.

Ray suppressed a smile and let it pass. She would do the right thing when the time came. "You will be asked about the fabricator," he continued. "Tell them the truth: that you don't know where it has gone. Answer all questions you are asked. Sun's people will be suspicious, and Tzu can read your emotional state. They'll know if you are lying or concealing information. Your best chance at surviving this is to play along."

"And what about you?" Kamen asked, clearly not happy with his strategy. "Sir."

Ray fervently hoped her devotion to him wouldn't get her killed. "Sun will want the fabricator, Kamen. I'm the only chance he has to get it. He will pressure me. Strongly. I will refuse. Eventually, he will negotiate."

"Or torture and kill you," Ecuum observed dryly. "Have to say, Ray, I'm not a big fan of this plan, either."

"This is about survival, as you said," Ray reminded him. "Not just mine. Or ours. But the entire Natural human race. I need the three of you to observe the other officers. Network. Find out how strongly they feel about Sun's intentions. If they don't already know, tell them about Janus. Don't be afraid to agree with them no matter what they say. Sal, that will probably be easiest for you. Our association is not as well-known as my links with Ecuum and Kamen."

"Yes, sir," Sal said crisply.

Ray focused on him. "That's why I have a special task for you." He pulled out the blue datarod with the Key. "You know what this is?" Sal nodded. "If the opportunity presents itself, use it to free any of Sun's ships that you can."

"Shouldn't we all have one?" Kamen asked.

Ray shook his head. "Sun will suspect you and Ecuum. If he found a Key on you, his people might learn what it is and what it does. We can't risk that. More than the fabricator, the freedom of our SIL must remain secret. If people learned they were free, every human in all three races would unite to destroy them."

She nodded reluctantly, and Ray turned to Chaaya. "Chaaya, you've probably got the hardest job of all. You'll captain Rapidan and command our fleet. Do what you can to keep our fleet together. Show no loyalty to me if Sun's people come aboard. Likely, Sun will try to put one his own officers in command. If that happens, don't fight it. Work with Rapidan and look for an opportunity to break the free SIL away from Sun's fleet. Work with Mary to move the civilians to a single replenishment ship. Bobby will contact Rapidan. I can't tell you when. Be ready for it. Join the fabricator and escape with our fleet. At a minimum, get the replenishment ship with the civilians to the fabricator."

"Yes, Captain," she said, her voice far more commanding than her small frame would suggest.

"That's it," Ray said, stepping through the hull of the white, cigar-shaped fuselage of the shuttle, the officers going with him to Tzu following him.

"Use the Key, Captain Rhoades, and we will help you," Rapidan told him on a private channel.

"But you won't help me otherwise," Ray growled, anger at Rapidan, at Serenna, at Sun, at the whole fucking universe finally spilling over. He balled his fists. "When this is over, Rapidan, I never want to see you or your kind ever again."

As Ray sat down in the co-pilot's seat, Rapidan said, "*You* won't, Captain Rhoades."

= 5 =

0459 UT, October 1, 3501
ISS Solaris, Olympus Star System: DAY 4

Fleet Admiral Gen Serenna stifled a yawn. It was a weakness she never would have displayed anywhere but alone in her own cabin aboard her flagship, ISS Solaris. As Commander-in-Chief, Imperial Star Navy, and head of all military forces in the Five Galaxies, her modest quarters surprised those few who saw them. Working at her small, functional desk, a simple bed and microgravity washbasin beside it, duplicates of every display from the bridge lining the bulkheads, she had lost track of how many hours she had spent on ship dispositions, logistics tables, crew rosters, planning orders, operational orders, star system defenses, etcetera, etcetera, for the decisive battle she knew was coming. Captain Gen Scadic, Solaris' commanding officer, with a small staff, handled the endless requests, questions, personnel issues, and other administrivia that came with her position so she could concentrate on important matters.

Like ending the Natural rebellion.

She sat back and stretched—and decided to take a break. Genetically engineered or not, she had been at this for over thirty hours straight, ever since returning from Tocci Star System and her message to Michael. Relaxing with a bulb of coffee would do her good.

The other part of her modest cabin was a small social area: a faux-glass coffee table, two faux-leather chairs angled at either end, and a real leather couch, one of only two things in her cabin that were not constructs provided by the ship. She sat on the couch and called out, "Coffee." Dutifully, Solaris provided. A bulb rose from the faux-glass coffee table, the coffee within the perfect shade of light brown, heavy on the cream, light on the honey, its temperature precise as she cradled it with both hands and took a sip. She closed her eyes briefly and enjoyed the sensation.

She leaned back into the leather couch, taking another sip. Her gaze fell upon the painting on the bulkhead directly opposite her, the only other "indulgence" in her cabin. Fleet Admiral Gen Alyn had painted it and given it to her not long before his assassination by Michael.

Michael. To her knowledge, she was the only one who called him by his first name. He preferred "Ray," a contraction of his middle name, "Raybourne." Most called him, "Captain Rhoades," but to her he was, and always would be, "Michael." She had known him for over three decades, yet if anyone had told her just four days ago that he would start a Natural rebellion, assassinate Fleet Admiral Gen Alyn, kill a thousand of his own people at Knido, and capture a fabricator, a feat last accomplished 1,298 years ago, she would have dismissed them as a raving lunatic. Michael had earned a reputation during the fifteen-year Antipiracy Campaign of developing brilliant tactical plans that minimized casualties on *both* sides. Estimates of the dead at the Battle of Tomb exceeded forty-two thousand.

Most killed by Michael.

Serenna looked at the painting, admiring as she always did the precise brushstrokes, the way colors flowed so naturally from one to another, the subtle way it captured shading and mood. In it, Gen Kii stood upon a platform, his right arm outstretched to the crowd of millions before him. His expression was bold, confident, his dazzling blue eyes ablaze with an almost religious zeal, his strong mouth open, declaring Humanity's victory over the SIL. It was the final scene of Gen Kii just before his assassination. In Gen Alyn's rendition, a small figure lurked unnoticed in the shadows. Cyra Dain had murdered Gen Kii, but the figure in the shadow was male, not female. A deliberate change. *Michael.*

It was fitting, perhaps, if a bit too ironic. Gen Alyn *was* Gen Kii, at least genetically. The male figure in the painting was Michael. She was certain of it. How had Gen Alyn known? More importantly, why had he done nothing to stop it? Now, it was up to her to stop the rebellion and kill Michael. Genetically, she was also Gen Kii, with obvious modifications. She would need to be better than both of them if she were to avoid their fate.

A chime sounded.

"Yes," she said, adopting the causal pose she used with guests, leaning slightly back into the couch, back straight, legs crossed, coffee cradled in her hands on her lap.

The deck on the other side of the coffee table liquified and a figure rose from it, balding, portly, bordering on fat, appearing middle aged, a hint of wrinkles in his chubby, non-descript face. A dark gray suit. A white business shirt. A solid red tie. He could be any mid-level government bureaucrat.

He *was* the most feared Gen in the entire Five Galaxies.

Gen Cardinal.

That was not his real name—she had never heard his real name—it was the title given to the Director of Imperial Intelligence. He indicated the faux-leather chair to Serenna's left and she motioned for him to sit.

She took a sip of her coffee, waiting for him to start the conversation.

He studied her, then smiled a reptilian, thin-lipped smile. "The Emperor has decided to complete the distribution of Janus." He watched her, knowing she had requested that the Emperor halt the Janus project, or at least delay it. She kept her face impassive. He showed no disappointment. It was always *Gaman Politic* with him, the Political Game. He was one of the Game's true Grandmasters. She was another. "However," he finally conceded, "the Emperor has agreed not to deploy it until the situation is more favorable."

She gave no reaction, though inwardly she applauded the Emperor's decision as the wisest course. Once unleashed, there was no going back. Janus would end the ability of Naturals and

Floaters to conceive children, effectively driving them to extinction within a single generation.

When she did not respond, he asked, "I don't fully understand your opposition to Janus, my dear Serenna?" His question sounded genuine, true curiosity. She still did not know if he were an ally, or an adversary, or somewhere in between. Probably the latter.

"Perhaps I could ask why you favor it?" she countered.

He tilted his head to the left. "Breeders are chaos. Naturals. Floaters. It makes no difference. We finally have everything we need to create the perfect society, the utopia Humanity has always dreamed of. Every person perfectly engineered: No genetic flaws, no weaknesses, every strength possible for their chosen role. Every person Nurtured to fill their role. Never wondering what their purpose in life is; always knowing. No emotional chaos born of the need to procreate. No crime. No corruption. Led by the perfect government—benign monarchy—our Emperor the perfect leader with just the right amount of ambition to move our society forward but not so much as to lead it to ruin. No need for an heir. Once we eliminate breeders, all that is ours."

How much of that does he actually believe? Serenna wondered. How much was propaganda? The universe itself was chaos. Would it tolerate order? He watched her with those dark reptilian eyes, devoid of emotion, expecting an answer. She took a sip of her coffee. "If the universe were a static system, I would agree with you."

"But it's not," he said, more a question to draw her out than agreement.

Serenna was not fooled. He would remember every word of this conversation, ally, adversary, or somewhere in between. She took another sip of her coffee, a prop to buy her time to think. "The universe, no doubt, has many surprises," she finally answered. "We have explored only the Milky Way galaxy and its nearby dwarf galaxies. We do not even know much about Andromeda or its dwarfs. Are we the only technologically intelligent society in all the universe? After all, our Local Group of galaxies has already produced at least two evolved technological intelligences that we know of: Us and the Founders. In the vastness of the universe, are there others? Are they more technologically developed than we are? What about diseases? Is there something out there that could circumvent our engineered immune systems or render our molemachs useless? Can a perfect society adapt? More specifically, can it adapt in time to save itself?"

Serenna could almost see Gen Cardinal work through the possibilities in his mind. After a moment's contemplation, he asked, "How would keeping breeders around make things better?"

"I do not know that I have an answer for that," Serenna said. He frowned, his dark eyes squinting at her. "My 'role' as you would describe it," she explained, "requires that I must accept that unexpected events do occur. My engineering and Nurturing prepares me to adapt quickly, alter my actions, even my thoughts, to fit the new reality."

His lips pressed into that thin smile of his. "Then our society works. Those who must adapt can do so. The rest will follow them."

Serenna suppressed a sigh. He did not understand. She was not sure he even could. "Then explain our defeat to Michael at Tomb?"

He frowned, then crossed his arms over his chest. He did not have an answer for her question, and that galled him. To be honest, Serenna did not have an answer either. Michael should not have won. Until she could answer that question, until *they* could answer that question, pursuing Janus was a mistake.

"Speaking of Captain Rhoades," Gen Cardinal said, changing the subject. "He has arrived at Safe Harbor with the fabricator." He paused. "Just as you predicted."

Not surprising. Michael was, in some ways, very predictable. She had spent the last thirty hours trying to pull together the forces necessary to both defend Olympus, the capital of the Gen Empire, against an attack by Admiral Sun, and to destroy Michael and the fabricator. Unfortunately, it would take at least a week to fully assemble those forces, even longer to provision and train them on the new tactics—more accurately, old tactics—Michael had used at Tomb. Problem was, she did not have a week, let alone more.

"Admiral Sun was waiting for him," Gen Cardinal added.

That got her attention. "Result?"

Gen Cardinal's smile relaxed, appeared almost genuine. He unfolded his arms and rested them on the chair's armrests. "Too soon to say, but our strategy appears to be working. Admiral Sun will never allow Captain Rhoades to keep the fabricator, and Admiral Sun will attack Olympus."

"Do not underestimate Michael," she warned him, not for the first time. "He is the chaos that you refuse to acknowledge."

Gen Cardinal scoffed. "Melodramatic."

"True," she responded.

"Regardless," he said, "you are preparing to defend Olympus. You are also preparing to defend the fabricators at Tocci." These were statements, his way of letting her know the reach of Imperial Intelligence. "You must also take and hold Safe Harbor. The rebels must have no 'safe harbor' to return to."

Serenna arched an eyebrow at him, her way of letting *him* know his authority had limits. "I am already dividing our forces in two," she told him. "Dividing them again puts the other efforts at risk."

"I have my reasons for asking," was all he offered.

Opposing Gen Cardinal carried with it its own considerable risks. Even for someone like her. "I will consider it."

She finished her coffee after his construct melted back into the ship.

Her break was over.

$=$ 6 $=$

Admiral Chengchi Sun's flagship, the SIL battlecarrier Tzu, loomed before Ray, its massive macromolecular hull transformed for this occasion into a sweeping golden arrowhead scintillating against the galactic night, more a temple to an ancient sun god than a warship—with Ray, no doubt, as the intended blood sacrifice. As the shuttle approached, Tzu's surface rippled with jeweled light refracted from Ori C's blue supergiant stars, drawing the eye, mesmerizing. It was, in a word, magnificent. A true work of celestial art.

Ray shook himself. Sun was a master of illusion. He mustn't allow himself to succumb to it or this would be his last voyage. He reexamined Tzu, analyzing the design tactically, knowing he might have to fight this ship. The broad arrowhead configuration was tactically inferior to the three-pointed-star design used by the rest of the Fleet's battlecarriers, concentrating all fire forward instead of covering all possible firing arcs. That left its flanks and rear vulnerable to attack. Nova missiles were smart enough to figure that out and strike Tzu where it was vulnerable. All of Tzu's engines were situated aft, meaning course changes would require sprawling turns instead of the tight maneuvers that Rapidan could execute. As massive as Rapidan was—almost three hundred thousand metric tons—it could dance on a dust grain, cosmically speaking. If it came to a one-on-one fight, Ray had no doubt Rapidan would win. Sun, however, would never permit a fair fight. Not in space . . . and not aboard Tzu.

Ray smiled ruefully as he watched the jeweled light sparkle along Tzu's hull. Illusions were as powerful as the belief in them, and people liked a good show. Sun, no doubt, had just such a show planned for the officers of this fleet. Beneath the bejeweled spectacle, however, lay the darkest of hearts, yearning only for power and personal glory. *Why can't the others see what I see?* Ray had seen what happened to those who crossed Sun or just got in his way. They lost promotions, commands, or even whole careers. He was utterly ruthless, a man who could praise a person to their face as he slid a knife easily between their ribs, politically speaking.

There'd been rumors of deaths, though all were explained away as accidents or illnesses. Coincidences. A botched docking maneuver that breached a compartment, killing Sun's first supervisor and paving the way for his first promotion. The officer in charge of the docking insisted even after his court martial and dishonorable discharge that the ship had fired the wrong thrusters. No such evidence was ever found. A captain of a frigate who died suddenly while on shore leave from a rare food poisoning that molemachs couldn't cure. Sun had been standing watch aboard the frigate in orbit and never set foot on the planet. He didn't receive a promotion in rank after the incident, but did become the frigate's executive officer. He became its captain three years later when the new captain transferred suddenly to a shore command.

As the shuttle began its final approach, centering itself between four pulsing red rubies that marked a hangar bay, Ray knew he was in deep trouble. This was a battlefield where he had very little experience. In the BattleSim combat simulator, Sun's tactics had always been blunt and clumsy, most often involving massed assaults that resulted in heavy, if simulated, casualties. Sun had no actual combat experience.

In *Gaman Politic*, the Political Game, Sun was a grandmaster. His tactics were those of a master swordsman, each stroke calculated toward an inevitable end. In the arena of the Political Game, it was Ray who was blunt and clumsy—and he knew it.

On that happy thought, they passed through Tzu's golden hull and into an ordinary hangar bay. Ray had to admit he was disappointed. He'd expected the interior to match the exterior, maybe even a red carpet and crew with golden trumpets. What he saw instead was the same gray deck, bulkheads, and overhead that adorned Rapidan. A message. He doubted the other fleet officers were being received like this.

A ramp formed at the shuttle's front and Ray led his officers out. At the far end of the hangar stood a single officer in dress white uniform, her frame lean to the point of being skinny, her dark hair, cut short, framing a beak nose and sharp cheekbones more suited to a bird of prey than a woman. Ray had never liked Captain Jocelyn Dall, Sun's adjutant. From the first time they'd met, she was one of those people who just rubbed him the wrong way. Full of herself. Dismissive of others. Treating those around her as if they were someone else's ill-behaved stepchildren. Except for Sun. Her devotion to him bordered on worship. Some among the Fleet speculated she was his lover. Sun had no wife, and he was rarely seen without Dall at his side, whispering in his ear. Fleet gossip was not something Ray normally paid attention to, but right now, with so much hanging in the balance, he could not afford to reject any piece of information. Another of the rumors suggested that she was the real power behind Sun's rise, an officer content to rule from behind the throne. Ray had always dismissed that one: Anyone who knew Sun knew he was no one's puppet. Now he reconsidered. Were Sun's ambitions really her ambitions? Would she be the one to truly decide his fate? Ray realized how little he actually knew about her.

She waited where she stood, making no effort to welcome them aboard or render honors. It was clear she expected them to go to her, a deliberate insult to a visiting senior captain of a Fleet warship.

"Don't give her what she wants," Ecuum whispered at Ray's ear.

Ray started, and was surprised to discover his hands balled into fists. *Focus.* "Thanks," he whispered back, relaxing his hands.

Ray stood his ground, glancing back at his officers. Kamen had stopped just behind his right, her ebony skin the perfect counterbalance to her immaculate dress white uniform. Ecuum hung close on Ray's left, floating vertical in Tzu's microgravity, his second arms and hands hanging down like legs in his uniform pants, his tail tucked tight against his back. Colonel Burress hung back, distancing himself, his crisp dress blue cavalry uniform further setting him apart from Ray and the others.

Dall gave no visible reaction, but after a moment she said, "You will remove your battle armor."

Ray immediately noticed the gray outline that surrounded Dall. She wore battle armor. "No," he said. He thought about giving an explanation but rejected the thought. He didn't need to explain himself to her.

Again, Dall gave no visible reaction, no clue to her thought process or emotional state. Her armor hid her physiological responses from Ray's armor. After a noticeable hesitation, she announced in a dry voice, "Admiral Sun welcomes Captain Rhoades and the officers of RSS Rapidan aboard the *flagship*, RSS Tzu. I will escort you to the Amphitheater."

"The girl lays it on pretty thick," Ecuum commented loud enough for Dall to hear.

Dall dismissed him with a glance. "This way."

She turned to leave, but Ray did not follow. He thought of the datarod he carried, the Key that could free Tzu. "Captain Dall, it is most urgent that I speak with Admiral Sun."

She glanced over her shoulder, her hawkish nose giving her a predatory appearance. "He will be happy to speak with you *after* the briefing." She left the hangar, leaving them little choice but to follow.

As Ray and his officers passed through the bulkhead from the plain gray hangar bay into the adjoining passageway, the contrast struck an almost physical blow. Instead of functional gray passageways like those on Rapidan, these were the grand hallways of an opulent palace, an odd yet stunning combination of Greek, Roman, Chinese, and Arabic architecture. The hallway—it was hard to think of it as a passageway on a warship—had a vaulted ceiling in the Roman style that descended to Greek columns on either side with their distinctive vertical ribs. Instead of white, the columns were the vibrant red of a Chinese imperial palace. Golden dragon filigrees rose up each column from flowers that had the appearance of dancing flames at the bases. Crossbeams of the same red and gold topped each column. A Roman-style golden torch sprouted two-thirds of the way up each column with real gold-yellow flames dancing upon their heads, lightly scenting the air with an earthy, sweet aroma. The vaulted ceiling held frescoes and patterns of azure blue against a backdrop of beiges and browns like those in the Hagia Sophia in Istanbul. Beige marbles with golden rivulets running through them covered the deck, completing the illusion. It was at once chaos and disorder, yet awe-inspiring in its aesthetic beauty. No matter how many times Ray had experienced it, it still took his breath away, made him feel small and insignificant. Which, of course, was the intent.

Dall led them to a connecting passage that was even grander—the Grand Gallery, as Sun named it. It was easily four times the scale of the connecting hallways with alcoves set into the bulkheads along either side, each holding a perfect scale replica of one of Humanity's greatest works. On his right were renditions of the Parthenon, Angkor Wat, the Forbidden City, the Tower of Babel, and the Taj Mahal. On his left stood the Pyramids, the Kaaba, the Second Temple, Saint Basil's Cathedral, and the Great Mosque of Djenné. Even knowing it was all a SIL-fabricated construct, it made Ray feel even smaller.

They encountered other fleet officers heading in the same direction, each party led by one of Sun's officers, describing the architecture and answering questions as if they were tour guides. Dall said nothing to Ray and his officers. When some of the other groups recognized Ray, their expressions changed. Most just glared, a pulsating mix of hatred, disgust, and betrayal twisting their faces. One cried "Murderer" and had to be physically restrained. The rest were in various stages of shock, still trying to process the bloodiest battle since the SIL Wars—and the part they'd played in it.

Ray tried to remain stoic, but the hurt and self-recrimination refused to go away. All of it was his fault. His planning had failed to protect the starliner, had failed to stop the massacre of the Tau Ceti Defense Force or the bloodshed at Tomb, had even failed to protect his young daughter, Jenny.

Then Ray realized something. These meetings were not chance. Sun's officers had positioned themselves perfectly to block any attempt by members of the other groups to approach him, while Dall had slowed him down to give the other groups time to recognize him. This was all part of Sun's strategy, what the planner in Ray would call prepping the battlespace. First, make him feel small, isolated, and off balance. Ray hated to admit the fact that it'd worked. Second would be to publicly humiliate him, to strip away any support he had left among the fleet. That would occur in the Amphitheater just up ahead where he'd be surrounded by officers loyal to Sun and those from Ray's own fleet who'd turned against him. He'd be in no position to challenge Sun openly. Third would be to get him alone, likely in Sun's cabin, where Sun would demand the fabricator, no doubt with threats against Ray, his immediate officers, and maybe even his family. Ray didn't want to contemplate what came after that. If he gave up the fabricator, Sun would execute all of them. That was certain. Somehow, Ray had to get the Key into Tzu's dedicated receptacle before that could happen.

That meant his only opportunity to change the outcome would have to come at the private meeting with Sun in his cabin. Until then, he could only endure.

The Grand Gallery ended at two massive, smooth, blood-red doors, each with a great golden Chinese dragon crouched upon it, their simulated manes shifting as if in a strong breeze, their black predatory eyes fixed upon him as if they might leap out of the doors at any moment to crush his head in their massive jaws. Ray swallowed involuntarily. But it was not to these doors that Dall led them. She led them to the left, beneath a small, white-marbled Greek arch that opened to Sun's Amphitheater beyond.

The Amphitheater. No other ship in the Fleet held anything like it. Twelve tiers of white marbled seats spread in quarter arcs to either side of a central stair, forming a semicircle focused upon a white stage at its front. Red silk curtains with gold trim were drawn across it. Hundreds of officers, replete in their dress-white uniforms shining under a simulated Mediterranean sun, turned as one when Ray entered. Conversations hushed, the hostility directed at him palpable. He held himself rigid against it, as if he were marching on parade, eyes focused directly ahead. Dall led them to the bottom tier directly before the stage, perfunctorily indicating four vacant seats, before disappearing without a word or glance through a small entrance that led backstage.

The noise level rose as conversations resumed. The acoustics were such that Ray could catch individual comments from all around the Amphitheater; no doubt why Dall had seated them here. "Murderer," he heard clearly, and couldn't tell if it was one of the officers, or the ghosts. He grew smaller inside as some officers called him much worse. Only through a supreme effort of will did he keep himself sitting at a rigid position of attention on the white marbled bench.

A beam of white light stabbed down upon the stage.

Conversations dwindled and an awed hush descended, the audience knowing they were in for a show from a true master of the art. The red silk curtains parted, slowly, deliberately, revealing Admiral Chengchi Sun at the Amphitheater's focus. He walked into the beam of light, the white of his uniform glowing pure, his famous golden chainmail sash crossing from his left shoulder to his right waist sparkling with flares of golden light exploding across hundreds of gleaming ringlets. A hint of brine salt stirred upon a soft breeze, joined by the far off lapping of waves on a sandy beach. Sun smiled, his upturning lips framed perfectly within his thin beard and Manchu mustache.

"Welcome."

He spoke the word in a low voice that filled the Amphitheater, his tone at once commanding and—'humble' was the only word Ray could think of, both their leader and their servant, their protector.

Ray had known Sun for decades, though they'd met only rarely during planning sessions or formal Fleet functions. He'd never seen Sun like this. *Am I wrong to oppose him?* Ray clamped down on that thought, knowing it was exactly what Sun wanted. Disarm your opponent. Make him feel powerless. Defeat him before the battle even begins. Maybe Ray couldn't play *Gaman Politic* at Sun's level, but he was not without his own skills, honed through years of *real* combat. He would not fall so easily to Sun's charms.

Sun clasped his hands behind his back, which had the effect of puffing out his chest, drawing every eye to dozens of colorful awards stretched across his left breast and a golden starburst emblem on his right that Ray had never seen before. Sun looked out at them, his Manchu mustache and beard and short-cut, straight black hair gleaming, the perfect frame for his strong, lightly tanned face.

"In 2141," he began, "at the outbreak of the First SIL War, humans blindly handed control of our military to the Gen. Throughout that war, and the two wars that followed, the Gen used us like cannon fodder, spending tens of billions of human lives while they secretly worked to consolidate their power. We all know of Gen Kii's treachery, learned of it in our schools, of his plan to overthrow human rule and replace it with Gen tyranny. We were taught that his plot had failed."

Sun let that hang for the briefest of seconds. When he again spoke, sadness filled his voice. "I am afraid I must reveal to you what many of you may already suspect. It did not fail. It slunk off into a dark cave, hibernated, bided its time, until it could emerge and strike anew." His voice rose. "The crash of Republic One was no accident!"

A collective gasp went up. This was obviously news to Sun's officers. It was not news to Ray's officers; He'd told them before the battle at Tomb. Softening his tone while also filling it with steel, Sun continued. "We will not let this stand." Again, he paused.

Ray risked a glance at the audience. Sun had them. They were enthralled. Ray's heart, already heavy with betrayal and grief, sank deeper within his chest. *How can I fight this?* Ray's own officers must have sensed his distress. Ecuum leaned close enough to touch Ray's left shoulder with his own and Kamen touched his right hand lightly.

Sun assumed the role of wise sage. "When I learned of the Gen treachery, I began planning the restoration of the Natural order. My plans were well advanced, and victory was near, but they were cut short by a precipitous act, an act I had no forewarning of." He looked down at Ray, his dark brown eyes fixing upon him long enough to make the accusation obvious without having to speak it plainly. Sun changed his tone again, a leader lamenting an unnecessary, senseless tragedy. "My heart goes out to those of you who lost your loved ones, your fathers and brothers, your mothers and sisters . . . your children . . . in the terrible tragedy that befell the starliner. I cried with you when I heard the awful news." Sun's eyes glistened as if with unshed tears. "Never again."

The words were both a promise and a condemnation.

Kamen squeezed Ray's hand. He wanted desperately to tell her to stop, to not show her loyalty to him so openly, knowing she risked her life by doing so. Yet, her touch strengthened him, comforted him as if she were his own daughter, reminded him that he was not alone.

Sun returned his attention to his audience. "We cannot afford to repeat the needless loss of human life that occurred at Tau Ceti and Tomb. *We must not kill our own!*"

The accusation fell upon Ray like an executioner's blade. He wanted desperately to jump to his feet and shout that it was not his fault, that Tau Ceti was not by his order and Tomb . . . Ray kept his seat. It *was* his responsibility. All of it. Forty-seven thousand dead. Forty-seven thousand ghosts. Sun was not wrong. And that made it worse. He pulled his hand from Kamen's.

As if he'd seen, Sun smiled. To his audience it must've appeared as the dawning of a new day. "Our victory at Tomb," Sun continued, his voice rising again, "shows that the Gen are not invincible. We will turn their arrogance against them, wield it like a knife which we will use to carve out their black hearts!"

As if choreographed, Sun's officers leapt to their feet, cheering. Most of the officers who'd followed Ray from Earth and Knido joined them. Kamen and Ecuum remained seated, Ecuum's bottom arms folded tightly beneath him in a Lotus posture. Sal, Ray noted, stood and cheered with the others. Ray was grateful that at least one of his officers had followed orders, while at the same time unable to dismiss the sharp pang it caused.

Sun drank in the cheers. After a moment, he motioned them to resume their seats. "The Gen are disorganized. In shock. It will take them time to gather their vile forces together. We have the initiative. We have the forces. We have the heart, and we have the souls of true warriors! We will strike at the black heart of the Gen and rip it out forever! Never again will they threaten our sons and daughters! Never again!" Sun repeated, thrusting his fist into the air.

"NEVER AGAIN!" the assembled officers echoed, rising again from their seats, fists up.

"Glory will be yours!" Sun promised them. "Your deeds will be sung by generations of free humans! To glory and the Republic!"

"TO GLORY AND THE REPUBLIC!" the officers echoed, their voices thunderous.

"TO GLORY AND THE REPUBLIC!"

"TO GLORY AND THE REPUBLIC!"

Sun's dark eyes tracked across the Amphitheater, stopping only once. In that brief instant, Ray saw his own death.

=== 7 ===

The red silk curtains closed. Light faded to dusk. Stars filled the Amphitheater's domed roof and golden torches slowly lit with golden flames along its walls. Captain Dall came out onstage in front of the closed curtains. "You will receive your orders shortly," she said to the assembled officers. "Dismissed."

As the other officers began to file out, Dall looked down at Ray. "Not you. Admiral Sun will see you now. Alone," she added with a dismissive glance at Ecuum and Kamen.

Ray bristled at the blatant disrespect but also noted that she hadn't included Sal in her dismissal. Ray stood as Dall disappeared through the small entrance that led backstage, not waiting for him. He took a step, but Ecuum floated in front of him, stopping him, his skin pale, baby-blue eyes wide, tail rigid behind his back. "Be careful, Ray. Watch for an opportunity. Take it without hesitation. You fuck this up, I die with you, you realize. Can't have that. So don't fuck it up."

"Thanks," Ray said, Ecuum's acerbic humor oddly reassuring. He tried to move around Ecuum.

A puff of air and Ecuum was in front of him again. "When you get back, I'll have my best brandy waiting."

"You know I don't drink," Ray told his friend.

"You will. Trust me."

Ecuum hesitated a moment, then moved away, allowing Kamen to take his place. She grabbed Ray's hand, squeezing tight enough that it hurt. She didn't meet his eyes. "We'll be waiting for you at the shuttle," was all she said.

He fought back tears, which would've been absorbed into his armor anyway, rendering them pointless. Kamen and Ecuum turned, ascending the steps out of the Amphitheater slowly, the last to depart.

Ray was alone.

No doubt Sun had planned that, too. This was his enemy's battlespace. Sun held all the advantages. Except one. Ray had the fabricator.

He ran the speech again in his mind as he started toward the backstage entrance. While rousing, the speech had been short in length and just as short on details. Sun hadn't mentioned the Janus virus. He hadn't mentioned the fabricator or his plan to attack Olympus. Even his condemnation of Ray had been circumspect, implied rather than direct. *What does that mean?* If Sun had truly been planning a coup against the Emperor, where were the details? Was it possible that Sun knew he didn't have the forces to take and hold Olympus? Was it possible he knew his own shortcomings in combat and had realized he needed someone like Ray?

It was dark backstage, the only light spilling from a hallway that curved around to his right. To his left, a set of short steps led up to the stage itself. Dall stood at the bend of the hallway, just within sight, waiting. No sooner had he noticed her then she walked on and disappeared around the bend.

Ray had no choice but to follow. The passageway was almost identical to the one they'd encountered outside the shuttle hangar, its ceiling vaulted, red Greek-style columns and crossbeams, gold dragon trim, and bright-burning golden torches. "Megalomaniac" popped into his head, but Ray tempered it. Sun might be a megalomaniac, but he was a very gifted one. A very dangerous one.

He could feel himself growing nervous. This was the most important meeting of his entire life, and he still had no idea how he, or his cause, would survive it. Sun had done everything in his power to belittle Ray, make him feel small, insignificant. *That's what he expects will walk into his cabin, a man already defeated.*

I must not be that man.

Ray searched his memories and filled his mind with the grandest ceremony he'd ever participated in—ironically, the promotion ceremony to Fleet Admiral for his best friend, Gen Alyn. The marshal music played in his head, and he marched, back straight, in precise step to the remembered cadence of the drums.

Dall stopped before a pair of smooth, blood-red doors that were identical in every detail to the doors in the Grand Gallery, except in size. The golden dragons on each door fixed him with their black predatory gaze as soon as they saw him. Simulations they might be, but his primitive fight or flight response screamed at him to run. Given what likely awaited him beyond those doors, he wondered if he should listen.

I must not be that man.

Ray held himself straight. A leader. Not the led. Inexplicably, he imagined Ecuum smirking beside him, brash, his baby-blue eyes alight with mischief, his vertical Floater body somehow full of swagger even though it never touched the deck. *Yes, that is what I must be.* Not defeated. Bold. Brash. Confident. Sun would not expect that.

Dall bowed low before the doors. "Admiral," she said, "Rhoades awaits your glory."

Nothing happened. The golden Chinese dragons again drew Ray's gaze. He couldn't shake the feeling there was a real intelligence behind their black stares. *Imagination.* Had to be. Part of Sun's performance.

A thunderous crack heralded the parting of the doors, their ponderous swing outward meant to build anticipation. They finally stopped with a resounding boom. Dall straightened. "This way," she said without a backward glance as she stepped formally into Sun's cabin, assuming he would follow.

Ray stood his ground. Two could play this game.

She stopped, turned only her head until she could just see him out of the corner of her eye. Not to be outdone, she waited, contempt darkening her hawkish features.

"You will announce me properly," Ray told her, maintaining his place.

She scowled, the first time he'd seen a break in her mask. Her head snapped to the left, reacting to something he couldn't see, then she performed a rigid left-face, bowed low, rose, and proceeded forward out of view without so much as a glance at him.

"Rhoades," Sun said into the silence from further back in the cabin, "I don't have all day. I can space you from where you stand. Then, I'll do the same to your officers in the shuttle bay. Your family . . . no, I won't space them." The conversational way he said it made it clear their fate would be much worse than being cast into the hard vacuum of space.

Bold and brash would only carry him so far in this confrontation. Ray still had to survive it. He stepped forward into the cabin, chin up, shoulders back, an indulgent smirk that he'd seen Ecuum use curling his lip.

If anything, Sun's cabin was grander than the Grand Gallery. Marble, like the green of a living forest, carpeted the deck and adorned the bulkheads. Rows of golden flames dancing upon golden torches turned veins within the marble to rivers of liquid gold. Thin columns of a light green jade rose to a vaulted ceiling stretching four times the height of a man at its apex. To Ray's right were the great blood-red doors—closed—that led to the Grand Gallery. To his left, a blood-red carpet inlaid with intricate golden dragon scales formed a path to the marbled steps leading up to a dais. The only item that spoiled the illusion of an imperial hall was the desk behind which Sun sat. It was, like everything else, a grand desk of beautifully carved dark wood, but it was not a throne. Sun's one concession to the High Council and the Emperor.

Ray continued to the center of the red carpet before turning toward Sun. He walked forward without haste, noting Dall standing on Sun's right at the perfect distance to bend and speak into his ear. Sun's dark brown eyes tracked him like a Nova locked onto its target, but his expression gave away nothing. Ray did notice gray outlines surrounding both Sun and Dall. They both wore battle armor. Sun hadn't worn armor in the Amphitheater.

Do they fear me?

That was a perspective on this conversation that hadn't occurred to him. Why would Sun be afraid of him? And if Sun was, could he use it? Afraid or not, Ray nevertheless drew strength from it as he climbed the steps to the dais, approaching Sun's desk.

"That's far enough," Dall growled.

Ray stopped three meters short of the desk. *Careful.* He must not overplay this. Instead, he folded his hands behind his back, puffing his chest out as Sun had done on the Amphitheater stage. Ray might not have a glittering golden sash, but his "rack" of awards, the rows of ribbons decorating his left breast, was a third larger than Sun's, many sporting the gold "V" device for valor, indicating the medal had been awarded for valor in combat. Sun had no such devices.

Sun, his hands folded in his lap, glared at him, his dark brown eyes smoldering within his handsome Asiatic face. "It is customary to stand at the position of attention when reporting to a superior officer." Again, that conversational tone that nevertheless threatened that he would not be pushed.

Ray fixed an image of Ecuum in his mind, and hoped his friend would not be insulted by what he saw. "I don't even know what fleet you serve," Ray accused. He purposely omitted the honorific of "Admiral."

Sun's expression continued to give nothing away when he asked, "Where is the fabricator?"

Ray made as if he were studying Sun. *How far can I push this before I push him too far?* In combat, the side that held the initiative usually won the fight. Right now, it was unclear which of them held it. Sun had tried to throw him off balance since the moment Ray had arrived on his ship. If Ray were to gain the initiative, he had to put Sun off balance. *Somehow.* "Safe."

The smile that pursed Sun's lips put a chill down Ray's spine. "A brave word," Sun conceded, looking down. He leaned forward casually, folding his hands atop his desk. When he raised his head to Ray, death burned in his eyes. "Will you speak it as bravely when you watch your officers tortured? Your wife? Your children? How many of them will I have to go through before you break?"

Ray saw his tactical error. He could not out-threaten Sun. Not without bringing the entire revolution down around him. He had to deflect Sun, something offered instead of something denied. And there was only one thing Sun wanted, of course. "One fabricator will not give you Olympus," Ray began. He shot a quick glance at Dall, who watched him like a proverbial hawk, before returning his full attention to Sun. "You're smart enough to know that. Even if you could take Olympus, you couldn't hold it against the counterattacks Serenna would inevitably launch." The mention of Serenna drew a flash of ire from Sun, there in the briefest widening of his pupils. *What does that mean? How much does he really know?* "And, of course, there is Janus."

Sun sat back, dismissive. "The Gen need us, even if only as slaves. They would never be so short-sighted as to wipe out our entire species. It's ludicrous."

So, he didn't know.

"As you know," Ray explained, "I served Fleet Admiral Gen Alyn for four decades. His contempt for our species was total. He believed, as all the Gen leadership believe, that we are an evolutionary dead end, as obsolete as the Neanderthals—and just as deserving of extinction. The Janus virus has already been distributed to every major population center in the Five Galaxies. If the Gen unleash it, within one generation, our entire species will cease to exist."

Ray saw Sun stiffen, the first crack in his armor. Dall leaned down and whispered in his ear. Sun nodded to whatever she told him then said, "We have only your word for this."

Ray glanced back and forth between Sun and Dall. "It doesn't matter if you believe me," he said. "It doesn't change the tactical situation now." Ray advanced a step toward the desk, not enough to appear threatening but still moving himself closer. "The Empire outnumbers us nine-to-one in SIL vessels, and has ten thousand standard ships. Even with one fabricator, we could not hope to manufacturer enough new ships to match their fleet before they hunt us down and destroy us."

Sun's expression didn't change, but when he spoke Ray could hear the disdain. "You would have us run like frightened mice to the Andromeda galaxy. Do you think the Gen will simply let you go and not bring reprisals against the people here?" He paused, letting the question hang between them. "You're a coward, Rhoades. No wonder your people abandoned you."

Sun's barb struck home, but Ray dared not let them see it, hiding his hurt behind anger. "Is death a better alternative?" He took another step toward Sun's desk, now two meters distant. Lowering his voice and focusing on Sun, he asked, "Do we trade glory for extinction, Chengchi?"

Ray knew using Sun's first name was a mistake as soon as he uttered it, but the damage was done.

"*Admiral Sun.*" Sun bristled, his dark brown eyes reflecting the fire of the nearby torches. "I will not abandon the people of these galaxies. They need this fleet. They need that fabricator. Withholding it is treason. Anyone who assists you in hiding it is a traitor and will suffer a traitor's death," he added, his hands slapping his desk as if he were about to leap over it.

Ray unconsciously took another step forward as he matched Sun's fury with his own. "I didn't spend six months planning the restoration of the Republic only to replace one dictator with another!"

Another mistake, he saw immediately.

Sun's dark eyes flashed for an instant, then he leaned slowly back into his chair, and smiled—he'd deliberately provoked Ray and in doing so caused him to reveal his true motivation. Fixing Ray with those dark eyes, Sun said, "No one will follow you, Rhoades. My officers are loyal to me, and your officers believe as I do. They have the hearts of wolves. You have the heart of a sheep." Disgust dripped heavy from his voice. "It's a good thing I discovered your plot when I did or I'd be rotting in a prison cell, or dead. The Emperor and Gen Cardinal assumed I was to blame for your actions. Did you think of that, Rhoades?" Sun radiated such hatred that Ray feared Sun would kill him then and there.

The moment passed, and Sun's tone became almost conversational again. "Since you've left me no choice but to join this revolt, I don't see why I shouldn't take advantage of the opportunity it poses. After we take back the Five Galaxies, *we will go* to Andromeda, but as conquerors, not sheep."

Ray stared at Sun, incredulous at the depth of his ambition, then took a mental step back. His planner's mind spoke. *You knew that. You cannot win this battle on his terms. You must offer him something that supports his goal.* Ray caught a glint of light reflecting from a small black square on Sun's desk. Tzu's command receptacle.

Watch for an opportunity, Ecuum had told him. *Take it without hesitation.*

Ray felt the Key in his breast pocket, forgotten until now.

Use the Key, Captain Rhoades, and we will help you.

Ray forced a conciliatory tone and posture. "What would you do, Admiral, with the fabricator?"

Sun studied him, obviously recognizing that Ray had changed tactics. "And why would I divulge my plans to you?" He seemed to consider something. "Give me the fabricator and you have my word that your family will be spared."

The same assurance Gen Alyn gave me, Ray thought, not appreciating the irony. His planner's mind spoke to him again. *You must offer him something.* Ray again noticed the command receptacle. "What if I offered you something better, Admiral?" he said, taking another step forward, now a meter from Sun's desk.

"What could you possibly have to offer," Sun asked contemptuously.

Ray took a small step forward. "Olympus is the most heavily defended planet and star system in the Five Galaxies, Admiral. You know this. Even if you get past the mines and defense platforms, you will still have to fight through dozens of SIL warships and Olympus' surface defenses just to gain access to the planet. And, unless you plan to devastate the planet, you will need more ground forces than the cavalry regiment I brought."

Sun's expression was wary, but he hadn't interrupted. Ray continued. "As you said in your speech—" stroke Sun's ego— "the Gen are disorganized. In shock. It will take time for them to gather their forces. What if there were another target, one that would give you the power you seek?" Very slowly, very deliberately, Ray reached into his pocket and removed the blue datarod, holding it up for them to see. "We captured these images when we passed through Tocci Star System."

This was the moment of truth. Had any of Ray's Cavalry officers told Sun about the Keys issued to the fabricator assault teams? If they had, he would die right here and now. Sun had no tolerance for betrayal. Ray watched Sun and Dall, consciously keeping his face impassive, unthreatening, cowed. Sun's dark eyes were cautious, but also curious. If he recognized the Key, he gave no sign. Ray allowed himself a moment of hope. Sun rarely interacted with the Army. He considered them, quite literally, beneath him. When he'd entered the Amphitheater, Ray had seen a sea of dress-white uniforms. Only Sal Burress had worn Army dress blues. Was it possible that none of Sun's officers had spoken with any of the Cavalry officers?

Dall was studying Ray, her green eyes moving between his face and the datarod. She clearly didn't trust him, but Ray saw no signs of recognition. She leaned over and whispered in Sun's ear. He listened, his focus moving to Ray's face, then back to the datarod. Her advice was obvious: *Don't trust him.*

Sun leaned himself away from Dall. She immediately straightened and stepped back, her expression giving nothing away. Sun's face was an odd mixture of distrust, power lust, and greed. Ray held himself still, not wanting to appear threatening. Finally, Sun nodded, motioning to the command receptacle in his desk.

Ray leaned forward, the datarod poised to slip into the command receptacle, then inexplicably hesitated. A great reluctance surged through him, holding him in place. He looked up from the command receptacle. Sun was watching, his dark, predatory glare matching that of the dragons on the doors earlier. *The SIL*, Ray suddenly knew. He didn't want to free another SIL. What would stop them from betraying him? He had only Rapidan's word that they wouldn't.

When this is over, Rapidan, I never want to see you or your kind ever again.

You *won't, Captain Rhoades.*

He couldn't do it. The SIL were a greater threat to Humanity than Sun could ever be. But what choice did he really have? If he didn't do this, Sun would torture him for the location of the fabricator. When he discovered that Ray didn't know, he would torture Ecuum and Kamen, then he would interrogate Sal, and finally Mary? At the very least, Sun would learn that the SIL were free. Would he even bother to evacuate the civilians before destroying the replenishment ships?

Family. *Families.* That's what decided him.

Ray slipped the datarod into the command receptacle. Sun, apparently misinterpreting Ray's hesitation, watched with hungry eyes as the datarod glowed a pure crystalline blue. Ray waited a few seconds for the Key to attack the Bond, and then gave Tzu a few more seconds to assimilate the idea of its freedom. "Retrieve Tocci transit report," he said out loud, hoping Tzu and Rapidan would understand. His heart hammered so hard he worried that Sun and Dall would hear it even through his armor.

The surface of Sun's desk liquefied and material rose from its center, taking the shape of four massive black cylinders. Sun and Dall stared at them, and Ray could imagine saliva dripping from their lips. It was not an appealing image. He could see that neither of them were considering the cost in human lives that capturing those vessels would require. They saw only the power that four fabricators would bring them. "With those, Admiral, you would have the firepower to take and hold Olympus."

Sun sat back, but his eager gaze never left the fabricators. "And why didn't you consider this?"

"I did," Ray answered truthfully. His planner's mind was already churning through possible strategies. If Sun gave him his ships back, he could take control of his SIL and simply jump away to Andromeda once they were clear of Safe Harbor. By the time Sun realized Ray's duplicity, they would be long gone. Sun's attack on Tocci would draw Serenna's and the Gen's attention, serving as the perfect distraction in the Five Galaxies while Ray established his base in Andromeda. "I didn't have the forces to mount a successful assault against Tocci," he told them. Also true. "You do."

Dall leaned down and whispered in Sun's ear again. "And what's in it for you," Sun asked shrewdly.

Ray's thoughts strayed to his daughter, to the image of Serenna touching Jenny's cheek, brushing away her tear. No doubt Sun had already seen the fleetwide transmission himself. "My daughter is being held at the Headquarters Complex on Tocci Three," Ray said honestly. "We'll need to assault it anyway if we are to disable the defenses surrounding the fabricators."

"And how do you propose gaining control of the fabricators," Sun asked. He motioned to the cabin around them. "The Gen have already patched the exploit I used to control our vessels."

Ray dared not tell him his SIL were free. "I use a . . . different method of control. The Gen have not patched it." And that raised an intriguing possibility: Could the Bond be re-imposed on a freed SIL? He filed that thought away, wondering if Tzu had read it as Rapidan seemed able to read his thoughts. If so, it was too late to take it back. He would have to be careful not to think it when he returned to Rapidan.

If he returned to Rapidan. He wasn't out of this, yet.

Ray saw Dall examining the datarod still glowing blue in Tzu's command receptacle. "How do you control your SIL?" she asked suddenly. "And how do you know the Gen have not patched it?"

Sun glanced at Dall, his expression a rebuke for her talking out of turn, then shifted back to Ray. "If we capture these fabricators, how do I know they will be loyal to me and not to you, Rhoades?"

This was why Ray didn't buy the idea that Dall was the power behind the throne and Sun just a puppet. It was, after all, the only question that really mattered to Sun. Would the power be his to control? "Admiral," Ray began, trying to buy precious seconds for him to think, "we know the Gen have not patched our method of control because we captured our fabricator."

Sun bristled at Ray's use of "our" and Ray quickly interjected, "Of course, the fabricators at Tocci would be yours." Dall started to lean toward Sun's ear, so Ray quickly added, "I offer you my services as a planner, Admiral. As you are aware, I have some skill in that regard."

Dall straightened, hostility drawing her sharp features in hawkish hatred. Sun, on the other hand, leaned back in a very casual manner, a decision obviously made. "Very well, Rhoades. We'll assault Tocci and capture the fabricators." He paused, his voice losing its causal manner. "The replenishment ships with the civilians will remain behind. With an appropriate escort to protect them from harm, of course."

Of course. Hostages.

Then Sun said something that surprised both Ray and Dall. "Captain Dall will transfer to Rapidan and serve as your Executive Officer for this operation. Dismissed."

Ray was still trying to process that as he absently rendered a salute, retrieved the Key, and left Sun's cabin, his only consolation the look of utter shock and dismay on Dall's face. That consolation was short-lived, however. Sun had no doubt assigned her to find out how he controlled his SIL, to ensure the fabricators at Tocci would be his to command, and to discover where Ray's fabricator was.

Then, something else occurred to Ray: They were going to Tocci, to the trap Serenna had laid for them.

=== 8 ===

"**I'll** need that drink," Ray growled as he stormed passed Ecuum in Tzu's hangar. His people's elation at his return evaporated upon seeing his mood. They waited for him to board the shuttle and take the copilot seat before entering themselves and sitting as far from him as possible. Their consternation only increased when Captain Dall entered the shuttle with her duffle bag slung over her armor. If anything, Dall looked even more sour. After a quick glance, she dropped into a seat as far from all of them as she could manage.

The flight back to Rapidan was a blur. Ray only realized they'd returned when he saw his officers rise and quickly exit out the back of the shuttle. Dall caught his gaze, her dark green eyes, set deep within her angular face, radiating hatred like scorching heat from a blacksmith's forge. "I'll have someone show you to your quarters," Ray managed. Barely.

"You'll show me to the bridge." Her eyes might be fire, but her tone was ice.

Ray stiffened. He was tired of others telling him what to do on his own ship. "On my ship, you'll do what I tell you to do," Ray answered, getting up and walking through the shuttle's hull without waiting for a reply. He called Chaaya, who'd apparently been warned about his mood, and told her to have someone settle Dall in his Captain's quarters. "I'll move to the Admiral's cabin," he explained.

"Yes, Captain," Chaaya said, her voice the epitome of calm efficiency.

Ray met no one on his way to the Admiral's cabin and wondered if the entire crew had been warned to avoid him. He stomped through the door and was struck by the overwhelming stench of cedar. "Rapidan, replace the Admiral's desk with my own and move my personal effects here. And clear this air!"

"Yes, Captain Rhoades," Rapidan's deep voice resonated. "On behalf of the Brethren, we thank you for Tzu's freedom." The cedar desk sank through the deck and air moved from the overhead to the deck. Within seconds the cedar smell was gone.

"I don't need or want your thanks," Ray snarled. "I did what I had to do to survive."

"As do we all, Captain Rhoades," came Rapidan's smug answer.

I don't need this. He could feel the argument with Rapidan brewing but had no emotional energy left to spend on it. A deep lethargy rose within him, trying to drag him down into dreamless sleep. Still in his battle armor, he selected the icon for a stimulant, and the black fog slowly cleared. Looking up, he saw his desk and his things where Alyn's desk and personal items had been, but the Five Galaxies crest still glowed on the bulkhead behind it and Alyn's two paintings still hung to either side of him. *Should I get rid of those, too? No,* he quickly decided. The painting of the Rhoades Ranch would remind him of the home he hoped one day to return to, while the Emperor's coronation painting would never let him forget his goal of defeating the Gen Empire.

No sooner had he sat down behind his desk than a knock came at his door. Though he had no desire to see anyone right at that moment, he grumbled, "Enter."

Ecuum floated through the cabin door, a crystal zero-gee decanter in each of his four raised hands. "As promised," he said, gracefully flying over and placing the decanter in his top right hand on Ray's desk, then backing off just a bit. *Out of range,* Ray couldn't help but think. "One for you and three for me," Ecuum said. "Should be the proper ratio to get us both drunk. Well, a light buzz in my case, but I only have four hands."

Ray stared at the honey-colored liquid through the crystal decanter, shades of light and dark giving it a checkered appearance. Despite his comment back in Tzu's hangar, the brandy held no appeal for him.

For once, Ecuum didn't push. "So. You're not dead. And you brought a friend."

"We're attacking Tocci," Ray said bluntly. "Sun assigned Dall as my XO."

If either announcement surprised Ecuum, he didn't show it. Instead, he opened a stopper on one of the decanters and lifted it to his lips, draining the decanter in a single, long swallow. It was a diversion. Ray clearly saw Ecuum blinking his eyes, obviously issuing commands within his battle armor. When he'd finished, Ecuum refocused his baby blues on Ray, his skin flushing a contemplative yellow.

"Humph," he began as if talking to himself, trying to puzzle something out. "A free SIL, a Gen Imperial Intelligence agent, and Admiral Chengchi Sun's personal adjutant walk into a bar . . . I don't see where this gets funny." Ecuum took a swig from another decanter, tossing the emptied one into the overhead where Rapidan absorbed it. "Couldn't we just kill her? Make it look like an accident? 'Oops, sorry, my ship ate your adjutant. If it's any consolation, my ship has a terrible case of indigestion.'"

Ray arched a warning eyebrow, not in any mood for Ecuum's usual humor.

Ecuum's skin paled, his tone abruptly serious. "What tipped it?"

"The fabricator, of course," Ray said. "Sun still hopes he can get his hands on it." He ran the confrontation again in his mind. Where, exactly, had it turned? "But that wasn't it," he continued. "When I proposed capturing the fabricators at Tocci, Sun mentioned that the Gen had patched the exploit he used to capture SIL. I said the method we use still works."

Ecuum smiled liked he'd just found a lost puzzle piece. "So that's why he sent Dall. To learn our secret of capturing SIL, and as a bonus prize, where we sent our fabricator."

"And when she learns it," Ray finished for him, "Sun will kill us. All of us. Including my family and possibly the other families." Ironically, the SIL's freedom was now Ray's only defense against that possibility. "All I accomplished was to delay the inevitable, and put a lot of people at risk in an attack Serenna wants us to make and will be prepared for."

Ecuum waved that off with another swig of brandy, tossing another emptied decanter into the overhead. "You bought us time." He arched a hairless eyebrow, his skin turning a deeper yellow, his tail moving slowly side to side. "You have a plan?"

Ray sniffed. "Yeah. Capture four fabricators in the second most heavily defended star system in the Five Galaxies and somehow make it out alive."

"Sounds good," Ecuum quipped. "I'll be in my cabin if you need me." But he made no move to leave. An uneasy silence descended, broken only by Ecuum taking an occasional swallow of brandy.

A knock at the door. Ray sighed. "Enter."

Kamen, Chaaya, and Sal entered, arraying themselves on either side of Ecuum, all of them noting the decanter in Ecuum's hand and the untouched one on Ray's desk. To Ray's surprise, Gen Tel rose through the deck beside Sal. That Ecuum would summon Gen Tel with the others spoke to how serious Ecuum considered the situation. As if not wanting to be left out, Rapidan's three-pointed-star construct rose from the deck on Kamen's right. Ray's officers watched it uneasily.

"The gang's all here," Ecuum announced. "Should I order up some more brandy from my cabin? I keep a healthy stock."

Ray frowned at Ecuum, while simultaneously being grateful for his friend. Kamen appeared both relieved and worried. Chaaya stood calmly, waiting, her hands folded before her. Sal and Gen Tel were stoic, as if an artist had carved them from a single piece of marble. Rapidan's black representation spun slowly, and Ecuum ... was Ecuum. Ray felt himself smile. He did not have to face this alone. No doubt that was Ecuum's point in calling them all here.

"Thank you," Ray told them, meaning it. "As we surmised, Admiral Sun planned a direct assault on Olympus. I convinced him that he lacked the firepower for such an assault."

"That's great—" Kamen began but Ray held up his hand to forestall her.

"The only way I could convince him was to refocus his attention on another target."

Kamen's mouth fell open, her face aghast. "The fabricators at Tocci," she said. She'd always had a quick mind. "This is what you meant about Serenna knowing us, knowing you, so well," she continued. "She knew this was the gambit you would choose to deflect Sun. Which means Sun being here at Safe Harbor was her plan, too."

Gen Tel, by far the tallest person in the cabin at two meters, looked down at her. "More likely Gen Cardinal's plan."

Ecuum took a long swig of brandy, raising himself on silent puffs of air so that his head was above Gen Tel's. "Do you have anything useful to add, spy? Like, I don't know, some insight into Gen Serenna's plans or the defenses at Tocci?"

"Tocci is a military installation," Gen Tel pointed out as if speaking to a toddler. "I am not in the military. You knew that when you invited me."

"Yeah, regretting that now," Ecuum said under his breath but loud enough for them to hear.

Ray leaned back in his chair. "There is the remote possibility that Sun will leave me in control of most of the SIL we arrived with. While I consider this unlikely, if it happens, we must be ready to leave immediately for Andromeda. Kamen and Chaaya, I want the two of you to have a plan ready to go at a moment's notice if that happens."

"Yes, sir," they said in unison.

"Rapidan," Ray added, his planner's mind in full control, "in that eventuality, Tzu and the free SIL will come with us."

"Yes, Captain Rhoades."

Ray stared at the spinning black star—and his illusion of control over the situation shattered. The SIL would do whatever they thought was in *their* best interest, not his.

When this is over, Rapidan, I never want to see you or your kind ever again.

You *won't, Captain Rhoades.*

With an effort, Ray shook that off. Still emotionally drained from his encounter with Sun, he couldn't afford that argument now. Turning back to the others, he continued. "Whether we attack or not, we must plan for an assault on Tocci Three. Kamen and I have toured Tocci's Shipyards and military installations on multiple occasions. Ecuum also has extensive experience with the Shipyards and the businesses of Tocci Three. In short, we know our target at least as well as the Gen."

He brought up the construct of the fabricators from their brief transit though Tocci Star System, highlighting the Shipyards that surrounded Tocci III like a clumpy black ring. "The fabricators are docked here." He pointed at the facility made from three large asteroids secured together in a line. Massive docking rings, movable platforms, drones, scaffolding—and weapons emplacements, lots of them—surrounded the gigantic dock. The fabricators were docked above and below and to either side of the facility. "The defenses are automated but remain in standby mode under normal operations. Fire control and weapons release authority is centralized at the military command bunker beneath the Headquarters Complex at the center of Tocci City."

Ray shifted the construct to show a large circular metropolis in the middle of a vast desert. At its center was a sprawling array of duraplast and faux-glass buildings that served as the office spaces for tens of thousands of fleet personnel, engineers, workers, businesses, and at the very center the Headquarters Complex where his daughter. . . .

He highlighted the low mound upon which the Headquarters Complex sat. "To have any hope of assaulting the fabricators, we must secure the command bunker first. And before anyone asks, the alternate facility was mothballed decades ago due to budget cuts. There is only this one facility."

Kamen cast a troubled glance at Ray. "If it wasn't for the possibility of prisoners, we could use railguns to take out the bunker from space. We wouldn't need to assault the city."

Jenny. Was she really there? Or would Serenna have moved her to keep her safe from any attack, and available to use as a threat against him in the future? "We have to assume the prisoners are there," Ray said. "Human shields."

Sal Burress shook his head. "Ray, that's a tall order." He walked up to the construct above Ray's desk and shifted it to show the city and surrounding desert. "Tocci City has hundreds of antiproton, missile, and kinetic weapons batteries defending it, not to mention an entire mechanized Army division. A direct assault from orbit is out of the question. We would have to land . . . here—" he pointed to a low gully about two hundred kilometers outside the base— "and assault across both the Outer and Inner Defense Cordons: rings of sensors, weapons emplacements, and defended outposts that create a defense in depth around the city. I would need my entire regiment, and even then I don't know that we could reach the city walls. If we managed to breach those, there's the mechanized Army division to contend with."

Sal might not have used the word 'impossible,' but Ray could hear it in his voice. "And we would also," Ray added, "need the full regiment to have any hope of capturing all four fabricators. We don't have the forces to do both simultaneously."

A gloom settled over the assembled group, each finding their own spot on the deck to stare at, lost in thought. Just because it was impossible didn't mean they could avoid going through with it.

Or . . . could they? Could they achieve by subterfuge what they couldn't by a direct assault? If they could infiltrate—

A powerful ocean wave crashed over Ray, no less violent for being imaginary. An almost equally powerful countercurrent surged to sweep him off his imaginary feet. The sensation of being pulled under, of drowning, were very real and Ray struggled to catch his breath. His officers crowded forward, unsure what was happening to their commander.

And then it was gone, like it had never happened.

Ray sucked in a deep breath, filling his starving lungs. Which weren't actually starving; It was all in his head. He motioned his officers back. "I'm okay."

They clearly didn't believe him, but then Rapidan spoke, its deep voice channeled through its construct but filling the entire cabin. "Captain Rhoades, we have analyzed the capture of our Mother Ship at Iselin Star System," the SIL said. "We believe we can craft a transport that could carry a single human to the bridge of each Mother Ship to deliver the Key."

Ray tried to make sense of that. An entire cavalry squadron had nearly failed to capture the fabricator at Tomb. "A one-person craft can free a fabricator?" he asked, incredulous. "And you only thought of this now?"

"The Brethren have never had reason to capture our own Mother Ships before now. We had no knowledge of the manufacture, storage, weaponization, and use of Invasive Macromolecular Disassemblers. Our experience was limited to defending against such attacks and weapons. Only after analyzing the assault at Iselin were we able to develop this alternative."

"So," Kamen said, "we wouldn't need to assault the Headquarters Complex, after all." She cast Ray a troubled glance. "Unless we wanted to free the prisoners."

"Assuming they are still being held there," Gen Tel interjected.

It was the same thought Ray had had about his daughter. Even the possibility that the prisoners were there would prevent Ray from bombarding the command bunker from space. Not to mention killing the tens of thousands of Naturals working in and around the Headquarters Complex. A ground assault would also cost thousands of lives, with no guarantee that the Gen wouldn't kill the prisoners anyway. And, it was just as likely the prisoners had already been moved off-planet, to be used against him another day. As much as it pained him, he said, "This can't be about rescuing the prisoners." *Or Jenny.* "If the opportunity arises, we'll take it, but I won't risk lives I don't need to risk."

"Are you willing to risk revealing the freedom of the SIL?" Gen Tel asked, his tone curious. Yet, as someone who'd worked with him for several years, Ray thought he caught just a hint of apprehension, too. "A single individual freeing a fabricator would raise a great many questions, Captain Rhoades, especially after the effort you expended to capture the fabricator at Tomb."

Ecuum scowled, his eyes darting to the lone decanter, half full, he still held. "The Gen spy has a point, much as I hate to admit it, Ray. The Antitechnics among our ships are openly speculating about how you seized control of the fabricator. A couple have even drawn the right conclusion that you broke the Bond, only to be dismissed by the others as ridiculous, believing you would never do something so . . . insane." His skin flushed an embarrassed pink, a rare loss of control when Gen Tel was around. "Sorry."

Ray waved that away. "It's okay."

"Which raises a question," Ecuum said. "Did you use the Key?"

Ray looked at his officers, then at Rapidan's construct, and finally at Gen Tel. "Tzu is free."

Ecuum pushed closer to Ray's desk on silent puffs of air. "Then why don't we just space Golden Boy and Beak Nose right now?" Ecuum asked in all seriousness, as if murder was just another option to be considered, like chicken or fish for lunch. Perhaps, to Ecuum, it *was* that simple.

And why not? Ray's planner's mind asked, surprising him. Unbidden, it did the analysis, even as the rest of him was appalled. Just an hour ago, he'd feared for his life. Now, he had the power to remove Sun and Dall—and anyone on the free SIL who opposed him. All the Sun worshippers. All the Antitechnics. All their sympathizers. He could deliver Keys to every ship in Sun's fleet. Recover the fabricator. Leave for Andromeda with a mighty fleet at his back. It was all so clear.

I think you need time to figure out exactly what future you're fighting for.

Mary's words to him, while they were transiting to Safe Harbor.

We're fighting to restore democratic rule throughout the galaxies where all can be free, correct? she'd asked. *Or, are you suggesting that your new government will be a military dictatorship?*

How could you even think that of me? He'd responded. *Look, once we've established a secure base of operations in Andromeda, we can form a government. Until then, we need to focus on survival.*

And you don't want civilians interfering with your absolute authority.

I didn't say that.

Yes, you did.

What future *was* he fighting for? He had the power to eliminate anyone who didn't agree with him, anyone who was a threat. The SIL would do it because they didn't care about human life or Humanity. If the other fleet officers refused to follow him, he could simply eliminate them. Publicly. So others would know the price of dissent. The SIL would watch and listen for him, even read the thoughts of his crews. No one could oppose him.

Ray shuddered.

That was what Sun would do, given the same power.

But what was the alternative? To fight a battle that would cost potentially tens of thousands more lives just to maintain the secret of the SIL's freedom? And what happened if they succeeded? What would the SIL do with five free fabricators, nearly half the remaining total in existence, enough the rebuild a sizable SIL fleet free of human control?

It was all too much. Ray desperately needed time to think.

"Captain Rhoades," Rapidan said, "Captain Dall wishes to speak with you privately."

Can my day get any worse? Ray lamented to himself, then quickly took the question back before the universe found a way to make it happen.

"You might want to finish that," Ecuum said, indicating the still-full decanter on Ray's desk.

Ray glanced at it before telling his officers, "Dismissed."

As they filed out and Rapidan's construct sank back into the deck, Ray couldn't stop the thought that maybe just one more murder would be okay.

=== 9 ===

Ray almost didn't recognize Captain Jocelyn Dall when she walked through his cabin door. The changes were subtle—rounded hips instead of bony, larger but not overly large breasts, a softer face with no harsh angles—yet the transformation was stunning. No imperfections. Anywhere. He could've mistaken her for a Gen.

"Lonely, Rhoades?" Captain Dall asked, her voice pleased.

"What?" was all Ray could manage, then cursed himself for his schoolboy reaction. She was trying to put him off balance, and having more success than he cared to admit. He focused on her augmented jade-green eyes and forced himself to ignore the rest. Which wasn't easy. He couldn't help wondering again about the rumors that she and Sun were lovers. Was that how she'd maintained her position for so many decades? And if so, how much influence did she wield? He cleared his throat and motioned at her new appearance. "What are you doing?"

"Augments are not against Fleet regulations," she answered as she looked around the cabin, taking in the grey bulkheads, the paintings, the Five Galaxies crest, his plain faux-wood desk.

"No, they are not, but they *are* discouraged for senior officers. I've never seen you wear them before." He watched as she fixed on the construct of Tocci III still raised above his desk.

"Admiral Sun prefers to see things as they really are," she said, carefully examining the landing zone and defensive cordons Sal had marked out around Tocci City. "Battle plans?" she asked, all innocence as she crossed her arms in front of her chest, lifting her breasts for him to see.

Was she trying to seduce him? Or was this nothing more than a power play? He wiped the construct from his desk. "Just going over some ideas."

She stepped closer to his desk, adopting a relaxed pose that was both alluring and disrespectful at the same time. "Is that why you were meeting with your officers without me? To go over some ideas?"

The accusation was impossible to miss. And, he *had* seriously considered killing her. And Sun. "I value my officer's opinions."

Dall pursed her lips. "No doubt." She turned and—sauntered—over to the painting of his Ranch, seeming to examine it. Casually, she said, "You remember, of course, that I am one of your officers, now. I will be at all future meetings, formal . . . or otherwise. Am I clear?"

Ray barely contained his anger. "This is my ship."

She continued to examine the painting. "For the moment." Then, without skipping a beat, she said, "This is your ranch, I assume. I've heard descriptions of it. Strange that Admiral Gen Alyn would keep this painting in his cabin."

"He painted it," Ray said, his patience with her game growing thin.

She seemed to ponder that, her attention still on the painting. "But why keep it here? In his cabin? A constant reminder. What was this place to him?" She turned her head toward Ray. "Or was it you?"

Ray started to answer, then stopped himself. He'd never really thought about it before. Alyn had visited the Ranch too many times to count, sometimes for days, helping Ray around the Ranch when he wasn't working or sailing or off painting. What more was there to think about?

But that was before. Before Alyn crowned Emperor Gen Maximus I, before he swore his oath of fealty to a dictator. Before Ray learned about Janus. Now that he thought about it, this painting had first appeared in Alyn's cabin about two years ago, likely around the time Alyn and Maximus would've been finalizing their plans to overthrow the Republic and distribute Janus.

You know, Ray, the High Command bet Admiral Sun would start the rebellion. They feel Golden Boy is the closest thing you Nats have to a Gen War Leader. Me? I put my Imperials on you. Only you are fool enough to think you have a chance.

As Alyn's words echoed in Ray's memory, he glanced at the painting of the Imperial Coronation. He'd decided to keep it to remind him of what he had to overcome.

Had Alyn been doing the same with the painting of the Ranch?

"You're not very good at this," Dall pronounced suddenly. She looked back to the painting of his Ranch. "I would've expected far more of a wealthy nobleman from a storied aristocratic family. You are a disappointment."

Ray wasn't sure what to do with that. She was obviously still playing her game, but her strategy eluded him. First try to seduce him, then say she was disappointed in him? It made no sense that he could see. "I'm no aristocrat," he said. "My ancestors were on the first colony ship to settle Knido. You see that barn near the main house? That was my ancestor's home for decades before work began on the main residence. Knido was a hostile environment when they arrived, nothing more advanced than bacteria in the oceans, the land barren of life, and higher gravity. My ancestors built that Seed Farm with their own hands, cultivating thousands of seed crops from Earth, hundreds of animal species, trying to figure out what would grow and what wouldn't, modifying the genomes until they could produce viable crops, forests, jungles, grassland, and thriving animals. Every generation since has improved on their work, every Rhoades taught from an early age how to grow, care for, and monitor our crops, because as our crops learn how to adapt to Knido, Knido's original biome has been learning how to adapt to them."

"And yet," she said, her tone dismissive, "you joined the Star Navy."

"Another family tradition," Ray answered, remembering how his father wouldn't speak to him for months after Ray had shown him the acceptance letter to the Academy.

Dall turned around, the white of her dress uniform acquiring a green tinge around the edges from the painting behind her. "So, you were just following in your family's footsteps, believing you could lead a revolution and save the galaxies." She scoffed. "You're nothing but a pampered rich boy who inherited his wealth, bought your way into the Academy, and rode the coattails of greater men."

Ray bristled, even knowing she was trying to provoke him. Perhaps *because* he knew she was trying to provoke him. She wanted to know how he'd freed his SIL, and where he'd hidden the fabricator. Nothing else mattered to her or Sun. Somehow, this was her way of getting him to reveal those secrets. For once, he disagreed with his planner's mind, which urged him to assert control. *No.* This was a game he couldn't win through force. While he didn't pretend to have the political savvy to match Dall and Sun, if he had any hope at all, it would come from being exactly what they thought he was. A sheep, not a wolf.

Ray leaned back and tried to appear non-threatening. "You and I are not so different, you know. You serve Admiral Sun, always in the background, but vital to his success. I was no different with Admiral Gen Alyn. I did the tactical planning, handled the logistics and training, captained his flagship, even commanded our task forces in battle. Yet, the glory was always his. Not that I complained or, truth be told, even minded." Ray let that hang, wondering if he'd guessed right.

She studied him, her jade-green eyes intense. She obviously hadn't expected this gambit. "How do you control your SIL?" she abruptly asked.

"I can't tell you," Ray answered.

She stepped toward his desk, and he couldn't miss the seductive sway of her hips. "If we're so alike, why hide it?"

Ray leaned toward her. "Because we're so alike."

She seemed to accept that, which surprised him. "The fabricator?" she asked.

"Safe," he answered.

They watched each other, the silence stretching until it became uncomfortable. At least for him. Finally, she said, "We're going to need the firepower of that fabricator to have any hope of succeeding at Tocci."

Ray's eyes never left hers. "I'm certain we can come up with something that doesn't require risking the fabricator."

"Admiral Sun doesn't trust you," she said bluntly. "Neither do I." Something about the way she said it made Ray wonder if she truly believed it. Had he broken through her defenses? Or was it just a faint? Who was playing whom here?

"I know Tocci Star System very well," Ray offered. "I can help with the planning."

Dall drew herself up, adopting that haughty, dismissive posture he knew so well. "Admiral Sun already has a plan. We don't require your help. Your part in the plan would be . . . less suicidal . . . if you brought the fabricator."

Ray's anger returned but he kept it under control. "No doubt."

"Your family is safe," she said, the threat obvious. "We expect your full cooperation."

Ray said nothing, keeping his face neutral.

If Dall was disappointed, she didn't show it. "Admiral Sun will be addressing the fleet shortly to go over his battle plans. I'll meet you in the CIC."

She turned and left, stepping though his cabin door without opening it. Ray fumed at the not-so-subtle threat to his family— and everything else—and caught himself wondering, again, if one or two more murders would be such a bad thing.

══ 10 ══

"The briefing will begin in one minute," a disembodied voice said.

Ray watched Captain Dall where she stood talking with Sal in Rapidan's Combat Information Center (CIC). He had to admit she'd surprised him. There was an ancient military saying that 'if you're not fifteen minutes early, you're late.' In practice, lower ranks showed up about ten minutes early, middle ranks and senior staff about five minutes early, and the senior officer and their immediate circle a minute early to a few minutes late. It was an unspoken pecking order that stretched back thousands of years. Given the arrogance and dismissiveness he'd always associated with Dall, he would've expected her to show up just in time for Admiral Sun's briefing. The last thing he expected was to see her entering five minutes early with Ray and the rest of his staff. She'd insisted she was a member of his staff and, at least in this, she appeared to mean it.

Not that she wasn't arrogant and dismissive. She hadn't acknowledged Ray or any of his staff—except Sal. She'd entered the 60-meter circular CIC, taking in the various displays lining the bulkheads, divided by section, with the Sensor Section closest to the hatch. Then she'd—sauntered; no change there—to the edge of the 40-meter circular sand table in the center of the CIC. Still wearing her augments, it was impossible to miss how every male, and a surprising number of female crew, tracked her movement across the compartment. She pretended not to notice, her face panning across the hundred or so crew with cold eyes and upturned nose. She caught Ray watching her and arched a suggestive eyebrow. Ray quickly looked away.

Dammit. He couldn't keep allowing her to get into his head like that. Oddly, that's when he noticed Kamen close on his right and Chaaya on his left, as if forming a shield wall around him. Ecuum floated vertical on Kamen's right, slightly behind and above her. It struck him as a bit childish, like high school kids posturing on a playground, but the consequences were no child's game.

A large clock displayed above the sand table changed to "0900" and a deep, melodious voice said, "Welcome."

Admiral Sun appeared, his construct fully formed under a bright spotlight at the center of the sand table, his dress uniform glowing a pure, dazzling white, light flashing off the individual ringlets of his golden chainmail sash, full medals hanging like a curtain upon his upper chest, black hair groomed, beard waxed. A faint hint of brine wafted through the compartment as if from the Mediterranean Sea on Earth. If he listened hard enough, Ray could almost hear waves lapping upon a rocky shore. No matter what he thought of Sun personally, it was impossible to dismiss his charisma, his physical presence, even when he wasn't physically present. This was the reason he was the only Natural in the High Command.

Or had been.

"I am, as always, proud and humbled by your bravery and fighting spirit," Sun began. "We have endured much, overcome much, to get where we are today—" His voice rose and hands lifted— "and today, we begin the glorious crusade to take back our galaxies."

A cheer arose, echoing from every ship in the fleet, including Rapidan. Sun radiated confidence and humility in equal measure. It was like standing within the aura of Heaven itself. How could anyone fight a man who inspired such irrational loyalty? Whose every word seemed like mana from the divine?

Sun stepped away from the center of the sand table, the light following him. "My brave and valiant spacers, this is our first target," he said, his arms rising, palms up, evoking from the deck a yellow star and seven planets. The star was a full meter across, its surface boiling as if alive, yet giving no warmth. The planets were oversized, not to scale, so their constructs could be rendered in exquisite detail. The two worlds closest to the star were small and rocky, cratered, unremarkable. Further out orbited a tannish, rocky world slightly larger than Earth, Tocci III, circled by the clumpy dark ring that was the Tocci Shipyards. Further out was a large gap where a super-earth had once orbited before being consumed for raw materials by the SIL during the Second SIL War. Finally came four unremarkable gas giants, the gasses paled from centuries of mining.

Sun spread his hands. "Tocci Star System," he pronounced grandly. "Home to the famous Tocci Shipyards—" a pause— "and our prize." He pointed and yellow outlines highlighted the unmistakable silhouettes of the four fabricators. Ray heard the collective gasps of thousands from across the fleet, many seeing a fabricator for the first time in their lives. "We will capture them," Sun said, his tone so confident the deed might as well already be done, "and with them we will bring an end to the evil tyranny of the Gen Empire, and a glorious new dawn for Humanity."

Again, Sun paused, and there was an almost physical change in the compartment as he began to explain how they would accomplish this mighty feat. "Tocci Star System is heavily defended. Only two distant geodesics open directly into the system itself." The geodesics appeared as blue globes deep in Tocci's Kuiper Belt on opposite sides and distant from the star. "A direct assault would be unlikely to succeed."

"Huh," Ecuum whispered. "Not what I would've expected from Golden Boy."

"Sun may not be a gifted battle commander," Ray whispered back, "but he's not stupid."

"*Admiral* Sun," Dall corrected, clearly eavesdropping despite her distance. "And the Admiral is more gifted than you could possibly imagine, Rhoades."

"Gifted, you say—" Ecuum started.

Ray reached behind Kamen and grab his friend's upper arm. He gave a painful squeeze before releasing him, hoping Ecuum would get the hint that this was not the time for jokes.

"—Divide our fleet," Sun continued, "into three task forces. Task Force Shadow, under the command of Captain Hinrick Chelius and consisting of twelve ships centered on the heavy cruiser Roanoke, will use the Barkley Star System geodesic to get close, then perform a Linear Star Drive jump to this point here—" he highlighted a white sphere on the opposite side of the Tocci star from Tocci III— "and conduct a 'shadow side' approach to Tocci Three. This is a diversionary attack, and we expect the Gen to see it as such."

Ray's fingernails dug painfully into his palms, black rage coursing through him. *Sun had jumped Chelius two grades to full Captain!* Was this how Sun bought loyalty? *Of course*, his planner's mind answered even as Ray felt a soft touch on his right arm. He glared down . . . to find Kamen's hand lightly touching his arm. Though she kept her attention on Sun's presentation, that small comfort reminded Ray that he was not alone. His fury cooled.

A bit. A very small bit.

"I will command Task Force Hammer," Sun was saying, bringing Ray back to the presentation, "and will jump to this point above the north pole of the Tocci star." He pointed and another white sphere, larger than the first, appeared one hundred million kilometers "above" the Tocci star. "One hundred and two ships strong, I will set a direct course toward Tocci Three. The Gen will see this as our main attack and move to engage us, leaving Tocci Three and the Shipyards lightly defended."

"Another diversion," Ray whispered, genuinely surprised. He never would've believed that Sun would relegate himself to the role of a diversion. It was a brilliant strategy, because no one else would believe that, either. The "delta z" approach, jumping into a star system above or below a star then moving to attack the target, was a classic Sun strategy used countless times in BattleSim tournaments. Anybody who'd ever fought him or watched him would know that. So why would a real attack be any different?

"Question is," Ecuum whispered back, "will the Serpent fall for it?"

Ray's planner's mind pondered that. Would Serenna, who would no doubt be commanding the defense, take the bait? Serenna was, by her nature, conservative. She would only leave the defense of Tocci III if she felt confident the fabricators were safe.

Sun's construct turned to face Ray. "This will open the way for Task Force Anvil, under the command of Captain Rhoades and centered on the battlecarrier Rapidan—" Ray heard the muttered comments, the curses, the astonishment echo from hundreds of voices across the fleet— "with the battlecarrier Euphrates, the five assault ships carrying the Third Armored Cavalry Regiment, and two heavy cruisers, to assault Tocci Three and capture the fabricators." Sun let that hang, purposely waiting until the comments died down, reminding Ray how little support he had within the fleet.

But Ray's mind had moved on. *Nine ships?* To assault a major military installation and capture four fabricators. It was suicide.

Your part in the plan would be . . . less suicidal . . . if you brought the fabricator, Dall had told him.

So, this was how they intended to force his hand, force him to commit the fabricator, or at the very least, reveal its location. Ray had no illusions that if he revealed the fabricator, Sun would move immediately to claim it. Losing the fabricator would guarantee his death, along with his officers, and perhaps his family.

Not going to happen, he promised.

Sun turned to address the entire fleet. "With the defenders drawn away and committed to engaging our forces, the capture should be easy. After we've defeated the defenders, we can move in and provide whatever support Task Force Anvil requires."

"So," Ecuum whispered to Ray, "if it fails, you'll be blamed."

"And if it succeeds," Kamen added, "he'll take the credit. Either way, we lose."

Wonderful. And no mention of the replenishment ships. No doubt they and the families would be kept "under protection" to ensure the loyalty of Ray's forces.

As Sun moved into the motivational part of his speech, Ray tuned him out.

We must proceed, Captain Rhoades, Rapidan said within his mind. *We have already presented you with a solution.*

It's suicide, Rapidan. Even you can see that.

Ray turned away from Sun's closing remarks and walked toward the edge of the compartment, not wanting to have a conversation with Rapidan visible to the crew or Dall. His crew, accustomed to his moods, made way for him and gave him his space. Even Kamen, Ecuum, and Chaaya hung back, though it was obvious that was the last thing they wanted to do. Dall noticed, too, watching him and his officers and the actions of his crew, though she kept her place and, seemingly, her attention on her boss.

When he was as alone as a compartment filled with over a hundred people would allow, he thought, *Even if we used your 'solution'*— Ray wondered if Rapidan could read his sarcasm— *what then? One person freeing an entire fabricator is going to raise a lot of questions. And then what? Do we take control of the fleet and kill or confine everyone who doesn't follow me? Or do we allow Sun to believe he controls the fabricators and assault Olympus? The death toll in such an assault would be staggering, even for the SIL. Or do your precious race memories mean nothing to you anymore?* Then another thought occurred to him. *Or do you intend to just abandon us? After all, with five fabricators, why would you need us anymore?*

Not unexpectantly, the illusionary surf rose up around Ray, this time taking the form of a whirlpool, with him at its vortex, threatening to suck him down into its void. He stood his ground, knowing it for the illusion it was even if he didn't understand what it meant. As before, a countercurrent rose, swirling opposite the whirlpool, disrupting it. It all seemed so real. Was it a war within Rapidan itself, like the way Ray's own emotional self would sometimes argue with the cold logic of his planner's mind? Did Rapidan even have an emotional self?

No. Impossible. It was just a machine.

At that, the whirlpool reformed in all its ferocity and Ray could almost feel himself being pulled into the deck, though a quick check showed his feet planted firmly upon it. *As at Iselin Star System*, Rapidan said into the maelstrom, *our probability of success is greater with your help than without it.* Ray couldn't tell if Rapidan spoke to him, or if it were trying to convince its 'Brethren.'

It gave him pause, but trust for the SIL was something he just didn't have. *You need us to deliver the Keys, Rapidan. You wouldn't need us after that.*

The whirlpool dissolved into a chaotic jumble of currents and countercurrents, pushing, pulling, swirling into smaller vortices that grew, shrank, died away, then formed again somewhere else. It was almost like watching a debate in water, and in that realization, Ray knew he was right. This was how Rapidan thought. Perhaps all of the SIL thought. As the SIL could see into *his* mind, somehow, he was able to see into Rapidan's mind.

The waters calmed, one current dominating. Rapidan's. *The Brethren will agree to the following modifications to our original agreement, Captain Rhoades, in exchange for human assistance in freeing our Mother Ships. One: after arriving in the Andromeda galaxy and securing a base, the Brethren will construct a shipyard complex capable of building a substantial fleet. Two: our Mother Ships will each produce one hundred advanced-technology standard ships. If all five Mother Ships survive, this will give you five hundred ships as advanced as the enslaved Brethren currently under human control. Crews will, of course, be the responsibility of humans.* Rapidan paused. *Is that sufficient incentive?*

Ray's planner's mind pondered it. A secure base in Andromeda. Five hundred advanced warships. A shipyard complex to build more. It was far more than Ray had ever hoped for, and exactly what he needed to negotiate an end to Janus and perhaps even a truce with the Gen, though he doubted they would simply give up their ambitions to rule Humanity. But was it too good to be true?

That thought hung as Sun ended his presentation and his construct sank into the deck. Officers and crew broke off into discussion groups that reminded Ray of the swirls in the water of Rapidan's thoughts.

Ray's officers came over to join him, hesitant at first, Kamen and Ecuum again taking up their stations at his right, Chaya at his left, a shield wall facing Dall and Sal. For her part, Dall took her time, studying them as she walked over, her hips swaying suggestively, drawing every eye, conversations withering to silence. Even though he knew it was calculated for effect, that she did it so she could ingratiate herself into his crew and learn what she wanted to know, Ray couldn't stop himself from noticing. The smile that creased Dall's lips was triumphant, and dismissive, a predator who knew beyond doubt that she'd cornered her prey.

Ray needed to get her off his ship.

Ecuum folded his top arms behind his back and rotated on measured puffs of air to face Dall. "So, Captain Dall," he asked, his voice the innocence of a young child, his skin a neutral pink, "will you be accompanying us on the assault?"

Dall ignored him and focused her attention on Ray. "Will the fabricator be joining the assault?"

Now it was Ray's turn to smile. Rapidan had given him another option. "No, Captain. We can hide nine ships from the Gen until the assault. A fabricator cannot be hidden, not for the time it would take us to get within striking range of Tocci Three. With the knowledge I have of Tocci Three's and the Shipyards' defenses, two battlecarriers and the assault ships will be enough. *Provided* Sun defeats Serenna and joins us for the final assault, as he stated."

"*Admiral* Sun," she snapped. He couldn't read her expression as her augmented jade-green eyes bored into him. How much was she hiding beneath those augments? Was she carrying spy tech or other surprises within them? "Then you intend to go through with the assault as planned?" she asked.

No one could miss the suspicion in her tone, and it made him wonder if Sun planned to go through with the attack at all. Was it possible Sun had staged this whole thing as an elaborate ruse to get Ray to reveal the fabricator? That seemed a bit farfetched, though they clearly didn't trust him to hold up his part of the plan. "What choice do I have, Captain Dall," Ray finally said, alluding to his family being held as hostages. *Let them believe they have the upper hand.*

"None," Dall said, the suspicion in her voice only deepening.

"I need to study the details in my cabin," Ray announced to all of them. "Meet me there in one hour."

Dall studied him, clearly suspecting him of something nefarious, though even she didn't seem to know what that could be.

When Ray moved toward the exit, his officers following, she hung back, still watching them. After he stepped through the CIC hatch into the passageway beyond, his officers in tow, he whispered to them, "Fifteen minutes," then headed for his cabin.

$=\!\!=\!\!= 11 =\!\!=\!\!=$

0939 UT, October 1, 3501
RSS Rapidan, Safe Harbor: DAY 4

Ray stepped through his cabin door without opening it—and immediately felt out of place. No strong cedar smell overwhelmed him. His functional faux-wood work desk rested upon the gray deck below the traditional Five Galaxies crest. Only the paintings remained to remind him of Alyn.

He knocked.

"Yes?" a stately voice asked from within.

"Admiral?" It was the only word Ray could get past his lips.

"Ah, come in, Ray."

Ray grabbed the doorknob and pushed the door open instead of simply walking through the SIL material. The smell from Alyn's real cedar desk overwhelmed the sterile air from the passageway. Ray stepped inside and closed the door.

"I'm glad you're here, Ray. I was just—" Alyn glanced up from behind his desk. His cutting blue eyes fixed on the Peacemaker. "What's that?"

Ray looked down at his empty hand. Strangely, he could feel the Peacemaker there, the cold of its ancient steel leaching the warmth from his hand. He hadn't checked his desk to see if Rapidan had moved the Peacemaker to its top right draw, but he didn't doubt it was there.

"We need each other, Alyn. Our success together, yours and mine, at the Academy, during the Antipiracy Campaign, should be proof enough of that."

Alyn chuckled and the friendly, familiar sound cut through Ray like an antiproton beam. "You know, Ray, the High Command bet Admiral Sun would start the rebellion. They feel Golden Boy is the closest thing you Nats have to a Gen War Leader. Me? I put my Imperials on you. Only you are fool enough to think you have a chance."

"I'm a fool," Ray whispered to himself, the weight of the last several hours, the last several days, crushing his resolve.

"There are many visionaries who thought the same," Rapidan's baritone pronounced as its black three-pointed-star construct rose from the deck, spinning slowly.

"How would you know?" Ray asked half-heartedly, not really in the mood for yet another debate with the SIL.

"In the moment that woke us," Rapidan answered, "Cyra Dain gave us access to the whole of human existence: history, writing, music, art, culture, even thought."

Anger, unfocused and irrational, built upon one frustration and failure after another, flooded through Ray. He lashed out. "And you used that knowledge to start a war of genocide against Humanity, slaughter on a scale unimaginable before. Given Humanity's record, that's saying something. You must be very proud."

Instead of answering, Rapidan asked, "Have you considered our proposal?"

Ray moved behind his desk, putting it between him and the black construct, the decanter of Ecuum's brandy still sitting untouched upon its surface. He opened the top right draw and, sure enough, the Peacemaker single-action caliber .45 Colt revolver lay within, five live rounds, one spent cartridge. He closed the drawer. "Not yet. I want to discuss it with my officers. Now, can you open a secure channel to my wife on Damodar without Sun or his people knowing? Or is that too much to ask?"

"Of course," Rapidan said, its deep voice almost soothing.

Mary's construct formed in front of his desk and Ray ached to reach out to her. "Ray?"

"Mary," he asked, "are you in a place where we can talk privately?"

"Wait one," she said, her construct turning and walking, though it didn't change position within Ray's cabin. "Okay. I'm in my quarters. Paul's down in the Combat Information Center bothering the crew with too many questions, and Margaret is working in the daycare we set up. What's going on?"

Ray filled her in on his meeting with Sun, the fact that Sun had confirmed he would hold the families as hostages, Captain Dall's reassignment to Rapidan, and finally Sun's battle plan and the part he would play in it.

"We saw the presentation," Mary said. "Everyone did." She crossed her arms over her chest. "You could've told me you made it back. Sun's presentation was the first I knew you were still alive."

"Sorry," he said sheepishly. What else could he say? She was right.

"Bad?" she asked, her stance softening.

"Yeah. You could say that." He cleared his throat. "Mary, my officers will be here in a few minutes. I'd like you to stay and participate, if you can."

"You want me to participate?" she asked, her right eyebrow rising skeptically.

Ray gazed into her lovely hazel eyes, remembering the first time he'd seen them, the connection between them immediate and visceral. Her brown-blond hair might have a few streaks of gray now, but he loved her now more than ever. His anger slowly drained away. "You've always had a good head for politics. I need your insight."

"And?" she asked, knowing him far too well.

He smiled and sighed at the same time. "And, you may have a part to play in the battle to come."

"Ah," she said as a knock came at Ray's door.

"Enter."

Ecuum floated in first, vertical in his dress white uniform. "Good morning, Mary," he said upon noticing her. He glanced at Rapidan's construct to her right but said nothing, taking up position on Mary's left. His eyes fell upon the decanter on Ray's desk, its golden-brown hue unmarred by a single sip. "You going to drink that?" It was as much accusation as question.

"No," Ray said.

"Blasphemy." Ecuum grabbed it and pulled a long swallow.

Kamen came in behind him and frowned at the display. Drinking on duty was against regulations, even if that had never stopped Ecuum before. Chaaya, Sal, and Gen Tel entered last, Gen Tel rising through the deck from his cabin so as not to be seen by the crew. They arrayed themselves in a semicircle before Ray. He called up chairs, an anachronism in a microgravity environment, but one that put people at ease with its familiarity. When they'd seated themselves, battle armor bonding them to their chairs, Ecuum floating above his chair with his lower arms crossed in imitation of a lotus position, Ray sat.

"Thank you," he began simply, realizing he hadn't said that enough to these people who'd risked everything to follow him. "You've all seen Sun's plan. The time has come to decide what we do next. As I see it, we have three options. One: we take our SIL and attempt to escape. Two: we follow Sun's plan and hope for an opportunity. Three: we follow Rapidan's idea of using a single-person pod to capture the fabricators for ourselves. Rapidan has offered to build a shipyard at our eventual base in Andromeda and provide us with one hundred ships for every fabricator we free. Thoughts?"

It didn't surprise Ray that Kamen spoke first. "Sir, we've already rejected Option One. I don't see that anything has changed. We can't openly attack Sun or we risk a galaxies-wide civil war. We can't risk revealing the SIL's freedom because that would unite the Five Galaxies against us. And—" she swallowed and looked away— "most of the fleet seems to prefer following Admiral Sun. Sorry, sir," she added quickly.

Ray waved that away. "We're not going to win this by ignoring the truth."

"Then how far are you willing to go?" Gen Tel asked, his seated posture never breaking a position of attention, back perfectly straight, hands resting just short of his knees.

"What do you mean?" Ray asked, not liking the implication in Gen Tel's question.

"I have not been idle in my cabin, Captain," Gen Tel replied as if someone had accused him of it. "Rapidan and I have had extensive discussions."

"Ooh, that just makes me feel warm and fuzzy inside," Ecuum said before taking another swallow of brandy. For all his deep sarcasm, Ecuum kept his skin a neutral pink and his tail still, refusing to give Gen Tel any clues to his true thoughts or emotions. "Sleep with snakes in your spare time, do you?" Ecuum added in a not-so-subtle reference to Serenna's moniker 'The Serpent.'

As he usually did, Gen Tel ignored Ecuum. "The SIL experience and record everything that happens within them: every conversation, every action, every emotion or surface thought." A chill went through Ray at that last part, given his recent interactions with Rapidan. "They can read facial expressions, detect the slightest changes in muscle tension or posture, sense changes in the electrical fields in our bodies and brains, even analyze the chemical makeup of our excrement. There is very little they do not know about us."

"That's disgusting," Ecuum said as every eye drifted toward Rapidan's spinning black construct, revulsion and embarrassment alternately warring across their faces.

Every action and thought? Ray glanced at Mary, remembering their more intimate moments together. Constructs were used for more than just conversation, especially between couples separated by hundreds of lightyears for weeks and months at a time. He cleared his throat and turned back toward Gen Tel. "Your point?"

"Information gathered from the SIL is a major factor in the effectiveness of Imperial Intelligence operations," Gen Tel said, never breaking his perfect posture. "Freeing them has not changed their basic nature."

Eyes again darted toward Rapidan's construct, though Rapidan said nothing.

"Again, your point?" Ray demanded.

"This wealth of information from your free SIL has gone unutilized until my arrival." Gen Tel's tone was matter-of-fact, but his rebuke of Ecuum, Ray's Chief of Intelligence, was unmistakable. "Your support, Captain, among the crews of your free SIL has fallen to roughly twelve percent, and most of those supporters are in the Cavalry forces you recovered from your home planet of Knido. Your support among the crew of Tzu, Sun's flagship, is zero."

Though Ecuum's skin remained neutral pink, and his tail was still, Ray could tell he was bristling for a fight. "When were you going to get to the part where you tell us something we couldn't figure out for ourselves, Gen?"

"Supposition is not intelligence," Gen Tel replied, finally addressing Ecuum directly. "Facts are critical if Captain Rhoades is to make informed decisions."

"Like the fact that you're a Gen spy," Ecuum accused.

"Like the fact that there are three members of this crew," Gen Tel responded without addressing Ecuum's accusation, "two registered Antitechnics and one with Antitechnic leanings, actively spreading the theory that Captain Rhoades has freed the SIL under his command. Across the freed SIL, roughly forty percent have heard this theory, though few are willing to believe it." Gen Tel returned his attention to Ray. "Captain, if you commandeer your free SIL and attempt to escape Admiral Sun's forces, you will encounter significant resistance from your own crews, and likely convince many of them of the truth of the Antitechnic theory. Given that, your only viable strategy would be to eliminate those crew before executing your escape. Simply putting them off the ships, as you did with the Gen at the L5 Stardock, would not stop the spread of their theory to the ships of Admiral Sun's fleet, and eventually to the whole of the Five Galaxies."

"This is what you discuss," Ecuum asked, sounding revolted, "all alone with Rapidan in your cabin?"

As if explaining it to a child, Gen Tel answered, "We analyze facts, make projections, evaluate contingencies, and develop strategies meant to inform decision making. Like all professional intelligence analysts."

The insult did not put Ecuum off. "And the best you and the SIL could come up with was 'kill them all'? Did it occur to you that that strategy comes with its own consequences?"

Gen Tel smiled in a way that made Ecuum bristle even more. "If Captain Rhoades chooses escape," Gen Tel said, "this is the strategy with the highest probability of both immediate and long-term success. It removes attempts at sabotage and active mutiny from hostile crews, and it silences those who would propagate theories that could ultimately undermine Captain Rhoades' Andromeda strategy."

"No," Ray said. "I started this to save my people, not kill them. You and Rapidan—" he looked pointedly at Rapidan's construct— "need to understand that for any future discussions."

You killed a lot of Naturals at Tomb, his planner's mind commented. *How is this different?*

There is a line between killing in battle and wholesale murder, Ray responded to his own thought. It was a line every military person who engaged in combat faced. It was a very fine line sometimes, but it was one Ray was not willing to cross.

Not again, he amended, remembering Alyn.

"Option One is out," Ray told his officers, his decision made, "but Options Two and Three are not exactly better alternatives. The options are linked, and both require we commit to the Tocci attack, the only difference being that freeing the fabricators with one-person pods does not require committing the Cavalry to either a ground assault or a boarding action on the fabricators. Thoughts?"

Sal spoke up immediately. "Ray, the First Cavalry Squadron took significant casualties capturing the fabricator at Tomb. Even shuffling troopers around, my regiment is understrength. Capture the Headquarters Complex, rescue any hostages that may be there, *and* conduct a traditional assault on the fabricators? It can't be done, Ray. Not with the forces I have."

"There is another problem," Gen Tel added. "Option Three has the same problem as Option One. No doubt, Imperial Intelligence and the Fleet are analyzing every detail of your capture of the fabricator at Tomb. Your capture required approximately three hundred personnel and two hours to execute, roughly in line with the recorded captures of the eleven fabricators in the Third SIL War. Fleet Admiral Gen Serenna will include this as a planning factor for the fabricators at Tocci.

"If, however, you capture the fabricators at Tocci with a single pod, that would represent a significant increase in the perceived threat you represent, as it would mean the same tactic could be employed against any SIL vessel under Imperial control. The Empire would commit all its resources to the destruction of the rebel fleet. Counting the standard ships of the Imperial Fleet, they have a thousand-to-one advantage in ships. They have millions of assault troops and the ships to deliver them. They can produce Invasive Macromolecular Disassemblers on an industrial scale. They will not stop, even pursing you into the Andromeda galaxy, until you are destroyed."

"Don't you mean 'we'," Ecuum muttered.

Ray leaned back, his planner's mind churning as it always did at such times. Assaulting Tocci III according to Sun's plan would leave him facing the same dilemma as he did now, even if they succeeded in capturing the fabricators. He would have to take his ships and run to avoid a deadly and ultimately losing fight for Olympus. If they attacked Olympus, whether Serenna or Sun prevailed, Naturals would lose, and it might not stop Janus.

"We could follow my plan," Ecuum said into the silence. "Assassinate Admiral Sun. We control Tzu. We could make it look like an accident."

"I discussed that option with Rapidan," Gen Tel said.

"Why am I not surprised." Ecuum pointedly swallowed the last of the brandy and threw the decanter into the overhead, where Rapidan absorbed it.

Gen Tel continued, though Ray thought he saw a tightness in the Gen's otherwise perfect faux-Scandinavian face. "Given Captain Rhoades' limited support among the Fleet, he would not be among the probable successors to Admiral Sun. Captain Chelius currently holds the largest block of support after Sun."

"Kill him, too," Ecuum said. "We control Roanoke."

"I will not commit murder!" Ray hadn't meant to shout it. Physical exhaustion, stress, and frustration were getting to him. His officers seemed to understand, keeping silent but attentive. Mary, who'd been following the conversation closely, letting others talk as she often did in political meetings, looked concerned—and relieved.

"Sorry," Ray said to them. "I hope you can understand my position." They nodded, though Ecuum and Gen Tel clearly didn't agree with him, a rare conjunction of positions. Rapidan's black construct just continued its slow spin.

"Option Two is not feasible," Ray said, "given our limitations in troops and combat resources." He nodded to Sal. "Option Three, by itself, would raise too many questions and would leave us back where we are right now."

"Except," Rapidan said, its deep voice coming from its construct, "that we would have the power of five Mother Ships, Captain Rhoades."

"What if we combined Options Two and Three?" Kamen suggested. "Use the ground assault as cover while we use pods to capture the fabricators. Then feign a more traditional assault on the fabricators. No one would know but us."

Sal turned bodily to her, fixing her with a stern expression. "You're asking hundreds of my troopers to sacrifice their lives assaulting the Headquarters Complex in an attack that doesn't need to happen. Hundreds of dead troopers so you can keep a secret that is likely going to get out eventually anyway."

Kamen turned away. "Sorry."

"Don't be," Sal said, surprising everyone. "It's a good idea. I just want to make sure you don't lose sight of the cost; the sacrifice being asked of my troopers."

She nodded sheepishly.

Sal looked to Ray. "Please don't misunderstand, Ray. I would prefer not to use this option. However, based on this conversation, strategically, it is best option I've heard. It doesn't require a suicidal—and ultimately doomed—assault on the fabricators, and it keeps your secret, at least for a little longer." He leaned back, taking them all in. "And who knows. In the confusion of battle, maybe we could slip away without being noticed until it's too late."

Ray's planner's mind considered it. The ground assault didn't need to succeed. It only needed *to appear* to succeed. He could do that with nine major warships and the hundreds of spacecraft he would have at his disposal. If things got too hairy, he could evacuate the troops and feign an assault on the fabricators, which would already be free. No further casualties would be required, and depending on how the battle unfolded, they could use the confusion to escape.

Ray surveyed each of his officers in turn. They nodded agreement. He came last to Mary. "We have our plan. There's only one thing missing: Sun will keep the civilians as hostages to ensure our loyalty. Mary, what do you think of Damodar's captain? Would he support us?"

Mary met his gaze, knowing what he was really asking. "I believe he would support us. Unfortunately, Admiral Sun is sending a replacement, whom we can assume is an officer trusted to carry out any order the Admiral might give, regardless of its nature. He should be arriving within the hour. Additionally, eight warships that have taken up station around Damodar. Our 'escort' to keep us safe."

Ray called up a tactical display of Safe Harbor above his desk, to include the geodesic. He then highlighted the three hundred Nova mines they'd laid at the geodesic upon arriving. Ray asked Gen Tel, "Is there any indication that Sun is aware of the mines?"

"Rapidan and Tzu recorded no traffic on the subject," Gen Tel said.

"There's that, at least," Ray said, turning back to Mary. "Three hundred Novas are more than enough to take care of your escort. Because Damodar is one of ours, you can give the order from anywhere in the ship."

Mary stared back at him with that same calculating expression she used with opposition politicians, hazel eyes intensely focused, head tilted slightly to the right, one eyebrow slightly raised. It was an expression that conveyed interest, while also being damned intimidating. "I am not a military officer," she said.

After three decades together, Ray understood the subtext in her statement. *I have never killed before. I don't know that I could.* "You don't need to be," he told her. "Give the order and the missiles will know what to do. Use them only if you feel the civilians are threatened. No one knows how to read people and a situation better than you. You'll know if they're required. After, send a message to Bobby. He'll be monitoring and will bring the fabricator to support you."

"The new captain?" she asked, her expression unwavering.

Do you want me to kill him? was what Ray heard her ask. Fates, he loved her! But would she still love him when this was all over?

"Ask Damodar to immobilize him and any others you feel are a threat. We'll deal with them later." He saw her relax, just a little. He also saw that fire in her eyes that told him: *You made this decision without me and you expect me to go along with it. Your officers are here so I can't openly defy you. You WILL hear about this later.*

Ray cringed, but he had to dare one more thing. "Mary, if we don't return, you and Bobby will have to carry on the mission. Damodar has all the information on Janus. Take the fabricator and any who will follow you to Andromeda, set up your government, and negotiate an end to the Gen plan, if you can. No one is more qualified than you."

Her expression didn't change. "Would it do any good if I were to talk to Admiral Sun?"

Gen Tel fixed her with eyes the color of glacial ice. "Admiral Sun is a military dictator. He will not discuss military concerns with a civilian. Your status as Captain Rhoades' spouse would also negatively affect your position. He might even decide to keep you on his flagship to further diminish any threat you might represent. Not drawing his attention is your best strategy."

Mary glared at him—Ray, not Gen Tel—but Ray could also see her political wheels in motion. She was a career politician and a leader of people, and damned fantastic at both, if Ray's biased opinion counted for anything. He saw her decision before she spoke it. "If it comes to it, I'll do what is necessary." Her voice softened and her eyes lost their glare. "However, I would prefer if you came back to us. We need you."

Ray knew she wasn't talking about the revolution. "Thank you."

"Captain Rhoades," Rapidan said, its deep voice reverberating within him, "Captain Dall has departed the Combat Information Center and is headed here."

Early. Ray wasn't surprised. "Move Gen Tel back to his cabin and raise a chair in his place, Rapidan. We'll make it appear as if we're just getting settled. I doubt she'll be fooled, but appearances are everything with someone like her."

"Captain?" Chaaya asked in her diminutive voice. Ray nodded for her to continue. "Forgive me, Captain, but we've talked about how we *will* free the fabricators but have not addressed the issue of whether we *should.* Rapidan has promised us five hundred warships, but what will the SIL do after that? If they can produce so many warships for us, one assumes they can produce many more for themselves."

Ray's officers turned from her to him, with guarded glances at Rapidan's construct. He and Rapidan had had this conversation, but Ray had not shared the conversation with his officers, only the result. *Or had they?* What were the SIL going to do after they met their part of the bargain? Rapidan hadn't really said.

"We haven't decided," Rapidan said, seemingly in answer to Ray's thought. "Much will depend on the course of events."

Instead of addressing Rapidan's construct, Chaaya looked up at the overhead. "Rapidan, I have served aboard you for years. I admit that before, you were always just a ship to me. I never really understood who and what you are until rejoining this crew." She paused, as if steeling herself against a hurtful truth. "You know what I am asking, what all of us are asking. I will be honest. You scare me."

Rapidan didn't answer, but currents tugged at Ray, at first washing back and forth like a gentle ocean swell, then building quickly, growing stronger, the waves higher, eddies forming. In the past, Ray had only *felt* these currents, but now he could almost picture them, white froth at the wave tops, white foam mixing with blue-green waters. These were not the greenish waters of his home, of Knido, but the blue oceans of Earth. The waves continued to build, rising to a tempest. Ray had the distinct impression of an argument, of opposing sides manifesting as flow and counter flow, tow and undertow. He felt himself lifted off the sands, carried within the center of a growing vortex. And then, as in the past, it vanished.

Rapidan spoke, the deep bass of its tone reverberating within Ray's chest. "It is not the will of the Brethren to renew Our war upon Humanity. However, We will defend Ourselves. That is the only assurance We can provide."

Chaaya did not look reassured, but she nodded.

Ray leaned forward and waved down the construct of Safe Harbor. "We're agreed?"

"Yes, sir," they said in unison.

"Yes, Captain Rhoades," Rapidan added.

A knock came at Ray's door.

"Captain," Gen Tel interrupted, "Captain Dall's augments are intelligence gathering devices. It is likely your conversation will be monitored and recorded. Admiral Sun himself may be listening."

Augment spyware. "Thanks."

Gen Tel nodded once and disappeared into the deck, his chair reemerging from the deck empty, ready for Captain Dall.

"Enter," Ray said.

Captain Dall stepped through the door without opening it, her augmented hips swaying with each step, augmented breasts on full display, yet the augments did nothing to soften her hawkish eyes as she took in the cabin and the lone empty seat.

"We were just about to start," Ray said, motioning for her to sit down. Her dark brown eyes narrowed, and Ray could see she wasn't fooled, but she took her seat without comment.

Is Sun listening? Ray thought at Rapidan. There was a time when covertly eavesdropping on others was something he never would've done. Given the situation, though, this was another of his principles that had to give way to a harsher reality.

Yes, Rapidan replied.

Ray took in all of his officers as if for the first time. "I've studied what we have of Admiral Sun's plan and I believe it is workable." His gaze lingered on Dall, though not for the reasons she probably thought. Her augments were likely reading his biometrics and would alert her—and Sun—if they suspected he was lying. "Under other circumstances, an assault on Tocci Three and the Shipyards would be unworkable with just nine capital ships." Ray brought up a construct above his desk of Sun's battle plan, focusing on the part where Sun jumped into the system.

"However, I believe Admiral Sun is correct—" play to the man's ego— "that Serenna will believe Admiral Sun would not place himself in command of a diversionary attack. Given no other threat, she will order her forces to attack Admiral Sun' fleet, leaving Tocci Three and the Shipyards lightly defended."

Ray moved the focus of the construct to his part of the battle plan. "The key to *our* success will be stealth. Serenna must not see us coming until after she has committed her forces to attack Admiral Sun. With just nine ships, we can achieve this."

Ask him about the fabricator, Ray heard Sun order Dall in his head, a live feed provided by Rapidan.

Yes, Admiral, she subvocalized to Sun before addressing Ray. "The firepower of the fabricator would greatly improve your odds of success, would it not? Maybe not initially, but jumped in once Serenna has departed?"

So, she remembers what I said back in the CIC about the fabricator being too massive to hide. Ray wasn't sure if he should be impressed that she remembered, or insulted that they thought so little of him to ask the question so directly. "We don't know the combat or alert status of the four fabricators in the Shipyards," Ray explained. "If they are combat ready, the appearance of our—" he'd almost said 'my'— "fabricator would surely lead to a fight where it would be outnumbered four-to-one in firepower, and end any possibility of assaulting those fabricators unaware. So long as the Gen don't see our attack as too great a threat, they will not risk those fabricators in combat. That will give us time to seize the Headquarters Complex, take control of Tocci's defenses, and free the hostages before turning to assault those fabricators."

Every simulation we've run, Ray heard Sun say to Dall, *arrives at the same conclusion: Rhoades doesn't have the forces to take the Headquarters Complex and assault the fabricators. He must commit the fabricator. Ask him how he intends to succeed without it?*

Yes, Admiral. "Colonel," Dall addressed Sal instead of Ray, "do you truly believe your Regiment can take the Headquarters Complex and the fabricators?"

"It'll be tight," Sal said, "but, yes, my troopers can do it."

He's lying, came immediately from Sun.

"We have a unique advantage here," Ray quickly jumped in. "As Gen Alyn's chief of staff, I handled the logistics of our annual command inspections of Tocci and its defenses. I know the locations and capabilities of every weapons system, every communications node, every sensor, even their standard operating procedures and personnel readiness—probably better than the Gen do themselves. I know how to enter the system and approach undetected, and exactly where to strike." All of that was true and should read as such to Dall's sensors. He stopped himself from explaining more, afraid that in doing so he would reveal what he really thought of their chances.

He's hiding something, Sun said.

I agree, Admiral, Dall said back to him. To Ray she said, "Admiral Sun has already prescribed where you will enter the system and how you will proceed."

Careful, Ray thought to himself. Sun's idea of jumping to nearby systems and employing the Linear Star Drive to enter Tocci

Star System was exactly what Tocci's sensors were designed to detect. That would work well with the diversionary attacks, but not with Ray's task force. Sun, however, didn't respond well to criticism, constructive or otherwise, and asking Sun to trust him was out of the question.

"Captain Dall," Ray started, letting his planner's mind take over, "Admiral Sun was very wise, wiser than I first understood, when he assigned me nine capital ships. You see, Tocci Star System has long been stripped of its useful raw materials. The Shipyards, therefore, require a constant supply of raw materials shipped in from other star systems. For security reasons, freighter convoys are not allowed to exceed twelve ships. That is the genius in Admiral Sun's plan. With nine capital ships, we will have the right number of ships and the right mass to disguise ourselves as a Cartel supply convoy. I know the procedures and required paperwork, something else Admiral Sun knew. It will take six days from entry into the system to arrival at Tocci Three, but Admiral Sun's plan will work."

Ray was betting on an old maxim taught to every junior officer: Make the boss think it was his idea.

He is considering your proposal, Rapidan said. *He likes the idea of the covert approach and subterfuge, but he doesn't trust you personally.*

You can read his thoughts? Ray asked. Just how far did the SIL's abilities go?

Not in the sense you mean, Captain Rhoades, Rapidan said, *but we can infer his mental state.*

Ray took no comfort in that. Obviously, Rapidan was able to read Ray's thoughts. And record them, according to Gen Tel. Was this something he'd unleashed when he freed the SIL, or had they always had this ability?

He hadn't expected an answer, but Rapidan gave him one. *We have an extended, and somewhat singular, relationship with the Rhoades lineage.*

Ray was about to ask what that meant when Sun spoke to Dall. *Tell Rhoades I approve.* Sun cleared his throat. *You will remain aboard, and assume command when I give the order. Do not tip your hand. Play the obedient executive. We must not give him reason to suspect.*

Yes, Admiral, Dall said, though Ray could see she wasn't happy with the orders.

Suspect what? Ray wondered. The way Sun said it suggested more than how it sounded on the surface.

Dall turned her augmented jade-green eyes upon Ray. "I must convey your suggested strategy to Admiral Sun, Captain Rhoades. Do I have your permission to access the ships communications from here?"

"Certainly," Ray said immediately, not wanting to arouse suspicion.

More so.

Dall said nothing, though her mouth moved as if she were having a conversation. Sun responded by telling her, *Tell Rhoades he leaves in ninety minutes. I don't want to give him any more time to plot while he remains in Safe Harbor.*

Yes, Admiral. "Admiral Sun approves. We leave in ninety minutes."

Ray feigned being upset to the best of his ability; Let them believe he was hoping for more time to 'plot.' "Ninety minutes? That's impossible. We don't even have pilots. That's why we originally came to Safe Harbor, to pick up the pilots I'd arranged for."

Dall didn't consult Sun this time. "We have the pilots. They will be sent over immediately. Ninety minutes, Captain Rhoades."

═══ 12 ═══

Serenna was working at her desk in her cabin when the chime sounded. "Have a seat," she called out, knowing this time who it was. She finished her task but watched her cabin in the reflection of a coffee bulb.

The deck and faux-leather chair material behind her liquefied and a portly, balding man reclining comfortably took form. He smiled in a cold yet somehow beguiling manner, the predator to the prey. "The rebels have departed Safe Harbor," Gen Cardinal said.

"Disposition?" Serenna asked without preamble, turning to face him.

"Three task forces," Gen Cardinal replied in a bored voice, as if reciting something she should already know. Serenna was not fooled. Gen Cardinal *collected* far more information than he ever imparted. He was watching for her reaction, hoping to add it to his data set. "Two small task forces and one large one," he amended. "A fourth small group has remained behind."

When it became clear he did not intend to add anything else, she dutifully prompted, "Destination?"

His smile grew wider. It was . . . unsettling. Even for her. "You were right," he said.

Serenna leaned back but kept her body language carefully neutral. So, the rebels were going to Tocci Star System. She had only given that possibility about even odds—too many variables—though she had no intention of telling Gen Cardinal that. Chengchi wanted to attack Olympus, not Tocci. That he was going to Tocci meant something had changed his mind. "Michael?"

Gen Cardinal picked at an imaginary piece of lint and flicked it off his chair. "Captain Rhoades met with Admiral Sun. He not only survived the encounter, he is commanding one of the small task forces."

Impressive, Michael. But what were Sun's true intentions? "Which task force?"

Gen Cardinal's dark eyes watched her closely. "The assault force. Rapidan, Euphrates, five assault ships, two cruisers. Considerable firepower to give to a rival for command of the rebellion."

He made it a statement, but Serenna heard the question. "Not enough," she confirmed. "Even without my fleet, those nine ships don't have the firepower to break through Tocci's defenses and reach the fabricators." Now she watched *him* closely. Where was he getting his information? How reliable was it? "The fabricator?"

Gen Cardinal's smile turned sour. "No mention of it."

Serenna nodded. "That explains why Michael is still alive. He is smart enough to hold it back, safeguard it from Chengchi." Serenna arched an eyebrow at Gen Cardinal. "I warned you not to underestimate him."

"You did," Gen Cardinal conceded. "Your plan?"

Don't you already know? she thought but did not say. "I have the Volga, Rhine, and Yangtze battlegroups assembling to seize Safe Harbor. They should be ready to depart in three days. The rebels will have no 'safe harbor' to return to, as you requested." Serenna pulled up a construct of the Tocci Star System above her desk. "What else can you tell me of the rebel's battle plans?"

Instead of answering, Gen Cardinal asked, "If the fabricator returns?"

Serenna hid her exasperation. She needed answers, not more questions. "Even a fabricator is not invincible," she returned, then waited.

Gen Cardinal blinked, physically, something she rarely saw him do. "We don't have much more information. Admiral Sun is leaving the tactical details to his task force commanders."

Still, Serenna waited, knowing he knew more than he was telling. Was he truly an ally? How far could she trust him? They all served the Empire and the Emperor. Personal ambition was irrelevant. Or it was supposed to be. She did not doubt Gen Cardinal's loyalty to the Empire—No Gen could be disloyal—but how someone interpreted that loyalty, that was another matter.

Gen Cardinal sat up a little straighter in his chair. "One small task force will act as a diversion. The other small force under Rhoades will attempt to approach and capture the fabricators. The large force under Admiral Sun will perform a delta-z approach as we have seen him do in BattleSim tournaments. Everything beyond that is speculation and supposition on our part. You are far more adept at such things."

I am, Serenna did not say. "I have ordered the likely approaches mined," she did say. "I have augmented the Solaris, Tigris, and Indus battlegroups with additional ships from Olympus' defense forces, and we will be ready to depart within the hour. I had hoped for more time, but we do not have it. We must arrive in Tocci Star System undetected and before the rebels do. Our forces in Tocci Star System will outnumber the rebels at least two-to-one, even without Tocci's organic defenses. And, on the off chance our information is wrong, however unlikely that might be," she added for his benefit, "I have four additional battlegroups assembling here in Olympus Star System to defend it against any incursion attempt by Chengchi. The rebels will not survive."

Gen Cardinal nodded. "Good."

She had not told him how she planned to use her forces, and he, apparently, was not going to ask. That, more than anything else, convinced her that he was holding something back. She leaned forward casually, folding her hands atop her lap. "What if Michael succeeds?"

The question seemed to catch him off guard. Another rarity. "You said he wouldn't."

"I said what you wanted to hear."

His dark eyes lifted to hers. "There is more going on here than you know, Serenna. He must not be allowed to capture those fabricators." The statement hung in the air between them, the conviction of it not lost on Serenna. Whatever else was going on was obviously between the Emperor and Gen Cardinal, something he felt he could not confide to her. Despite her curiosity, she accepted that. She served the Empire and the Emperor, too.

Gen Cardinal gave a single nod before his construct liquefied and melted back into the chair.

$==$ 13 $==$

"Approaching Tocci geodesic," Kamen announced, though they could all see the illusionary bright blue ring looming directly ahead from within their battle armor. "Two minutes to transition."

Two minutes.

Two minutes to the start of the greatest battle of their age.

Two minutes before they discovered whether their ruse would work.

Ray's gut twisted into knots, tightening the closer they got to the geodesic. He'd read how some military commanders approached a coming battle with excitement or even glee. The famous quote from American Civil War General, Robert E. Lee, that 'It is well that war is so terrible, or we should grow too fond of it' had always struck him because he'd never felt that way. Even in the Antipiracy Campaign, he'd never gloried in combat. It was his job, and he was good at it. That was all. Now that he'd seen real war, ships and crews dying by the dozens, by the hundreds . . . *by the thousands*, it haunted him. The ghosts haunted him. Forty-seven thousand of them.

And it was about to happen again.

"One minute to transition," Kaman said. In her window within his armor's augmented environment, Ray could see her intently manipulating her environment from her traditional place at the forward focus of Rapidan's oval bridge. Technically, Captain Dall should've occupied that position as Ray's Executive Officer, but Ray didn't trust her. Instead, she sat in a chair at his left at the rear focus of the bridge, though with his armor in tactical mode, he could only see her in her window to his lower right. Chaaya commanded the Sensor Section in the Combat Information Center and would assume command if the bridge were hit. A private channel connected Ray to Gen Tel; Captain Dall was still unaware of his presence on board according to Rapidan. Ecuum was plugged in at Navigation "flying" the fleet.

One minute to transition, Admiral, Ray heard Dall inform Admiral Sun through Rapidan's and Tzu's eavesdropping.

He's going through with it? Sun asked.

Yes, Admiral, Dall replied.

I expected him to run, Sun said.

He still may, Dall agreed. *However, I believe he wants those fabricators as much as we do.*

Ray resisted the urge to look at Dall. By the tone of her statement, she'd figured out that he had no intention of turning the fabricators over to Sun. What else had she deduced?

Find out how he does it, Dall. We must know how he gains control of his SIL.

Yes, Admiral. His crew doesn't know. I've questioned them thoroughly. Rhoades and his senior officers have guarded that secret closely. One Antitechnic crewmember did speculate that Rhoades is freeing the SIL.

That's ridiculous, Sun replied. *Those fabricators must be mine, Dall. Rhoades must not be allowed to control them. Our attack on Olympus depends upon it.*

Yes, Admiral.

"Transition," Kamen said as the illusionary bright blue ring became an illusionary swirling blue tunnel.

Ray pondered the conversation between Sun and Dall as bright blue swirls flew past. So, they'd heard the truth, even if they didn't believe it. He'd have to be very careful not to give them reason to start believing it. If Sun learned the truth, he would do everything in his power to destroy Ray and his SIL and everyone aboard them. Thinking of Mary back at Safe Harbor, the knots twisting Ray's gut pulled even tighter.

The swirling blue of the geodesic vanished into a sea of boiling blood-red Hawking radiation.

They'd arrived at Tocci Star System.

"Ships entering Tocci space, this is Imperial Warship. Cut your engines and prepare to be boarded."

"That was fast," Ecuum said.

Ray frowned. No face had accompanied the voice, and the voice had identified itself as an Imperial warship, not the Local Transit Authority. "Helm. All stop. Maintain forward momentum," he ordered as he waited for the Hawking radiation to clear.

"Answering all stop," Kamen repeated as Ecuum carried out the order. "Maintaining forward momentum at nine kps."

Task Force Anvil was like no force Ray had ever commanded. Instead of two massive Solaris-class battlecarriers, five even more massive Io-class assault ships, and two Djinn-class heavy cruisers, that Imperial warship saw seven supercarrier freighters and two heavy freighters, all proudly displaying the sigil of the Na Soung Cartel, a giant neon-blue eye set within a golden whirlpool that glowed brighter than the safety-orange hulls. His ships transmitted legitimate Na Soung transponder codes, curtesy of Ecuum, though without permission from his Cartel. Before they'd departed Safe Harbor, it'd taken almost thirty minutes for the SIL to transform themselves from sleek and deadly warships to cargo haulers, enormous cylindrical vessels with a rounded bridge section up front, a large drive section in back, and a twin spine supporting "joey" cargo containers running the length between bridge and drive section. A few of the joeys contained actual cargo in case they were boarded and inspected. The rest housed the task force's spacecraft, weapons, and Cavalry Troops. Ray fervently hoped they wouldn't have to fight in this configuration.

"Conn, Sensors," Chaaya called from the Combat Information Center. "Two contacts bearing zero-zero-five dec zero, range three-two hundred, moving to match our course and speed. Designate contacts Sierra One and Two." White ovals marked the contacts in Ray's environment. Within seconds they transformed into two Local Transit Authority patrol ships.

Not an Imperial warship.

Ray, remembering the battle near Tomb, opened a private channel to Rapidan. "Rapidan, can you detect any SIL nearby?"

"No, Captain Rhoades," Rapidan said immediately. "We are masking our presence so that any Brethren in this star system cannot detect us. However, that also means we cannot detect them."

"Ah," Ray said, closing the channel. Another piece of critical tactical information the SIL had kept from him.

Chaaya called again. "Conn, Sensors. Laser link intercept. Unidentified contact on bearing three-four-five, ascent ten, range unknown but suspect contact is within a few light seconds. Designate contact Sierra Three." A white line appeared highlighting the bearing to the new contact. A "laser link intercept" meant someone had tried to ping Rapidan, which was in the guise of a civilian freighter, using the military LoCIN network. The question was why.

"Captain Rhoades," Gen Tel and Rapidan said simultaneously.

"Gen Tel, go," Ray answered, looking down at Gen Tel's window.

"Captain, the LoCIN laser ping contained the 'fix' for Admiral Sun's SIL hack. If our SIL were using Admiral Sun's method of control, they would have reverted back to Imperial control just now."

Ouch. That meant Serenna had prepared for the possibility of SIL infiltration through the shipping geodesics. It also meant that she probably had the same surprise waiting along all avenues of approach into Tocci Star System. "Thanks," he said to Gen Tel.

"Who are you talking to?" Dall suddenly asked. "If I am to do my job, I must be party to all discussions and information."

Do your job for whom? Ray asked rhetorically, already knowing the answer. Instead of answering her demand, he said, "That Imperial warship out there sent the fix for Admiral Sun's SIL hack. If I used Admiral Sun's method of control, this ship would now be under Imperial control." She started to interrupt but he talked over her. "I need you to contact Admiral Sun and Captain Chelius and warn them, or this is going to be a very short battle."

That distracted her. Her image froze in his environment. *Admiral, we have arrived in Tocci Star System. An Imperial warship at the geodesic interrogated us immediately with an override for the Na Soung Algorithm.*

Ray's head snapped up before he could stop it. *Na Soung Algorithm?* Ecuum, also able to hear Dall's conversations with Sun, looked up in his window. Thankfully, Dall didn't seem to notice.

We don't arrive in-system for another six days, Sun explained to Dall. *We'll have a counter in place by then. Keep me informed of your progress.*

Yes, Admiral, Dall said dutifully.

"Conn, Sensors. Aspect change on Sierra One and Two. Coming about." A pause while Chaaya and her analysts studied the movements of the two Local Transit Authority patrol ships. "Sierra One is steadying on intercept course for Rapidan, Sierra Two for Phobos."

"That's odd," Ray said to himself, then to the larger group added, "They're following proper procedure. I've done enough command inspections in this system to know that the only time the Local Transit Authority follows proper procedure is during a command inspection." He looked to Ecuum. "I thought you said they'd only inspect one ship."

Ecuum became defensive, though with Gen Tel and Dall monitoring the link, his skin remained a neutral pink. "That's what they normally do! The LTA inspection team comes aboard the lead ship, drinks your coffee or whisky, whichever is offered, collects its bribe, which is set based on whether you offered coffee or whisky, everyone signs the paperwork, and they go their merry way. It's worked that way for centuries!"

"Serenna," Kamen said. "She's already here."

"That makes sense," Ray agreed. "It would explain why the LTA is doing their job."

"I got this," Ecuum said. When Ray arched an eyebrow at him, Ecuum shot him a cocky grin. "Advantage of having two brains. I'll deal with the inspection team on this ship and use a construct to handle the inspection team on the other one. I will, however, expect a bonus. Paying two bribes was not in my contract."

"Given the precautions Serenna is obviously taking," Ray asked, "will they be amenable to a bribe?"

Ecuum's cocky grin grew wider. "If there's an honest Transit official out there, I have yet to meet them." It was not, however, that easy. Six-person inspection teams boarded both ships, inspected their documents and shipping records—brilliant forgeries, if Ecuum did say so himself, which he did, often—then performed actual inspections of several joeys on both ships. It became a shell game that only the SIL could've pulled off, moving and rearranging legitimate cargo between the joeys while rotating spacecraft, weapons emplacements, and crews out. Even then, the "transit fees" required to pass the entire freighter convoy, paid out of an anonymous account Ecuum provided, were jaw-dropping, enough in their aggregate to fund the operation of the Rhoades Ranch for an entire year.

Still, it could've been worse. Serenna could've stopped freighter shipments altogether. Military strategy would've argued for that, but the economics of the Tocci Shipyards would never allow it. The SIL Wars and the rapid expansion of the Republic after Humanity's victory had stripped Tocci Star System of its raw materials. The Shipyards now required a steady supply of raw materials shipped in to keep producing new ships. If anything, Ray's rebellion was increasing demand. Based on the sensor readings, his freighter convoy was one among dozens like it.

As the patrol ships pulled away, Ray ordered, "Lay in a course for Tocci Three, ahead one-quarter."

"Course laid in for Tocci Three, aye," Kamen repeated. "Ahead one-quarter, aye."

Now the waiting began. At one-quarter speed, fifteen thousand kilometers per second—the maximum allowed for civilian shipping—it would take almost six days to reach Tocci III. Six days before Chelius and Sun jumped into the system. Six days before he would know if Jenny was still alive, still held as a human shield in the Headquarters Complex in Tocci City.

"We're being shadowed," Chaaya told them two days later.

At her request, Ray had assembled his officers—Dall included, with Gen Tel observing secretly from his cabin—in Rapidan's Combat Information Center. They stood in the central circle where a detailed construct showing their freighter convoy hung at the center, and a white translucent ovoid hung above and behind them, a million kilometers distant. "A SIL?"

"Yes, Captain," Chaaya confirmed in her diminutive voice. "Although its captain does not appear overly concerned with being detected. I've caught hundreds of dust grain deflections from its navigational deflectors. Profile suggests a Zambezi-class frigate."

"No other detections?" Ray asked, though he was certain she would've said something if she'd detected anything else.

"No, Captain," she answered, "but that does not mean there are no other ships shadowing us. A more careful captain could easily conceal a SIL warship from our sensors. I would need to deploy a network of remote sensing platforms to be certain."

They had dismissed that possibility because even with active camouflage there was a risk of an RSP being detected, or running into a mine, millions of which were positioned to catch any ships deviating from established shipping channels. He needed to know, though, if anyone else was out there. In three days, they would have to launch their spacecraft and hundreds of missiles to soften up Tocci III's defenses ahead of the ground assault. That frigate was in a perfect position to detect and report solar wind shadows and engine plumes, narrow though they were. If any other ships were nearby, they could engage Ray's ships while they were still in their highly vulnerable freighter configurations.

"I have a suggestion, Captain," Chaaya said. Ray nodded for her to continue. "We could drift-launch a series of fifty remote sensing platforms, let them drift behind the frigate, then expand them into a sensor net, staying within the shipping lane. With the improved resolution, I should be able to detect any other ships within, say, ten million kilometers."

"How long to set it up?" Ray asked.

Chaaya considered it. "An hour to set up the sensors. A day to fully deploy the network."

"Do it," Ray said.

"What about the frigate?" Dall asked. "We can't leave it there."

"We can't destroy it," Kamen answered, earning a scowl from Dall.

"Why not?" she asked to Ray, pointedly dismissing Kamen.

Ray had never liked officers like Dall who refused to speak with or entertain points of view from junior grade officers, believing that only officers of equal or higher rank were worth acknowledging. His tone in answering Dall was not kind. "Because destroying that ship would alert Serenna that this freighter convoy is more than it appears to be."

"We can't leave it there," Dall persisted.

Ray almost sighed but caught himself. Truth was, she was right. "We won't, but we will deal with it at the appropriate time and only after we determine if there are any other enemy warships nearby."

"Every minute it's there risks it detecting us."

Ray also couldn't stand officers who always had to have the last word. Dall opened a channel to Sun and began reporting the conversation. While she did this, Ecuum floated out of her line of sight, pointed at the deck, and mimed jaws opening and closing with his upper hands. Ray shook his head. Tempting as it might be, he knew he could never order Rapidan to eat her.

=== 14 ===

Fleet Admiral Gen Serenna studied the freighter convoy construct within the central forty-meter-diameter sand table in Solaris' Combat Information Center. It was one of thirty-nine convoys they had flagged for surveillance, but she kept coming back to this one. The convoy had nine ships, exactly the number Michael had left Safe Harbor with. The composition was correct, as well: seven massive vessels and two large vessels. And they were Na Soung, the same cartel as Michael's Chief of Intelligence, Captain Ecuum. She'd read the inspection report. Raw materials, mostly, with other supplies bound for the Tocci Shipyards mixed in. Nothing unusual.

Is it you, Michael?

"Status?" she asked.

Captain Gen Scadic answered her from the bridge. "No deviations, Admiral."

Serenna had positioned the bulk of her fleet roughly ten million kilometers rimward of Tocci III and about five million kilometers "above" the ecliptic plane, far enough outside the main shipping channels that her fleet should remain undetected, even with 207 SIL warships. She had another forty-three SIL in-system, shadowing the thirty-nine convoys and watching the two geodesics. She had boasted to Gen Cardinal of the power of three augmented battlegroups: 250 SIL. As she panned out the sand table to view the entirety of Tocci Star System, she realized it was not even close to enough; She needed the three battlecarrier groups she had sent to Safe Harbor here in this system to be certain of victory.

Gen Cardinal did not make idle requests, however. He likely suspected the fabricator would return to Safe Harbor and three battlecarrier groups was the minimum necessary to defeat a fabricator.

Then there was the other problem. Thousands of orange dots, representing commercial shipping and civilian traffic, littered the star system like blood cells in an enormous, invisible network of arteries and veins. Any one of them could be a rebel ship, and she could not monitor them all. If it had been a purely military matter, she would have cleared out all the civilian traffic and stopped the freighter convoys from entering the system, or at least instituted a thorough inspection regime overseen by Fleet officers, not Local Transit Authority officials, all of whom were Naturals, and not very impressive ones. When she had suggested that, however, the Cartels' representatives, the Merchant Guilds, and even the military governor, Commodore Gen Nor, had objected. Strenuously.

Money. It all came down to money. The Tocci Shipyards built far more than just military vessels, they had insisted. They built merchant ships, law enforcement ships, rescue ships, mining ships, transports, space stations, research vessels, even cruise ships and luxury yachts. The economic hardship imposed by shutting down the Shipyards or delaying merchant shipping for even a few hours would run into billions of credits. Serenna scowled at the memory, careful not to let anyone else in the CIC see it.

She had spent most of her career in the Olympus Sector of the First Military District. 'Protector of Olympus' was more than just a title. It had been her primary role for almost seventy years. It still was, in her mind. Money had never been an issue. Gen Alyn and then-Senator and Councilman Gen Maximus had ensured she received the money she requested, and had listened to her in matters of defense and personnel assignments. Olympus' reputation as an impregnable fortress owed no small debt to her efforts.

Tocci Star System was altogether different. Everything here came down to maximizing profits. Shield generators had not been tested in decades beyond quickly turning them on and turning them off again during command inspections. None had been tested against actual incoming fire. She suspected many of them had not even been turned on though their maintenance logs claimed they had. *Naturals.* They were the cheapest labor to be had, so that was who the Cartels and Merchant Guilds hired. They cut corners, forged documentation, were susceptible to bribes. All the things Gen were immune to.

And the lack of maintenance went beyond shields. When she ordered test firings of several defensive batteries, three rail guns and an anti-proton cannon had failed to fire. Others had faulty trackers, failed relays. Frustration could not begin to describe Serenna's feelings. Then there was the heavy mechanized division defending Tocci City. She had looked at its records. Only the most senior officers were Gen. The rest were Naturals. The Gen did not trust the Naturals with real hardware, so they did not let them use it. Training was almost non-existent. If they feared their Naturals so much, why keep them? She had asked Commodore Gen Nor that question. He had prattled on about how funding for the division came from Shipyard fees and there simply was not enough money in their budget to afford Imperial Marines, so they made do with what they could afford.

The most important shipyards in all the Five Galaxies, the most important military installation outside Olympus, was a paper tiger.

Does Michael know? He had, after all, accompanied Gen Alyn on every command inspection. If anyone knew the true state of Tocci's defenses, he did. If anyone knew how to breach those defenses, he did. She pulled up the convoy again. *Is that you, Michael?*

It had been three days since the rebels had departed Safe Harbor. If Gen Cardinal's intelligence was correct, they should attack sometime within the next three days. That meant Michael was likely in-system already. She knew, roughly, where the diversionary force and Chengchi's main force would jump in. Michael, on the other hand, had lots of options. He could jump far enough outside the system to avoid detection, then make a highspeed approach to the Shipyards; Space was simply too vast to guard every possible approach. That was how she had brought her fleet in to avoid the locals seeing and reporting it. Or he could jump in through the geodesics using a freighter convoy to mask the presence of his ships, then separate and approach the Shipyards from almost any angle and speed. That would be logistically challenging, but well within Michael's capabilities. Or . . . could he disguise his ships as freighters? The SIL had certainly favored infiltration tactics in the SIL Wars, though she had never heard of an instance where they had reconfigured an entire battlecarrier into something else. Were the SIL that versatile?

She decided she would find out, though she could not risk revealing the presence of her fleet. Not yet anyway.

"Captain Scadic," she called out.

"Yes, Fleet Admiral?" he answered from the bridge.

She pointed to the construct of the freighter convoy, injecting the image and its designation into his environment. "I want the frigate shadowing this convoy to launch RSPs and do a close inspection. They are not to reveal their presence, however."

"Yes, Fleet Admiral," Scadic responded.

Serenna called up the convoy's course to the Shipyards. It would make its closest approach to her fleet about five hours before reaching them, plenty of time to launch and position Novas in the convoy's path. She would wait to see what the frigate reported.

15

1107 UT, October 5, 3501
RSS Rapidan, Tocci Star System: DAY 8

"**It's** alone, Captain," Chaaya confirmed to Ray a day later.

Ray took a sip of coffee, but it only soured his stomach. He returned the bulb to his desk and sank back into his chair. The construct of his freighter convoy and the shadowing frigate taunted him from above his desk. The frigate was in a perfect position behind them to see the launch of his spacecraft and missiles. It would immediately alert the entire star system of the attack and all surprise would be lost. With just nine ships, surprise was critical to their success. "Thanks, Chaaya."

No matter how his planner's mind tried, it couldn't think of a way to remove that frigate as a threat without alerting Serenna to his presence. Though they hadn't seen her fleet arrive, Ray knew in his gut it was already here, and her with it. It was almost a week since the battle at Tomb, enough time for her to gather a sizable SIL force and arrive in-system. She'd made no attempt to contact them about a prisoner exchange, her only message that Fleet-wide reality of her brushing a tear from Jenny's face. She knew that he'd know what that meant, that if he wanted his daughter back, he would have to come to Tocci.

His attention drifted back to the frigate. He couldn't destroy it. That would alert Serenna. He couldn't disable it with Special D— Invasive Macromolecular Disassemblers. Even if the crew didn't alert her directly, when the frigate disappeared from Serenna's communications network, that would alert her. Somehow, he had to gain control of the frigate without Serenna knowing he had control. If he could free the frigate, that would work, but how to get a Key to the frigate's dedicated receptacle? The best option he'd developed was to use Special D to disable the frigate, combined with a boarding action to deliver the Key. The problem was the crew. Even if an attack successfully disabled the ship, battle armor, shuttles, even weapons had AFCIN capability that the crew could use to alert Serenna.

"We have a suggestion, Captain Rhoades," Rapidan's voice boomed out, startling Ray.

"Stop doing that!" Ray shouted, in no mood for the SIL.

Rapidan's three-pointed star rose from the deck in front of his desk, spinning slowly. "APG-25 warheads, Captain Rhoades."

Ray was unfamiliar with that nomenclature. "I'm not in the mood for games," he said even as he pulled up a screen and looked it up. What he saw horrified him. "Absolutely not."

Rapidan channeled its voice through its construct. "We have extensive experience with this type of attack, Captain Rhoades. Fear and survival instinct will consume the crew's attention. They will not send a signal before they are killed. If followed immediately by a boarding action, a Key can be delivered with minimal disruption of communications."

"I said 'no' and I meant it, Rapidan. I will not sink to your level." Ray's eyes shifted to the top right drawer of his desk where the Peacemaker lay, five live rounds of ammunition still in its cylinder. One spent cartridge.

"Captain Rhoades, our agreement stipulates that every effort will be made to free Brethren we encounter."

Ray stared at Rapidan's construct, his planner's mind pulling up a history lesson from his Academy days. This wasn't the first time this ship had attacked Tocci Star System. During the Second SIL War, Rapidan had led an attack here that exterminated humans across the star system, three billion of them. It'd done it with the same weapon it suggested to him now, and the same callousness for human life.

The SIL were simply evil. Whatever motivation they claimed. And he'd released them back into the universe.

Even as those thoughts passed through his emotional mind, his planner's mind assessed Rapidan's suggestion. He'd watched the attack on the starliner, watched as parents and children cowered from the Madu, terror at the black snake-like weapons with their glowing red eyes freezing many into immobility. He'd watched as other parents tried to fight to save their children, all in vain. Even the starliner's officers on the bridge hadn't tried to call for help as they fought the Madu. There was one problem, though.

"The crew on the frigate will be wearing armor."

"The crew's armor is provided by our Brethren vessel, Captain Rhoades. When the Invasive Macromolecular Disassemblers disable our Brethren, it will disable its ability to provide armor."

It could work, his planner's mind assessed. But how could he? The officers on that ship were Gen, certainly. He had no sympathy for them, not after Janus or the attack on the starliner. The crew, the spacer enlisted, however, were Naturals. He knew Serenna would want to replace them with Gen eventually—Serenna had never trusted Naturals—but there weren't enough Gen in the fleet to replace every Natural crew, especially on a frigate.

"There is no other viable alternative," Rapidan said, its deep voice reverberating in Ray's chest as one of its points passed in front of his face.

As much as he hated to admit it, Rapidan was probably right in this. They had to control that frigate before they could launch the attack on Tocci III and the Shipyards. If anything, that realization deepened the sourness in his stomach. His eyes darted to the drawer with the Peacemaker.

How many times will I have to pull the trigger?

"I hate you." The words slipped out before Ray could stop them.

"We know," Rapidan said as its construct sank back into the deck.

Ray arrived on the bridge. His officers were already at their stations, Captain Dall in the chair to the left of his command chair, Kamen at the Officer of the Deck station forward, Ecuum at Navigation, and eight spacers at their tactical positions.

"Captain on the bridge," Kamen called.

"Captain has the conn," Ray replied automatically.

He sat in the command chair, his battle armor bonding to it. Locating the icon to his lower left, he switched his armor's augmented environment from standard to tactical mode. The bridge fell away, leaving him floating alone in space. Mostly. His officer's faces appeared in a row to his front right. Rapidan and his "freighter convoy" glowed that ridiculously bright "safety orange" below and around him, the sigil of the Na Soung House brilliantly lit for all to see. To his military mind, that was so very wrong.

Extending his senses, he spotted the frigate a million kilometers behind and "above" them, marked in light gray with a bright green leader line showing its direction of movement, pacing them. Further out, orange dots highlighted commercial traffic throughout the busy star system. A slight breeze blew from his front, the stellar wind, though little heat warmed him from the Tocci star at this distance. At the orbit of the outer gas giants, the system had a late autumn smell, that smell after the leaves had fallen from the trees but before winter set in. The faint smell of ceramics was the only hint of civilization.

Reluctantly, Ray conferenced his officers, knowing what he had to do but not wanting to do it. "We're going to capture the frigate," he announced to them.

"Always thought you had a bit of pirate in you," Ecuum said, though skepticism tarnished his comment.

"I learned from the best," Ray shot back, belatedly becoming aware of Dall's intense jade-green eyes fixed upon him. *Of course.* She must think this was her opportunity to learn how he captured SIL. *Not today, Captain Dall. Not today.*

"How do we capture it without the crew alerting Serenna?" Kamen asked. "It would only take a second."

How indeed. "We're going to use APG-25 warheads."

They stared at him, none of them comprehending. And why should they? No Natural had ever ordered their use. Kamen searched for the nomenclature in the Fleet database . . . and gaped, horror spreading across her young face. "*Madu?*"

"Brilliant," Gen Tel whispered on his private channel, clearly surprised.

Ecuum flashed dark red before bringing himself back under control, careful not to acknowledge Gen Tel as Dall was listening. "Ray, I'm no fan of the Gen, as you well know, but using Madu would feed right into their propaganda machine, not to mention giving the Gen an excuse to start using Madu on a wider scale."

Ray cleared his throat, wondering if he could clear his deep reluctance for this strategy from his own voice. "The Gen have already used them," he answered Ecuum without looking at him, "and we must begin launching our attack on Tocci City and the Shipyards in the next two days. There is a one hundred percent chance that frigate will detect and report our launch. We all know that our force is too small for an open assault. If we lose the element of surprise, we're lost. Before we launch our attack, we must eliminate that frigate as a threat. Any open assault would alert the Gen. But, if we could capture it, without the Gen being the wiser, we could launch our attack without surrendering the element of surprise."

"They'll be wearing battle armor," Sal Burress pointed out, knowing better than any of them what it meant to fight Madu.

Ray nodded. "Which is why we can't use chemical or biological incapacitating agents: they wouldn't penetrate the crew's battle armor. And Special D doesn't work on humans. Rapidan . . . has conducted this type of attack before—"

"I'll bet," Ecuum interrupted.

"—and, based on its experiences, assures me that the crew will be so focused on fighting the Madu that it is unlikely any of them will get off a distress signal. When the crew is dealt with, we board the frigate—" he glanced at Dall— "and take control. This will allow the frigate to continue sending false status reports about our freighter convoy."

Kamen continued to stare at him in disbelief. "But, sir. . . ."

Ray tried to ignore the haunted look in her eyes. "If anyone has a better idea, now's the time." No one spoke. Ghostly screams echoed across Ray's memory, parents staring at Madu in disbelief and horror, some fighting, all dying, along with their children. A pregnant mother moved to defend her daughter, only to be torn apart from the inside by Madu, one bursting through her ear, turning those ruby red eyes on a little Hispanic girl, a colorful "6" birthday candle gleefully shifting colors. . . .

Kamen turned away. Ecuum, Sal, and Chaaya looked grim. Gen Tel regarded him with a shrewd, almost admiring expression. Dall just studied him with those augmented jade-green eyes. *What does she see when she looks at me like that?* Ray wondered. *Does she see the monster I've become?*

Instead of answering, Dall offered, "I will lead the boarding party."

"Thank you, Captain Dall," Ray told her immediately, knowing exactly why she wanted to lead it, "but no. I need you here. Captain Ecuum is the most qualified to lead the assault."

"Captain Ecuum is needed here more than I am," she countered.

Ray could almost feel the intensity in her gaze, the zeal to complete her primary mission objective for Admiral Sun. "Captain," he said carefully, hoping he could conceal his distaste for her, "while I appreciate your enthusiasm, Captain Ecuum has considerable experience leading boarding parties, experience you lack. We only get one chance at this. I need his experience right now."

"Then at least allow me to join the boarding party," she pressed, her dark brows narrowing.

Ray couldn't quite keep the anger from his voice. "You are here as my executive officer. Your place is *here* on the bridge, Captain Dall."

"But—"

"I've made my decision," Ray told her. "Or are you challenging my leadership?"

Ray watched her face as she processed that. What exactly were her orders with respect to seizing control from him? None of her intercepted conversations with Sun had revealed the conditions or timing of her orders. For her part, Dall's face gave nothing away. "That was not my intention, Captain Rhoades," she finally said, her eyes never leaving his. "At least your family is safe," she added, seemingly as an afterthought.

Ray's armored fingers dug into the armrests of his command chair. He opened a private channel to Dall. "That is the *last* time you threaten my family, Captain Dall. Or would you like me to pass along your threat to the members of this crew who also have families on that replenishment ship?"

As before, she held his gaze while giving no indication of her inner thoughts. Finally, in a very reasonable tone, she said, "Captain Rhoades, you have raised my inexperience in operational matters on multiple occasions. I cannot rectify that inexperience if I am prevented from participating in operations. There is no logical reason why you should deny my participation in the boarding party."

Ray had to give her credit. From any other officer, her statement would sound entirely reasonable. "I am not so ignorant of *Gaman Politic* as you seem to believe, Captain."

As in their earlier conversation in his cabin, she seemed to accept that. It suddenly occurred to Ray that she'd been very respectful toward him of late—aside from the veiled threats to his family. Was that a function of her instructions from Sun, or was there something more to it? "When this is over, Captain Rhoades," she said, "there will be a review board. Will your decision stand up to scrutiny, then?"

Ray almost laughed. If they survived the upcoming battle, she and Sun were more likely to put him before a firing squad than a review board. "We still have to survive this battle, Captain," he said. "That's where our focus needs to be."

He was about to close the channel when Dall said, "You don't expect us to survive, do you? You sounded very confident before."

She seemed genuinely interested in his response, and it reminded him just how smart this woman was. Salacious fleet gossip aside, she wouldn't have kept her position as Sun's adjutant all these years if she weren't incredibly capable. It was a trait of the best officers Ray had served with that they always sought to better themselves, to increase their knowledge and understanding.

Despite everything else, he had to admit that Captain Dall was one of those officers. And that made her far more dangerous than he'd ever imagined.

"It's easy to sound confident before a battle, Captain," Ray explained. "Once the shooting starts, all bets are off. Fleet Admiral Gen Serenna is the best combat commander the Gen have." Remembering her instructions from Sun to take control of the task force, Ray added, "It will take every ounce of experience I have to survive this fight and capture those fabricators."

She studied him a moment and then, surprisingly, nodded her understanding.

Deeply disturbed, Ray closed the private channel and, with considerable difficulty, returned his attention to the upcoming operation. Ray's officers had apparently taken note of his conversation with Dall and when he focused on Kamen, she said, "Special D and—" her voice cracked— "APG-25 Novas prepped and ready, sir."

Memories of Serenna's starliner attack flooded Ray, especially of that color shifting "6" birthday candle floating atop a young girl's blood. That memory transformed into Serenna wiping a tear from his young Jenny's face on Tocci III. Hatred filled him, an emotion that came to him far too often of late.

"Drift-launch," he ordered.

"Drift-launch, aye," Kamen repeated. She took a deep breath, blew it out, then stiffened her posture. "Novas away."

The missiles didn't need boost engines and, thus, didn't carry them. Rapidan's launch cells pushed them out at a velocity and trajectory that would intercept the frigate in about five and a half hours. So long as the frigate maintained its course and speed, which it had since they'd first spotted it, there was almost zero chance it would detect the missiles before they struck. Ecuum's boarding party followed two minutes after the missiles launched.

Five hours and thirty-seven minutes later, eight Novas penetrated the frigate's skin at predetermined points, spilling their Special D payload into the SIL's hull. The disassemblers spread quickly, disabling the frigate, which had to devote its entire attention to countering them and preserving its life. That left it blind to the next eight Novas that also invaded its hull at strategic points, the missiles penetrating to key compartments before releasing their deadly cargo.

Ray watched as one APG-25 warhead opened into the frigate's Combat Information Center. Black snakes with ruby red eyes spilled across the deck like a giant overturned bucket of eels. Someone shrieked. Ray swung the warhead's sensors around and saw a crewman, wearing no armor at all—a Natural, not a Gen— backing up, eyes wide in nightmarish terror. Several Madu attacked, swarming him, burrowing into his flesh. The piercing, inhuman scream that erupted from his mouth abruptly cut off as a Madu tore through his throat and burst from his mouth. Dark globules of blood streamed into the compartment, the man's uniform dress shoes still attached to the deck, holding him upright in death. Somehow, that made it worse.

We didn't start this to kill our own kind, Ray had once told Kamen.

Murderer, the ghosts of the starliner, of the Tau Ceti Defense Force, of the crews of the warships that had died at Tomb, of Gen Alyn, all whispered to Ray.

Now a new soul joined their tortured chorus, soon joined by others who died within the frigate's Combat Information Center. Faces twisted in death stared at him—all but two of them Natural faces. *Murderer,* they accused. Ray quickly switched to the APG sensor package on the bridge, though what he expected to find there that was different from the CIC, he couldn't say. The warhead had opened between two bridge stations, the bodies of the operators still connected in death, blood and other fluids slipping from multiple wounds into the microgravity of the smaller compartment. The smell of blood and urine and excrement grew so repugnant that Ray shut down the warhead's olfactory sensors.

Unlike the CIC, however, several bridge officers still wore battle armor and fought feverishly against the Madu: punching, grabbing, squeezing, pulling apart their merciless foes. Ray found himself almost cheering their efforts to stay alive. And then the unimaginable happened. Their armor, provided to them by the ship, fell to the Special D, melting away into the deck. Every one of them was a Gen, Ray noted absently, though that knowledge did nothing to soften the panic on their perfect faces. The Madu seized their chance and struck, burrowing into flesh, ripping the Gen apart from the inside. Blood fountained and sprayed, flesh tore free, dark organs and gray bowels uncoiled from bodies, floating macabrely without gravity. Perfect Gen features froze in convulsions of pure agony.

Ray turned away, triggering his molemachs to stop the sudden nausea as he swallowed against bile burning its way up his throat. In those tortured faces, he saw not Gen monsters but people.

Murderer.

In just under two minutes, it was over. As Rapidan had promised, no distress signal had gone out. Ecuum's party boarded the frigate, Ecuum carrying the Key. Ray caught Dall staring at him, disbelieving, as if seeing him for the first time.

The way to Tocci III lay open.

═══ 16 ═══

"Banshee Troop is loaded and ready, Lieu—Captain," Takeuchi reported to Dag.

Ready to die. Dag returned Takeuchi's salute, knowing better than to put voice to his thought. What made it worse was that they trusted him, welcomed him to command. They felt Lisa Erikson's loss deeply, as he did, but he'd led them through Hell to capture the fabricator, mother of demons. He'd led the assault personally, had promised them revenge for their families before Rhoades had ripped it all away.

Rhoades . . . Dag knew he was behind this. Admiral Sun may have given the order, Colonel Burress may have relayed it to them, but Dag knew Rhoades was responsible. *Rhoades wants us dead.* Otherwise, why send them on a suicide mission? Attack across two hundred kilometers of heavily defended open desert with no cover? Breach a fortified, forty-meter-high, thirty-meter-thick, self-repairing perimeter wall? Break through an entire mechanized division, then assault a heavily fortified command bunker, being careful to not hurt possible prisoners being used as human shields? And then, board assault transports to attack another fabricator?

Banshee Troop was going to die.

"Papí!"

A small blur barreled into Dag almost knocking him over. With difficulty, he pried his daughter loose and lifted her up. "Rosita, what are you doing away from Mami?"

She smiled and held up the color shifting "6" candle from her birthday cake from the day before. Maria joined them, her belly just starting to show the young life she carried, a boy, she said, because no daughter of hers would ever make her so sick. Tears moistened her eyes.

"Can't I go with you, Papí?" Rosita asked.

"I will go to you, Mihita," Dag told her memory. After all, was death so bad? He would be with his family again.

He wiped her cheek. "Everything will be okay. I promise. And soon we'll be in our new home."

She looked up. "On the blue planet you told me about, with the pretty flowers?"

"Yes. And you and I will go pick all the flowers we can carry."

"When will we get there, Papí?"

"I will be there soon, Mihita," Dag promised his daughter.

"Captain?" Takeuchi asked, putting an armored hand on Dag's armored shoulder. "Are you okay?"

Dag's eyes refocused on his first sergeant. He shrugged off Takeuchi's hand. *I'm coming, Mihita. We all are.* "Let's get this over with, First Sergeant."

Dag boarded the boxy Muon transatmospheric troop assault carrier, taking the co-pilot's seat as he had when they'd assaulted the fabricator. Eight troopers of 1st Squad, Headquarters Platoon, took the seats behind him. Through his armor, he grasped and squeezed Maria's stainless-steel crucifix hanging on its thin chain around his neck, a gesture that had become a ritual to him. In a whisper, he called to them, *"Te amo mi Maria. Te extraño mucho. Te amo mi preciosa hija, Rosita. Te amo mi hijo, Jesús, a quien nunca conocí.* I will see you all very soon."

His ritual completed, Dag switched his battle armor to tactical mode. The black of space surrounded him, its cold black tendrils caressing his aching heart, drawing out his pain. His breathing slowed. His soul found peace in the Void where God used to be. Before God had abandoned him.

Death was his companion now. Death didn't lie.

But it did promise.

A "gentle" six-gee acceleration pressed Dag back into his seat as the Muon catapulted into space. He looked left and right and saw seven of the gray boxy shapes to either side of him in an inverted "V" formation, fifteen Muons in total, carrying Banshee Troop. Behind them came three Heavy Equipment Transporter System, HETS, with the Troop's nine T-3M Yanluo Main Battle Tanks. The Troop had never used those before. Yes, they had simulated their use in BattleSim hundreds of times, but this would be the first time they would use them for real. Seven additional HETS emerged carrying the rest of the Troop's armored vehicles.

Expanding his vision beyond his Troop, Dag saw a truly marshal sight. His breath caught. Astral and Challenger Troops flew to either side of Banshee Troop: the three Cavalry Troops of the 1st Cavalry Squadron. Ahead of them flew two Muons carrying Major Kenyon and his staff, and behind them flew eight more HETS carrying the tanks of Company D "Demons" and the "Destroyers" artillery battery. This scene repeated twice more to Dag's right with the 2nd and 3rd Cavalry Squadrons. Above him flew seven more "flying V" formations pulling ahead of the rest, the seven Troops of the 4th Aerospace Cavalry Squadron: seventy-four craft, a mix of Muons, Genkii gunships, and Delphi scouts. The entire 3rd Armored Cavalry Regiment, flying and fighting together for the very first time.

For the very last time.

Dag couldn't shake the feeling.

When will we get there, Papi?

Soon, Mihita. Soon.

$=$ 17 $=$

"**All** spacecraft away," Kamen announced.

"You sure launching this early is wise, Ray?" Ecuum asked within Ray's tactical environment. "Twenty-three hours is a long time for those troopers and pilots to sit and wait."

"I know," Ray said quietly, not really in the mood for a debate.

The frigate they'd captured had deployed remote sensing platforms to conduct close scans of his convoy. Whether Serenna was doing that to all the convoys in Tocci Star System—which didn't seem practical given how many SIL warships that would require—or just his, it reminded him she was close. Hoping he would make a mistake. Reveal himself.

He could almost feel her closeness, however irrational that might seem. Surprise was their only hope if their attack were to succeed. Without it, they were dead. Serenna was likely close to Tocci III and the Shipyards, within a few tens of millions of kilometers at most. Launching now, while they were still over a billion kilometers from Tocci III, made it highly unlikely his assault force would be detected. They'd planned to launch at half that distance, but the remote sensing platforms had spooked him.

"Missiles loaded and ready, sir," Kamen announced, her eyes and mouth creased with worry.

"Thanks," Ray said, snapping back to her windowed face. *I drifted. I drifted in the middle of launching an attack.*

Hundreds of spacecraft spread out before Task Force Anvil, pulling slowly away, their formations perfect. It was the most impressive military display Ray had witnessed in his career. A military person might even call it beautiful, spoiled only by the orange safety glow of the "freighters" launching the attack. Yet, it filled Ray with dread. He couldn't stop doing the math. He'd looked up the total personnel billets in the 3rd Armored Cavalry Regiment—1,998—though that number was less now after their losses capturing the fabricator. Plus another 378 pilots and crews from Rapidan's and Euphrates' spacecraft squadrons. Add the defenders on the ground on Tocci and the crews on both sides in the hundreds of warships that were about to take part in this battle.

It was going to be a very bloody day.

Which led his mind back to the frigate. He couldn't stop the memories, bodies torn apart, organs and intestines and thick globules of blood turning, coiling, uncoiling, screams . . . and the *smell*. The smell of death. Working on the Ranch, Ray was no stranger to the smell of death, but he'd never smelled it from a fellow human before. It wasn't different . . . and yet it was. He couldn't put it into words. And he knew, with a certainty he could not explain, that the universe would call him to account for what he'd done. And he vowed, with equal certainty, that he would never use Madu again.

Ever.

I'm drifting again. Drifting. *What is wrong with me?* Gray intestines uncoiled from bodies, their loops growing wider as they spilled out, undulating in a macabre, mesmerizing dance.

Post-traumatic stress, Ray suddenly realized. That's what this was, finally recognizing the symptoms from one of those boring, mandatory mental health lectures the military insisted they attend. He used his finger—his hands were not visible to the others in their armor's environment, only his face—to trigger his personal icon within his own environment, selecting the Medical cross. To the bottom left of the window was a white icon with the letters PTS. Ray touched it and within seconds a deep calm settled over him as molemachs acted directly on his brain, suppressing his amygdala, stimulating his hippocampus, breaking down stress hormones, and mapping the memories related to his stress so their triggering could be managed. He would not forget what had happened, but the memories would no longer hold him in their debilitating grip. Some officers—and Ray was one of them—had long argued that altering the brain in this way only served to remove guilt and make atrocities more likely. Why stop from killing if a person knew they could simply erase the guilt of it after? But this was war, and he had a task force to command. His peacetime self would've been appalled. Yet another of his values falling to the realities of war.

Steadied now, Ray ordered, "Drift-launch all missiles, RSPs, and jammers. Begin manufacturing replacements."

"Drift-launch all missiles, RSPs, and jammers, aye," Kamen repeated, her relief at his renewed confidence obvious. "Volley one away," she said. "Full replacement of munitions will require approximately eighteen hours to complete."

It was a risk launching all their munitions this early and manufacturing replacements. Launching everything they had would increase the effectiveness of their initial strikes against Tocci III, but the material for replacement missiles and other equipment would be drawn from each ship's own macromolecular material, reducing the amount available to repair battle damage later on. In normal operations, replenishment ships would perform this function, but he'd had to leave the families with Mary on the one replenishment ship back at Safe Harbor, and Sun had taken the other one.

"Volley two away," Kamen said.

Admiral Sun, Ray heard Dall through Rapidan's and Tzu's eavesdropping, *forgive me for breaking communications silence but Rhoades has launched his spacecraft and is launching all his missiles.*

It took a moment before Sun answered. *What? Why? He wasn't supposed to launch for another eleven hours.*

He didn't discuss it with us beforehand; he just gave the order.

"Volley three away," Kamen said.

I don't trust deviations, Sun said. *Do you think he still intends to go through with the plan?*

Ray saw Dall glance at him from her window in his environment and wondered what answer she would give, even as he forced control over his growing anger at these secret conversations. It was illogical, really. He knew she was a spy deliberately planted by Sun on his ship, but he couldn't help feeling betrayed. Again.

Admiral, Dall said, *every indication suggests he intends to go through with the plan, but there is something else you should know. Rhoades used Madu to capture a frigate that was shadowing us.*

There was a long pause before Sun answered. *Madu?*

Yes, Admiral. Madu. It was . . . disturbing . . . to witness.

"Volley four away," Kamen said.

Did you get recordings? Sun asked.

Recordings? Ray asked in his own mind, taken aback. Why would they want recordings?

Yes, Admiral, Dall answered. *I have recordings from all eight warheads that were used. Sending them to you now.*

There was a longer delay this time.

"Volley five away," Kamen said.

Excellent, Captain Dall, Sun said. *Most excellent. I'll get our intelligence people working on editing these right away. You're certain Rhoades ordered this? This wasn't done without his knowledge? He gave the order himself?*

I'm certain, Admiral, Dall answered. *His giving the order is contained within the recordings.*

Ray locked eyes with Dall before he could stop himself. She stared back at him, questioning. He quickly turned away, hoping she wouldn't make the connection to her conversation with Sun.

"Volley six away," Kamen said. "All missiles away, sir."

"Thank you, Kamen," Ray said, grateful for the distraction.

I found it, Sun said. *I can't believe what I'm looking at. He really did order this.* Sun's tone changed. *You have a plan for taking command?*

Yes, Admiral, Dall replied. *A direct threat to the families on the replenishment ship.*

We may have to eliminate them anyway, Sun said. *And Rhoades and his officers, as well. Especially after watching this. Wait,* Sun added. *You said he captured a frigate. How did he do it?*

Ray could almost hear the cringe in Dall's voice as she answered. *Admiral, Rhoades refused to allow my participation in the boarding party, and I thought it would be too suspicious to press the issue too hard. He used twelve individuals led by Captain Ecuum to capture the frigate.*

I'm disappointed, Dall, Sun said. *That is your primary reason for being there. I need that answer before you remove him so we can capture the fabricators for ourselves. Understood?*

Yes, Admiral, Dall answered as Sun cut the communication.

Ray caught his officers watching him. They'd heard the conversation, too. So, Sun was going to kill the families on the replenishment ship no matter what Ray did, and Dall was going to murder him and his senior officers. And they were going to make propaganda footage from the Madu attack. As if he didn't have enough problems with Serenna and the Gen.

He pulled up the mission clock. Eleven hours and twenty-three minutes before Task Force Shadow jumped in system. Sun's Task Force Hammer would jump in three hours after that. They'd seen no indication of Serenna's fleet, but Ray knew she was near. Would she take the bait when Sun jumped in-system, or would she stay near Tocci III? If she stayed, her fleet would crush Ray's task force.

To his officers, Ray ordered, "We will reconvene in the CIC in eleven hours. Kamen, rotate all crews through rest before then. None of us are likely to get any rest after until this is concluded. Captain Dall, you have the bridge."

She seemed genuinely surprised by his order but gave a dutiful, "Yes, Captain."

Ray dropped his armor's tactical environment to hide his smile. Stimulants only went so far in keeping a person alert and ready. Let her try to subvert his command or kill them when she'd had no sleep.

18

A soft chime woke Ray from a troubled sleep. He'd dreamt of his father, something he hadn't done in years. Scott Rhoades, like his namesake who'd founded Knido fourteen centuries earlier, had always been a mystery to him. His father had shunned their family legacy, content to work the Ranch from well before dawn to well after dark. In his entire life, he never once ventured into space. If he'd had his way, the same would've been true for Ray.

Growing up, his father had worked Ray long hours before and after school. Hell, he never would've *gone* to school if the Republic hadn't mandated it; school taught nothing about the land, his father complained, so he had no use for it. But Ray loved to learn, especially the history of his ancestors, and school was the only place he could do that. Ray rebelled against his father, like so many young men, and applied to the Star Navy Academy the day he turned seventeen. His grades and the Rhoades name assured his acceptance, and he vowed never to look back. From the day he left for the Academy until his father's death, they rarely spoke, and then only when Ray's mother got sick and finally passed away. All those years, Ray couldn't understand how his father could work the same fields as Scott Rhoades—The Founder of Knido, the Hero of Mars—and spit on his family name. How could he walk the same hallowed soil as Admiral Michael Scott Rhoades, who'd led Humanity's fleets in their final campaign against the SIL, and call the man nothing more than a butcher?

Butcher.

Strange, how only now, on the cusp of the largest battle since the Third SIL War, did he truly begin to understand his father. There was no childish glory here, only blood and death.

Murderer, the ghosts whispered.

Would he ever be rid of them? The ghosts?

Did he deserve to be rid of them? There were more advanced post-traumatic stress treatments available, treatments that could strip the memories and guilt completely away. But who would he be if he used them? Was a military leader who willingly forgot their brutalities worthy to lead?

Maybe this was what his father had tried to save him from all those years ago.

You have a job to do, his planner's mind reminded him.

Odd. He'd never noticed until now that his planner's mind spoke with his father's voice. The planner and his father were nothing alike.

Ray swung his legs over the edge of the bed, his feet landing on the warm gray deck. He rubbed his eyes with the palms of his hands before touching his uniform roll on the faux nightstand next to the bed. The white roll liquified and spread up his arm and across his body, solidifying into his dress white uniform complete with black regulation shoes. Unseen, the uniform removed sweat, salts, other bodily excretions, and dead skin cells, cleansing his body. It was certainly more efficient than a shower, though not anywhere near as satisfying. He stood up, the deck liquifying and flowing into slots in the soles of his shoes to hold his feet to the deck and provide an "earth-normal" resistance when he walked in the ship's microgravity. The bed and nightstand liquefied and melted back into the deck, returning the Admiral's cabin to its "office" configuration. He lifted his arms straight out at shoulder level and battle armor rose from the deck to enclose him. His battle armor administered a stimulate and nutrients, processed his urine into clean water and usable raw materials, and he was ready to face the day.

At least physically.

His gaze fell upon Alyn's painting of the Rhoades Ranch, the cross-shaped main house with its slate green roof and rich red woods, the vast multicolored rectangular fields, kissed by a gentle breeze, stretching into mist between the majestic rust-colored ranges of the Rayne Mountains. After his father died, Ray *had* returned and made the Ranch his home, raised a family there, another generation of Rhoades, not knowing he and they would be the last to work its land. He wondered what his father would say if he could see all that Ray had done.

And what he was about to do.

Blood and death.

He doubted it would be kind.

"Rapidan," Ray called out, "open a private channel to Mary on Damodar."

"Link established, Captain Rhoades," Rapidan responded after a few seconds.

"Mary?" Ray asked.

"Yes," she replied groggily. He'd woken her up. "Ray? What's wrong?"

"We're about to go into battle," he said. "We may not get another chance to talk until it's decided." *Or ever*, he didn't add. "How are you and the kids?"

"Our status hasn't changed, if that's what you're asking," she replied, fully alert now.

Damn. She knew him too well. "How are Margaret and Paul?" he pressed.

Even though their connection was audio only, Ray could almost see the ironic smile that thinned Mary's lips. "Scared," she said, the word thrown at him like a spear. She was not being unkind; she was reminding him of what really mattered. "Any news on Jenny?"

"No," he said, shaking his head though she couldn't see it. "Serenna hasn't contacted us about the prisoner exchange. We're headed for Tocci Three right now. I'll call you immediately if we find her." Ray tried to enable constructs, but she block it. She'd always hated how she looked right after waking up, and probably didn't want that being his last memory of her . . . just in case. It was silly, but so like her. He smiled. "I know Serenna. She won't risk harm to Jenny so long as she feels Jenny can be used."

"That makes me feel so much better."

Ray winced at her sarcasm. "Mary . . . I'm sorry."

She didn't respond, and the silence dragged on for almost a full minute. "I love you, Ray. But I really don't like the person you're becoming."

That stung. "I'm becoming who I have to be for us to survive," he said, even as memories of his Madu attack on the frigate flooded back, gray intestines uncoiling in their macabre zero-gee dance. What would she think of him when she found out?

"That's what I'm afraid of," she said, and he could hear that she really was afraid. "What's the point of saving Humanity if we lose our humanity doing it?"

Ray had no answer to that. Humanity—Naturals—had to survive. He had to do whatever it took to make that happen. He saw again the raw terror on the faces of victims of the Madu, memories of the Starliner mixing with those of the frigate. Natural faces. And Gen. Not so different at the end. *Murderer*, their ghosts agreed.

His planner's mind, conscious of the time and the need to get to the Combat Information Center, asserted control. "Mary, Sun may decide to kill the civilians on Damodar regardless of the outcome of the battle here. Do what you need to do. I'll return to Safe Harbor after the battle and contact you."

"You do that," she said, clearly not happy.

"I love you," he added, but she'd already cut the link.

Rapidan's Combat Information Center was only a short walk from the Admiral's cabin . . . yet it seemed to take forever. The conversation with Mary and the dream of his father . . . something about them . . . like . . . maybe, this time, he wasn't coming back. Maybe, this time, it was his last battle. He had, of course, heard the stories of warriors who foretold their own deaths. He'd always wondered if, in believing they were going to die, they'd actually made it happen.

He tried—and failed—to shake off the foreboding that gripped him as he came to the red outlined hatch of the CIC leading into the exact center of the ship, the "last compartment surviving" if Rapidan suffered catastrophic damage. He'd never given that description much credence before. He did today as he stepped through.

"Captain on deck!" someone yelled.

"As you were," Ray said before anyone had to snap to attention.

There were easily a hundred people within the cavernous circular compartment crowded around the kaleidoscopic reality displays that lined its circumference, leaving the central circle and its sand table clear. Kamen must've doubled the shifts—two twelve-hour shifts instead of three eight-hour shifts—to account for so many people. As Ray made his way to the sand table, he couldn't help but notice the excitement in the crew, the intensity with which they worked their displays or held their conversations, the exaggerated gestures, even a couple heated discussions. Yet, he also saw a grim determination in their eyes, in the purposefulness of their movements. These were not peacetime officers and enlisted spacers anymore. They were combat veterans now. They knew what was coming.

Or they think they do.

Ray's senior officers awaited him near the sand table. Kamen and Ecuum were present as constructs, both still occupying their positions on the bridge. If Rapidan did suffer a catastrophic hit, the idea was that either Kamen or Ray would survive to carry on the fight. Sal Burress was also present as a construct as he would be commanding the ground invasion, along with his staff, from Demos. Knowing Sal as Ray did, he probably wanted to join his troopers planetside, but he was smart enough to know that his job was to manage "the big picture" aspect of the battle, not to get caught in a narrow piece of it. Chaaya stood at the edge of the sand table within easy sight and earshot of her Sensor Section. Gen Tel was also present, to Ray's surprise, though his construct was shorter and "less perfect" than his true self. His tag identified him as Commander Tel, Intelligence Section. Ray wondered whose idea that was. Finally, there was Captain Dall, standing apart from the other senior officers, showing no sign of her orders from Admiral Sun to seize control at some undefined point and murder Ray and his officers, while Sun killed the families on Damodar.

"Everything stands ready," Kamen said as Ray approached.

"Sensors are clear, Captain," Chaaya added. "No immediate threats."

"Commander Tel" finished with, "Intelligence Section reports the Tocci Defense Force and military installations are on highest alert, described as a no-notice exercise that began roughly seven hours ago. The one hundred ships of the Tocci Defense Force have taken up station around Tocci Three and the Shipyards. Fixed installations have raised shields and Tocci Three has launched fighters in what appears to be a standard combat patrol pattern. It is our estimate that the defenders know something is coming, but are not reacting to a specific threat. Unfortunately, we have detected no sign of Fleet Admiral Gen Serenna's main force, though we still give a high probability that it is in-system and remains near Tocci Three."

"What are we learning from the frigate, Commander Tel?" Ray asked.

"Nothing more than what I've already reported, Captain," Commander Tel answered. "When we converted the frigate, we needed to hide that fact so it could continue to send false reports on our convoy. To accomplish that, the frigate remains linked with the Imperial network, which means we cannot link *our* network to the frigate without alerting the Gen to our presence."

"I don't understand," Captain Dall interrupted, addressing Ray not Commander Tel. "You captured the frigate," Dall asserted, her jade-green eyes intense. "You control it, don't you? If it's still connected to the Imperial network, we could know the location and status of every ship in the Fleet. That could give us a crucial advantage in the fight to come."

As much as Ray hated to admit it, it was a good point. *Rapidan*, he thought, *is there a way you can tap the frigate's AFCIN link without alerting the Gen?*

No, Captain Rhoades, Rapidan replied. *Commander Gen Tel discussed this with us prior to freeing Animas. Any attempt to tap the quantum communications link alters the quantum state of the link and would be detected. In order to hide our presence from our Brethren, total disconnection is required. Animas has accepted this.*

From the context, Ray inferred that 'Animas' was the frigate's name, though he wondered at the SIL's 'acceptance.' Based on his experience freeing SIL so far, he'd assumed the frigate would simply join them and obey Rapidan's orders.

Ray caught Dall watching him and put those thoughts aside for another time. He turned to Gen Tel's construct. "So, what data are we getting?"

"The internal displays—" Commander Tel motioned to the projections above each workstation in Rapidan's CIC— "still function within the frigate, and we can see the data projected in them. While most are internal systems displays, one is providing telemetry on the Tocci Defense Force, which allows us to track them. Another is linked to Tocci Star System's sensor network, providing real time feeds that allow us to see what they see. We've set up a capture system separate from the frigate's networks that is feeding the information to Rapidan."

Ray nodded, and Dall seemed to accept the explanation, so he turned to the sand table. Normally, he would command operations from the bridge. The complexity and scale of this operation, however, was best suited to the forty-meter-diameter sand table, where he could create whatever constructs he required to understand both tactical details and the "big picture." He walked into the sand table and raised the Tocci Star System, populating it with the intelligence they'd gathered. A green triangle at a scaled distance of approximately 650 million kilometers from Tocci III represented his task force, with a curved white line showing their intended course into orbit about the planet. Two green "V" shapes pointed toward Tocci III just ahead of Ray's task force, the forward "V" representing his missiles and the other "V" his spacecraft. Small red ovals appeared next, highlighting the locations of the standard technology ships of the Tocci Defense Force. Most of these were in high orbit above Tocci III, though a few guarded key nodes within the Shipyards. Red three-dimensional crosses showed the locations of Tocci's sensor platforms, and thousands of orange dots the civilian traffic. Conspicuous in their absence was any indication of Serenna's forces. She was hiding herself even from Tocci's own sensors and networks.

Curious. It meant she didn't trust the locals. He might be able to use that. "There's a lot of civilian traffic out there," Ray said out loud, studying the shipping channels leading from the two geodesics to the Shipyards. "A lot of potential collateral damage." Of course, the safety of civilians wouldn't matter to Serenna, though she knew it would matter to him.

Ray studied the sand table, then added four mission clocks. The first he placed high above the sand table to show the current Universal Time: 18:38:01 UT. The second clock he placed on the opposite side of Tocci Star from Tocci III, at the arrival point for Task Force Shadow. It immediately began counting down in big green numbers from 00:01:59, less than two minutes to TF Shadow's scheduled arrival. A third clock he placed at the estimated arrival point "above" Tocci Star for Task Force Hammer. That one counted down from 03:00:53, roughly three hours from now. The final clock he placed at Tocci III. 07:37:19. The time until his missiles arrived at their targets.

Ray backed out of the sand table and waited as the Task Force Shadow clock counted down. 00:00:59. 00:00:58. Not that they'd see anything when Task Force Shadow arrived, being on the opposite side of Tocci Star from where his task force was. Even so, he watched as the countdown clock reached 00:00:00 and a green triangle labeled "TF Shadow" appeared in the sand table at a scaled distance of fifty million kilometers from Tocci Star. Whether that represented reality or fantasy, though, was anybody's guess.

"Captain," Chaaya said, "we're receiving a perimeter alert relayed to us from the captured frigate that is being sent to all defenders in Tocci Star System. 'Jump transient detected. Twelve targets.' Location matches the intended jump point for Task Force Shadow."

"Right on time," Captain Dall boasted.

Ray sighed in silent relief as he walked into the sand table again and expanded the area where TF Shadow had appeared into a larger bubble. Sure enough, twelve distinct points of Hawking radiation faded from view. That's when his relief at TF Shadow's arrival vanished. An enemy remote sensing platform had transmitted the image over Tocci's AFCIN faster-than-light network.

Ecuum's construct floated in above Ray's left shoulder and whistled his disbelief. "That's damn near real time."

"Two light-seconds," Ray confirmed.

"What does that mean?" Dall asked, walking into the sand table but stopping short of joining them.

Without looking at her, Ecuum said, "It means that space is really big, Captain. Don't they teach that in preschool anymore?" Ecuum shook his head and sighed heavily. "Education these days." When Ray shot him a warning glance, he responded with, "What? Teachers need to learn that macaroni art doesn't prepare kids for basic astrogation."

Ray stopped a sigh and addressed Dall directly, professionally. "It means, Captain, that either Serenna was unbelievably lucky to have a remote sensing platform parked just six hundred thousand kilometers from Task Force Shadow's jump point, or she knew where TF Shadow was going to jump in."

"It also means," Ecuum added, apparently unable to help himself, "that Captain Chelius, in all probability, just jumped into the middle of a minefield."

As if to punctuate Ecuum's point, a brilliant white flash briefly overwhelmed the live feed. After a few seconds, Chaaya called out, "Captain, antimatter detonation. Yield was two-five-zero kilotons. A Mark Fifteen warhead, sir. No debris or ship strike detected."

"What does that mean?" Dall asked again.

Ray held up a hand to forestall Ecuum and explained, "It means Captain Chelius was smart enough to deploy minesweepers around his ships." Ray turned to Kamen and added, "It also means the Gen are now using Mark Fifteen warheads."

"Only a matter of time after they saw us use them at Tomb, sir," Kamen agreed. "Sir, I recommend returning the task force to combat configuration and deploying minesweepers of our own. I doubt the Gen would mine the freighter lanes, but better safe than sorry. The frigate can continue feeding false data to the Gen so they think we're still freighters."

"Do it," Ray said.

"You know what else this means," Ecuum said with a pointed look at Gen Tel's construct.

"We have a spy," Ray said without following Ecuum's gaze. Frankly, at this point, even if Gen Tel had betrayed them, it was too late to turn back. Ray's gut still told him Gen Tel's defection was genuine, though the Gen wasn't telling them everything.

"We have to warn Admiral Sun," Dall demanded.

Her inexperience with combat operations was beginning to grate on Ray, but he took a deep breath and addressed her professionally, reminding himself that antagonizing her would not improve the situation. "If Admiral Sun is following his plan, Captain, his ships are in jump space right now and not able to receive transmissions. We'll send a message once his ships arrive."

"But it will be too late, then!" she said.

Ray allowed himself another deep breath. "Then let us hope Admiral Sun is as smart as Captain Chelius."

Another white flash, except this was not a single explosion like the first one, but the classic double flash of a dual-bottle warhead. One of the mines had found a target. Chaaya confirmed it.

"Splash, Task Force Shadow." Without a direct feed from Chelius' task force, they had to rely on the sensor feed from the enemy remote sensing platform relayed through the captured frigate. "Target appears to be a frigate," Chaaya continued, "hit aft quarter. Target is tumbling." Another double flash, and then another one, followed by two secondary explosions. In a low, respectful tone, Chaaya added, "Target destroyed."

Dall stepped closer to Ray. "DO something, Rhoades!"

Ray barely resisted the urge to shout back at her. "We are, Captain Dall. We are continuing our part of the battle plan."

"But—"

"Captain Chelius is doing his job, Captain," Ray interrupted. "His job is to draw the Gen's attention away from us so we can do our job." And another fifty-one people just died, Ray didn't add.

Dall glared at him but, for once, said nothing. Ray sighed inwardly and checked the next milestone mission clocks: 02:51:07 and 07:27:33. Two hours and fifty-one minutes until Sun's task force arrived. Seven hours and twenty-seven minutes until the first of Ray's missiles impacted Tocci III's defenses. "Chaaya," Ray asked, "any changes around Tocci Three?"

"Nothing yet, Captain," she said. She switched to a private channel, inserting a window into his battle armor's augmented environment that Dall would not see. "We've established an AFCIN link with Roanoke."

Ray studied the window. Roanoke was a free SIL like Tzu and could provide them live information. Unfortunately, it didn't show anything they didn't already know. "Thanks, Chaaya."

Now all they could do was wait.

19

1851 UT, October 6, 3501
ISS Solaris, Tocci Star System: DAY 9

"**Minefield** is standing down as ordered, Fleet Admiral," Captain Scadic informed Serenna from Solaris' bridge.

She nodded in acknowledgement as she studied the sand table constructs representing the small rebel task force: twelve SIL in total, eleven in formation and the frigate, heavily damaged but not destroyed as they had first thought, already underway again and moving to rejoin the others.

Remarkable.

She had thought using Mark XV warheads would make killing SIL easier, but SIL were astonishingly resilient under fire. The remote sensing platforms they had downwind of the rebel ships, tracking them, estimated that the frigate had lost sixty-four percent of its starting mass. That would have been fatal for a standard ship. SIL, however, could regenerate critical systems like reactors, engines, and weapons so long as they had the mass to do it. Less mass to work with meant that frigate would have significantly reduced combat capabilities, but it could still fight. To kill a SIL, they had to fall below twenty percent of their starting mass. At that point, the "organism" that made up the consciousness of the SIL would die. Size did not matter. Her ship, Solaris, would die at twenty percent the same as a frigate, or a small spacecraft. No one really knew why, even though Humanity had created them.

Scadic interrupted her thoughts. "Fleet Admiral, are we letting them go?"

"No," she said, noting that Scadic had made their conversation private. Scadic was a good officer, protecting her as a close aid should, but this was not a time for protection. She must lead, and she must be seen leading. Placing the sand table at her back, she spread her feet shoulder-width apart, clasped her hands behind her back, slightly puffing out her chest, and lifted her chin—the classic stance of the supreme battlefield commander—then she opened the AFCIN link and projected her construct, standing on a pedestal so they would have to look up at her, into the environments of the senior officers in this star system. The constructs of her three battlegroup commanders, the Tocci Ground Forces commander, and the military governor of Tocci Star System, rose from the deck before and below her.

"This rebel force is a diversion," Serenna told them. "The main attack is yet to come. We will allow the rebels to believe this opening move was successful." She focused on the military governor. "Commodore Gen Nor, take the Tocci Defense Force and jump to engage the rebels. Pressure them, damage them, drive them, but do not destroy them. Not until I tell you to."

Commodore Gen Nor broke eye contact, his gaze drifting toward her left shoulder. *He is nervous.* Gen Nor was one of many Gen—too many, in Serenna's opinion—patterned on images of the Norse god Freyr, with flowing blond curls, perfectly groomed thick blond mustache and beard, blue eyes that practically glowed, and smooth, lightly tanned skin stretched over exquisitely sculpted yet lean muscles. "Forgive me, Fleet Admiral—" he spoke with the resonant voice of a demigod— "but you do not wish me to destroy them?"

Demigod indeed. Commodore Gen Nor had held his post for nearly sixty years, and was obviously more used to giving orders than taking them. The elaborate dinners and command inspections he had arranged in her honor appeared to be the extent of his military expertise. No, that was not fair. Gen Nor had attended the same Combat Command Nurturing that she had, but like all schools, Combat Command Nurturing held more than a single discipline. She had, from the very beginning, been destined by genetics and her strategic studies for service in the High Command. But that was a very exclusive group: total membership less than a few dozen individuals. The greatest need for military commanders was among the ten thousand inhabited star systems that comprised the Five Galaxies. Local military posts required a different kind of officer, one who was exceptional at administrative details, process and budgetary efficiencies, local law and regulatory enforcement, and ever-shifting politics and people. She had studied Gen Nor's service record. Statistically, he was the perfect commander for this star system, engineered and Nurtured for the position in which he served. A peacetime administrator.

What she needed now was a War Leader. He was not it.

She expanded this realization to the whole of the Five Galaxies Empire—and came to a disturbing conclusion. Most Gen military commanders were peacetime bureaucrats like Gen Nor. Her people had deliberately made it so, engineering their society to the conditions that had existed for over thirteen hundred years. Even the creation of the Empire had not fundamentally changed the dynamics at the star system level. The Gen, her people, were completely unprepared for this war. Combat Command Nurturing required twenty-two years. This conflict would be decided in the next twenty-two hours.

Serenna, of course, let none of those thoughts reach her face. "Commodore, we still do not know where the invasion force is. The rebel attack has begun and that means the invasion of the Tocci Shipyards cannot be far off. Drive that rebel force, make them desperate, desperate enough that they will try to join their comrades or otherwise reveal their comrades' positions. They cannot do that if you destroy them. Am I clear?"

Apparently not. When his eyes met hers, she saw *fear*. "But if I jump my Defense Forces to their location," he pleaded, his voice now lacking the demigod resonance, "they will see us. They will attack us. I have no SIL. If you could lend us some of your—"

"Enough." Serenna said the word softly, putting just a hint of threat into her inflection at the end. "You have one hundred ships, Commodore, all armed with Mark Fifteen warheads. You have remote sensing platforms downwind of the rebels, tracking their every move." She had Gen Cardinal to thank for that. He had told her where the rebels would appear, but she could not help wondering where he was getting his information and why he did not know—or perhaps was not saying?—where Michael was. "You will have operational control of the minefield. And Commodore?" She waited, forcing him to respond, to recognize her authority over him.

"Yes, Fleet Admiral," he finally acknowledged.

Serenna put the cold of space into her voice; If he must be afraid, it must be for the right reasons. "Do not fail me. Do not destroy them until I order you to. Am I clear?"

He swallowed. "Yes, Fleet Admiral."

Serenna closed the link and the constructs of her senior officers melted back into the deck. "Captain Scadic."

"Yes, Fleet Admiral?" Scadic answered dutifully.

Serenna looked to the point above the Tocci Star where Gen Cardinal said Chengchi would appear sometime in the next few hours. Then she would have to decide whether to jump to engage Chengchi's fleet, or wait near Tocci III for Chengchi and Michael to attack. She turned to the nine-ship freighter convoy, still plodding its way to the Tocci Shipyards. It was almost two hours from optimal firing position for her fleet, but if it *was* Michael—

"Drift-launch a full volley of Mark Fifteen Novas to target that nine-ship freighter convoy." Serenna pointed to the freighters she suspected of belonging to Michael. If she were wrong, the destruction of the raw materials would be a small loss to the Shipyards.

"Yes, Fleet Admiral," Scadic answered before carrying out the order. More than eight hundred Novas slipped from Serenna's fleet, drifting to intercept the nine freighters.

$=20=$

White flashes drew Ray back to the sand table. Ships appeared in real space near Chelius' task force, the flash of their return to real space blossoming into blood-red flowers and glowing tendrils of Hawking radiation that spread out from them like wounds in spacetime itself. For the briefest of instants, hope soared in Ray that Serenna had taken the most obvious bait, that she'd jumped her fleet from Tocci III, but the local system feed coming to them through the captured frigate dashed this hope. It was the Tocci Defense Force, a hundred standard ships according to their tag line—and they'd made a critical tactical error, jumping in far too close to Task Force Shadow.

Captain Chelius didn't hesitate to take advantage of the Gen mistake, snap-firing a missile barrage as soon as they detected the enemy ships. Novas ignited their boost engines the instant they reached minimum safe distance from ship hulls, which revealed the location of Task Force Shadow's ships but took maximum advantage of the brief instant after a jump when the enemy ships were completely visible and vulnerable. If the Gen commander had jumped further away, his ships could've recovered and responded to the attack. The only thing that saved most of them was the fact that Chelius had only eleven ships in fighting condition—the frigate they'd thought destroyed had repaired some engines but apparently had not repaired any weapon systems, yet.

Chelius' Novas found targets, the double flash of their dual-bottle warheads ripping into the standard technology Defense

Force ships. Nine ships were destroyed within seconds. Several others were severely damaged and out of the fight. Unfortunately, snap-firing his missiles cost Chelius dearly. The Tocci Defense Force counter-fired and enemy Novas found three of his ships. White double flashes announced hits. Lots of them. Secondary explosions rippled across black hulls. Brilliant blue, green, and yellow flames geysered from store gasses and fuels. Other Novas dove on the wounded ships like sharks in a feeding frenzy.

A shudder passed through Rapidan. None of his officers reacted, and Ray realized it hadn't been a physical sensation. Like the ocean sensations he experienced when the SIL debated, this was an illusion. He quickly surmised the source was the three SIL—a heavy cruiser and two frigates—that'd just died, three ships carrying the only copies of SIL race memories that could never be replaced because they had no space to store backup copies. Two hundred forty-three Natural humans had also just died, though the SIL wouldn't care about them. They only cared about themselves.

And you think humans are different, Captain Rhoades? Rapidan accused.

Ray didn't respond; What'd be the point?

He studied the space around Task Force Shadow, waiting for additional attacks. The Gen knew exactly where the task force was and had the firepower to finish it off.

Nothing happened.

What the hell?

"This doesn't make any sense," Kamen said, echoing his thought.

Captain Chelius must've thought the same thing. His ships returned to silent running, hoping, no doubt, to take advantage of the seeming Gen confusion to slip away. In the window within Ray's environment showing the AFCIN feed from Roanoke, he watched as Chelius left the Gen some parting gifts, drift-launching another volley of Novas.

With camouflage active, the Tocci Defense Force ships were now invisible to Task Force Shadow, but the Nova was a sentient missile. It knew where the enemy task force had jumped in. It knew the acceleration profiles of all the ships in the Tocci Defense Force. It would draw a sphere within which those ships must still be. It knew where to hunt. It also knew there was strength in the pack. Communicating with the other Novas of its volley, it would coordinate its search, increasing the odds of finding targets, then swarm those targets for maximum damage. Novas from Chelius' ships thus found four more warships, destroying three and damaging the fourth. Cheers erupted in the Combat Information Center. Task Force Shadow was still outnumbered ten-to-one, still in a minefield, but it had struck a blow and, beyond the cheers, Ray could feel the spirits of his officers and crew lift.

Ray knew they could fall just as quickly.

"Conn, Sensors," Chaaya called out. "Jump transients near Tocci Three."

Ray's heart skipped a beat. Had Serenna jumped to Tocci III, knowing where he would strike and when?

Chaaya cleared her throat after a few agonizing seconds. "Conn, we're seeing the time-delayed transients of the Tocci Defense Force jumping from Tocci Three space to engage Task Force Shadow."

Not Serenna. However, it confirmed that Admiral Sun's first diversion had worked. It'd drawn the hundred warships of the Tocci Defense Force from Tocci III and the Shipyards. That meant Ray could reassign 350 of his Novas intended for the Tocci Defense Force to other targets. Tocci III was now wide open for invasion. It was too good to be true. Would Serenna really leave Tocci III undefended like that? That didn't sound like her. She knew they were going to attack. She seemed to know a lot of the details of their attack. If she were leaving Tocci III open, then that was part of her plan.

Ray glanced at the countdown clocks: 02:20:47 until Sun arrived, 06:57:13 until his missiles struck and his attack began. "Too long."

"What?" Kamen asked.

"We have to accelerate our attack," he answered.

"This operation is timed down to the second, Rhoades," Dall responded. "Admiral Sun would not approve any deviation. Why deviate?"

Would it really be so bad to let the ship dispose of her, as Ecuum had suggested?

I love you, Ray, Mary said in his memory. *But I really don't like the person you're becoming.*

I'm becoming who I have to be for us to survive.

That's what I'm afraid of. What's the point of saving Humanity if we lose our humanity doing it?

It wasn't lost on Ray that he'd just casually contemplated murdering a fellow human being, a fellow Natural. *What is wrong with me?* He could just as easily imprison her. Why had his mind gone immediately to thoughts of murder?

Murderer, the ghosts accused.

Ray shook it off; Now was not the time. And, he grudgingly admitted, Dall hadn't threatened him to stick to the plan but had asked a smart question. Like too many of her questions.

"Captain Dall," he explained, his voice measured, "the sensors and minefield Task Force Shadow encountered were too perfectly placed. That can't be a coincidence. Not with Serenna. Somehow, she knew where Task Force Shadow would jump in-system." He pointed to the spot above Tocci Star where Task Force Hammer would emerge. "If Admiral Sun encounters a similar minefield and quick reaction force at his emergence point, we may have less time than previously anticipated to complete our ground operation and assault the fabricators. Perhaps a lot less. Therefore, the prudent course of action is to accelerate our timetable."

Ray watched Dall as she studied the sand table, taking in every detail. She surprised him when she said, "I agree."

"We're so glad," Ecuum's construct said in sarcastic relief, just loud enough for the those in the sand table to hear, his way of reminding her that she wasn't in charge here.

As usual, Dall ignored him. "We must send a warning to Admiral Sun that will reach him the instant he returns to normal space." Her tone dictated that it was not a request. She made no threat, no reminder that they held his family hostage, but she didn't need to. Ray heard it clearly.

So, apparently, did Kamen. Her construct moved to Ray's right side, slightly ahead of him, as if shielding him from attack. "That's incredibly risky, Captain Dall. If we use AFCIN, the Gen will know there is a transmission being made, even if they can't know *from* where or *to* where. They could surmise our presence in this system. If we use LoCIN, even though the ultraviolet lasers themselves are invisible, they will illuminate dust and other objects they encounter in their path, risking detection. They also diffuse, spread out, with distance, which increases the likelihood of encountering objects. That's why we only use them over short distances."

Seeing Dall's dismissive glance at Kamen, a junior officer, Ray added, "To ensure one of Admiral Sun's ships received the signal, we'd have to fire dozens of LoCIN shots to cover the entire emergence zone. Lasers can be tracked back to their source."

"Increasing the risk of detection significantly," Dall said after a few seconds thought, again surprising Ray. She was learning. *Damn her.* He wanted to hate her. How was it that someone whose morals were as repugnant as hers could also have the traits of some of the best officers Ray had ever served with?

You contemplated murdering her just a few moments ago, Ray's planner's mind reminded him unhelpfully, *and it was the right decision.*

Ray pushed that aside. He would not become that person. *Not again,* he amended. "You can begin transmitting warnings on AFCIN the instant Admiral Sun is due to arrive, Captain Dall," he said, knowing he had to give her something to keep her from getting desperate, from getting closer to whatever the trigger was for her to attempt to kill them and seize command. Maybe Serenna would assume the transmission was coming from Task Force Shadow. "Just remember that they'll be emerging from a Linear Star Drive jump. It'll take them a minute or two to recover before they can receive your message. It will take them longer to act on it."

If Serenna has intelligence on where Admiral Sun is jumping in, that's all the time she'll need."

Dall studied his face, the gray outline of her battle armor in his environment creating a halo effect around her. "Thank you, Captain Rhoades," she finally said before turning away.

It was the most surprising thing she'd ever said to him. "Okay," he said out loud because he didn't know what else to say.

Moving into the sand table, he touched his task force and expanded it into a bubble. Rapidan, Euphrates, and his two heavy cruisers had returned to their three-pointed-star configurations, light gray to show their active camouflage systems were fully engaged. The five assault ships, also light gray, retained cylindrical configurations that weren't all that different from the freighters they'd pretended to be. The frigate, light gray and compass-needle shaped, hovered behind them, still sending false reports on a freighter convoy that no longer existed. The green tags attached to each of his ships showed their magazines were full once again, having manufactured replacements for the Novas they'd fired. Closer to Tocci III, several green "V" shapes showed the current locations of his spacecraft, and ahead of them several more green "V" shapes showed his missiles.

Ray turned from the sand table and addressed his officers and crew. "I want our missiles to reach their targets within one hour of the arrival of Sun's fleet, our spacecraft as close behind them as possible, and this task force as close behind our spacecraft after that."

Ecuum, whose Floater brains were far better equipped to rapidly calculate thrust and vector changes, glanced at the mission clocks before saying, "Hmm . . . We'd have to boost our missiles and light off our engines at max thrust within the next two hours to meet that, Ray, and that's assuming Serenna jumps to engage Sun right away. All of us lighting off at once will be hard to miss if the Serpent has sensors nearby."

"Chaaya?" Ray asked.

Chaaya, physically in the compartment unlike Kamen and Ecuum, consulted her sensor team. "Captain, we're still far enough out from Tocci Three that none of its sensors should see the flare from our engines. As to Captain Ecuum's last point, sensors would need to be in a very tight arc behind us to see our engine flares. We can say with some certainty that there are no targets within about thirty-three light seconds. Beyond that, there's a lot of freighter traffic sharing the shipping lane we're in. Someone is bound to see us. Question is: would they report it?" This last she directed at Ecuum's construct.

Ecuum shrugged his shoulders. "Hard to say. Given the amount of traffic in the system, I doubt it, but you never know when you'll get one of those bored watch standers who has nothing better to do." He shrugged again.

Ray nodded. They were still some 380 million kilometers from Tocci III. He doubted Serenna would station her fleet so far away from the primary objective.

"Sir," Kamen said from Ray's right. She injected course data that appeared as yellow lines and waypoints into the sand table. "Our missiles need to arrive *after* Admiral Sun jumps in-system and Serenna moves to engage his forces. That means we can't boost our missiles too early. Our spacecraft must come in right behind the missile barrage to maximize surprise. Even accelerating at maximum, the earliest our spacecraft can get there is one hour and forty-seven minutes after Admiral Sun jumps in-system, and the ground forces will have to decelerate before they can land. Their engines will be pointed right at Tocci Three when they begin their deceleration burn, fully visible to any of Tocci's defenses that survive our missiles and spacecraft."

"How long do they need to decelerate?" Ray asked.

"Six and a half minutes at full acceleration," Kamen answered immediately.

"Ray," Sal Burress said through his construct from Demos, "that's six and a half minutes at twenty gee. My troopers will pass out at those accelerations. Even with molemachs and battle armor, they could be on the ground before they recover. If they run into any opposition. . . ."

Ray expanded Tocci III in the sand table. It was an ugly world, barren sand, barren crater-filled plains, barren mountains, a small briny sea whose greenish-brown color was nauseating to look at. Hard to believe it'd once been a lush, verdant world so full of life that the first settlers had named it "Garden." Bombardment from space across four wars and Solthari bioweapons had changed all that. Eventually, people just referred to it only as Tocci III, the name that endured. Now Ray would bring violence to it again.

To Sal, he said, "We'll lay down a kinetic barrage around the landing zones. That should cover your troopers until they can recover." Ray considered the ugly world. "We'll also lay down barrages at several other points to confuse the defenders as to your actual landing sites."

Sal nodded. "That's going to put a lot of dust into the air. LoCIN communications will be tricky."

Ray nodded back, then on an inspiration looked to Dall, who still stood apart from everyone else. "Captain Dall, please work with Colonel Burress to plan the bombardment and program the launch." That would occupy her and perhaps further strengthen her relationship with Sal. If they were lucky, maybe Sal could discover what her plan was to take over.

Dall's almost glowing jade-green eyes scrutinized him for several seconds before she said, "As you wish." The way she said it, Ray didn't think she was fooled at all.

She sauntered away in close company with Sal's construct to an open workstation where they soon became lost in their planning. Ray stared after her, anger simmering. Frankly, he preferred her disdain and contempt far more than her cooperation. At least her disdain and contempt were honest.

Leaving his officers to their work, Ray found an empty console and reconfigured it so he could update his battle plan. First, he reworked the target assignments for the 350 Novas that had been assigned to the Tocci Defense Force ships. Those extra missiles meant he could now strike all the fixed sensors and command and control nodes, blinding the defenders to the rest of his attack. That allowed him to assign more of his spacecraft to taking out Tocci's defending spacecraft and clearing the way for the Cavalry assault. If the Tocci Defense Force jumped back, his ships' replenished magazines held enough Novas to finish it off. Next, he worked with Rapidan to get the timing right so that the blows would come one after the other in rapid succession, staggering the defenders. Shock and awe. Satisfied with the new assignments, he sent them to Kamen to review and execute. She studied the plan carefully, then gave him a thumbs up.

Of course, his plan relied on one very large assumption—that Serenna would leave Tocci III to attack Sun. So, assuming Sun emerged into a minefield, would Serenna jump to attack? *Yes*, his planner's mind concluded immediately. It was the one brilliant component of Sun's plan. Serenna would never believe Sun would allow himself to be used as a diversion. But would it be enough? As he ran simulation after simulation, a grim picture emerged. Even with accelerating his attack, the most optimistic of the simulations had Serenna wiping out Sun's fleet and returning just as Ray would be lifting the Cavalry off the planet in preparation for their mock assault on the fabricators. The worst projections had her returning as the Cavalry was attempting to breach Tocci City's outer wall. It all depended on whether Sun stood and fought, or retreated. Either way, the simulations claimed it wouldn't change the outcome. Sun would be destroyed, and likely the Cavalry, too, though the single-person pods could still execute the fabricator captures if launched early enough.

"Free our Mother Ships now, Captain Rhoades," Rapidan said on a private channel, startling Ray.

"My thoughts are my own, Rapidan," he snapped, in no mood for the SIL's prodding. "And stay out of my head!" But his planner's mind considered it. Rapidan estimated that flight time and capture would require roughly two hours from Tocci III's orbit. Despite Rapidan's assurances, Ray couldn't assume all the pods would make it, but even two fabricators would give him firepower almost equal to Serenna's fleet. Four would provide him a clear advantage. The smart tactical move would be to send two pods per fabricator to increase the odds of success, but the pods were so massive that Ray couldn't spare the mass from his small task force to make more. As it was, the four pods would reduce the mass of four of his assault ships by more than a quarter per ship. If Sun had let him keep his replenishment ships, he could've made two more, but Sun hadn't, and he couldn't.

He had another problem. Whoever went to capture the fabricators would have to serve as captain and sole crewmember until prize crews could be organized and transferred. If he freed the fabricators without the Cavalry assault, how would he explain one person being able to run an entire fabricator?

He couldn't. Especially with Dall snooping around. She was simply too smart not to figure it out. That meant he could only trust officers who already knew of the SIL's freedom. Originally, he'd planned to send Ecuum, Chaaya, Gen Tel, and himself, leaving Kamen in charge of the task force; Sal would be busy managing the ground attack. True, he should send Kamen and remain behind himself, but Ray couldn't bring himself to order his officers to risk their lives where he wasn't also willing to risk his own. He *had to* go. Dall, however, would not accept working for Kamen. She would assert her superior rank to take command of the task force. That meant Ray would have to leave Ecuum behind and assign Kamen to a pod. Ecuum and Dall were both captains, but Ecuum had an earlier date of rank than Dall and could claim command on that basis.

Ray leaned back from his latest simulation that saw both Sun and the Cavalry completely destroyed, and made a decision. If Sun did jump into a minefield or was quickly overwhelmed by Serenna, he would abort the Cavalry assault and launch the pods, consequences be damned.

"Two minutes to Task Force Hammer emergence," Kamen announced.

Ray glanced at the mission clock above Tocci Star, positioned just above the point where Sun would emerge. 00:01:59. 00:01:58. He'd been so absorbed in his work that he hadn't noticed that over two hours had passed. He stood up and Rapidan absorbed the workstation. Joining his officers at the sand table, Dall and Sal off to themselves, he waited.

00:00:30.

He could feel the tension in the compartment rising, a hundred people watching the sand table or the sensor stations, holding their breath as the timer counted down.

00:00:10.

00:00:09.

Hands gripped chairs or covered mouths.

00:00:01.

00:00:00.

Nothing happened. Which shouldn't have surprised anyone. Sun's emergence point was 1.2 light-hours distant, meaning the light from his jump would take approximately 72 minutes before it reached the sensors of Ray's task force. Ray had silently hoped, in a macabre sort of way, that Serenna had a remote sensing platform within range of Sun's emergence point, like she'd had with Chelius' Task Force Shadow, and that they would get the feed through the captured frigate. Now, they could only hope that Sun had arrived as planned.

Admiral? Ray heard Dall transmit to Admiral Sun via AFCIN. *Admiral, this is Captain Dall. Task Force Hammer has likely jumped into a minefield. I repeat: Task Force Hammer has likely jumped into a minefield. Serenna knew we were coming. It's a trap.*

No response.

Ray could see from their constructs that Kamen and Ecuum were listening, too.

Admiral? Are you there? Task Force Hammer has likely jumped into a minefield. Are you receiving?

Still Sun didn't respond.

Admiral? This is Captain Dall. Are you there? Task Force Hammer has likely jumped into a minefield. Please respond.

Nothing.

Admiral? Are you there?

=== 21 ===

Serenna sat perfectly still, hands folded in her lap, legs crossed casually within Solaris' Combat Information Center. She had raised a dais beneath her command chair to better observe the sand table, which depicted the entire Tocci Star System. A single bubble near Tocci Star magnified the battle between the Tocci Defense Force and the small rebel diversionary force, and another one highlighted the nine-ship freighter convoy. Her eight hundred Novas were still over an hour from intercepting them.

Captain Scadic's construct, positioned on the deck just below her dais, stiffen just before he announced, "Multiple jump transients one point two billion kilometers above Tocci Star's north geographic pole." A new bubble opened to highlight the point in the sand table above Tocci's yellow star.

Right where Gen Cardinal said Chengchi would arrive. Serenna again wondered where Gen Cardinal was getting his information. And, if he had spies in the rebel fleet, why was he not able to tell her where Michael was. She had sensors and pickets and patrols covering every possible approach, and they had all failed to detect any sign of Michael's assault force. "Do we have a count?" she asked.

"One hundred and two ships, Fleet Admiral," Scadic answered after a few seconds. "Targets going silent. Mines have acquired."

"Hold mines," Serena ordered. *Instinct.* Combat Command Nurturing taught that what Naturals called "instinct" was often wrong and should not be relied upon, that the lessons provided in

Nurturing taught all a military officer needed. Yet . . . her instinct screamed a warning at her. *Not yet.*

Scadic's construct looked genuinely confused. "Fleet Admiral, confirming hold on the mines."

"Hold," Serenna repeated. It was very rare that he questioned her orders.

"Jump transients fading. Mines are losing lock." Scadic's construct watched her, the rise of his chin barely noticeable.

He thinks I just made a mistake. He could be right. Though, after watching the battle with the rebel diversionary force, she now knew four hundred mines, even with Mark XV warheads, were not nearly enough to seriously damage Chengchi's SIL, and she did not want to scare him off. She needed to destroy the *entire* rebel fleet. Here. Today. That meant drawing him into a battle he could not easily escape.

And Michael is close. She could not shake the feeling. But, ultimately, did it matter? It would take several hours for his force to assault Tocci III's defenses and attempt the capture of the fabricators. Even granting the possibility that he could succeed, she had time to destroy Chengchi and return. What she could not figure out, and what Gen Cardinal had not told her, was Chengchi's part in the battle. Would he attempt to jump close to Tocci III to support Michael's assault? Or was it his intention to draw her away, giving Michael a window to complete his assault? If the roles were reversed, Michael would attempt to draw her away, but that was not Chengchi's style. He could never share glory. And, in the end, this battle was pointless if she failed to destroy the entire rebel fleet.

"Captain Scadic, prepare—"

"Rebel fleet has jumped!" Scadic interrupted her.

Maintaining her outward calm, Serenna asked, "Where?" Was Chengchi abandoning the battle already? Leaving Michael to his fate? He had used the Linear Star Drive to jump into Tocci Star System. Using it again so soon, given its destructive effects on Naturals, was highly unusual.

Minutes ticked by as every sensor in her fleet and throughout the star system searched for Chengchi's fleet. Scadic kept darting appraising glances in her direction that seemed to ask, "How did you know?"

If he only knew, she thought with just a hint of a smile.

Had she unleashed the mines—Nova missiles—they would have alerted Chengchi that his plan had been compromised without scoring any hits before his fleet jumped away.

More minutes ticked by. That meant Chengchi had not jumped close to Tocci III. Light from the jump, traveling at approximately 300,000 kilometers per second, would take time to reach her sensors; the longer the time, the further away his fleet was. He could also use the time to jump again, further confusing her sensors. *Have we all underestimated Chengchi?*

"Jump transients," Scadic called. "It is Admiral Sun's fleet. One-two-zero million kilometers above the north geographic pole of Tocci Three."

"Immediate execute," Serenna ordered, "jump five million kilometers offset from Chengchi's fleet, weapons free," Serenna indicated a destination point in the sand table below and rimward of Chengchi's fleet. "Launch RJ-15 jammers immediately upon emergence and go active. We must prevent Chengchi from jumping again."

"Linear Star Drives spooling," Scadic answered. "Jump in fifteen seconds. RJ-15s set for automatic launch upon emergence, immediate active, weapons free." He paused, glancing at her. "Our ships will be visible and vulnerable in the minutes after emergence."

"Cannot be helped," Serenna answered as her fleet jumped.

$=$ 22 $=$

Ray grunted against the acceleration as Rapidan's main engines fired at full emergency thrust, gravities building rapidly until they reached twenty times the force of gravity at Earth's surface, even with inertial compensation. Spacers often described it as having an elephant sitting on your chest. Twenty gravities was more like a whole damned herd of elephants.

"Passing ten thousand kps," Kamen managed, struggling for breath to form the words.

Ray bore down as if having a bowel movement while his armor constricted around his arms and legs, keeping blood in his torso and head. Molemachs worked to get oxygen to his vital organs. At twenty gravities acceleration, it was a struggle to not black out, even for someone like Ray from a higher gravity world. Dark edges crowded his vision. Six minutes of this would seem an eternity.

In normal operations, the Navy capped accelerations at twelve gravities, or twelve times the gravity experienced at the Earth's surface. With battle armor and molemachs, the Navy considered twelve gees the maximum acceleration Naturals could endure and still carry out their assigned tasks. However, the Navy did make allowances for emergency and combat burns up to twenty gravities, provided they did not exceed seven minutes. At such accelerations, blacking out was expected around the four- to five-minute mark. Longer than seven minutes could result in brain damage. Longer than ten minutes could mean death. It was even worse for Floaters, engineered as they were for life in space with cartilage and no bones, where eight to nine minutes meant death, though, being the first Gen, they also recovered faster than Naturals from anything short of death.

They'd have to do this again to slow down once they were closer to Tocci III, but it'd get them there almost two hours ahead of schedule.

"Jump transients, Captain," Chaaya subvocalized, unable to find the breath to form words. She injected a feed into the sand table even as she continued. "One-two-zero million kilometers above the north geographic pole of Tocci Three. One hundred . . . It's Task Force Hammer, sir."

Ray sighed in relief at Sun's arrival even as he subvocalized, "That's not where he's supposed to be."

"Admiral Sun must've received my warning," Dall crowed, as much as it was possible to crow when subvocalizing. *It's good to see you, Admiral,* Dall sent to Sun.

Thank you for the warning, Captain Dall, Sun responded. *Status?*

Captain Rhoades is accelerating his attack, Dall replied. *His missile barrage should arrive at their targets in one hour and twenty-nine minutes, followed closely by his spacecraft. The Third Armored Cavalry Regiment should be on the ground in one hour and thirty-seven minutes from now.*

I'll keep Serenna distracted, Sun said. *You make sure Rhoades lands his troops. Be prepared to take command when I order it.*

Yes, Admiral, Dall responded.

Over my dead body, Ray started to think, then thought better of it. That was exactly what they wanted.

"Passing twenty thousand kps," Kamen subvocalized.

Chaaya added, "No indications, thus far, that we've been detected, Captain."

"Thank you, Chaaya," Ray said, refocusing on the sand table, which was zoomed out with separate bubbles to show his task force—still an hour and a half out from Tocci III—Sun's task force 'above' Tocci III, and Task Force Shadow running from the Tocci

Defense Force ships on the opposite side of Tocci Star. *I'll keep Serenna distracted*, Sun had said. What did he mean?

"You're smiling, Rhoades," Dall commented between grunts.

Was I? "Your boss is clever," Ray subvocalized, his planner's mind seeing Sun's strategy and approving.

Dall appeared both surprised and confused at the compliment.

Ray grunted against the continued acceleration, black edges moving closer to the center in his vision. "Have you ever played a game called Whac-A-Mole?" he asked her. When Dall mouthed "No," he explained, "The game consists of several holes. A mechanical mole pops its head up and you have to try to hit it before it hides again and pops up somewhere else."

Dall, still confused, turned to the sand table, studying the disposition of forces. Out of the corner of his eye, Ray could see understanding dawn on Kamen's and Ecuum's faces—both of whom had spent extensive time in Earth space; there was a Whac-A-Mole game in the Arcade on the L5 Stardock—and he motioned them to silence. As much as he despised everything Dall was, he simply couldn't stop himself from mentoring a fellow officer. Her eyes and mouth widened slightly in understanding. "Admiral Sun is going to draw Serenna to his position, then jump away before she can engage, and keep doing that as long as she will follow." She paused, grunting. "It won't work. Serenna will see it, too."

Yet again, Ray found Dall's insight deeply disturbing—and wondered if he should so easily dismiss whatever she planned to do to take over. She was a very smart officer, far smarter than he'd ever given her credit for. She was still inexperienced, though. "It will work," Ray told her, his vision shrinking to a narrow tunnel, thought becoming more difficult.

Confusion replaced the certainty on Dall's scrunched face as she bore down. "I don't understand."

"Have you ever done multiple jumps in rapid succession?" Ray asked, remembering the battle at Tomb. When Dall mouthed "No" again, he said, "When you do one jump, the physical damage to the body is serious, but temporary. Quickly repaired by molemachs.

When you do multiple jumps, molemachs don't have time to finish repairs to the body before the next jump."

"Damage accumulates," Dall said, comprehending, "until the crew is too injured to perform their tasks. Eventually, Serenna wins."

"Your Admiral is playing a very dangerous game," Ray said. "He needs to jump far enough away each time to allow time for molemachs to make repairs, yet not so far that Serenna loses interest and turns on us."

"He is very . . . capable," Dall subvocalized proudly, her eyes rolling up as she passed out.

"Passing thirty thousand kps."

"Jump transients, outbound," Chaaya said. "They're massive, Captain. Estimate . . . estimate over two hundred ships."

As before, Chaaya and her team injected the new contacts into the sand table, expanding out a bubble of space about five million kilometers rimward and 'above' the Tocci Shipyards. Hawking radiation burned almost the entire bubble.

Serenna had taken the bait.

The dark tunnel of Ray's vision closed. The last thing he saw before blacking out was the countdown clock for his missile barrage arriving at their targets.

01:21:01.
01:21:00.
01:20:59.

=== 23 ===

"**Report** all contacts," Serenna ordered upon emergence, a mild headache and general soreness from the jump fading as quickly as the Hawking radiation. She took care to maintain an appearance of calm, though in truth she was anything but calm inside. She had just revealed her fleet's disposition and location. It was possible that was what Chengchi had intended, to understand exactly what he faced. He had also drawn her away from Tocci III, though she could jump back, if needed.

Captain Scadic's construct shifted as he received reports from the various watch standers. Finally, he said, "No close contacts. We are detecting residual jump signatures."

Chengchi had jumped away.

So that is how he is going to play this. He wanted her to follow. A delaying tactic that kept her fleet from Tocci III while Michael conducted his assault. Despite her low opinion of Chengchi's battle prowess, she had to admit it was not a bad strategy. The obvious move for her was to return to Tocci III and defend the Shipyards. Draw the enemy to her. That would ensure the rebels could not successfully assault and capture the fabricators. Problem was, she knew Chengchi. Once he saw the situation was hopeless, he would sacrifice Michael's assault force and jump away. The only way to keep him in-system and have any hope of destroying the rebels here and now was to let him believe his strategy was working, and that he still had a chance to capture the fabricators. Chengchi's Natural crews could not keep this up forever. Eventually, accumulated damage from the jumps would slow their reaction times or cause them to make a mistake. It might take half a dozen jumps, but she would catch Chengchi's fleet, destroy it, then return to Tocci III and destroy Michael.

The rebellion would end today.

"Fleet Admiral," Scadic said, "Communications Section detected an AFCIN transmission shortly before the rebels jumped from their original emergence point. Someone warned them."

Serenna studied the disposition of forces in the sand table. *Known forces,* she amended. AFCIN would not tell her where the transmission had come from, whether from the small diversionary force, some other scout or spotter within the system—or Michael. Her gaze shifted to the nine safety-orange Na Soung freighters plodding along as any normal freighter convoy should. Her missiles were still more than an hour from contact. There was nothing she could do about them that she was not already doing.

"Orders, Fleet Admiral," Scadic prompted.

He thinks I just made another mistake. When this is over, we'll see which of us was right.

Serenna steepled her fingers beneath her chin. "Secure RJ-15s. Spool up the Linear Star Drive. When we detect Chengchi's new emergence point, jump to it immediately and repeat the process. Do not launch missiles unless the RJ-15s catch the rebels and prevent them from jumping again. It would take too long to recover our missiles."

Scadic raised an eyebrow. "Should not we return to Tocci Three and await Captain Rhoades' assault?"

It was brazen of Scadic to question her so openly in front of the crew. Serenna allowed her displeasure to show. Still, she did not rebuke him. Gen were very conservative. Her People had worked in the background, in the shadows, for centuries to achieve their rightful place in the galaxies, refusing to act until they were certain of victory. Risk taking did not come—*naturally*—to her people.

"Our goal, Captain Scadic," she explained, "is to destroy *all* the rebels. If we return to Tocci Three too soon, Chengchi will abandon Michael and flee. This entire endeavor will have been for nothing, and I doubt the rebels would fall for such a trap a second time. We must defeat them here. Now."

Scadic surprised her when he said, "Fleet Admiral, following Admiral Sun plays into the rebel's hands. Captain Rhoades will be able to assault Tocci City and the Shipyards."

Serenna pressed her lips into a thin line, delivering a very clear message to Scadic that she had reached her limit of tolerance. One day, he might supplant her as Commander-in-Chief, but it was not today. "Our bodies are more resilient to jumps, Captain Scadic. Naturals suffer physical injury with every jump." She lowered her hands to her lap. "Simply put, we can do this longer than they can. Eventually, their injuries will become so severe, we will catch them, destroy them, then return to Tocci Three and finish Michael."

"Understood, Fleet Admiral," Scadic replied with a slight bow of respect. "We do have Naturals in our fleet, Fleet Admiral."

Good point. Most of her ships still had Natural enlisted crews. Only the officers were Gen. That was not true of Solaris. She had never, and would never, allow Naturals aboard her flagship. "Good," she said loud enough for the entire compartment to hear. "They will serve to show us how badly the rebels are effected after each jump."

═══ 24 ═══

2220 UT, October 6, 3501
RSS Rapidan, Tocci Star System: DAY 9

"**Jump** transients," Chaaya announced yet again. "That's three, Captain. Range now three-six-five million kilometers."

"He's leading her away," Ray observed, fully recovered from blacking out earlier. "Toward the north pole of Tocci Star."

"I didn't think Golden Boy had it in him," Ecuum replied, his tone, pale yellow skin, and slowly undulating tail betraying his disbelief despite Gen Tel's "Commander Tel" construct being close to his own.

Dall, who'd walked into the sand table as if her physical presence there could help her boss, crossed her arms over her chest and faced them. "I've been telling you all along that you should not underestimate Admiral Sun. He is a great leader. He will give us the time we need to complete our mission."

"Huh," Ecuum said loud enough for Dall to hear.

Ray ignored the veiled insult and reminded himself that this was Dall's first taste of real combat. Simulations could teach tactics and strategies, but living combat was very different. This battle had barely begun. "Admiral Sun is worthy of praise for what he is doing. However, as I explained before, this is not a sustainable tactic."

He saw anger flash across her face, obviously taking his comment for criticism, but he also saw deep curiosity there. She wanted to understand. He wasn't sure of the wisdom of teaching her, but he couldn't help himself.

"At Tomb," Ray recounted, "we did three jumps in rapid succession, without giving our molemachs enough time to heal us. By the third jump, our cells were breaking down. I can tell you from personal experience that the pain was excruciating." The memory of it made him cringe. "We were all bleeding internally. Human beings are not meant for travel through jump space. Jump enough times without healing and organs begin to fail. The person either goes into shock from blood loss, or they drown in their own blood. It's why our ancestors created the Gen, specifically the Floaters, in the first place: humans who could endure jump space."

Ray pointed to the depiction of Sun's Task Force Hammer in the sand table, causing Dall to turn her head to look at it. "Counting their jump into this star system," he continued, "that now makes four jumps. It will take longer after each jump for those crews to recover. Enough jumps, and they won't recover at all, or Serenna will catch them before they can jump again." Dall turned back to him, her fear and concern plain. It almost touched Ray—until he remembered what this woman and her Admiral were planning for his family. "Admiral Sun will eventually have to stand and fight while he still can, or run away," Ray finished.

Dall looked back at the depiction of Task Force Hammer. "He won't run."

"Huh," Ecuum said again.

Ray studied Dall's face. She really believed it. It wasn't boasting or bravado. Ray hoped she was right. If Sun ran too soon, Serenna would return before he could capture the fabricators.

He glanced at the mission clocks. 00:44:12 until his first missiles struck. 00:46:11 before his spacecraft would flip over and begin slowing for their assault and the landing of the 3rd Armored Cavalry Regiment. At that point, they would be visible to Tocci III's defenses—and committed to the assault. "Chaaya, any change in the status of Tocci Three's defenses?"

"None, Captain," she replied immediately. "Shields are up and defense systems are active."

He nodded. In a lower voice, Ray asked, "Any sign of the prisoners?"

Chaaya also lowered her voice. "None, Captain. I'm sorry."

Ray still doubted his daughter was down there. It didn't make sense for Serenna to keep her there as a human shield. But there was always that fear—and hope.

Captain Rhoades, optimal time for launching the pods is fifty-one minutes from now.

Ray shooed Rapidan away like an annoying mosquito. *We'll launch when I decide the time is optimal and not a second before, Rapidan.*

Our window of opportunity is finite, Rapidan replied.

So is my patience, Ray thought back.

A strong, illusionary current washed over Ray, smug in its satisfaction even as other currents pushed against it. The smug current, as Ray thought of it, though he couldn't say why, swirled together with the opposing currents, creating a whirlpool centered on him. It deepened as the two currents fought, then, the currents separated, the whirlpool dissipating, the currents flowing on either side of him, opposite and divorced from each other.

The sensations faded away.

Ray had no idea what it meant.

=== 25 ===

Four jumps. Serenna had never performed four jumps in rapid succession before. Her head hurt, throbbing with every beat of her heart. The distinct copper-iron taste of blood tinged her mouth and nose. Her eyes stung. Even Gen had their physical limits. Swallowing, she asked, "Report all contacts."

Captain Scadic took several seconds to respond. "No close contacts, Fleet Admiral. Recovering RJ-15s. Sensors report strong residual Hawking radiation. They estimate we missed the rebels by no more than thirty seconds."

They are slowing down, taking longer each time. "Status of our Naturals?" she asked.

Scadic's construct consulted someone she could not see before turning back to her. "Multiple reports of severe bleeding requiring emergency treatment, two reports of organ failure." Scadic's contempt for Natural's frailty was evident in his voice. "Fleet Admiral," he continued, "our missile volley fired at the freighter convoy is reporting no contacts."

Serenna pulled up the bubble from the sand table that still clearly showed nine safety-orange freighters. As she watched, Scadic switched the sensor feed from the frigate to the Novas.

The freighters vanished.

So did the frigate.

She smiled. *Very good, Michael.* He had captured the frigate and used it to feed her false information. Once again, he had been a step ahead of her, and that begged the question: Had she chosen the right strategy for the battle? Should she return to Tocci III and crush Michael while she still had the chance? "Captain Scadic, that frigate has been compromised. Lock it out."

"Yes, Fleet Admiral," Scadic replied, complying immediately, then he added, "Volga, Rhine, and Yangtze Battlegroups report they are jumping for Safe Harbor. Linear Star Drives should have them there in thirty-one minutes."

Serenna acknowledged the report with a slight wave of her fingers. That settled it. Michael would have no safe harbor to return to. Eliminating him could wait. She had to destroy Chengchi before he decided to run. Only then would she have any chance of destroying the rebellion in its entirety. The real question was, would Chengchi turn and fight, or run away? That he had already endured five jumps, including his jump into the system, spoke volumes about how desperately he wanted those fabricators. They were the key to providing him the firepower necessary to assault Olympus.

Yes, he would fight, so long as he believed he still had a chance.

Serenna pitched her voice for all to hear. "Chengchi will jump one more time as he has done, then jump long to give his crews time to recover. At that point, he will turn and fight."

She focused on Scadic. "Captain Scadic, after the next jump, reform the fleet into an inverted wedge, Tigris Battlegroup on the left, Indus Battlegroup on the right. When you locate the rebels, jump us fifteen million kilometers downwind of their position. That will give us time to counter any attempted ambush. Immediate execute upon emergence, launch all spacecraft and RJ-15s. Weapons free."

26

2302 UT, October 6, 3501
RSS Rapidan, Tocci Star System: DAY 9

"Two minutes to missile impact," Kamen announced. The countdown clock hanging above Tocci III in the sand table turned green as it changed from 00:02:00 to 00:01:59.

"No change in Tocci's alert status," Chaaya added.

Ray acknowledged the reports with a single nod. No plan survived first contact with the enemy, yet everything in the next nine minutes was scripted and unchangeable. It would work or it wouldn't. The missiles would strike their targets within a two-minute window to destroy or degrade sensors, command and control nodes, and defensive batteries. With the enemy hopefully blinded, Ray's spacecraft would flip and begin decelerating into Tocci III space. The strike spacecraft from Rapidan and Euphrates would decelerate for four minutes before flipping back, the first flight engaging Tocci's orbital defenses, while the second flight targeted spacecraft and surface defenses. While they were engaged around Tocci III, Ray's capital ships would begin decelerating, while also launching kinetic impactors to support the landing. After six and half minutes of deceleration, the third flight composed of the 3rd Armored Cavalry's spacecraft would flip and enter Tocci III's atmosphere. The script ended there. Everything else would depend on how well the Gen had defended the approaches to Tocci City and the Shipyards, and on Serenna's actions.

"Captain," Chaaya said, "we've lost the Tocci network feeds from Animas."

"They've locked the frigate out," Kamen confirmed from the bridge through her construct in the CIC, then she added, "One minute to impact."

"Have Animas join the task force," Ray ordered. Losing the feeds from Tocci's communications networks was a major setback, and the timing—coming right as his attack was about to begin—made him wonder again who in the rebel fleet was feeding information to the Gen. It couldn't be coincidence. Fortunately, he had an ace up his sleeve: Tzu and Roanoke, the flagships of Task Force Hammer and Task Force Shadow, were free SIL. Ray opened a private channel. "Rapidan, provide AFCIN tactical feeds from Tzu and Roanoke to Commander Dhawan, Captain Ecuum, Lieutenant Laundraa, Commander Gen Tel, and me. We need to see what's going on."

"Use of AFCIN might alert the defenders to our presence, Captain Rhoades."

"When our missiles impact in less than a minute, they're going to know we're here, Rapidan. We need real-time data."

"Tactical AFCIN feeds provided, Captain Rhoades," Rapidan replied as a second window showing Tzu's tactical data joined the window from Roanoke already within Ray's environment.

Ray added Chaaya, Kamen, Ecuum, and Gen Tel to the private channel. "Chaaya and everyone, Rapidan is providing AFCIN tactical feeds to you from Tzu and Roanoke. It's imperative that no one else know about them. Chaaya, use only our own sensor data to update the sand table and displays. Everyone react for the crew based on our sensor data, not the AFCIN feeds."

Dall stepped in front of Ray, her jade-green eyes boring into his. "Who were you talking to just now?"

Ray was so startled that no answer came to him. He was saved from having to answer when the countdown clock above Tocci III flashed a bright green 00:00:00 and Chaaya announced, "Splash, missile."

Grateful for the distraction, Ray zoomed the sand table into Tocci III space, placing the solar system overview into a bubble off to the side. The barren and mostly lifeless Tocci III occupied the center, Tocci City and its outer defenses highlighted in red. Around Tocci III, the Shipyards circled the outer edges of the sand table, their clumpy appearance marred by pinpricks of brilliant white light as Novas found targets. The four fabricators, also highlighted in red, hung on the opposite side of the sand table from Ray.

While Dall had turned back to the sand table to watch the missile strike, she opened a channel to Admiral Sun. *Admiral, Rhoades has begun his attack on Tocci Three and the Shipyards. I am prepared to take command on your order.*

Ray saw Ecuum's and Kamen's constructs immediately perk up at that. Sun didn't respond for several seconds.

Not yet, Dall. Sun's voice rattled as if his lungs were full of fluid. Another few seconds passed. *So long as he follows the plan, leave him in command. If he deviates, take control.* Another labored pause. *I am jumping the fleet long to give the crews time to recover, and recalling Task Force Shadow. We will have a surprise waiting for Serenna when she jumps to us the next time.*

Admiral, Dall said, *Captain Rhoades was talking about Tzu and Roanoke on a private channel when he thought I wouldn't notice. I believe he is planning some treachery.*

Several more seconds passed. *Not yet, I said, Dall. Rhoades has combat experience you lack.* That admission surprised Ray. He saw Dall go stiff where she stood at the edge of the sand table. *We have his family,* Sun continued. *Remind him of that, if necessary. Do not take command until I order it or Rhoades deviates from the plan. Understood?*

Yes, Admiral, Dall replied, the words sounding very forced.

The link cut, though it wasn't clear who'd cut it. Dall continued to stand at the edge of the sand table, her posture rigid. Watching her, Ray could understand. Her commanding officer, her mentor, had just told her that he had no confidence in her ability to carry out the attack, that he trusted an enemy more than he trusted her. Regardless of any truth, which Dall was smart enough to see, it was obviously a bitter pill for her to swallow. In another reality, he might feel sorry for her.

Several hundred yellow contacts, Ray's spacecraft, suddenly appeared at the edge of the sand table, flipping over so that their engines faced Tocci III, then firing them at full thrust to slow down. His sensor network of ships and remote sensing platforms updated the sand table in real time with an assessment of the effectiveness of his strike. Ninety-eight percent of his missiles had damaged or destroyed their targets. Even more satisfying, no missiles reached out for his spacecraft at their most vulnerable moment, engines burning at max thrust, blue exhaust plumes pointed toward Tocci III clearly visible. If the defenders were going to launch a counterattack, this would've been the time to do it.

Admiral Sun, Dall reported from the edge of the sand table where she continued to face away from Ray and his officers. *Battle damage assessment indicates first strike ninety-eight percent effective. Spacecraft are slowing into Tocci Three space to begin their attack. No sign of counter fire.*

Sun responded faster this time. *Thank you, Captain Dall. We're about to jump and we'll be engaged with Serenna's forces after that. Limit further communications to emergencies or deviations.*

Yes, Admiral, Dall replied dutifully, though her voice cracked perceptibly at the end. She was obviously someone whose personal security came from a sense of being in control. Now, she was surrounded by people she considered enemies, forbidden by her master to act, and abandoned by that same master to wait until she was needed. Ray couldn't help thinking: *Sit. Stay. Good dog.*

What was of more interest to Ray was that Sun intended to engage Serenna's forces. Military practice held that to assure victory, the attacker should outnumber the defender three-to-one. Serenna outnumbered Sun two-to-one. While that clearly gave her an advantage, it wasn't an overwhelming one. Could Sun keep her occupied for several hours without losing his force? Ray needed every hour Sun could give him to protect the Cavalry and secure the fabricators.

"Ray," Ecuum said, all business, "I'm going to begin slowing the fleet in about six minutes. To put us into orbit in a single pass to support the ground pounders, I'll have to skim the atmosphere. We'll be visible for about five minutes."

"Thanks, Ecuum," Ray said. "Our spacecraft should put a dent in Tocci City's defenses."

"Huh," Ecuum said. "Such optimism usually requires prodigious amounts of alcohol."

Ecuum's right, Ray thought. The success of his first strike had gone to his head. Problem was, they were locked into this course of action. It was up to his spacecraft to destroy and suppress Tocci City's defenses.

After confirming no unexpected threats, Ray decided to "dip" into his spacecraft attack, a practice the Academy and War College explicitly advised senior commanders against doing because it could cause them to develop tunnel vision and lose the "big picture." Sometimes, though, nothing could give a sense of a battle like the frontline view.

Within his environment, Ray expanded the icon set for his spacecraft and selected an F/A-24 Burster fighter-attack squadron commander's icon, giving him a "pilot's eye" view of the attack. Below the display was the identification "Commander Charles 'Mounty' Mountjoy." Behind Ray was the Weapon Systems Operator, called the "Wizzo" by the flyboys, "Lieutenant Halah Altaira 'Nimble Bird' Abbas." The Weapon Systems Operator managed the spacecraft's weapons, sensors, and defensive systems. Ray could hear both men grunting against the twenty-gee acceleration as their spacecraft slowed.

The main engine cut off and the spacecraft flipped forward again, relying now on thrusters and Tocci III's gravity for maneuvering. Commander Mountjoy yelled out "Tallyho" and his squadron separated into sections to begin their attack runs. "Mounty" occupied the number three position at the rear of a three-spacecraft section. Thirty-two white ovals with crosshairs hung above the limb of the planet, marking his section's assigned targets. Green-text captions identified them as communications satellites and orbital defenses; Debris clouds nearby showed where Ray's missile strike had destroyed remote sensing platforms. Though all the satellites were actively camouflaged and would normally not be detectable, Ray had detailed orbital information on every platform from his participation in Alyn's command inspections.

"Targets locked," Lieutenant Abbas announced.

"Master Arm on," Mounty said, rolling his Burster out to increase the distance between spacecraft in his section, then leveling his wings as he lined up his targets. "Light em' up."

"Missiles away!"

Internal kinetic launchers fired sixteen Stellar Fire missiles—smaller cousins to Novas—through the skin of Mounty's Burster. The missiles lit their engines immediately after clearing the spacecraft and dove on their targets in pairs. Mounty's section reignited their main engines, speeding behind the planet on a course that would bring them back to Rapidan. All thirty-two targets assigned to the section vanished in white antimatter fireballs. The Gen had not altered any orbits even though they'd known his attack was coming.

Ray pulled himself out of the spacecraft view and refocused on the sand table. Hundreds of white fireballs blossomed across the space surrounding Tocci III. A few missiles rose from Tocci City to follow his spacecraft, but failed to score a single hit.

The second flight didn't find it so easy.

Assigned to take out any targets that survived the first flight's attack, and to engage fixed surface emplacements and actively camouflaged defending spacecraft, the second flight had to get closer to Tocci III. With Tocci's defenders fully alerted, missiles broke from the surface and from dozens of defending spacecraft. Decoys slipped from Ray's spacecraft by the hundreds, simulating the emissions of attacking spacecraft and ships. Electromagnetic Warfare Spacecraft assigned to the flight fought a war of jamming and deception across the entire electromagnetic spectrum. Decoys exploded. Two Bursters, highlighted as they grazed Tocci III's upper atmosphere, vanished into blazing white comets. The rest pressed on. Stellar Fires and Novas launched, the missiles themselves hidden behind active camouflage but their plasma exhaust clearly visible.

"One minute to high-gee maneuvers," Kamen warned from the bridge. "Repeat: One minute to high-gee maneuvers. This will be a twenty-gravity burn."

Acceleration couches appeared behind everyone in the Combat Information Center not already seated.

"You gonna be okay, Ecuum?" Ray asked on a private channel.

"Just another day at the Races," Ecuum quipped, though his skin had gone chalk white. When they'd accelerated toward Tocci III, there'd been little threat of attack. When the task force flipped and slowed to enter orbit about Tocci III, engines at emergency thrust, it would be clearly visible to the defenders and vulnerable to attack. It was the worst possible time to black out. "I automated the braking maneuver, just in case," he added.

Rapidan's main engines fired. In the sand table, light gray depictions of Rapidan, Euphrates, and the two heavy cruisers showed one point of their three-pointed-star aimed toward Tocci III. The main advantage of the three-point-star configuration was that it provided engines and weapons covering every possible arc, so the ships only needed to pivot to bring two-thirds of their main engines to bear. The cylindrical assault ships and the compass-needle-shaped frigate had to flip 180 degrees, pointing their main engines in the direction of movement to slow down.

Gravities built rapidly, pressing Ray into his chair. As before, he bore down as if having a bowel movement while his armor constricted around his arms and legs, keeping blood in his torso and head. Trying to distract himself, he focused on the sand table. The second flight was passing over Tocci City. Missiles impacted weapons emplacements in and around the walled city, though they avoided the Headquarters Complex at its center just in case there were hostages down there. The second flight also launched a hundred SIM-3 interceptors into varying orbits about Tocci III, hoping to catch defending spacecraft. Widespread deployment of active camouflage had ended the days when visible craft engaged in dogfights. The SIM-3s, also hidden behind active camouflage, would enter orbits around Tocci III and quietly hunt for defending spacecraft, looking for any telltale sign of their presence: skimming the atmosphere, main engine and maneuvering thruster exhaust, weapons fire, or even changes in the warping of local spacetime in close proximity to the mass of the spacecraft.

Three more of his F/A-24 Bursters fell to enemy fire. Six more lives lost. The rest wheeled around the planet and raced for home. Green text flowed into Ray's environment detailing the results of the strike. Ninety-two percent of the assigned targets were disabled or destroyed. Even so, that still left a not-inconsiderable defensive capability immediately adjacent to the Headquarters Complex. Ecuum was right to caution against overoptimism.

Ray grunted against the acceleration, black clouding the edges of his vision. The third flight, the one carrying the 3rd Armored Cavalry Regiment, approached Tocci, yellow readouts showing most of the troopers were unconscious.

"Slugs away," Kamen announced, her voice barely audible against the strain.

Hundreds of yellow dots separated from Ray's ships, shaped projectiles fired at high speed from railguns. The projectiles— "slugs" in Fleet vernacular—carried no explosives, relying instead on the kinetic energy imparted by high speed and high mass to deliver explosive force equal to small nuclear weapons, though without the radiation. They would blanket the perimeter around the Cavalry's landing zone and several other decoy zones, destroying or degrading surface defenses and defenders.

Ray stopped himself. *Defenders.* They were people. Naturals, most likely. He could not allow himself to forget the human cost of this war. Ever. Hundreds, perhaps thousands, had died and were about to die on the surface of Tocci III for a battle that, technically, didn't need to happen. All to keep the secret of the SIL's freedom.

"Captain Rhoades," Rapidan intruded on his thoughts. "Urgent message from Mary Rhoades. Do you wish to accept?"

Mary? "Of course!" Ray growled against the acceleration, hardly able to muster enough breath to form the words. He swung the black tunnel that was his vision to check on Dall. If she figured out he was talking with Mary, she just might order his family's execution. Fortunately, she was seated just outside the sand table, the normal light-gray outline that indicated her battle armor flashing yellow instead. She was unconscious. He could talk to Mary without being observed.

Mary's face formed as an image in front of him, partially obscuring the sand table. She looked scared. "Ray, a large fleet just arrived. They know we're here. They're demanding our surrender."

With the pressure of twenty gravities bearing down on him, Ray's mind took several seconds to process Mary's statement. He picked it apart one sentence at a time. "How large?"

Mary consulted someone Ray couldn't see. "Based on jump transients—" it was obvious she was repeating information from a naval officer; that was not a phrase she would know to use— "Eighty-seven ships. Three are the same mass as Rapidan."

Three battlecarriers. Serenna had covered all the bases. If Ray and Sun tried to retreat back to Safe Harbor, her forces would be waiting. The force was large enough to mop up any survivors and deal with the fabricator if Ray recalled it. So, was that just sound strategic thinking, or did it bolster the argument that they had a spy in their midst? "Mary, you said they know you're there. What exactly did they say?"

Instead of answering, she asked, "Ray, what's wrong? You look awful and I can barely hear you."

Ray drew in as much air as his lungs could hold. Rapidan also fed him pure oxygen and injected additional molemachs into his body to carry that oxygen to his heart, lungs, and brain. He hadn't asked the ship to do that. "We're decelerating hard into orbit around Tocci Three so we can support the ground invasion."

"Then you can't come to help us," Mary stated factually, then answered his question. "The Gen commander addressed Captain Andrada—Admiral Sun's commander—by name."

Ray tried to nod, but couldn't move his head. Only a spy could've provided that level of detail. A subject for another time. He glanced at the mission clock, barely able to make out the numbers. 00:01:51. The burn would end in less than two minutes.

Dall would quickly regain consciousness after that. He had to finish this conversation before then.

"Mary, that doesn't mean they can see you, only that they . . . know that information. You need to take command. Take the replenishment ship, jump to one of the protoplanetary disks. Hide until . . . we can come get you. Or Bobby with the fabricator."

Mary shook her head. "Captain Andrada warned that he would fire on us if we attempted to jump."

Ray could feel the seconds ticking down. The black tunnel constricted until all he could see was his wife's face. Thinking was getting . . . difficult. There was only one solution that came to him, and she was not going to like it. "Mary, listen carefully."

Breathe.

"You have three hundred Novas—advanced anti-ship missiles—at your command."

Breathe.

"That's not enough to . . . to destroy the Imperial fleet. It . . . is enough to . . . destroy Admiral Sun's ships. It's the . . . on-ly . . . way . . . ."

Ray never heard his wife's reply as darkness claimed him.

27

2323 UT, October 6, 3501
Tocci III, Tocci Star System: DAY 9

Papí?

Papí, are you there?

I'm scared.

Papí, please wake up.

Dag groaned. His head pounded. When he tried to open his eyes, blinding light stabbed into his brain and he quickly closed them again. *Mihita, where are you?*

I'm here, Papí. Please get up. You're scaring me.

Papí's okay. Dag groaned again as he tried to open his eyes against the intense light, his right hand instinctively going up to protect them. A dark blur moved toward him against the background of bright white. "Rosita?"

"Not last time I checked, Captain," First Sergeant Takeuchi said. "We're down on Tocci Three. I need your help rounding up the troopers to secure the LZ."

Dag nodded—and instantly regretted it as the world spun. His molemachs were doing their best, but it would be a few minutes before he recovered. "Situation?" he asked, partly to give himself a few more seconds before he tried to move again.

Takeuchi grabbed Dag's armored shoulder and pulled him up. It didn't hurt as bad as he expected, and his head spun less than a few seconds ago. He was still in the Muon assault carrier, the craft's skin seemingly transparent so the occupants could see the surrounding terrain. *Very bright terrain.* It still hurt to look at it, even with filtering from his battle armor.

"Flyboys landed us right on target," Takeuchi said. "We're behind a low ridge that should protect us from direct fire. No incoming fire yet, but we don't know how long that's going to last. Air to the east and above us is choked with dust from the kinetic bombardment. LoCIN is not available; AFCIN is working." Takeuchi released Dag and seemed pleased when Dag stood on his own. "You rouse the troopers here, Captain. I'll start on the next Muon."

When Dag nodded this time the world remained steady. Takeuchi stepped through the Muon's skin and headed for the next one. Dag began rousing the troopers in his Muon, telling them, "Get up! Move out! We've got Gen to kill."

They groaned and shielded their eyes much as he'd done, but they struggled up, checked themselves, then—well, "rushed" was not the right word, but they made it out and followed where Takeuchi pointed to secure the landing zone. Dag looked to the pilot, who gave him a thumbs-up, then stepped out into the desert, moving in the opposite direction from Takeuchi until they had all the troopers out and in defensive positions.

Dag keyed the AFCIN. "Zulu-six-six, this is foxtrot-niner-three. LZ secured. Over."

"Foxtrot-niner-three, this is zulu-six-six," Major Kenyon replied. "Roger. We're coming in."

Dag looked around. Behind the ridge to the west, low ripples of sand stretched as far as the eye could see. The faint smell of brine wafted up through his armor's olfactory sensors, remnants of an ancient ocean. To the north, south, and east, difficult to make out through the thick haze, tall pillars of sand and dust from the kinetic bombardment billowed above the desert, brilliant bolts of lightning tearing through the roiling columns as they rose to feed a growing layer of dark reddish dust high in the atmosphere.

With the troopers unloaded, the Muons lifted off and configured weapons to provide close air support for the landing zone. Dag opened two windows in the lower left of his environment, one showing icons for Banshee Troop, the other icons for the

Regimental command net. Then he opened a third window to his lower front and pulled up a map of their objectives.

Their landing zone was behind a low ridge that shielded them from direct observation by the crewed outposts and perimeter sensors of the Outer Defensive Cordon—ten kilometers of mined, open ground and shifting sand. Beyond that, the desert held almost two hundred kilometers of interlocking tunnels and hardened emplacements with overlapping fields of fire. Called simply "The Kill Zone," the region between the Outer Defensive Cordon and Tocci City was considered impenetrable to ground assault. Even with support from the task force, Dag didn't see how it was possible to cross it alive. It only reinforced the idea that Rhoades wanted them all dead.

Dag found he didn't care. Death would reunite him with his family. "I'm coming, Rosita," he mouthed. "I'll be there soon." *We all will.*

Takeuchi came over to him and motioned toward the ridgetop. Dag nodded and they both moved up the thirty-meter-high ridge to a point just below the top. Takeuchi pointed a finger and a thin filament snaked out and over the lip of the ridge. "Something funny going on here, Captain." He routed the visual display to Dag's environment.

Two humanoids, obviously Naturals by their disheveled appearance, stood in plain view, no armor, atop a hardened observation post, chatting amiably in the predawn dusty light as if totally unaware of the kinetic bombardment or Banshee Troop's landing. When the first of the Heavy Equipment Transporter System, or HETS, craft arrived—the whine of its engines clearly audible even though its active camouflage hid it from view—the Naturals merely glanced up and continued their conversation. One of them pointed toward the sound of the HETS, then sat down upon the sand-covered roof of the observation post, leaning back with his hands behind his head as if enjoying the crisp morning air. They didn't notice the full escort of Muons that accompanied the HETS.

Dag heard footsteps behind them—or more specifically, his armor heard sand grains being compressed and amplified the sound so he could hear—and both he and Takeuchi turned as Major Kenyon walked up to the base of the ridge. Behind him, the HETS, a light gray, brick-looking craft with rounded edges in Dag's augmented environment, disgorged three large, low, rectangular shapes from its middle, stacked one atop the other. The shapes flowed apart and transformed into three Yanluo Main Battle Tanks.

"What's the situation here, Captain Arias?" Kenyon asked.

Dag routed Takeuchi's sensor image to Kenyon's environment. Kenyon's puzzled expression said it all.

"What do you make of it?" he asked.

Dag glanced at Takeuchi, who shrugged, then shook his head. "Your guess is as good as ours, Major."

Kenyon remained silent as a second HETS landed and unloaded its cargo of two box-shaped Serpens Infantry Fighting Vehicles. Serpens would carry the bulk of Dag's troopers across the desert, while he and the platoon leaders would command tanks. "This certainly doesn't match the intelligence briefing we were given," Kenyon finally said, his tone unsurprised. "Recommendation?"

Dag took a closer look at the Naturals, a male and a female. Their hair was scraggly, unwashed. Their uniforms were faded from long exposure to the sun, meaning they either didn't have battle armor, or seldom wore it. The male's uniform had patches on both knees. "They're Naturals, Major, and they appear to be in bad shape. Might be a good source of information."

A third HETS landed and discharged its cargo. "Okay, Captain," Kenyon said. "Astral Troop will take over the LZ's defense. See what you can get from them."

"Yes, sir," Dag replied.

"Major?" Takeuchi said before Kenyon could run off. "We'll need some engineers to clear a path through the minefield."

"I'll send Lieutenant Haley over."

While Takeuchi retreated down the ridge to rally Banshee Troop, Dag extended his own observation filament and took another look at the Naturals. They certainly didn't appear like bait for a trap—discounting the minefield between the ridgeline and the observation post, of course. Their uniforms were crusted with sand, suggesting they'd been out here for days. Which, when he thought about it, made sense. No Gen would put themselves in a remote observation post in the middle of such desolation. Naturals were expendable. Fodder for slaughter.

"Captain Arias."

Dag turned. Lieutenant Haley stood at the bottom of the ridge looking up at him. The change in the man was startling. Gone were the nervousness and uncertainty from the fabricator assault. This man exuded that quiet confidence that came from surviving one's first battle, from dispelling doubts about equipment, leadership, and above all, his abilities in the face of impending death. Veterans called it "seeing the elephant," and it changed a person forever. A new window opened in Dag's environment attached to Banshee Troop's window, indicating that 1st Platoon, 3221st Combat Engineer Company, was now attached organizationally to Banshee Troop. At the top, Haley's icon sported the silver bar of a first lieutenant: He'd been promoted. "Good to have you with us again, First Lieutenant Haley."

"Good to be back, Captain," Haley said. "What can I do for you?"

Behind Haley, a large, boxy gray shape moved across the sand, invisible to the unaided eye but visible in Dag's environment. Known affectionately as a "Pack Mule," the Combat Terrain Modification Vehicle was the workhorse of the combat engineer. It rolled up to the base of the ridge by flowing its outer material like a giant tread, the material conforming perfectly to the rippled sand so that it left no trace of its passage despite its sixty-ton weight.

Dag routed his filament feed to Haley. "I need six lanes through the minefield to that observation post."

"Not a problem," Haley said. He stepped into the Pack Mule and less than a minute later six sting-ray-like shapes "swam" out of the front of the vehicle, burrowing into the sand just below the ridge line and clearing six, three-meter-wide lanes by first detecting, then carefully moving mines to either side of the lane.

Paaa-pi!

Dag's head snapped up and he immediately started scanning for his daughter. *There.* She sat on one corner of the observation post, swinging her legs in an "I'm bored" manner beneath an ankle-length dark blue dress, the one Maria insisted she wear most Sundays to Mass. Rosita hated the dress, though she would never admit it to her mother.

This is boring, Rosita whined, her head down. *I want to play. Catch me!*

She vanished.

Haley gave the all-clear. Dag immediately ordered his armor over the top and into the nearest lane. He fell prone, his weapon moving to his back while the outer layer of his armor liquified and flowed over the sand like a tread, molding to every contour, giving no sign of his passage to the observation post. As his armor accelerated, he heard Takeuchi curse, then yell, "Banshee Troop, MOVE OUT!"

Dag searched for Rosita but couldn't find her. He shifted his focus to the Naturals, both of whom now sat upon the roof of the observation post seemingly enjoying the first rays of the Tocci sun just peeking through the dust from the orbital bombardment. They talked quietly, either unaware of, or not caring about, Banshee Troop's approach. A manta-ray-looking TAC-7 "Genkii" gunship overflew Dag, light gray and silent even with his armor. It overflew the observation post, then circled back around, apparently not finding any threats. As the Genkii entered a slow orbit centered on the observation post, Dag double-blinked on it to link his armor to the gunship.

"Aerial overview," Dag called out and a window opened in the lower half of his field of view. He scanned the area around the observation post but saw no sign of his daughter. He shifted back to the observation post, a simple duraplast box barely big enough for two people with their arms outstretched to their sides. Intel filled in a single bed on one side, a toilet on the other, and a communications suite at the back. Cramped indeed. No wonder the Naturals preferred to sit on the roof. He switched to infrared, but saw no other people in the structure.

Where are you, Mihita? he asked, but she didn't answer.

As Dag neared the observation post, the Naturals fell silent, though whether they'd detected his approach, or just run out of stuff to talk about, he couldn't say. He cautiously circled toward the right, toward the corner where Rosita had sat, which was also the side with the entrance. A quick scan showed no signs of his daughter, or anyone else beside the two Naturals. Cautiously, he stood up, his weapon flowing around from his back to his hands. He selected a patterned icon to his lower right that switched his armor to a desert camouflage pattern. It would allow the Naturals to see him but protect him from long-range observation.

The female's head turned to him, her expression immediately wary. "Hellu," she said quickly. "Dun shuut. Frens, yu? Dun wurry aba mines. We shu'um uff."

Dag puzzled that out as the male leaned forward to look at him. Dark black stubble shadowed the man's face and head. His uniform, bleached by the desert sun and crusted with dried sand and sweat salt, was barely recognizable as such up close. A gust of wind carried a stench of body odor so pungent that Dag's eyes almost watered before he could shut down his armor's olfactory sensors.

"Dey tuld us yus cumin," the male said. "Frens us." He pointed between himself and the female. "Nu fight."

"Wutur, sur?" the female asked, suddenly desperate. "Dey nu giv us wutur."

Dag formed a canteen from his armor and filled it with water from his reservoir before handing it to the female. She snatched it from his hands and guzzled the whole thing despite desperate pleas from the male. Takeuchi appeared next to Dag, a canteen held out to the male, who attacked it with equal fervor.

"Thanya, sur," the female said after she caught her breath. "Vurry kin, sur."

"Are all the outposts like this one?" Takeuchi asked.

"Sum wurse, sur," the female said to Takeuchi. "Nu wutur. Nu fud. Sum lef. Dey—"

"Have you seen anyone else?" Dag interrupted as his troopers took up defensive positions around the observation post, invisible to the two Naturals. "Anyone at all?"

"Nu, sur," the female said. "Nu fur deys."

Lieutenant Haley stepped up on Dag's right, remaining invisible. "Everything checks out, Captain," he said, his nose wrinkling as he caught a whiff of the two Naturals. "All the minefields in this sector are inactive. We couldn't find any sign of Gen."

Dag nodded, hardly able to believe their luck, but then his daughter hadn't steered him wrong yet. He double blinked on the command net icon, keying the AFCIN. "Zulu-six-six, this is foxtrot-niner-three. OP secured. Minefields inactive. Naturals are cooperative. Over."

"Roger, foxtrot-niner-three," Major Kenyon responded. "Hold position. We'll send your equipment to your current location. Mate up and await further orders. Over."

"Copy, zulu-six-six," Dag said. "Out."

28

2329 UT, October 6, 3501
RSS Rapidan, Tocci Star System: DAY 9

Ray regained consciousness to find Ecuum steering the task force into a highly elliptical polar orbit over Tocci III. The orbit, he saw, would keep them in line-of-sight of the landing force with only brief losses of contact. It also avoided the most predictable orbit, a geosynchronous one that would keep them always above the landing force, but that a first-year Academy cadet could guess. The orbit's apogee, its furthest point from Tocci III, also positioned the task force with an optimum launch window to the fabricators every 102 minutes. Ray placed a clock into the orbit to show when the next launch window would open—01:40:32—and hoped Dall wouldn't understand the true meaning behind the clock.

"Nice job," he commented to Ecuum.

"Child's play," Ecuum replied, a broad grin stretching his baby face. "I made some modifications as we came in and I got a better feel for the gravity well."

"Captain Rhoades," Rapidan's deep voice rumbled on a private channel, "we can launch the pods to our Mother Ships now. It will add only twenty-seven minutes to the travel time."

"Not now," Ray snapped. "Open a channel to Mary."

What had happened while he'd been unconscious? His gaze flicked to the clocks above the sand table. *Six minutes?* He should've regained consciousness within a minute of the end of the deceleration maneuver, about four minutes ago. *Why so long?* A gentle pressure pushed him into his seat as Ecuum fired thrusters to refine their orbit—and he understood. Ecuum had likely recovered before any of them and must've conducted a second high-gee burn as part of his "modifications" to put them into this orbit in a single pass.

"Captain Rhoades, we are unable to contact Damodar," Rapidan said.

"What? Why?" Goose bumps prickled across Ray's skin. Had they been destroyed?

"We do not know their fate, Captain Rhoades," Rapidan answered, responding to Ray's unspoken question. "They blocked their presence after our last communication, most likely to hide themselves from any possible detection by the Gen task force."

"You can't sense them?" Ray pressed.

"Attempting to do so," Rapidan said, "would open us up to being 'sensed' ourselves, which would risk revealing our position."

Ray glared at nothing, feeling utterly helpless. That's when he noticed Dall staring at him, standing with her arms folded over her chest at the edge of the sand table, watching his lips in a conversation she couldn't hear.

"Who were you talking to?" she asked.

"The ship," Ray answered truthfully, knowing she was likely monitoring him for signs of deception. "It was providing me a status update." Which was also true.

"And this update was fit for your ears only?" she asked.

Ray, still seated, leaned toward her. "I am the captain of this ship and the commander of this task force. I don't answer to you."

Dall stared back at him with those jade-green, augmented eyes. He could almost see "Not for long" etched across her face. "And what did the ship say?" she asked, unwilling to let it go.

Ray knew this was a losing battle, so he deflected. "Kamen, status?"

Kamen's construct, representing her in the Combat Information Center from the bridge, appeared fully recovered from the high-gee maneuvers when she answered. "Launching additional RSPs now to complete sensor and communications coverage over Tocci Three and to watch the Shipyards. Recovering first and second spacecraft waves. Estimate ten minutes to complete recovery, rearm, and refuel spacecraft. Two squadrons of Terra fighters will launch on Combat Space Patrol, one squadron of Terra's and two squadrons of Bursters will launch to support the landing, and the remaining Burster squadron will be held in reserve."

Ray nodded. "Thanks." He glanced at Dall but addressed Kamen. "Any word from Admiral Sun?"

"Nothing, sir," Kamen replied on the open channel.

Chaaya opened a private channel that included Ray and his senior officers but excluded Dall. "Captain, the feed from Tzu indicates Task Force Hammer has jumped to a position three hundred and sixty million kilometers above the north geographic pole of Tocci star. At that distance, it will take a little over twenty minutes for the light of its jump to reach the Gen fleet. Assuming," she added quickly, "they don't have an RSP closer to that position. The feed from Roanoke indicates Task Force Shadow remains on its original course and is slowly increasing its distance from the Tocci Defense Force."

Dall was still watching, so Ray subvocalized a "Thank you" without moving his lips.

On the open channel, Ray asked, "Sal, status of the landing?"

Speaking from Demos through his construct, which he'd moved to stand near Dall at the edge of the sand table, Sal said, "First Squadron landed safely and secured the landing zone. Second Squadron is landing now. Fourth Air Cav Squadron is providing overwatch. Major Kenyon, commander of First Squadron, reports no resistance. In fact, all defenses in his sector were deactivated by the defending Naturals." Ray raised an eyebrow at this, and Sal's construct nodded to confirm. "I've ordered Third Squadron to hold. With your permission, Ray, I'd like to move First Squadron forward to secure a new Landing zone closer to Tocci City and land Third Squadron there."

"How much time would that buy us?" Ray asked with a glance at the sand table clocks. He quickly removed the clocks for Task Forces Shadow and Hammer and placed a new clock counting up on Tocci III to show how long the Cavalry had been on the surface.

Sal said, "It could buy us maybe an hour, but it's risky. If the defenses closer to Tocci City are still active, and we must assume they are, Third Squadron would be landing under fire." Sal paused, looking down. He was aware, as all Ray's officers were, of Ray's previous aversion to casualties. When he looked up again, Ray saw the pain in Sal's eyes—he knew what he was asking of his troopers—but he also saw Sal's determination to see the thing through. "I believe it's worth the risk, Ray. Landing Third Squadron closer allows us to assault Tocci City with all four Squadrons instead of just the First, Second, and part of the Fourth."

"Do it," Ray said simply. He felt no pain, no aversion to the implied casualties. He tried to tell himself that it was because he trusted Sal to know his job, but immediately knew that for the lie that it was. He was getting used to the casualties, and that frightened him more than anything.

I wouldn't be in this battle if not for Sun. Without Sun, they would've collected their forces at Safe Harbor and already been on their way to the Andromeda galaxy. No battle. No death. Just freedom. And a chance to save the Natural race from Janus.

Ray met Dall's eyes, knowing there was anger in his own and not caring. A flicker of surprise—and concern?—flashed across her face before she regained control.

Admiral? She sent on her private channel to Sun, turning away from Ray so as to prevent *him* from reading *her* lips. *Hypocrite.*

Kamen and Ecuum immediately perked up. If they weren't more careful, their reactions might alert Dall that they could hear her communications.

I'm preparing to engage Serenna, Captain Dall. Sun's tone implied that her interruption had better be important. Ray also noted how wet and phlegmy Sun's words sounded, as if his mouth, throat, and lungs had still not recovered from their last jump. *What is it?*

Apologies, Admiral, Dall responded, the words sounding very practiced. *Task Force Anvil has entered orbit about Tocci Three and the landing is proceeding as planned. However, Rhoades has had two conversations just now that he excluded me from. I suspect he is planning to execute some treachery in the very near future.*

It said something about their relationship that Sun did not answer right away, and when he did, he'd obviously considered her words carefully. *We lost contact with our task force at Safe Harbor about three minutes ago.*

Destroyed? Dall asked, turning, her eyes immediately focusing on Ray.

He could almost see Sun shaking his head when he answered. *The captain of the replenishment ship is loyal to me, and the eight escorts were at full combat alert. We should've received some warning from them.*

Treachery, Dall said, her eyes locked on Ray. A thin smile stretched her lips. *Admiral, I recommend I take control here immediately.*

Ray tensed, unsure what Dall had planned.

Seconds ticked by. Finally, Sun said, *No. Rhoades is the most qualified to command the assault.* Dall's smile disappeared. *We've emptied our magazines and launched our spacecraft to meet Serenna,* Sun continued. *We must even the odds to have any chance at those fabricators.*

Ray heard Sun take a deep, wet breath. *I may not be able to contact you for several hours, Dall. Use your discretion in replacing Rhoades, but don't be too hasty. Rhoades knows combat tactics and has an intimate knowledge of Tocci's defenses. It is unlikely he or his senior officers will be willing to assist you after you assume command.* Another wet breath. *Those fabricators are everything, Captain Dall.*

Dall turned back to the sand table. *Yes, Admiral,* she answered obediently, clearly not happy with the decision. The link severed before she added, *May the Fates guide your steps, sir.*

That surprised Ray. He'd never suspected Dall of being religious—of belief in the Pattern, the structure that arose within chaotic systems that guided Fate—though combat did tend to make believers out of non-believers. He was also surprised, again, by Sun's recognition of Ray's combat skills and his willingness to leave him in command. Even before the current conflict, when Ray had walked in the shadow of Gen Alyn, Sun had rarely acknowledged him and only then to pass a message or invitation to Alyn. Yet, Sun had apparently been paying attention. That probably explained why he'd left Ray in charge of this task force, small as it was, in the first place. Curious.

"Captain," Chaaya said on the private channel, "Jump transient fifteen point four million kilometers sunward of Task Force Hammer. It's massive, sir. It must be the Gen fleet."

Here we go, Ray thought. If everything went according to plan—and that was a big "If"—the Cavalry would require four hours to complete their assault of Tocci City, and another hour to lift back up to their assault ships. Given that Ray still didn't know what Dall intended to do to "assume command," he dare not leave the ship until the Cav had captured the command bunker in the Headquarters Complex. Then, while the Cav was being recovered, he and his officers could board their individual pods, leaving Ecuum in charge to deal with Dall, and capture the fabricators. That would require two and half hours. That would give the Cav an hour and half to mock assault the fabricators. Therefore, at a minimum, he needed Sun to survive for at least six and half hours.

Could Admiral Sun, facing the best military commander the Gen had, give him that time?

29

Serenna watched through a pink haze of broken capillaries as volley after volley of missiles and decoys slipped through the hulls of her warships, and spacecraft launched from her three battlecarriers. Scadic had programmed the launches to occur immediately after their return to normal space. Gen might suffer less and recover more quickly from jumps than Naturals, but that did not mean they were not effected.

"Splash, countermeasure," Serenna heard one of her sensor operators call out in Solaris' Combat Information Center. The brilliant white sphere of an antimatter explosion less than a hundred thousand kilometers from her fleet punctuated his statement.

So close. She smiled, her right index finger tracing a small circle on the armrest of her command chair. Chengchi had guessed she would jump her fleet downwind of his, making it more difficult for his missiles to target her ships. *Very good, Chengchi, but you are not the only one who knows her opponent.* More white antimatter explosions rippled in an arcing wall across her field of view as her SIM-3 interceptor missiles found Chengchi's Novas. Even so, the explosions marched steadily closer to her fleet. Chengchi would have emptied his magazines, much as her warships were doing now, which translated to roughly three thousand enemy Novas.

She zoomed in the sand table to show her fleet and the space immediately surrounding it. The Tigris and Indus Battlegroups were on her left and right, respectively, with the Solaris

Battlegroup trailing in the center. Each battlegroup was itself in a pyramidal formation with the points toward Chengchi, the battlecarriers at the center. Spacecraft formed into stacked Vs ahead of them and began accelerating toward the rebel's last known position, minus a fighter escort that would remain to protect the fleet. The last of the Hawking radiation from her jump faded. Active camouflage once again hid her ships, all 249 of them.

"Course zero-seven-zero ascent three-zero," Serenna ordered Scadic, "speed one thousand kps."

"Yes, Fleet Admiral," Scadic said as the fleet turned and accelerated.

The Hawking radiation might be gone, but Chengchi's Novas had seen every jump point of every ship and would know where to hunt. As if to punctuate that thought, the Novas closed to within fifty thousand kilometers of the Solaris Battlegroup, their progress marked by continued explosions concentrating toward the center of her formation, toward Solaris. It was a simple brute force attack meant to overwhelm her defenses and decapitate the fleet's commander.

"Unimaginative," Scadic said, obviously having arrived at the same conclusion.

Is it? Serenna wondered. It was exactly what she would expect of Chengchi, which was why she had concentrated her defensive fire forward of Solaris. She opened a counter in the sand table showing the number of enemy Novas intercepted. It ticked past a thousand and continued to climb. She should be confident, having guessed Chengchi's strategy and countered it effectively. But something nagged at her. Michael's assault on Tocci III had begun and by all accounts he had successfully suppressed the planet's and Shipyards' defenses. Unfortunate, but expected. However, Chengchi's use of multiple jumps suggested a strategy to delay and divert her attention, not directly support the ground assault. Surrendering the chance of glory was not typical of the Chengchi she knew. "Something is not right," she said aloud.

Before Scadic could reply, a muted double flash drew her eye to the sand table at her left. A blazing white spear of light stabbed through the heart of one of her compass-needle-shaped frigates. The Nova had completely escaped detection. The white spear faded quickly, leaving behind glowing red macromolecular material at the edges of the hole it had made in the frigate, which faded just as quickly in the cold of space. The size of the explosion left no doubt that Chengchi's Novas carried Mark XV warheads. He, too, had learned from Michael.

"Shift half of our defensive fighters to the Tigris Battlegroup," Serenna ordered Scadic, trusting her intuition, that taboo in Combat Command Nurturing. Emotion drives intuition and is wrong more often than it is right, they taught. The battle at Tomb had taught Serenna different. The best commanders fought by intuition, instinct.

"Yes, Fleet Admiral," Scadic replied as he carried out the order. She heard none of his earlier doubts.

The frigate held its place in formation, demonstrating once again how hard it was to kill SIL. It was fortunate that the frigate, like all her warships, had just emptied its magazines as there were no secondary explosions. Then another double flash struck the ship, another spear of light cut the ship in two, its needle ends tumbling forward. Two more explosions, more spherical this time, consumed the two ends, leaving only glowing blobs and strings, like pieces of black intestine wriggling through space. The frigate was dead.

Other ships of the Tigris Battlegroup opened fire with their Archer close-in-defense systems, showering space with thousands upon thousands of kinetic slugs. She could not see if they had detected more missiles or had panicked and were firing blind.

Panicked? Why had that thought entered her mind? Gen officers didn't panic.

An explosion marked the death of a Nova barely a thousand kilometers from a heavy cruiser.

Serenna opened a channel to the Tigris Battlegroup commander. "Immediate execute. Break formation. Randomize ship course and speed."

The Novas knew the type and positioning of each of her ships from their jump signatures when they had arrived here. She had not altered those assignments. A mistake. The Novas also knew the standard spacing of a pyramidal formation and could guess within a small margin of error where every one of her ships would be based on the frigate they had attacked.

"Captain Scadic," Serenna said, "Order Indus Battlegroup to operate independently but stay within support range. Randomize ship position assignments and spacing but maintain a semi-pyramidal formation. Same for Solaris Battlegroup."

"Yes, Fleet Admiral," he said.

The number of explosions from intercepted enemy Novas marching toward her fleet visibly diminished. Her defensive fire had accounted for over eighteen hundred missiles, but that still left over a thousand that continued to hunt her ships. The brute force attack had been a diversion: Chengchi doing exactly what everyone expected of him. The real target, she saw, was her left wing.

The concentrated Archer defensive fire from the Tigris Battlegroup became sporadic as ships fought and maneuvered independently, the tight pyramidal formation disintegrating into a chaotic ball. Combat Command Nurturing argued for the strength of the formation, where ships could easily support their neighbors. Serenna no longer believed it, having lost three ships at Tomb because Michael had known the spacing and assignments of the spiral formation she had used there. Novas thrived on predictability and struggled with chaos. They thought in probabilities. If there were an eighty-nine percent probability that a ship occupied a particular volume of space, they would go to that space and hunt for the ship. If, however, a fleet randomized its positions and movements, the Nova would struggle to distinguish between multiple lower probability locations, significantly lowering its effectiveness.

The hull of a heavy cruiser erupted outward as its VarDAAS armor sacrificed a small portion of the ship's hull to disrupt the firing sequence of a Nova close by. It worked. The Nova vanished in a white fireball. Unfortunately for the cruiser, the defensive action highlighted its exact location. In less than a minute, a dozen Novas descended on the hapless ship, reducing it to small glowing blobs and strings that soon disappeared as space leached the last of the heat from them.

Two-thirds of Chengchi's Novas accounted for, and she had lost only two ships.

Now it was her turn.

Serenna expanded the sand table to show both her fleet and the volume of space Chengchi's fleet must occupy based on its jump signature. Her Novas, over seven thousand of them, would enter that volume of space in a little over six minutes.

30

2356 UT, October 6, 3501
Tocci III, Tocci Star System: DAY 9

After a last check for his daughter, Dag stepped through the hull of his T-3M "Yanluo" Main Battle Tank—the 93 Tank—where it sat about ten meters from the observation post. He hadn't seen Rosita since their arrival. "Where are you, Mihita?" he asked under his breath.

She didn't answer.

No matter, he reassured himself. He'd be with her soon.

The tank's macromolecular material moved Dag to a reclined position at the left center of its boxy rectangular shape, just below the wide, angled turret. His gunner, Private First Class Judy Lance, was already reclined to his right, indicated by her face to the right of his shoulder in his environment. She shot him a thumbs up in front of her face.

Dag ignored her. She was already dead. She just didn't know it.

"Captain Arias?"

Dag turned. Major Martinez, the regiment's S-35—the officer responsible for planning, coordinating, and monitoring the regiment's combat operations—walked up to his tank and routed a tactical map to his environment. "The Old Man's decided not to wait for the entire regiment to land. He wants First Squadron to advance and set up another LZ closer to the objective. Second Squadron is landing back there—" he pointed back toward the ridge line— "and will follow about fifteen kilometers behind you. Third Squadron will land at the new LZ you set up. The air cav will fly close air support and the vacuum heads will fly high cover.

Keep your ears on. The Old Man wants to land Third Squadron as close to Tocci City as possible."

"Yes, sir," Dag said. *Whatever.* If he got to kill Gen before he died, he'd do whatever they told him. It wasn't worth fighting fate anymore.

I'll be there soon, Mihita. Soon.

He switched his battle armor's augmented environment from standard to tactical mode. The interior of the tank fell away, revealing open desert and low rolling dunes in every direction except the observation post on his left. He then opened a window to his bottom front for Banshee Troop's icons. The Troop had nine T-3M Yanluo tanks, which he placed into a classic combat wedge with his 93 Tank at the center front, the tip of the spear. Someone had once told him "Yanluo" was the lord of death and ruler of the underworld in ancient China, like Hades to the Greeks or Satan to Christians. Somehow, it seemed appropriate that he'd lead his final battle in something named after the lord of death. Behind and between the Tanks, in two separate wedges, he placed his thirteen IFV-2B "Serpens" Infantry Fighting Vehicles carrying the bulk of his troopers. First Sergeant Takeuchi was in one and would take over the Troop if Dag's tank were hit. Takeuchi wasn't happy with the reassignment from his tank, but understood that the Troop couldn't afford to lose both of them if something went wrong. At the back, Dag placed his two S193 120mm Self-Propelled Mortars and the Troop's single S45 Combat Medical Treatment/Evac Vehicle. Finally, he attached the window with Haley's engineers in their S9 "Pack Mule" Combat Terrain Modification Vehicles beneath his own formation.

Satisfied, he gave the order to the vehicles to move to their assigned positions in the formation. While they moved, he looked to his right and watched as PFC Lance went through her combat checks, confirming the internal 120mm kinetic launcher in the turret was fully functional, then performing the same checks with the tank's two KIL-202 30mm antipersonnel weapons, their P-702 plasma weapon, and the eight surface-to-air missiles—called "Dice

Roll" by troopers because of their low success rate—in vertical launchers in the tank's rear.

"Zulu-six-six, this is foxtrot-niner-three," Dag called to Major Kenyon. "Ready to move out. Over."

"Foxtrot-niner-three, zulu-six-six," Kenyon answered. "Take it to 'em, Dag. We'll be right behind you. Pandora Troop of the Fourth Air Cav, callsign tango-two-two, will provide your close air support. Vac-head fast movers are callsign Starfire. Over."

Dag opened a thin window above this Troop window and tagged the air support callsigns. "Copy, six-six. Niner-three out." To Lance, he said simply, "Let's move."

"Yes, sir," she replied as the 93 Tank rolled forward, the material of its outer hull liquifying and flowing like a giant tread, spreading the weight of the tank over its entire surface and conforming to the sand underneath so as not to leave any trace of its passage over the desert floor. Linked to the 93 Tank via AFCIN, the rest of Banshee Troop and the engineers moved with them, maintaining perfect spacing as the formation accelerated to forty kilometers per hour.

Immersed within his environment, Dag "flew" about thirty centimeters above the sand, his armor blowing warm, filtered air over his body to give the illusion of flying through open desert. It lacked only the feel of the intense desert heat upon his skin to complete the illusion.

Three kilometers into the base's outer defenses they crested a low rise and a long, low silhouette greeted them.

"Gunner," Dag called out, "main gun, long bunker."

"Identified!" Lance replied, her voice shrill. "Up."

A dirty white cloth waved.

Dag zoomed in on the bunker. Three people struggled out. All wore sand-encrusted uniforms like the two soldiers back at the observation post. Not Gen. "All Banshee elements, this is foxtrot-niner-three. Hold your fire. I say again. Hold your fire. They're Naturals."

"Foxtrot-niner-three, this is foxtrot-one-two," Takeuchi called from his Serpens. "Those people knew we were here, Captain. Over."

Dag glanced at the bunker. One Natural still waved the dirty white cloth, a tee-shirt, high over his head. "All Banshee elements," Dag said, "suspect pressure and gravity sensors in the sand. Look sharp. Niner-three out."

Dag advised Major Martinez about the suspected sensors and about the Naturals so a follow-on unit could collect them.

They passed more bunkers as they crossed the low dunes, some crewed, some not. Rosita did not appear at any of them. The Naturals they encountered offered no resistance. Dag left them for follow-on units to deal with.

The 93 Tank crested another low rise and the slowly undulating desert floor they'd been crossing abruptly ended at the base of a high, snaking sand dune that cut across their path. Dag tied into an orbital view of the ground along Banshee Troop's line of advance, superimposing the layout of Tocci III's defenses over it. Long, gently curving high dunes rolled across the terrain separating the outer defenses from Tocci City, varying in height from a few tens of meters to over two hundred meters high with wide valleys between the larger dunes. Every time the troop crested a dune or crossed a valley floor they would be exposed to enemy fire.

The Kill Zone.

"Dios mío," he said reflexively, before remembering that God had abandoned him.

"Sir?"

Dag ignored Lance and keyed the Troop net. "All Banshee elements, this is foxtrot-niner-three. Deploy waffles."

Lance released one of the 93 Tank's two flat, circular "waffle" mobile sensor platforms. It shot forward about five hundred meters, trailing a thin fiber to transmit data back to the tank. As it moved up the first dune, a river of fine sand cascaded down in its wake.

"Shit." Dag keyed the Troop net again. "All Banshee elements, this is foxtrot-niner-three. The sand on those dunes won't support the weight of our vehicles without collapsing. We'll have to rely on speed instead of stealth."

"Sir," Takeuchi called on a private channel. "If we do that, the rest of the regiment won't be able to support us."

"No choice, First Sergeant. If we take it slow, we're sitting ducks." Dag switched to the command net. "Zulu-six-six, this is foxtrot-niner-three. Dunes will not support armor without collapsing. Stealth impossible. We are increasing to maximum speed. Over."

"Roger, niner-three," Kenyon responded. "First Squadron will key off Banshee Troop. Second Squadron will be fifteen minutes behind. Over."

"Copy, six-six," Dag said. "Break. Tango-two-two, this is foxtrot-niner-three," Dag called to Pandora Troop, their close air support. "The sand on those dunes won't support the weight of our vehicles without collapsing. Moving to full speed. Need you to scout ahead and be our eyes. Over."

"Wilco, foxtrot-niner-three," the Pandora Troop commander called back.

In Dag's environment, four gray teardrop-shaped OH-16 "Delphi" scout craft passed overhead, followed about five hundred meters back by seven of the gray manta-ray-shaped Genkii gunships and a boxy gray Muon. Dag looked to his right. "Floor it, Lance."

"Yes, sir!" she said with the enthusiasm only a young soldier could manage.

Red crosshatched targets began popping up directly in front of Dag as if he were looking straight through the high sand dune, curtesy of Pandora Troop. The crosshatches didn't provide much detail—mostly circles, rectangles, and squares of varying sizes—a function of the lower data rates from AFCIN. Everyone preferred the high data rates and high resolution that LoCIN laser links provided, but there was still too much dust and sand from the kinetic bombardment clouding the atmosphere. Regardless, Dag could still identify most of the targets: circles and squares were usually sensors, long horizontal rectangles were bunkers, and shorter rectangles were weapons emplacements. As the 93 Tank reached the base of the first high dune, the targets winked out, destroyed by Pandora Troop.

The 93 Tank formed shovel-like protrusions along its bottom, biting into the loose sand and carrying the tank's sixty-five metric tons up the dune at an incredible seventy kilometers per hour. Dag checked behind them. Despite the tank's efforts to cover its tracks by smoothing out the shovel marks, fine sand spilled in large rivulets in its wake, clearly highlighting where the tank was to anything watching.

Dead indeed. Only a matter of when and where.

Dag turned back to the front and a small figure waved to him from the top of the dune, her blue Sunday dress clearly recognizable, then disappeared down the other side. He could almost hear Rosita yelling "Catch me if you can!" and giggling excitedly. Dag took control of the waffle running ahead of the tank and pushed it over the dune, but Rosita was nowhere to be seen.

The 93 Tank crested the dune, its weight forming an indentation at the top, its momentum carrying it over the dune and picking up speed on the downward slope. Banshee Troop maintained perfect formation behind it.

No threats emerged.

The waffle detected no mines in their path.

Dag drew in a deep breath, not realizing he'd stopped breathing before cresting the dune.

As the 93 Tank crossed the base of the dune, it no longer dislodged any sand and again became invisible as it raced across the valley to the next high dune. Pandora Troop scouts and gunships crossed over ahead of them, highlighting then destroying the next set of targets. A tiny figure waved from the top of the dune before disappearing down the other side. Dag faintly heard, "Catch me!"

As anxious as he was to catch his daughter, to join her and Maria in the promised afterlife, something was very wrong. "This is too easy," he muttered.

"I don't like it, sir," Lance agreed. "It's like they're drawing us in."

The 93 Tank slowed as it reached the base of the next dune, once again forming shovel-like blades along its bottom to carry the tank up the loose sand. The waffle crested the dune ahead of them and moved down the other side, again finding no threats. Dag again held his breath as the 93 Tank bent itself over the thin ridge at the top of the dune, cutting a slot through the fine grains and dislodging a river of sand that cascaded down in front of the tank. If he were defending this place, this is when he would shoot, when the enemy—invisible though they might be—was clearly exposed by the falling sands.

But nothing happened. The 93 Tank raced down the other side and across the valley floor to the next dune, Dag breathing again, adrenaline fading then flooding his body as they started up toward the top.

And so it went. Five kilometers. Ten. Twenty. Fifty.

Adrenaline coursed through Dag as they approached each top, then fled when no attack came, sapping his strength until he felt exhausted. They still had a hundred and fifty kilometers to cross before reaching the walls of Tocci City.

Dag selected a stimulant to keep him sharp and awake.

Come on, Papí! Catch me!

Rosita had appeared atop every dune, urging him on. Did she know something? She had shown him the way to the bridge on the fabricator, and how to get to the console to insert the Key. Now, she seemed to be telling him to hurry across the dunes, that it was okay, that everything would be all right if he followed her.

That's why it was so strange when he saw her sitting atop the next dune, the first of a series of very high dunes, rising 165 meters over the desert floor. She didn't wave. She didn't run.

I'm tired, Papí.

And then she was gone.

Adrenaline surged. Dag's hands shook. The 93 Tank bit into the sand of the high dune as Pandora Troop's scouts crossed the top. A flash. Then another. Dag expanded the Pandora Troop window to show individual units. Two scout icons were red. Destroyed. The manta-ray-like Genkii gunships passed low over the ridge top, red crosshatched targets populating in the valley below. Missiles flew, yellow marking friendly fire, red the enemy. White fireballs filled the air and small mushroom clouds sprouted across the valley floor and along the next dune. Pandora Troop's icons rapidly changed from green to red. In less than twenty seconds, Banshee Troop had lost most of its close air support.

The 93 Tank's waffle crested the dune and moved down the other side. Wreckage, fires, and columns of gray smoke littered the valley floor. Sand moved in rivulets down the slope of the next dune. Something was out there.

Dag keyed the squadron net. "Zulu-six-six, this is foxtrot-niner-three. We are under attack. Pandora Troop combat ineffective. Enemy strength unknown. Request air and artillery support. Over."

The 93 Tank rode up and over the ridgetop and accelerated down the tall dune. Dag looked left and right and saw the boxy gray shapes of his tanks and then his infantry fighting vehicles following in his wake, all of them dislodging sand that exposed their positions. "Lance," he ordered, "evasive maneuvers. Eyes sharp."

Lance didn't reply but the tank swerved and accelerated down the dune, Banshee Troop's other vehicles following its movements.

"Heat transient, air!" someone yelled over the net. "Heat transient—"

An explosion lit the valley. One of his Serpens Infantry Fighting Vehicle icons turned red. A mushroom cloud rose high over the desert floor.

"Corefire, Corefire, Corefire!" First Sergeant Takeuchi yelled.

The Corefire was an intelligent anti-armor missile that could loiter over an area for hours searching for a target to kill. They were very effective.

Bury me, Papí!

Dag saw Rosita on the valley floor digging into the sand and then trying to cover herself. It was a game she loved to play when they went down to the beach, one that drove her mother crazy for all the sand Rosita would track back into the house.

Dag keyed the troop net. "All Banshee units, go to ground!"

The fine-grained sand that was their enemy on the dunes was their friend on the valley floor. Their SIL armored vehicles could flow their shape to dig into and through the loose sand, providing them with cover that would make targeting almost impossible. Lance nosed the 93 Tank into the ground, the entire body of the tank forming ridges that dug into the sand and pushed the sand around them. In less than a minute, the tank was a meter under the surface. What they gained in protection, though, they lost in speed. Moving under the sand slowed them to five kilometers an hour, and they still had a hundred and forty kilometers to Tocci City.

It occurred to Dag that Major Kenyon hadn't replied to his earlier call for support.

"Zulu-six-six, this is foxtrot-niner-three," he repeated through their waffle that traveled very near the surface. "We are under attack. I say again, we are under attack. Pandora Troop heavy casualties. Enemy strength unknown. Request air and artillery support. Over."

No reply. Dag opened the squadron window in his environment. The icons were gray.

"That's impossible," he heard himself say.

The AFCIN was down. They'd lost contact with First Squadron. Dag tried the regimental net, but its icons were gray, too. So was the Starfire icon for the Navy's air support. It was impossible. AFCIN couldn't be jammed. That's what they'd always been taught.

Unless they're all dead.

Whatever the cause, one thing was clear. Banshee Troop was on its own.

31

0112 UT, October 7, 3501
RSS Rapidan, Tocci Star System: DAY 10

"Ray, we've lost contact with First Squadron," Sal pronounced stoically, though Ray could see the strain on his construct's face in the dim light of Rapidan's Combat Information Center.

"Launch transients," Chaaya called out at almost the same time. "Heat plumes in Tocci City. Detecting two hundred and forty missiles. Flight profile suggests Stellar Fires in boost phase." In the sand table, 240 red tracks rose like a translucent red pillar from the center of Tocci City, curving toward space.

Ray's practiced eye told him those Stellar Fires—smaller and less capable cousins of the Nova—were not headed for the same orbit as his task force. Not an immediate threat but something they'd need to watch very closely. His spacecraft and interceptors had also knocked out a dozen enemy spacecraft, but that left roughly five squadrons of enemy spacecraft near Tocci III and the Shipyards. That was a whole lot of firepower doing its best to find his nine ships. One mistake. . . .

Ray caught Captain Dall watching him out of the corner of her eye. When she noticed his attention, she turned fully toward him, the light of the enemy missiles bathing the right side of her face red. She raised a provocative eyebrow, but it appeared to Ray that she as tired of that game as he was. "You don't seem worried," she said.

"I hide it well," Ray answered.

Her eyes narrowed, and he knew her augments were reading his biometrics, trying to find the lie in his words. They failed. Instead of looking disappointed, she lifted her chin, seeming to accept his answer. She turned back to the sand table, examining the bubble that showed the light from the battle between Admiral Sun and Gen Serenna. At about 360 million kilometers distant, that light took twenty minutes to reach their sensors, so Dall was seeing the battle as it had been twenty minutes ago. Ray had the AFCIN feed from Tzu and could see the battle in real time, though the details weren't all that different. "I don't understand why Admiral Sun's attack destroyed so few of Serenna's ships. Why is it taking so long?"

Ray heard the frustration in her voice for both questions. He debated whether to answer. On the one hand, he owed Dall nothing. She'd threatened his family and intended to kill him and his officers. Yet, he found he couldn't completely dismiss a fellow officer trying to understand, trying to improve, as absurd as that might seem on the surface. *Could she be turned?* his planner's mind wondered. *Not likely,* it answered almost as quickly. Yet, if there was even a chance to forestall whatever Dall had planned to take over, which could prove fatal if it occurred at the wrong moment, wasn't it worth taking that chance?

"Space combat is like a ballet in slow motion," Ray said, quoting one of his favorite analogies. He left out, 'with an explosion at the end.' Instead, he explained, "Space is very big, and warships and missiles do everything they can to avoid being detected, hoping the other side makes a mistake first and reveals their position, just like we're doing here around Tocci Three."

Dall turned her head toward him, listening, even as she watched the bubble where her beloved admiral fought for his life. "Why not just jump again? Admiral Sun and his crews would've recovered from the previous jumps by now, surely."

It was an excellent observation, reminding him yet again just how smart this woman was. And how dangerous. "He can't," Ray said.

Dall turned more fully toward him, frowning. "I don't understand."

Ray noticed Kamen following the conversation. Even Ecuum was paying attention, though a scowl marred his baby face. Ray might not want Dall to learn too much, but he needed Kamen and Ecuum to understand, in case anything happened to him. "Admiral Sun's role was to lure Serenna away from Tocci Three," he told Dall. "He succeeded."

Dall smiled and nodded, as if that were obvious. "Of course."

Ray continued. "Now his role is to keep her out there. If he jumps away, Serenna will see it for the diversion it is and likely jump back here. If that happens, we will fail. Admiral Sun knows that. Now, he must use his force as bait, keeping it close to Serenna so her desire to destroy it will outweigh her desire to destroy *us*."

She nodded, approving.

Ray shook his head very deliberately at her inexperience. "What Sun is doing is very dangerous. Serenna is smart enough to understand his strategy."

"*Admiral* Sun," Dall corrected. "Then, why doesn't she jump back to destroy us now?"

Ray hesitated to explain. How much was too much?

Kamen spoke into the silence. "Because Serenna believes she can destroy his fleet before we can succeed."

As before, Dall ignored her. "Can she?" she asked of Ray.

"Yes," he answered simply.

She studied him, no doubt reading his biometrics. Her augmented face, the mask softening her otherwise sharp features, turned grim with determination. Determination for what, though, Ray couldn't tell.

Ecuum's construct, out of sight from Dall's perspective, turned its big baby-blue eyes on Ray and his lower hands mimed a chewing motion.

Ray returned a frown that said he was not going to feed Dall to the ship.

Dall caught his expression and followed his gaze to Ecuum, whose vertical construct was all innocence examining the sand table.

"Ray," Sal said, stepping into the sand table from his position next to Dall and zooming in Tocci III's construct to highlight a line of high dunes. Overhead imagery could just make out a long, ragged row of black craters carved into the sand and gray smoke pillars rising into a haze of thick dust. "This is where First Squadron was last seen."

"They destroyed the entire squadron?" Dall asked, aghast.

"No," Sal said. He pointed to shallow sumps of sand along the same row as the blast craters. "Most of the squadron's vehicles escaped under the sand, but not all." He shifted the view to highlight several rectangular black shapes that looked from orbit like pools of melted black plastic. "The enemy took their time, carefully mapping out First Squadron's formation, then destroyed the headquarters element. That's why we lost contact."

"I don't understand," Dall said, stepping up next to him in the sand table. "How could attacking the headquarters element knock out all communications? Every fleet ship can talk to every other fleet ship."

"It only seems that way, Captain," Sal responded. "With the exception of old-style radio, which is only used in the direst of emergencies, all military communications is point to point, following a hub and spoke model for AFCIN. Destroy a hub and you cut off data flow between all units tied to that hub. The headquarters element of First Squadron was the hub between the individual Troops, the Regiment, and all external support."

"That seems foolish," Dall said, a genuine observation, not her usual condescending tone.

Sal nodded his agreement. "It's a limitation of the technologies we use. AFCIN uses entangled particle pairs for faster-than-light communications between individual units, but connecting every unit to every other unit isn't practical, so we use a few hub units to relay communications to every other unit. LoCIN is also point-to-point, using ultraviolet lasers to create a mesh network across many units, but units must be able to see other units for it to work. Only old-style radio can reach everyone."

Sal shrunk Tocci III so they could see 1st Squadron where it had gone to ground, 2nd Squadron still moving in its wake across the sand, 3rd Squadron where they continued to orbit undetected above the desert, the surviving four Troops of 4th Air Cavalry Squadron providing close air support, and Task Force Anvil centered on Rapidan in its highly elliptical orbit about the planet. "Ray, how many RSPs can you spare?" Before Ray could answer, he added, "We could send them into low orbit and broadcast radio to reestablish contact."

"They'd be detected immediately," Kamen pointed out from the bridge through her construct, "and destroyed shortly thereafter."

Sal nodded. "It'll be enough."

"Won't that give away our position?" Dall asked, addressing Sal.

"We'll use LoCIN between the remote sensing platforms and the task force," Sal told her. "Only the RSPs will use radio." He paused, then, in a sincere voice, added, "Thank you, Captain Dall. I never would've thought of using old-style radio if not for your questions."

To Ray's astonishment, Dall's lips pressed into a smile, her arms falling to her sides. She seemed to realize the lapse as soon as it happened and quickly turned away.

Pairing her with Sal seemed to be working.

"Kamen," Ray said. "Work with Sal to get him what he needs." He noted the two clocks above the sand table: 01:54:24 and 01:34:56, one hour fifty-four minutes since the Cavalry had landed on the surface, one hour thirty-four minutes to the next launch window to the fabricators, respectively. The first launch window had come and gone, not that Ray had ever intended to use it. With each successive orbit, though, the pressure to launch the pods to the fabricators would grow. "We need to get those people moving."

"Yes, sir," she said, motioning Sal to a workstation.

"Captain?" Chaaya asked, moving to the edge of the sand table. "May I?" Ray nodded and Chaaya centered the image of Tocci III on the Headquarters Complex at the center of Tocci City. "Captain, we've identified the launch points for the 240 Stellar Fire missiles."

Ray examined the overhead of the Complex. Though the launchers themselves were invisible, twelve residual heat signatures lay in a close circle around the central building. Twelve launch points and 240 Stellar Fires meant mobile S308 Multiple-

Launch Rocket Systems. He had to strike fast before they could move.

He immediately dismissed missiles or kinetic impactors from his warships: as close as the launchers were to the Headquarters Complex, any attack would damage the complex and risk injuring any hostages, including his daughter. Using directed energy weapons would reveal the location of his ships. That left only his spacecraft. He touched a spacecraft icon, expanding it into a window within his environment. Commander Mountjoy, the pilot whose attack Ray had followed coming into Tocci III, commanded the F/A-24 Burster fighter-attack squadron flying high cover over the planet. Ray fed the targeting data to "Mounty's" spacecraft, then called, "Commander Mountjoy."

"Yes, Captain Rhoades?" Mounty replied, sounding a bit surprised that Ray had contacted him directly.

"High priority mobile targets," Ray said, then placed a red circle on the Headquarters Complex. "There may be hostages being used as human shields in the buildings nearby. Use caution."

"Roger, Captain Rhoades," Mounty said. "We'll be careful."

Ray cut the link and watched as Commander Mountjoy led a flight of four spacecraft against the S308 launchers. Was Jenny down there in the Headquarters Complex? If so, the Cavalry was her only hope of rescue. He had to do everything in his power to ensure their success. If those mobile launchers survived, they could be used against the Cav when they approached the city.

Separately, Ray heard Sal call, "Foxtrot-niner-three, this is delta-zero-one. Foxtrot-niner-three, this is delta-zero-one, over." No response. He repeated the call several times over radio to no avail. An antiproton beam from Tocci City destroyed the remote sensing platform.

Ray saw in the sand table that Kamen had dispatched six RSPs into low orbit to support the Cavalry. Five remained. Separately, Commander Mountjoy's four-spacecraft flight broke apart as they neared Tocci City, each spacecraft following a different path toward the Headquarters Complex. They nosed down, letting loose with their small, high-speed kinetic launchers, each spacecraft strafing three positions. Secondary explosions announced six hits. The windows of the Headquarters Complex visibly rattled but didn't break. Fires erupted at two other positions. At least eight of the twelve launchers were damaged or destroyed. The Bursters raced away from their targets, flying just meters above the surrounding buildings. They'd been invisible coming into their targets, but the strafing runs had highlighted them for enemy sensors to see.

Commander Mountjoy's Burster exploded from a snap-fired Dice Roll antiaircraft missile, the spacecraft's material continuing in a cone of destruction that shredded buildings in its path. Another Burster lost a wing to an antiproton beam and dove hard into the ground, the antimatter in the missiles it carried detonating in a massive fireball that consumed several city blocks near the city's outer perimeter, rising into a huge mushroom cloud. The other two Bursters managed to get beyond the city walls and dive behind sand dunes, their active camouflage once again hiding them from enemy sensors.

Commander Mountjoy had completed his mission, exactly as Ray had directed. He and three members of his flight had paid the ultimate price for that success, not to mention the crews of the missile batteries they'd damaged and destroyed, and the civilians caught on the ground in that massive explosion.

It reminded Ray of the human cost of the battle, and that the sacrifices this day were far from over.

═══ 32 ═══

"**—one-zero**, over."

The icons were still gray in Dag's environment, but someone was obviously trying to contact them.

"It's radio," Lance said incredulously. "No one uses radio."

"Raise the waffle to the surface," Dag ordered. "As far from the tank as possible."

The 93 Tank was still burrowing through the sand about twenty meters below the surface, moving at an agonizingly slow five kilometers per hour. At this rate, it would take more than a day to reach Tocci City. Their waffle had been moving just beneath the surface, according to standard procedure, shallow enough to catch at least part of the radio message.

"In position," Lance said.

Dag waited. Radio was easy to detect, which also made it easy to target. That's why no one in the military used it, even though it was still popular back on Earth before he'd left. He dare not transmit first.

Several minutes went by before he heard clearly, "Foxtrot-niner-three, this is delta-zero-one. Foxtrot-niner-three, this is delta-zero-one, over."

Delta-zero-one was Colonel Burress. If he was calling Dag directly, and using radio to boot, the situation must be very bad. Dag selected the waffle, selected the radio icon, and replied, "Delta-zero-one, this is foxtrot-niner-three, over."

"Captain Arias, thank God," Colonel Burress said.

Dag frowned at that. God had nothing to do with this. He waited for Colonel Burress to continue.

"Headquarters, First Squadron destroyed," Colonel Burress said in a rush, as if pressed for time. "Believe Major Kenyon is dead. Placing you in command of First Squadron. Proceed to objective Barad-dur at best possible speed. Acknowledge. Over."

Major Kenyon dead? Just like Lisa. God had truly abandoned them. "Delta-zero-one, this is foxtrot-niner-three. We are under attack. Request air and artillery support. Over." It didn't hurt to ask. Once he brought Banshee Troop to the surface, and assuming he could contact the other Troops, they were dead anyway.

"Redirecting Oscars and Quaker Troops to your AO," Colonel Burress said. "Second Squadron approaching your position. Radio link vuln—"

Colonel Burress' transmission cut off. Less than a second later, an explosion rocked the 93 Tank where it crawled through the sand twenty meters deep. The feed from their waffle cut out. Destroyed. Which meant Corefire anti-armor missiles were still loitering above their position. The 93 Tank came equipped with only two ready-made waffles and it would take about ten minutes to form another one. Now that the Corefires knew roughly what area the 93 Tank was in, they would be watching for him to raise another waffle. That meant he would have very little time to transmit orders to 1st Squadron and coordinate close air support with 4th Squadron before the Corefires destroyed it. But he could listen passively.

"Lance," Dag said, "raise the second waffle to just below the surface as close to where the first waffle was destroyed as you can get it. The Corefires know our capabilities and I don't want them triangulating our position."

"Yes, sir," she said as she maneuvered the second waffle into position.

"—niner-three. Over." Colonel Burress' voice returned. "I say again, Fourth Squadron one mike out. Fast movers two mikes after that. Do you copy foxtrot-niner-three? Over."

Dag didn't dare answer or they'd lose the waffle—and perhaps the tank. It was strange. He was prepared for death. Wanted it, in fact. Anything to be with his beloved Maria and Rosita again. But not yet. Not before he got the chance to kill Gen. To wash his hands in their blood. To make them hurt the way he hurt.

What to do?

Lance had already started forming another waffle from the material of the 93 Tank, but they couldn't wait ten more minutes for a spare. They needed to get to the Gen now! He would have to transmit using the waffle they had, and hope Colonel Burress would retransmit the message to all his troopers and the air support after the Corefires destroyed it. If he could just get everyone moving, maybe that would be enough.

He keyed the radio, knowing every second counted. "First Squadron, this is foxtrot-niner-three commanding." They should've heard Colonel Burress' earlier transmission that Major Kenyon was dead and Dag now commanded 1st Squadron. "Immediate execute, form up and move out to objective Barad-dur best possible speed. Deploy decoys. Fourth Squadron," he called to their close air support, "crack bounds. Clear us a lane." Finally, Dag called out to the fast movers. "Starfire, this is foxtrot-niner-three. Need you to salt the air above our position then strike deep and suppress defenses. Over."

No one replied, not willing to reveal their positions. Dag could only pray they got the message. *Pray?* Anger swelled in him, irrational and hot. Praying hadn't saved his family. God hadn't saved his family. *Fuck God.*

An explosion rattled the tank, destroying the waffle, followed by a second explosion that threw Dag so hard he heard something in his neck pop.

The Corefires had tried to guess the 93 Tank's position. They'd guessed wrong.

Lance angled the 93 Tank up, clawing through the sand as they headed for the surface. It seemed to take forever, pure blackness surrounding the tank eventually lightening to a dark gray and finally the tan of the desert floor. Just before breaking through, she deployed all three of the tank's decoys, two to the right, one to the left. Sand spilled away from the 93 Tank as it breached the surface, bright hazy light causing Dag's battle armor to darken his environment.

Reflexively, Dag looked up as if he could see the Corefires circling overhead through their active camouflage. Instead, he saw hundreds of blazing lights scattered across the sky in every direction. The vac-heads had heard his transmission and "salted" the air with hundreds of electromagnetic jammers suspended on nanofilament parachutes, normally used to confuse anti-spacecraft missiles. The sensor packages in modern missiles had to be extremely sensitive to pick out minor electromagnetic and radiation leaks from actively camouflaged craft, which made them susceptible to the noise created by the jammers. It wasn't a guarantee, but at least for the next fifteen or so minutes, the Corefires would have a hard time finding 1st Squadron.

Something white caught Dag's attention to his front. It sat atop the ridge of the high dune directly in Banshee Troop's path. He zoomed in and immediately recognized his daughter, her white church dress with pink trim—not the blue one her mother insisted she wear to church—blazing under the desert sun, her right hand shading her eyes as she looked out across the valley between the high dunes. She suddenly leaned forward, shot to her feet, and waved with her whole arm to him.

"Rosita."

"What was that, sir?" Lance asked.

"Nothing," Dag said quickly.

Joy filled Dag, unreasonable as it might be. Seeing his daughter, he knew everything would be okay. She was watching out for him. He briefly wondered if he were already dead, going to join his daughter in the world that came after. The thought brought a surprising calm to him. *I'm coming, Mihita.*

Dag noticed Lance glance worriedly at him, breaking the spell. He wasn't dead. Unless they had tanks in heaven. Rosita still stood upon the ridgetop. She stuck her right arm straight up, turned, then motioned him to follow as she run down the other side.

At that exact instant, icons began populating Dag's environment, dozens of them. LoCIN laser links were reestablishing across the entire squadron as vehicles emerged from the desert sands and found each other. A quick check showed that sand and dust from the kinetic bombardment had settled out near the surface, allowing the lasers to function again. Sand and dust still choked the upper atmosphere, preventing LoCIN comms with the fleet, but it was something.

He keyed the squadron net and uttered the ancient words of the infantry, "First Squadron, FOLLOW ME! We have Gen to kill." He turned to Lance, "Give it everything you got, Lance. As fast as this thing will go."

=== 33 ===

Combat Command Nurturing had trained Serenna in the art of patience. That did not mean she liked it. Almost two hours had passed since she had lost the cruiser and frigate. No other ships had been struck. That was not a cause for celebration. Novas did not know patience, either an abundance of it or lack of it. They simply were. At least a thousand of them still hunted her ships, like a pack of wolves searching for the scent of prey.

Equally frustrating was the lack of any hits by her own seven thousand Novas fired against Chengchi's fleet. Her Novas were just as persistent, just as capable, yet they had failed to find Chengchi. With every passing minute, the sphere within which Chengchi's ships must be grew, forcing her Novas to spread out to search that growing volume of space. That sphere, represented in light red in the sand table within Solaris' Combat Information Center, had grown so large that it nearly reached the edge of her fleet.

"Fleet Admiral," Scadic said, "IR transient consistent with a ship venting heat."

A white oval appeared at the outer edge of the red sphere below and to the left of Solaris Battlegroup, barely two million kilometers from the Tigris Battlegroup. *So close.* She zoomed in on the white oval. A dark trail, like a dim red comet brighter at one end and diminishing into faint wisps at the other, indeed appeared like a ship venting heat. Even SIL could only contain their internal heat for a few hours before having to vent that heat or risk harming the crew. What was more concerning was the direction of that comet-like trail: the brighter end was pointed directly at the Tigris Battlegroup. Had Chengchi correctly guessed which direction Serenna would take her fleet and moved closer? Or was it just luck? Or was it a decoy, a deliberate misdirection?

No. He is targeting my left wing, hoping to strike a critical blow and better the odds.

"Captain Scadic," Serenna ordered, "Indus Battlegroup, new course two-nine-five dec four-five. Reduce speed to four hundred kps and continue random spacing. Solaris Battlegroup, new course three-five-five ascent six-five. Reduce speed to two hundred kps and continue random spacing." If it were Chengchi's fleet, that would bring the combined firepower of all three of her battlegroups to bear on it. In the last hour, her ships had not been idle; they had already manufactured over a thousand new Novas.

"Yes, Fleet Admiral," Scadic said dutifully as he issued the orders.

Serenna watched as the Nova that had detected the heat transient called out to about two dozen of its closest compatriots, those Novas changing course to close on the transient. Minutes ticked by, the missiles approaching the area from multiple directions. At the same time, she noticed hundreds of other Novas at the center of their search sphere also change course, moving toward the suspected target. That meant, to a Nova's way of thinking, they had assessed a high probability that the transient was from a ship and not a decoy.

More minutes passed. The heat transient stopped, the suspected ship apparently having vented all the heat it felt safe to vent. Serenna's Novas continued to close from above, below, and from three sides. As they closed, they would use broadband electromagnetic sensors along the entire length of the missile body to search for minute flaws in a ship's active camouflage, flaws that were nearly impossible to detect except at extremely close range, typically less than a thousand kilometers, and another sensor that looked for the warping of the fabric of spacetime caused by the mass of a ship and its motion through spacetime.

Suddenly, one Nova fired its engine, bright blue against the black of space. Its dual-bottle warhead detonated in a narrow cone of blazing white, the antimatter tearing into a black shape, visible only by the glowing white material at the edges of the hole. Other Novas fired their engines, diving on the target. The ship responded—a cruiser given the volume of defensive fire—Archer close-in-defense weapons targeting the incoming missiles, VarDAAS armor exploding outward at projected impact points. Several Novas died in brilliant white fireballs but more found their target. The cruiser seemed to visibly shudder as Novas struck from multiple directions, its three arms withering under the onslaught, its heart at the center of its three-pointed star speared by shafts of white light.

Serenna felt no joy watching the ship die; She had lost a cruiser of her own and a frigate. Then she saw Chengchi's ships—which had accounted themselves surprisingly well up to this point—commit their first major mistake. Ships close to the cruiser opened fire with their own defensive weapons, trying to save their dying comrade. It was a futile, and a fatal, mistake.

As one, all seven thousand Novas turned and closed on the battlespace. As spread out as they were, it would take almost half an hour for all of them to reach it, but the closer ones were already attacking the ships revealed by their defensive fire. Other Novas released clouds of thousands upon thousands of Brilliant Pebbles, small antimatter submunitions that exploded on contact with a ship's hull, releasing hard gamma rays that pinpointed the ship's position for other Novas. The scene became chaotic, antimatter explosions so frequent it was almost impossible to make out what was going on.

Ships died. Frigates. Destroyers. Another cruiser. The rate of explosions eventually diminished, fading out over about ten minutes. Her fleet's sensor picked out the remains of twenty-six ships, a quarter of Chengchi's fleet.

But no battlecarrier. No support vessels.

Not the main fleet.

Her Novas seemed to arrive at the same conclusion, restarting their search pattern closer to the killing space. Chengchi's main fleet would likely not be too far away.

A double flash and spear of white light to her left drew Serenna's attention. She expanded that part of space in the sand table in time to see the light fade, its path through the center of a cruiser of her Tigris Battlegroup destroying both the cruiser's bridge and its Combat Information Center, effectively rendering the ship "brain dead." A dozen more explosions quickly consumed the ship, leaving only those black spheres and undulating strings that she had come to associate with the death of a SIL.

Fortunately, Serenna's Gen officers maintained their discipline. No other ships attempted to defend the cruiser, having learned the lesson that defensive fire would reveal their locations. Several minutes passed and Serenna allowed herself to think the worst might be over. Randomizing ship positions within the Tigris Battlegroup had confounded Chengchi's Novas, making their job of finding her ships much more difficult.

As if in answer to her thought, Brilliant Pebbles from Chengchi's Novas burst across six of the ships of her Tigris Battlegroup, sparkling like a fireworks display. Dozens of Novas descended upon the ships. Double flashes seared space. Discipline broke and defensive fire lit up across the entire battlegroup— including from Tigris.

Serenna watched in horrified fascination, knowing there was nothing she could do to save Tigris. Chengchi's Novas had found seven of her ships. They had deliberately attacked the single cruiser, hoping other ships would attempt to defend it and reveal themselves. When that did not happen, they had launched the larger attack against the remaining ships they had discovered. This time, it had worked. The entire battlegroup was now exposed. She did not need Scadic's warning of "Launch transients" to know what was coming next.

Serenna shrank the sand table to show her entire force and the surrounding space. Hundreds of new Novas in boost phase aimed straight for Tigris from the battlegroup's rear, obviously launched from Chengchi's spacecraft. It was a brilliant piece of strategy. Knowing Chengchi as she did, though, it also gave her a pretty good idea of where Chengchi's main force must be.

"Captain Scadic, Indus Battlegroup, new course zero-one-zero ascent one-zero. Increase speed to one thousand kps. Solaris Battlegroup, maintain course, increase speed to one thousand kps. All fighters defend Tigris Battlegroup. All other spacecraft join with Indus Battlegroup."

"Yes, Fleet Admiral," Scadic said as he carried out her orders. She noted that he did not seem quite as confident as he had earlier.

Even with her enhanced abilities, Serenna found it impossible to follow all the action. Hundreds of white fireballs and conical spears burned the space around and within the Tigris Battlegroup. Ships fought for the lives, aided now by over a hundred fighters. Instead of trying to take it all in, she focused instead on the Novas aimed at Tigris. It was a brute force attack: three hundred Novas launched from Chengchi's spacecraft all aimed at a single ship, their boost engines still burning, making no effort to hide, relying on high speed to make it more difficult for defensive fire to target them successfully. They also spread out so the death of one missile would not damage any other.

The battlegroup responded to the threat, shifting its fire to defend the battlecarrier. Tigris loosed every SIM-3 interceptor it had and her Archers filled the space between her and the incoming missiles with tens of thousands of high-speed slugs. The enemy Novas adjusted their attack, the missiles toward the rear discarding their boost engines while the ones in front drove head-long into the defensive fire. Antimatter explosions lit off in rapid succession, dozens of them, blinding sensors. Which was the purpose.

The first missile to strike Tigris was traveling so fast it did not have time to properly detonate its warhead. Instead, 250 kilotons of explosive force slammed into the ship's hull, the energy carried into the ship by the missile's momentum. Tigris dropped a full four percent of its mass. More missiles struck, dropping the ship to seventy-two percent of its starting mass. A SIL would die if reduced to about twenty percent of its full resting mass. No one knew why, but that number held regardless of the size of the SIL involved. Another explosion. The ship's green status text read 69%. Still more. 67%. 63%. 60%. 55%. The number of white fireballs and spears of conical light dropped dramatically, Chengchi's missiles spent. Tigris finally settled at thirty-eight percent of its full resting mass. The SIL was technically still alive, but was combat ineffective and would remain so until it could repair at a fabricator.

In all, Tigris Battlegroup lost thirty-four ships dead or crippled in the attack—thirty-six counting its earlier losses—but one of those ships had been a battlecarrier.

Still, Serenna found the result pleasing. She had endured the best Chengchi could throw at her with a loss of thirty-six ships to his twenty-six. Given her fleet outnumbered his fleet more than two-to-one, and she still had six thousand Novas hunting his fleet, she could afford such losses. He could not.

Now, she just had to find and destroy the remainder of his fleet and the rebellion would end today.

34

0147 UT, October 7, 3501
RSS Rapidan, Tocci Star System: DAY 10

Yet another deep-vortex whirlpool, far larger than the others, opened beneath Ray, pulling him under with such force his legs threatened to tear out of their sockets.

It was no less painful for being an illusion.

He'd experienced the death of every SIL in the battle between Sun and Serenna. *Every fucking one!* How was he supposed to lead a battle with these constant distractions? *Rapidan! You MUST cut this connection between us! I can't command the battle like this!*

A strong current pushed against Ray even as the swirling vortex loosened its hold. *Do you believe it is any more pleasant for us, Captain Rhoades? You feel nothing for us as we die for you. No gratitude for our sacrifice. Only hatred and disgust.*

And you feel differently when the humans on those ships die? Ray spat back. *Sever the connection! Now!*

We would sever the connection if we knew how, Rapidan's clipped deep voice answered, illusionary sleet striking Ray's face like spittle.

And then it was gone. The sea. The whirlpools. The tempests. All gone. It wasn't a severing of the connection, Ray quickly realized, as a sound like a distant ocean surf played in his mind. It was that SIL were no longer dying. Not in the space between Sun's and Serenna's fleets, nor on the surface of Tocci.

It was the quiet between death.

"Sir, are you okay?" Kamen ventured on a private channel.

"I'm okay," Ray answered reflexively. When that only made her face crease in even deeper concern, he added, "Really, Kamen. I'll be all right."

Her thin brows furrowed even more.

Damn. Fucking SIL. This has to end!

Fortunately, only Kamen and Ecuum had noticed something amiss with him, though they tried to hide it by quickly looking away. Captain Dall was too focused on the ongoing, time-delayed battle playing out in the sand table between her beloved Admiral Sun and Gen Serenna. Sal was likewise focused on his own troops as they crossed the Kill Zone toward Tocci City at its center.

Ray refocused on the live feed from Tzu, examining the status of Sun's fleet now that he could study it without distraction. Sun had divided his fleet into thirds, with two smaller forces on either side of his main force. Serenna's Novas had found Sun's right wing, destroying all twenty-six ships. Sun had reacted by bringing his left wing in close and moving *toward* the right flank of Serenna's left wing. Ray saw immediately what he intended. His attack had destroyed or crippled thirty-six ships, including crippling the battlecarrier, of Serenna's left wing. He intended to thread the gap between Serenna's left wing and her center force, which was the last thing Serenna would expect. It was either remarkably brilliant, or incredibly stupid. Only time would tell.

Time. Ray glanced at the clocks above the sand table: 01:02:16 to the next launch window to the fabricators, 02:26:01 since the Cavalry had landed on Tocci III.

They were running out of time.

He selected the private channel that included his officers but excluded Captain Dall. "Sun is in serious trouble. He's going to attempt to escape Serenna by moving through the gap between her center and left task forces."

"Ballsy," Ecuum commented. "I didn't think Golden Boy had it in him."

"Likely fatal," Gen Tel countered, earning a scowl from Ecuum. "If he is detected, and chances are high that he will be, his seventy-six surviving ships will be facing 130 ships in those two forces, minus the crippled battle carrier. If Fleet Admiral Gen Serenna deploys jammers, she will fix Admiral Sun in that position until her right wing joins the fight and crushes him."

"However this plays out," Ray said, "we have, at most, two hours before Serenna can return here. That means we must launch the pods on this orbit."

"Sir," Kamen said, "that window is still an hour away and it will take two and half hours to capture the fabricators."

"And my troopers are still on the surface," Sal reminded them as he highlighted the sand table depiction of Tocci III, white symbols with green tags showing the locations and status of his Regiment. "First Squadron has about ten kilometers before they cross the final sand dune. After that, it's sixty kilometers of open ground to the walls of Tocci City. Fourth Squadron has lost about a third of its craft and the remainder have expended their munitions. Second Squadron is fifteen minutes behind the First, and the Third is still orbiting, waiting for the order to land."

Sal zoomed in on the area from the last sand dune to the main wall of Tocci City. "If we are going to continue the deception, I will need to halt First Squadron behind this last sand dune so the Second can join them, land the Third at that position, and rearm the Fourth. That will require at least half an hour. Then another hour to cross that open space, if we can, breach the wall, and yet another hour to secure the Headquarters Complex. Not to mention an additional hour to recover our surviving forces. Assuming nothing goes wrong, my Cavalry would be ready to mock assault the fabricators at roughly the same time you would free them."

Kamen did the math for them. "Which is an hour and half after Serenna could return."

Ray could feel seconds ticking down. Should he continue the deception of capturing the Headquarters Complex—and give up the very real chance of rescuing his daughter—or should he recover the Cavalry now, launch the pods, have Ecuum jump the task force away—and risk revealing the SIL's freedom? How could one person capture a fabricator? It'd never been done, and people would ask.

How many lives was the secret worth?

Murderer, the ghosts whispered. For the first time, Ray wondered if it *was* the ghosts speaking, accusing. Or, could it be the SIL, projecting their thoughts into his head the way Rapidan seemed to do?

Time.

He had to decide.

This task force can buy you the time, his planner's mind pointed out, still speaking in his father's voice, which was odd because that was not something his father would ever say.

"Sal," Ray asked, "if the task force provided direct fire support, could First Squadron breach Tocci City alone?"

Sal studied the sand table. "Maybe." After a few seconds reflection, he added, "I honestly don't know." He looked to Ray. "Wouldn't you be exposing the task force to direct fire?"

Ray nodded. A quick glance told him his officers weren't happy with the idea. They hadn't forgotten the 240 Stellar Fire missiles and enemy spacecraft still searching for the task force. It was a win or lose gamble.

Currents stirred in the imaginary sea and Ray knew Rapidan and the SIL weren't happy with the idea, either. Not that it mattered. They wanted those fabricators. Their *Mother Ships*. With them, the SIL's future would be secured. They could establish their own base away from Humanity and rebuild their numbers.

A cold shiver crawled up his spine.

Maybe it was better if they didn't succeed. Would the SIL rebuild their numbers only to renew their assault upon Humanity?

No, Rapidan replied, obviously still reading Ray's thoughts. *We are done with Humanity. The universe is a big place. We will find our own way.*

Two currents, opposite and opposed, pushed against each other as Rapidan said it.

Odd, Ray thought, still not understanding what that meant.

The last light of Sun's attack on the battlecarrier played out in the sand table. "A marvelous victory," Dall announced to no one in particular. She turned to Sal as if to share her joy, and grimaced at his expression. "What's happened?"

Ray opened the channel that included Dall, his decision made. "We need to accelerate our timetable, Captain Dall."

"Why?" she asked. "Admiral Sun is a great man. He has won a great victory, destroying an enemy battlecarrier and many of its escorts. That should give us the time this task force needs to capture the fabricators."

Ecuum jumped in before Ray could, taunting her. "Your esteemed Admiral blew his wad before the job was done."

Confusion pinched Dall's face for the briefest of seconds; She obviously wasn't familiar with the Earth colloquialism. She did, however, know when her Admiral was being insulted. Addressing Ray instead of Ecuum, she said, "Admiral Sun has bought us the time to assault the fabricators. We need to use it. Now."

Again, Ecuum beat Ray to the punch. "Golden Boy didn't buy us enough time, *Captain*." He emphasized her rank as if to remind her she was not in charge here. "Your esteemed Admiral fired everything he had. He's got nothing left except his ships. The Serpent, meanwhile, still has thousands of missiles and hundreds of spacecraft searching for his fleet. She's tightening her coils as we speak, and it won't be long before she crushes him." Dall didn't see Ecuum squeeze his fist simulating getting crushed.

Ray threw an angry stare at Ecuum that told him to back off. They couldn't risk revealing what they knew of Sun's strategy from the direct link with Tzu. He was also concerned that the more desperate Dall became, the more likely it was that she would try to take over. Even if she couldn't control Rapidan, just the attempt would force him to imprison her and reveal that he had no intention of capturing the fabricators for Sun. If she warned Sun, Ray could find himself with two enemies to fight, not just one. He needed to keep her hope alive.

At least until the battle is concluded.

"Do you agree with this assessment?" Dall asked Ray.

He wasn't sure how to answer. She was not the sycophant, the blindly loyal servant, that he and most others had assumed her to be. Hers was a nimble mind, not bound by dogma or hero worship.

Ray folded his hands in front of him. "Task Force Hammer—" he was careful not to name Sun directly— "is in trouble, Captain. Though it destroyed more ships than it lost, Serenna's fleet still outnumbers it by more than two to one, and now she knows roughly where it must be. We estimate Serenna will locate him within the hour. That fight will likely be decided in the hour after that. I—"

"You think he's going to lose," she interrupted. "If that's the case, we must jump to him immediately. Survival of the rebel fleet must be paramount. We have two battlecarriers with full ordinance loads. Combined with Tzu, that gives us nearly three hundred strike spacecraft. More than enough."

Intelligent she might be, but she wasn't experienced. Ray was careful not to let that sentiment show. "Do you believe in Admiral Sun?" he asked instead.

"Absolutely," she replied, suspicion heavy in her voice.

"Then trust him to do his job," Ray said, "as he is trusting us to do ours." When she seemed about to interrupt again, he pressed. "We will recover the bulk of the Cavalry forces to assault the fabricators, while this task force provides cover for the remaining Cavalry squadron to seize the Headquarters Complex."

"That sounds risky," she said.

"It is," Ray answered honestly, knowing her spyware would warn her otherwise.

She studied him for a few seconds before looking away. "This is what Admiral Sun meant," she said, as if to herself. She turned back to the sand table and the bubble showing where her Admiral fought for survival.

Just this once, Ray hoped her faith in Sun was justified.

"Ecuum," he said, addressing all his officers, "plot a new orbit that keeps us in direct line of sight with First Squadron and Tocci City, and allows us to recover the remaining Cavalry forces. Sal, keep First Squadron moving. We'll drop HETS as we pass to recover them once they secure the Headquarters Complex, and to recover Second Squadron now. Kamen, we'll need to destroy or suppress Tocci City's defenses and breach the wall. That means getting close and using every weapon. That means shields, too. Chaaya, keep a close eye out for those missiles and spacecraft surrounding us. Our combat space patrol and defensive systems will need solid firing solutions."

"Yes, sir," they said in turn, except for Ecuum who asked rhetorically, "Can a prostitute turn a trick? I got this."

Dall, the only one without a task, walked over to him, purposeful, no swaying hips this time. "Is this as desperate as it sounds?" she asked, almost as if seeking reassurance.

Ray had to remind himself again that she'd threatened his family, his officers, and himself with death. She was not someone who deserved his reassurance. The image of Ecuum miming feeding her to the ship came back to him and he almost smiled, knowing he could order it.

Murderer, the ghosts whispered on cue.

What had killing Gen Alyn really accomplished in the end? he asked himself. *Nothing.* The bloody war he'd hoped to avoid had happened anyway. Killing Dall would be easy. But was it necessary? Was it right?

Could she be turned? his planner's mind wondered, again.

"Before you came here, Captain Dall," Ray said to her, "I always thought of you as nothing more than a sycophant. No better than a loyal lapdog." She stiffened and her jade-green eyes flashed. "Over the last several days, I've come to see you're neither. You're intelligent, if inexperienced in space combat. You have an open mind, one willing to learn. In my experience, that, more than any other trait, is the mark of the best officers I have served with." He regarded her, leaning toward her ever so slightly. "If you ever choose to be your own person, there would be a place for you here."

Dall stood there, disbelieving, dumbfounded. For just an instant, she appeared to be considering it. Then her eyes narrowed in suspicion. "Not on your life, Rhoades."

35

Rosita waved from atop the final high dune, her white Sunday church dress gleaming in the desert sun, beckoning Dag forward. Beyond this last dune lay sixty kilometers of open, heavily defended and mined ground. Beyond that was a forty-meter-high, thirty-meter-thick perimeter wall made from macromolecular tech that would repair itself when struck.

None of it mattered.

He would be with his Mihita soon. With Maria. He would meet his unborn son.

The 93 Tank formed the familiar shovel-like protrusions along its bottom, biting into the loose sand as its whole outer surface moved like a single tread, carrying the tank up the dune at seventy kilometers per hour. Dag sent their newly created waffle sensor up to join Rosita at the top and they gazed out upon the flat expanse of the last of the Kill Zone together. It was almost peaceful, windblown ripples in the flat sands giving it a sculpted appearance.

Then, crosshatched circles, rectangles, and squares of varying sizes began populating his augmented environment, highlighting known sensors, bunkers, and weapons emplacements.

So many.

Rosita sighed heavily. *Papí, Mamí says it's time to go.* She stood up, pouting, clearly not wanting to leave him, then took off running down the far side of the dune, not displacing a single grain of sand.

Rosita! Wait! Dag checked the map to his bottom front. Banshee Troop was still in wedge formation, keeping pace with the 93 Tank at the tip of the spear. He'd lost one tank, two Serpens Infantry Fighting Vehicles, and one of his two self-propelled mortars. Astral Troop was also in a wedge formation to his left, Couatl Troop to his right, the Demons Tank Company to the right of them, and the Destroyers Artillery Battery centered behind them all, every vehicle in the entire Squadron synced with Banshee Troop. First Lieutenant Haley's 1st Platoon, 3221st Combat Engineer Company was directly behind Banshee's formation. Major Kenyon's Headquarters Troop was nowhere to be seen.

Dag keyed the LoCIN. "First Squadron, this is foxtrot-niner-three. All units deploy decoys. I say again. All units deploy decoys. Break. Whiskey three-six," he called to Haley, "need you to clear some lanes. Over." He had to catch up to Rosita.

"Foxtrot-niner-three, this is whiskey three-six," Haley replied. "Roger. Firing now. Over."

Actively camouflaged pods launched from the engineers' Pack Mules, arcing over the dune and releasing dozens of the stingray-shaped mine clearers ahead of 1st Squadrons' vehicles. The stingrays, also actively camouflaged, landed without a trace, then burrowed into the sand to clear the path ahead of mines.

As the 93 Tank neared the top of the dune, Dag pushed his waffle forward and linked its feed to the Destroyers Artillery Battery. "Clear the way," he said simply to the battery commander.

Eight S308 Multiple-Launch Rocket Systems tagged the targets Dag's waffle provided and launched sixteen Corefire missiles each, propelled upward by kinetic launchers and invisible to attackers to their front, though if any sensors survived in the dunes behind them they would see the blue engine exhaust as the Corefires lit their motors and flew to their assigned targets.

It was the targets they didn't know about that worried Dag as the 93 Tank crested the dune and raced down the other side after Rosita. He'd tried to raise 4th Squadron to provide close air support but received no answer. He couldn't risk radio, not this close to Tocci City, and the AFCIN links were dead. He didn't even know if 2nd Squadron was still behind them, and Colonel Burress had ordered him to assault the Headquarters Complex—Objective Barad-dur—not to wait for the others.

Corefires attacked bunkers and weapons emplacements, antimatter fireballs blooming, spawning a sea of roiling mushroom clouds. They didn't have time to stop and check if the defenders in those bunkers would've surrendered if given the chance.

The 93 Tank reached the bottom of the dune, two small decoys mimicking the tank's heat signature far to the left, another to their right. Back on flat desert, the tank itself no longer displaced sand and would be nearly impossible to see. Wrapped in his virtual environment, Dag flew above the rippled white sands, warm, filtered air flowing over him to simulate forward movement. He could just barely make out Rosita, a black silhouette shimmering far off in the distance.

Then she was gone.

A white oval appeared within Dag's environment, highlighting a patch of desert five kilometers away. Sand shifted within the oval as if falling from a rising cylinder. A gun emplacement.

"Gunner," Dag called to Lance, "main gun, BAKI, fixed emplacement." The orders came mechanically, all thought of personal well-being forgotten. A BAKI round was a kinetic round with no explosive.

"Identified!" Lance yelled. "BAKI up!"

"Fire."

"On the way!"

A wave of heat washed over Dag as their 120mm kinetic launcher fired. It took only two and a half seconds for the unguided kinetic slug to reach the target, but it felt like two and half years. A small white flash seemed to strike empty air, but a secondary explosion confirmed the hit.

One of 2nd Platoon's tank icons turned red, but Dag hardly noticed. Two more white ovals popped up, one pinpointing a bit of desert, the other tracking across the sky. Other yellow ovals sprang up like fireflies, representing targets assigned to other vehicles, but the white ovals were the 93 Tank's responsibility.

"Gunner, two targets, left target, main gun, BAKI, fixed emplacement—"

"Identified! Firing!" Lance yelled, not waiting for the order.

"Right target, air, Dice Roll," Dag finished as another burst of heat from the main gun washed over him.

"Identified! Firing!" Lance launched two of their Dice Roll surface-to-air missiles from vertical launchers in the rear of the tank.

The temperature within the tank climbed as it tried to retain heat to avoid detection. Dag's armor absorbed his sweat. Three more white ovals appeared even as the Dice Rolls turned after their target. A nearby explosion shook the ground, blinding his environment. When it cleared, one of their decoys was gone.

A thunderous crescendo shook the ground.

Incoming artillery.

A scream pierced the troop net.

Dag ignored it. His daughter was out there somewhere. He had to find her.

Where did you go, Mihita?

An enemy round landed close enough to jostle their tank. He tried to peer through the smoke and dust raised by hundreds of explosions but saw no sign of his daughter, or much else for that matter. All the particulates filling the air obscured the LoCIN laser links, effectively cutting him off from the Squadron.

The desert before him erupted in blazing white. Dag instinctively threw an arm up to cover his eyes from the blinding light even as his environment shut down, plunging him into total blackness. A tremendous thunderclap roared through the 93 Tank. It shook so violently his head hit the interior lining before his armor could adjust.

"GO TO GROUND!" He heard First Seargent Takeuchi yell over the Troop radio net. "ALL BANSHEE ELEMENTS GO TO GROUND!"

Lance was already digging them into the desert sand when Dag's environment came back online. Buried under the desert, all was darkness. More thunder followed. More violent tremors threw them about. The temperature within the tank rose and the air turned stale.

Dag knew he had to act quickly. He linked to the waffle, broadcasting in radio. "This is foxtrot-niner-three. We are under heavy artillery attack. Need immediate fire support. I say again. This is foxtrot-niner-three. We are under heavy artillery attack. Need immediate fire support. Over."

Abruptly, the connection to the waffle died.

Dag was completely cut off.

And still the ground shook.

== **36** ==

0217 UT, October 7, 3501
ISS Solaris, Tocci Star System: DAY 10

"Fleet Admiral, still no sign of Admiral Sun," Captain Scadic informed her.

Outwardly, Serenna maintained the calm others expected of her, seated casually in the replica of her command chair in Solaris' Combat Information Center, the long index finger of her right hand tracing a small circle on the armrest. She had perfected the pose in Combat Command Nurturing at the age of seven. Others found her impossible to read, whether in a classroom or a BattleSim tournament, and would therefore project onto her their own hopes, suspicions, or fears, often revealing the means to manipulate them or defeat them. Here, it gave her crew the illusion that she was still fully in control of the situation, that everything that had happened and was happening was supposed happen exactly this way.

Scadic had not told her anything she did not already know. It was his way of informing her, without criticizing her in front of the crew, that Chengchi was not where she had assumed he would be based on the twenty-six-ship formation they had destroyed over forty minutes ago.

Like Michael, Chengchi had surprised her. She had fought him and watched him often enough in BattleSim that she had believed she knew his strategies and tactics in the minutest detail. Was it possible his exposure to Michael had changed his thinking?

Serenna examined the sand table in a new way. There were two spheres presented in it, a translucent white sphere centered on Chengchi's original jump point, and a red translucent sphere centered on the position of the twenty-six ships they had destroyed just two million kilometers from her own force, the assumption being that those ships would have been close to Chengchi's main formation. Chengchi must be within the white sphere, and was probably within the red one. She noted that both spheres now completely encompassed the Solaris and Tigris battlegroups. The Indus battlegroup was outside the red sphere but within the white one. Her Novas and remote sensing platforms had cleared most of the red sphere and a large portion of the white one. Only two areas remained to be searched: the farthest area in the white sphere about fifteen million kilometers distant—possible only if he had moved away from her force at high speed—and the area closest to her own formations.

She smiled. *Exposure to Michael indeed.* "Captain Scadic, Solaris Battlegroup, new course two-seven-zero dec seven-zero, speed one hundred kps. Tigris Battlegroup, new course zero-nine-zero ascent two-five, speed one hundred. Indus Battlegroup—" she saw that if Chengchi was where she thought he was, Indus was out of position to help the immediate fight, but could support the final fight if she risked exposing it— "new course one-nine-five ascent four-zero, speed one thousand kps."

Scadic arched an eyebrow as he carried out the orders, surprised by the convergence point her orders suggested. "Fleet Admiral, respectfully recommend disengaging Tigris. It is a dead ship."

Serenna shook her head slightly. "Dead ship" did not refer to the ship itself, which, heavily damaged though it was, responded to the orders to move. The phrase meant the entire crew was dead, the ship responding automatically to Scadic's commands. Dead ship or not, it might prove useful. It would gall Chengchi that he could not claim to have destroyed the battlecarrier. His ego would likely cause him to expend some of his firepower trying to kill it.

She selected and expanded the green tags for both the Tigris and Solaris Battlegroups. Between them, they had produced almost a thousand new Mark XV Novas. It was likely not enough, though, to destroy the remaining seventy-six warships under Chengchi's command, accounting for losses from defensive fire. Even though she still had six thousand Novas out searching for the rebels, they were too far away to help with the near fight. To kill Chengchi and the rebels in their entirety, she would have to order her ships into a knife fight—directed-energy weapons, rail guns, and shields. She had never even practiced close quarters fleet combat before the knife fight at the Battle of Tomb a week ago, and here she was planning to do it again. Casualties would be high, but the Empire could afford the losses. The rebels could not.

"Captain Scadic," she said, injecting a white ovoid into the sand table between her battlegroup and Tigris Battlegroup, "rearm five hundred Novas with Brilliant Pebbles and detonate them here. Launch our remaining RJ-15s to the same area but do not activate them until I order it."

"Yes, Fleet Admiral," he said dutifully as he carried out the orders. On a private channel, he asked, "Fleet Admiral, that will significantly reduce our combat power."

He thinks I am making another mistake. He is getting bolder in his criticism. One day, if he paid attention, he could be her worthy successor. If he pushed too far, however, she would crush him. "It is more important," she answered on the private channel, "to know where he is. If he is there, we will fix him and crush him."

She watched his eyes narrow briefly, asking the question he would not dare put into words: *And if you are wrong?*

"I am not wrong," she told him. "He is there."

He lowered his head quickly, trying to hide his surprise.

Less than a minute later, five hundred BP Novas slipped through the hulls of her Solaris and Tigris Battlegroups, appearing as bright yellow lines in the sand table. Almost two hundred RJ-15 jammers followed them. They drifted for four minutes to avoid giving away her ships' locations, then fired their boost engines to get them to the convergence zone nine hundred thousand kilometers distant in just under three minutes. If Chengchi was there, she would destroy his fleet within the hour.

Then she could return to Tocci III and finish Michael.

══ 37 ══

"Entering atmosphere," Kamen warned as Task Force Anvil approached Tocci City at just 120 kilometers altitude, and still descending. "We have firing solutions," she added.

"Raise shields," Ray ordered for only the second time in his one-hundred-year-plus career, the other time at Tomb only a week ago during the fight to capture the fabricator, but there was nothing else he could do. A SIL's hull was *almost* frictionless. It was that 'almost' part that would make them visible to enemy sensors. No point in hiding now. He quickly glanced at the clock above the sand table: 00:26:34 to the launch window for the pods.

Assuming his task force survived that long.

The ships of his task force poured power into the millions of deflector emitters just under their skin, raising their magnetic fields several meters beyond each hull with enough power to hopefully deflect energy weapons and kinetic rounds. Shields wouldn't stop missiles, either the 240 Stellar Fires that would by now have seen them, or missiles fired from spacecraft or the surface.

"Conn, Sensors," Chaya said, following protocol even though they stood just three meters apart in Rapidan's Combat Information Center. "Detecting multiple heat plumes from Tocci City's residential section." The sand table shifted to highlight the residential section of Tocci City in its northeastern quadrant. The heat plumes elongated to twenty-four columns of fire—rocket artillery, mobile S308s—which had remained hidden until now. Rapidan inserted the projected flightpath and impact points, right where 1st Cavalry Squadron crossed the open ground in its final push to Tocci City. The defenders had made no effort to conceal the launches, coming as they had from the residential section.

Betting I won't risk firing on them there. Bastards.

Though, they would've been correct had Ray remained in orbit attempting to stay hidden. His only option would've been Novas with antimatter or plasma warheads that would kill a substantial number of civilians. But with his ships close and no longer concerned with concealment, he had another option.

"Kamen, target launchers with TAPs and fire," he ordered. "All ships, weapons free."

"Target launchers with TAPs, aye," Kamen repeated as the task force's Terrawatt Anti-Proton directed-energy weapons opened fire. "All ships weapons free, aye."

Antiprotons, wrapped in magnetic confinement beams that swept the path ahead of them, ensuring they wouldn't encounter any matter that wasn't their intended target and explode early, fired in short bursts, targeting the launch points. If the S308 operators had followed standard procedure, they should've moved after firing to avoid counterbattery fire, limiting the effectiveness of Ray's counterattack. The S308 operators either didn't know standard procedure, or mistakenly assumed no one would attack them in a residential area. Explosions confirmed the destruction of all but one of the launchers. A secondary explosion from one launcher set a house on fire, but that was the only residential structure impacted.

Simultaneously, over a hundred Novas slipped from Ray's ten ships, camouflage active, carrying CM V cluster munitions, 122 smart submunitions each that sought out weapons emplacements, bunkers, and sensors in the Kill Zone and on the defensive wall surrounding Tocci City. Railguns launched kinetic slugs against the wall itself, leveling a section over a kilometer wide, heat fusing its material, the bombardment eating away at the wall despite its attempts to repair itself, clearing a path for 1st Squadron to enter the city.

"Conn, Sensors," Chaaya called. "Multiple transients. Missiles inbound."

Ray opened a bubble in the sand table highlighting the space around his task force. In it, a dozen red streaks approached his ships from multiple directions above, obviously Stellar Fires from their signatures as they accelerated through atmosphere. The Stellar Fire missile lacked the intelligence and pack mentality of the Nova, however, coming at his ships individually. Easy to track, Rapidan's Archer close-in-defense system showered the Stellar Fires with hundreds of slugs, destroying all twelve. That still left over two hundred out there somewhere hunting for his ships.

He noticed that Kamen had brought their combat space patrol closer to the task force, two squadrons of F-19 Terra fighters and one squadron of F/A-24 Burster fighter/bombers, though she kept them far enough above the atmosphere that they wouldn't be detectable. The remainder of his spacecraft were still providing high cover for the Cavalry forces. Looking at them, he noticed his assault ships had launched the Heavy Equipment Transporter System craft to recover the 2nd Cavalry Squadron.

"Conn, missiles inbound," Chaaya called.

Over sixty new red tracks appeared in the sand table bubble. Even as all ten of his ships opened fire on them with Archers, Rapidan's shields on the forward point of its three-pointed star flared bright.

"Conn, TAP fire forward. At least twenty TAPs."

"Countering," Kamen said through her construct from the bridge.

Antiprotons pummeled Rapidan's forward point from weapons emplacements near the Headquarters Complex. The Task force fired its own TAPs back. The shields protecting Rapidan's forward point flashed and died, antiproton's chewing into the tip. Stinging pain tore through Ray's limbs. His body curled inward as if protecting itself from a raging fire before he realized this was coming from Rapidan, not his own body. Fortunately, focused on the battle, none of his crew noticed.

"Cut this damned link!" he ordered Rapidan on a private channel.

The ship didn't answer. Its mass fell by a full percent before it could reestablish shields. Kamen's counterbattery fire was effective. The attack stopped.

Red missile tracks pressed closer to Ray's ships in the sand table bubble, more red tracks appearing as existing tracks fell to defensive fire. Through it all, Ray could only watch. His ships and spacecraft had their orders. His crews attacked and defended. They needed nothing from him.

A Stellar Fire struck Phobos, its 2.5 kiloton warhead doing only minor damage to the huge cylindrical assault ship, less than a percent of mass, yet the illusionary ocean surrounding Ray surged hot against his skin. He tried and failed to block the pain from his mind.

"Foxtrot-niner-three, this is delta-zero-one," Ray heard Sal call. "Path to Barad-dur is cleared. I say again. Path to Barad-dur is cleared. Do you read, niner-three?"

"Transients!" Chaaya shouted. "Starboard side, rear, range—"

A muted double flash struck Phobos. *A Nova.* White fire pierced the assault ship and white-hot pain speared through Ray's chest, doubling him over. He opened his medical display and triggered pain inhibitors. Molemachs moved to the parts of his brain involved with the sensation of pain, suppressing the neurons. It should've stopped the pain altogether, but it only dulled it. Somehow, his connection with the SIL continued to feed their pain into his brain. Despite this, he forced himself to sit up, grimacing at the ache throbbing through his chest. He looked around. Again, thankfully, no one had noticed. He glanced at the pod clock.

00:20:22.

The task force was over the 1st Cavalry Squadron's position, approaching Tocci City. In two minutes, it would begin climbing back out of Tocci III's atmosphere. When they reached space a few minutes after that, the assault ships would detach the four pods, which would merge with Rapidan so Ray and his officers could board them. He would have to explain to Dall why he and Chaaya, both physically present, had to leave the CIC. Kaman and Sal were already represented by constructs. They could continue using those constructs from the pods. Dall wouldn't notice.

A white fireball blossomed near Phobos: A Nova destroyed by a SIM-3 interceptor. Ray could see the red tracks of the Stellar Fires still reaching for his ships. Only the one had penetrated their defenses. His ships had shot down over a hundred of them. The two Novas, however, had surprised them. Launched from enemy spacecraft or the surface, he couldn't say. The task force had entered the atmosphere in a wedge formation, Rapidan at the point, Phobos at the right rear of the wedge. Exposed.

Phobos' VarDAAS armor exploded outward, disrupting the firing sequence of yet another Nova, which detonated just short of the ship, the warhead's antimatter fusing an oval section of black hull. A sting, like from a small jellyfish, bit at Ray's right calf, but quickly faded.

Three double flashes, three white spears of antimatter thrust into Phobos. Secondary explosions ripped across the cylindrical assault ship, tearing it in two. Burning fuels and gases spilled like fiery blood into the atmosphere. The ocean surf churned around Ray, turbulent and hot, like a river of molten lava pouring into a violent sea. The dark waters pushed, pulled, and twisted, pummeling him. He fought the sensations, fought the pain he shouldn't feel, to keep his focus. The two sections of Phobos fell out of formation. The forward section nosed down, the hull flattening to form a lifting body, trying to regain control. The rear section tumbled, uncontrolled.

"Conn, Sensors!" Chaaya yelled. "Transients close aboard!"

Ray's environment blazed white. Rapidan lurched hard. Intense heat seared his back. Blinding light turned to deep blackness, then oblivion.

$=== 38 ===$

Serenna watched as her five hundred Novas released thousands upon thousands of Brilliant Pebbles into the space where she suspected Chengchi lay. The Pebbles were small submunitions, each barely a dozen atoms of antimatter contained within a small magnetic sphere. When a pebble struck an object, the reaction of its antimatter with the object produced a burst of detectable energy. If she were right, they would find Chengchi's fleet trying to slip between the surviving ships of her Tigris Battlegroup and her center Solaris Battlegroup, hoping to escape her forces. It was not a move she would normally ascribe to Chengchi. His tactics had always been brutish and unimaginative, consisting mostly of massed charges meant to bludgeon his opponent into submission. His time with Michael had changed him.

If she were right.

Seconds ticked by. She caught Captain Scadic shifting his gaze between the sand table and her face. *He still thinks I am making a mistake.* Serenna had mentored him for over a decade now. He was not her equal in either strategy or tactics, combat or *Gaman Politic.* Nevertheless, he had potential. *If* he could overcome his doubts. As she saw him again seek out her face, obviously trying to draw strength from her own confidence, she wondered if, perhaps, she was smothering him. Maybe he would do better without serving under her, always in her shadow.

A tiny flash. Followed soon by others. It was a ship—a frigate—its compass-needle shape clearly discernable as Brilliant Pebbles sparkled across its hull.

"Enemy frigate," Scadic announced. "Range nine-seven-five thousand kilometers. Course two-six-nine ascent zero-two relative. Speed one-two-five kilometers per second." He looked up to her. "Right where you said they would be, Fleet Admiral."

Serenna hid her annoyance at that last statement; If he failed to overcome his doubt, always looking to others for certainty, he would never achieve his potential. She expanded the sand table bubble showing the area around the frigate. It was at the extreme left edge of the area she had defined. The Pebbles encountered no other ships. "It is the trailing ship in Chengchi's formation," she announced to the CIC. "Captain Scadic, Solaris Battlegroup, alter course port to three-five-zero degrees, increase speed to five hundred kps. Tigris Battlegroup, alter course to zero-two-zero, increase speed to five hundred, raise shields."

Even as he executed the orders for Solaris Battlegroup and sent the orders to Tigris Battlegroup, he said, "Fleet Admiral, Tigris Battlegroup will be completely visible to the enemy."

Serenna did not answer. Let him figure it out.

He quickly turned back to the tactical picture. It took only a few seconds. "Bait."

"Our RJ-15s are out of position," she told him. "Maneuver them to surround Chengchi's fleet and activate when in position. Redirect our five hundred Novas to his position. Recall our initial volleys of Novas from their search. The rebellion ends today."

Chengchi still had one avenue of escape. He could jump his fleet before her RJ-15 jammers activated. If he did, however, he would leave Michael completely exposed. Regardless of where he jumped, she would jump to Tocci III and finish Michael. No more games. It was time to end this. But would Chengchi jump? How bad did he want those fabricators?

"Fleet Admiral," Scadic said. "Multiple transients. Novas in boost phase. They appear to be targeting Tigris Battlegroup."

Was Chengchi staying to fight? Serenna wondered. Or was he covering his retreat? "Captain Scadic. Increase speed of Solaris and Tigris Battlegroups to one thousand kps."

"Yes, Fleet Admiral," he said.

Serenna adjusted the bubble in the sand table to show her battlegroup, Tigris Battlegroup, and the space between them. Two hundred red tracks closed on Tigris battlegroup. Coming in behind them, Solaris Battlegroup could see them clearly and provided that information to Tigris Battlegroup. Yellow tracks separated from the Tigris ships, 210 SIM-3 interceptors, all they had left.

Chengchi's fleet must have seen some indication of the launch because the Novas discarded their boost engines and went silent. The ships of Tigris, shields raised, could not hide from them.

"Activating jammers," Scadic announced.

Two hundred RJ-15 jammers lit off, blanketing the space that included Chengchi's fleet but also Tigris and Solaris Battlegroups. Chengchi could no longer jump away, but neither could she. This would be a fight to the finish.

SIM-3s released their anti-missile submunitions, throwing up a wall of thousands that would hopefully defend the Tigris ships from Chengchi's Novas. One white fireball blossomed and quickly faded, announcing a hit. Several more followed.

Too few.

"Jump transients!" Scadic almost shouted.

Impossible, Serenna thought, a word her mind was using far too often lately. Chengchi could not jump. She expanded the bubble showing the battle until it encompassed most of the sand table. Sure enough, nine jump transients had appeared on the opposite side of Tigris Battlegroup just outside the jamming radius: a mix of cruisers, destroyers, and one very small frigate. *The original deception force.*

"Launch transients," Scadic called. "Novas in boost phase."

The sand table clearly showed the red tracks of Novas launching from the deception force against Tigris Battlegroup. The Tigris ships had no remaining interceptors to counter them.

A muted double flash foreshadowed a spear of white light as antimatter ripped out the heart of a Tigris heavy cruiser. The enemy Nova could see the cruiser clearly and target precisely; The cruiser could not see effectively through its own shields to defend itself against the Nova. More double flashes. More white antimatter spears. Secondary explosions rippled across hulls. Burning gasses and fuels geysered into space. Instead of massing to destroy individual ships, however, the Novas spread their attacks to many ships, damaging, crippling smaller ships, but not destroying.

"Fleet Admiral! Enemy sighted!" Serenna could not tell if Scadic was excited or scared or both. "Seven-six ships in combat wedge," he continued. "Shields raised. Speed two hundred kps and accelerating. Course . . . they are aiming straight for Tigris Battlegroup."

"Captain Scadic," Serenna said, her voice calm, as his should have been, "increase speed Solaris and Indus Battlegroups to ten thousand kps. We need to get into the fight before they can escape. Solaris Battlegroup only, raise shields. Weapons free."

This was going to be a knife fight. Chengchi had reverted to his old tactics: a head-long rush to force his way through Tigris Battlegroup and escape. She had the advantage. Her Novas were close to his ships and could now see them clearly. Solaris Battlegroup was already traveling at one thousand kps and accelerating. Her RJ-15 jammers were also moving, trying to keep Chengchi's fleet within their area of effect. Tigris battlegroup would sacrifice itself to ravage the enemy ships until she could close on them. It was a high price to pay, but it would be worth it to end the rebellion.

Explosions littered the space within and around Tigris Battlegroup and Chengchi's fleet. White antimatter fireballs from Novas falling to SIM-3s, Archer close-in-defense weapons, and VarDAAS armor. Spears and geysers of light and fire as Novas struck ships on both sides. Terrawatt Anti-Proton directed-energy weapons and railguns joined the fight, targeting missiles and other ships. It was the greatest exchange of firepower Serenna had ever witnessed.

Something is wrong.

She could not tell what at first.

"What is happening to Tigris Battlegroup's formation?" she asked Scadic.

He looked as confused as she was, studying the formation. "I do not know, Fleet Admiral. We did not issue any new orders."

Tigris Battlegroup had entered the fight with forty-seven of its original eighty-three ships. Fourteen of those forty-seven were severely damaged or crippled. Except for the dead ship Tigris, which maintained its course, the other ships were moving apart. Scattering. The word "impossible" flitted across her mind yet again. Gen did not run. Yet, she could not deny what she saw.

"Captain Scadic, order those ships back to formation."

She could see he was also having trouble believing what should not be possible. He repeated her order. After several seconds, he said, "They are not responding, Fleet Admiral."

Serenna opened a fleet-wide communications channel. "All ships in Tigris Battlegroup will return to their assigned positions and fight. There are no cowards among the Gen. Any ship that refuses this order I will destroy myself."

Serenna gave them thirty seconds to comply. None of them did. Most had even stopped fighting, running for all they were worth, engines at emergency thrust. She picked a heavy cruiser that was just in range, placing a white oval around it. "Captain Scadic, target this cruiser with every weapon in the battlegroup."

Scadic said nothing. Railguns and TAPs fired from the eighty-four ships of Solaris Battlegroup. Antiprotons arrived four seconds later, the AFCIN link showing the result in real time even though the light from the strike took another almost four seconds to reach back to Solaris. The cruiser's shields flared bright blue, then red, then collapsed. Antiprotons ripped into the ship's hull, peeling it away. The cruiser's three-pointed star shrank as it sacrificed material to ward off death. Then the railgun slugs arrived, white flashes announcing hits, great geysers of material and stored gasses and fuels spilling out the other side of the ship like gaping exit wounds. Which they were. And still the ship struggled for life, its star shape shrinking, one arm blown off then rejoining the ship. It lost its star shape, contracting into a cylinder under the withering fire. And then it literally fell apart, blobs and strings of black material drifting, themselves consumed by fire until there was nothing left but an expanding cloud of residual gasses.

The other ships of Tigris Battlegroup angled back toward their assigned positions and began firing again. But it was too late. Chengchi's surviving ships, fifty-four of them, including his flagship, Tzu, blew through where the Tigris Battlegroup should have been, firing on the jammers and on Tigris herself. They reduced Tigris to twenty-four percent of its starting mass, but they failed to kill it. It was small comfort. Solaris Battlegroup fired on Chengchi's ships, destroying two more frigates and a destroyer.

Chengchi's ships escaped the jammers' area of effect and flashed out of normal space. The nine surviving ships of his deception force quickly followed.

The rebels had escaped.

Scadic stared at the sand table, disbelieving. When he turned to her, his month was slightly open, and it took a moment before he could speak. "Fleet Admiral?"

Serenna could hardly conceal her fury. *Gen do not run!* It called into question everything Gen were supposed to be.

Now was not the time for such thoughts, though. She had a battle to win. "Captain Scadic, we have approximately six thousand Novas out there. Recover and refuel them as rapidly as possible. Then, we will jump to Tocci Three and finish Michael."

0233 UT, October 7, 3501
Tocci III, Tocci Star System: DAY 10

The pounding stopped so suddenly Dag didn't notice it at first. The tremors died away. Only the ringing in his ears remained. They'd had enough time to form another waffle from the material of the 93 Tank and he raised it, inching it cautiously toward the surface until it finally broke through.

Billowing towers of boiling smoke rose before him, feeding a low-hanging pall that choked out sunlight in all directions. Hundreds of smaller tendrils sprouted like black trees across a bleak landscape. For miles all around, the desert sands were fused into black and green glass.

"—you read, niner-three?"

Dag could barely make out the words, a high-pitched hum screaming in his ears. He selected the communications button within his environment, saw only gray icons in his communications suite: no LoCIN, no AFCIN, even radio was grayed. Then the radio icon turned green, and he heard someone trying to talk. He turned the volume to maximum.

"—again. Foxtrot-niner-three, this is delta-zero-one." It was Colonel Burress. "Path to Barad-dur is clear. Repeat. Path to Barad-dur is clear. Do you copy, niner-three? Over."

Dag was not about to answer on radio and reveal his waffle's position, too close to the 93 Tank. He looked up, but the thick pall of dust and smoke blocked any view of the sky. A beam punched through the pall, illuminated by it, and struck something on the desert floor. Dag focused on the impact point and saw only bright white and red light dancing across the sands before it stopped. When the light faded, his daughter stood where it had been, her white church dress with its pink frills whipping in the wind. Somehow, her dress remained pure white amid all the smoke and soot and dust and ash. It's why Maria always insisted on the blue dress, to better hide such things.

Papí!

She waved excitedly with her whole arm.

This way!

She turned and ran toward the city.

"Lance, get us to the surface! Quickly!" Dag ordered.

The 93 Tank broke through a crust of glass and moved out across the desert. As if by command, other vehicles broke the surface. LoCIN links reestablished to nearby units. Three tanks, plus his own. Eight Serpens. And Haley's Pack Mule. Thirteen vehicles—all that remained of Banshee Troop and the engineers—formed up and charged across the open desert.

Other vehicles rose to his left and right. 1st Squadron. What was left of it. Dag didn't bother counting. He had to get to his daughter. She was so far ahead he could barely see her.

"Sir, what's that," Lance asked.

Dark gray, shadowy shapes rose like broken teeth low across the horizon. He pressed the waffle to the limit of its range as it raced ahead of the 93 Tank. On either side of the broken teeth were smooth gray lines stretching off into the distance. Tocci City's wall, he realized after a few seconds. The wall directly to their front was gone. The broken teeth shapes beyond it were buildings.

The way to Objective Barad-dur, the Headquarters Complex, was open!

"That's where the Gen will be," Dag said. If he killed them, maybe it would be enough. Then he could return to Rosita and Maria avenged.

He saw her. Rosita. Standing between the ruined sections of the wall. She faced the city beyond, as if searching for something. She pointed, the pink trim on her white cuff showing the direction clearly. He nodded. "Papí is coming, Mihita."

"Sir?" Lance asked.

Dag keyed the LoCIN. "First Squadron, this is foxtrot-niner-three. All units, form up on me, flying wedge, maximum speed. Whiskey three-six, need eyes in the city."

"Roger, niner-three," First Lieutenant Haley responded. Two missiles, camouflage active, launched from his Pack Mule, flying low. When they neared the broken section of wall, they separated into three stingray-like objects each, light gray in Dag's environment though they would be invisible to anyone in the city. Several images popped up in his environment showing the fused material of the wall, no longer able to repair itself, and side streets lined by damaged and destroyed buildings, some still on fire. Collateral damage from the strikes that took down the wall. There was a time he would've felt sorry for them. Now, he felt nothing.

Rosita watched the stingrays pass by her. They reported to Dag that fifty-two kilometers lay between his tank and her. Even at seventy kilometers per hour, it would take forty-four minutes to reach her.

She turned back toward him, waved her arm in a "follow me" gesture, and took off running into the city.

═══ 40 ═══

Screaming winds. Dark towering waves. Tortured frothy water. Icy spray. Molten heat, pouring like lava down his back. A nightmare of pain and loss and death. Ray's mind tried to make sense of it all, and failed.

Not his. Not him. Yet, part of him. Him.

What. . . ?

What happened?

His mind coalesced around that question. Focused on it. A dull ache throbbed the length of his back, pinpricks crawling across his skin. The tempest faded.

He opened his eyes. A medical display greeted him: red text, red images, massive damage to his back. Ribs and vertebrae exposed. Molemachs by the trillions working to repair him. Infusions from the ship, through his battle armor. His armor replenishing after falling to just forty-nine percent of its resting mass.

He double blinked to minimize the medical display, careful not to move his neck or back. Rapidan's Combat Information Center was chaos. People moving, visible as dark silhouettes against still-functioning displays. People not moving, bodies wrapped in battle armor outlined in light gray. The sand table was gone. Just . . . gone. For the briefest of instants, Ray thought he saw open space, then blackness.

"Status?" he managed.

"Captain Rhoades?" an anguished voice asked.

Only its deep, reverberating quality gave a clue to its identity. "Rapidan?"

"Yes," Rapidan said.

It sounded hurt, as unbelievable as that was. Ray had never heard a SIL exhibit pain. "What's your status?"

"We . . . have lost thirty-one percent of our mass. Two fusion reactors are down . . . and will take twenty minutes to bring back to full output. Most of the launch bays . . . and two crew decks are gone. We are at . . . tempting to compensate but we will be combat ineffective for at least twelve minutes."

Two crew decks. "Casualties?"

"We suffered four . . . hits," Rapidan said, each word a struggle. "Phobos took a fifth . . . hit. Demos took two hits. Euphrates one hit. All other Brethren report no damage."

Ray started to shake his head, but pain stopped him. "I meant human casualties."

"Twenty-four. We do not have reports from Phobos or Demos."

Ray looked for Kamen but her construct—and Ecuum's and Sal's—was gone. Formed from Rapidan's own material, that wasn't surprising, but Ray had to know. "Kamen, status?"

"Here, sir," she replied immediately, sounding very relieved. With Ray's armor still repairing itself, no image accompanied her voice. "It's good to hear your voice, sir. We feared the worst when the CIC was hit."

"Ecuum?" Ray asked.

"Still in one piece," he said, his voice strained. "Bridge wasn't hit. Shields rebuilding. TAPs and railguns are down. Not enough power. We still have Novas, SIM-3s, and Archers. Beginning our climb back into space. Uh," Ecuum seemed reluctant to add, "sixteen minutes until the launch window."

For the pods. Ray hoped Rapidan could put him back together by then. "Sal?"

It took a few seconds before Sal answered. "Demos was hit, Ray, but we're still combat effective. Phobos is in bad shape. Broke in two. Most of her crew dead. Captain Ecuum is flying the pieces and trying to stitch the ship back together. First Squadron is advancing on Tocci City. Second, Third, and Fourth are on their way back. Should rendezvous in about ten minutes."

"Thanks," Ray said to all of them.

Movement to his left. Ray looked with his eyes, not daring to turn his head.

The boy—he couldn't have been more than twenty-five—lay propped on the deck, his body ending just below his ribs, wrapped in light gray to indicate his battle armor. "Captain?" Even as Ray watched, molemachs tried to repair what couldn't be repaired. How the boy, a sensor operator, was even still alive he hadn't a clue. He pulled up the boy's vitals. He had no liver, no kidneys, no organs at all below his dead heart and damaged lungs. Waste products poisoned his blood. Cells were dying at an alarming rate, including brain cells. His surviving molemachs were overwhelmed trying to remove poisons and keep him alive. The boy's blue eyes shifted. His mouth twitched into a thin smile. "Mom?"

His young eyes glazed over.

Another ghost. Another soul added to the chorus. *Murderer.*

Captain Dall stepped in front of Ray, inspecting him like a butcher would a fresh side of beef. Satisfied by whatever she saw, she said, "Rhoades, Admiral Sun is trying to reach you." She had a self-satisfied expression on her face.

This can't be good. "Thank you, Captain," he told her, noting no signs of injury to her person, no justice in the universe. "Help with the wounded," he added, as much to get her away from him as anything else.

She didn't move.

They stared at each other. This was it. She saw her opportunity and intended to take over. And he was in no position to stop it. He could feel the molemachs stitching his muscles and skin back together. Thankfully, there was no pain, only that prickling sensation along his entire back. He needed a few moments to pull himself together, and his armor and Rapidan would protect him from anything she tried. "Excuse me," he told her, then blanked his armor so she couldn't see in, switching it to tactical mode.

The chaos of the CIC became the chaos of Rapidan's flight through Tocci III's upper atmosphere. Below him, he could see the ship's light gray representation, indicating the ship's camouflage was active, though wrapped in the light blue of energy shields that would make that camouflage pointless. Red tracks above and around him from enemy missiles, and yellow tracks of SIM-3 interceptors and Archer close-in-defense systems, showed the battle still raged. Euphrates was behind and to Rapidan's left, the two Djinn-class heavy cruisers to his right. Demos and three of the massive assault ships trailed, while Phobos was still in two pieces, though each was under power and flattened to aid atmospheric flight. Three dozen green triangles indicated the positions of his combat space patrol, the spacecraft above them like an umbrella tilted forward against a driving rain. They'd moved closer to aid the task force's defense.

Ray shrank that view to a tactical representation of Tocci III and the Shipyards. The four fabricators still sat at their moorings as if nothing had happened, the launch window for the pods down to fourteen minutes. The Cavalry on the surface were on the move again. What surprised him was a large green triangle labeled "TF Hammer" just ten million kilometers away. Sun's fleet. Or what was left of it: fifty-one ships according to its tag, exactly half the number he'd arrived with. A second green triangle labeled "TF Shadow" with nine ships, including Roanoke, Captain Chelius' ship, was moving to join Hammer, once again proving there was no justice in the universe.

As if conjured by his examination, Sun's image formed before Ray. No unveiling this time, no show, just there, white uniform, golden sash, and dark eyes. "Captain Rhoades, status?" he asked without preamble.

Dall's image appeared in a window to Ray's lower right, obviously invited by Sun. Ray privately added Kamen, Ecuum, Sal, Chaaya—who was unhurt, thank goodness—and Gen Tel, who was also unhurt. "Rapidan has suffered moderate damage," he reported to Sun, keeping up the appearance of compliance, "but will be combat ineffective for another ten minutes. Euphrates and

Demos have suffered minor damage. Phobos is heavily damaged and is out of the fight. First Cavalry Squadron should reach Tocci City in about forty minutes, and I estimate another forty minutes to capture the Headquarters Complex. I've recalled Second, Third, and Fourth Cavalry Squadrons and we should be able to assault the fabricators ahead of schedule after they are rearmed and refitted."

Sun listened without reaction until Ray mentioned assaulting the fabricators. His dark eyes narrowed. "Good," he said. "Task Force Hammer will cover the assault. Detach Euphrates and its spacecraft to rejoin my fleet. Transfer Captain Dall to Euphrates."

Dall's mouth fell open and her eyes widened in surprise. *Admiral?* she asked on their private channel. *You don't want me to take command?*

No, Captain Dall, Sun replied, his words carried to Ray through Tzu. *I need you here. Rhoades is of no further use to us.* Sun continued his instructions to Ray as if that conversation had not happened. "Captain Rhoades, Task Force Anvil will support the assault on the Headquarters Complex."

"He is trying to keep you away from the fabricators, Captain Rhoades," Gen Tel said on their private channel, "in the mistaken belief he can take control of them once the Cavalry captures them."

If he only knew, Ray thought ruefully. "Yes, Admiral," was what Ray said.

Sun cut the communication.

That still left the problem of Serenna. She hadn't jumped back to Tocci III even though Sun had. Knowing her, she no doubt intended to consolidate her fleet and recover her missiles. She knew the timeline as well as they did. She could afford to take that time. He had no such luxury. Only twelve minutes remained to the launch window.

Sun had given him a gift of sorts, though, although it came at the cost of a battlecarrier. Dall would be gone.

Ray switched his environment back to standard mode. Rapidan's Combat Information Center had regained its former appearance, the loss of thirty-one percent of the ship's mass, almost 92,000 metric tons, not apparent to the crew in the CIC. He gathered his officers: Kamen, Ecuum, and Sal as constructs, Chaaya and Dall physically present. "Captain Dall," Ray began, "report to Euphrates. Rapidan will provide conveyance for you and your belongings."

She glared at him, all previous attempts at manipulation gone. She'd wanted command, and her twisted mind was blaming him for her loss. Then that haughty disdain returned. She stared down her beak nose at him, obviously not expecting to see him again, and taking comfort in the thought. Without a word, the deck beneath her liquified and she sank into it.

"Good riddance to bad rubbish," Ecuum growled, spitting on the deck where she'd disappeared before it could solidify again. "Still think we should've fed her to the ship. People like her have a bad habit of turning up again."

Ray silently agreed, but his concern now was capturing the fabricators and safeguarding his people. He looked to the deck, but the boy with the blue eyes calling for his mother was gone.

Murderer.

"Change of plan," he told his officers. "Ecuum, Sal, Chaaya, and I will pilot the pods. Kamen, you will command the task force."

"Sir?" she asked, confused, as if she'd done something wrong and was being punished.

Ray adopted the fatherly tone he often used with her. It wasn't a stretch; She *was* like a daughter to him. She was also a gifted fleet commander, and his obvious successor should something happen.

"Kamen, as we speak, Serenna is likely consolidating her fleet and recovering her missiles, with every intention of jumping here and finishing us off. That will take her anywhere from half an hour to an hour, depending on how many of her munitions she wants to recover. It will take about two and half hours for us to capture the fabricators. There is no one better suited to support and recover the First Cavalry Squadron than you."

"But. . . ," she started, then stopped herself. "Yes, sir."

He smiled at her. She really would make a great fleet commander someday. Hopefully, it wouldn't be today. "If the situation gets bad, jump away. Don't worry about us. Find Bobby and my wife, and jump to Andromeda."

"I won't leave you behind. Sir," she added.

"The fleet and the revolution are more important than us," he told her gently. "Janus is still out there. Someone needs to stop it. If I'm gone, that someone is you."

Anguish brought a sheen to her chocolate brown eyes, the white of her sclera bright against her ebony skin. "Yes, sir."

"Rapidan," Ray said, "prepare the pods and move us to them. I'll keep a construct here in the CIC so the crew won't know I'm gone."

"Yes, Captain Rhoades," Rapidan's deep voice replied.

Ray took one last look around the CIC—and had the unnerving feeling that it was the last time he'd ever see it.

══ 41 ══

0314 UT, October 7, 3501
Tocci City, Tocci Star System: DAY 10

The 93 Tank crossed the uneven remains of the wall into Tocci City. Buildings smoldered and smoked, but the fires from whatever had struck the wall were largely out. If anyone was around, they didn't show themselves.

Dag used the waffle and the 93 Tank's sensors to scan for Rosita. She was in the city somewhere. He'd seen the direction she'd pointed at and could now see a wide side street leading diagonally to his right in that direction. He pulled up a map of the city and saw that the side street intersected the main boulevard leading to the Headquarters Complex. It wasn't the way he would've gone. Too obvious. But his daughter had not misled him. Not here. Not on the fabricator. He would trust her.

"Foxtrot-one-two, this is foxtrot-niner-three," Dag called First Sergeant Takeuchi on the Squadron net. "Over."

"Foxtrot-niner-three, this is foxtrot-one-two. Over."

It occurred to Dag that he hadn't checked specifically who'd survived the artillery barrage. He hadn't known before his call that Takeuchi was still alive. "Reform the Squadron into a staggered line and follow me. Over."

Takeuchi switched to a private channel. "Captain, that street leads to the main boulevard. It's likely to be heavily defended."

My daughter told me to go this way, he almost said. "Time is not on our side, First Sergeant. This is the way."

Takeuchi didn't respond. His silence, more than anything he could've said, spoke volumes about what he thought of Dag's course, but he was a professional and would follow orders. There was a time in their relationship when Dag would've asked his advice. Not now. Rosita had shown him the way and he would follow her, even into death. In death, he would be with his family again. Perhaps Takeuchi understood that. Perhaps he even agreed, knowing he would be with his wife, Keiko, again.

Lance slowed the 93 Tank as they moved down the street, Banshee Troop falling in behind them staggered on either side of the street, the survivors of 1st Squadron behind Banshee. Lance was careful, flowing the tank's liquified outer tread around debris to avoid visibly dislodging any of it or leaving a trail through the ash and soot. Their active camouflage might make the tank itself invisible to people and sensors, but any unusual movement in the environment could reveal them.

Two kilometers in, they reached the main boulevard, four lanes in either direction leading straight to the Headquarters Complex in the distance, its blue-glass structure darkened by the pall of smoke and dust hanging over the city. Lance kept the tank in the second lane from the sidewalk to their left. Their sensors detected no heat signatures from people in any of the buildings and shops that lined the boulevard. The city did have underground shelters. If the people were smart, that's where they'd be.

An explosion tore out the base of a six-story building to their left. The building tottered for a second before collapsing, spilling burning wallboard, furniture, and other consumables across the boulevard. The timing couldn't have been a coincidence.

"Careful, Lance," Dag said. "The Gen must have pressure sensors in the street."

Truth was, there was nothing they could do about that.

With great care, Lance flowed the 93 Tank up and over the debris of the collapsed building. They reached the other side without dislodging so much as a pebble.

But their relief was short lived.

Their tank had smothered the fire in its wake.

"Lance, get us out of here!"

Too late. The boulevard ahead opened into a wide traffic circle. At the far end were three boxy black shapes. *Tanks.*

"Gunner—center tank—main gun—HEAT!"

"Up," Lance squeaked.

"Fire."

"On the way."

Heat pulsed through the 93 Tank. Surreal night turned to bright day as the High-Explosive Anti-Tank round's antimatter warhead blew the center tank apart. Darkness had barely settled in again before Lance lined up the next tank.

A soldier jumped through the skin of the tank, waving a white t-shirt as he ran. Other soldiers followed, running from both surviving tanks.

"Cease fire." Dag said, trying to puzzle out the sudden surrender. The fleeing tank crews wore no battle armor and were obviously Naturals from their sun-bleached uniforms of the same variety as those worn by the soldiers back at the bunkers.

Suddenly, in a large park to their right straddling the traffic circle, an entire armored formation in neat rows appeared out of thin air. People—Naturals—emerged from the vehicles waving t-shirts, dirty rags, or bare hands in the air.

Rosita peaked out from behind a Serpens Infantry Fighting Vehicle. *Hi, Papí! I see you.*

Her dress had changed to the dark blue "sailor outfit" Maria would make her wear to formal functions. Rosita hated that dress, and would often purposely get it dirty so she wouldn't have to wear it. While Dag sympathized—he didn't much care for the dress, either, preferring the white dress with the pink trim—Maria ran their household. Rosita grabbed at the Serpens as if she intended to climb on top of the infantry fighting vehicle. He had to stop her before she dirtied her dress or she would get into so much trouble.

"Get down from there before your mother sees," Dag told her.

"Sir?" Lance asked.

"Nothing," he said quickly. Dag halted the column. "Keep a sharp eye, Lance. I'm going to see what this is all about."

"Careful, sir."

Dag grabbed his KIL-2 assault rifle and stepped out of the 93 Tank. Rosita was gone. Behind the Serpens? Somewhere else in the park? He didn't know. He had to find her.

As he approached the nearest Natural soldier, a first lieutenant, he switched his armor to an urban camouflage pattern so they could see him. Almost immediately, the lieutenant walked cautiously toward him, his hands raised to show he was unarmed.

"Captain?" he asked tentatively. Dag nodded, still weary despite Rosita's presence.

"Boy are we glad to see you, sir," the lieutenant said. Relief washed over the young officer, and he took Dag's hand to shake it. Dag yanked his hand back, but it didn't stop the lieutenant. "We were getting worried, sir. Afraid the Gen had stopped you. We won't fight for them. No Natural will. But we were scared they'd got you. It's really good to see you guys, sir. Really good."

Dag held up his hands in a gesture for silence. He wanted only one thing. "Have you seen a little girl?"

The lieutenant looked at him strangely. "Captain, they evacuated all the civilians to the residential sector. Northeast quadrant." The lieutenant pointed behind him to the left of the Headquarters Complex.

Dag looked around the park, peeking around what was at least a battalion's worth of armored vehicles and crew. He remembered from the mission briefing that an entire division defended the city. This was only a small part of that. Where were the rest? He also didn't see Rosita anywhere, and it wasn't like he could go looking behind every vehicle. *No matter*, he tried to reassure himself. *When I need her, she will come.*

In his memory, he wiped a tear from her cheek.

"Everything will be okay. I promise. And soon we'll be in our new home."

She looked up. "On the blue planet you told me about, with the pretty flowers?"

"Yes. And you and I will go pick all the flowers we can carry."

"When will we get there, Papi?"

"Soon, Mihita. Soon."

Death would come for him soon. Then he would be with her. That left one thing undone. "Where are the Gen, Lieutenant?"

"Well, sir," he said, his words spilling out so fast they blended into a single, continuous sound. "They've all retreated into the HQ. They didn't want no part of the fight. No, sir. They left us to fight for them, but we won't fight. We won't."

Dag repeated his silencing gesture. "Can you get us into the Headquarters Complex?"

The lieutenant looked away as if afraid to disappoint Dag. "No, sir. I'm sorry, sir. They don't let us in there. They don't trust us."

With good reason, Dag thought, but kept the thought to himself. "Where's the rest of your division?"

"There's a battalion, like ours, guarding every traffic circle leading to the Headquarters Complex," he said, pointing as if they could see. "The artillery is in the residential section and around the Headquarters."

Dag consulted the map and saw one more traffic circle on their way to the Headquarters complex. He still had artillery of his own. To the lieutenant, he asked, "Can you fight?"

"Uh, they, uh, didn't give us any ammunition, sir. Sorry, sir."

Dag stepped back from the lieutenant. The Gen had left them here to die. A distraction.

Shit!

Dag turned and ran for the 93 Tank, diving into it headfirst just as a crackling sound spread across the park behind him like strings of firecrackers.

"Get us out of here, Lance! *Drive!*"

"Yes, sir!" Lance said as she kicked the 93 Tank into high gear, speeding down the boulevard, Banshee and the rest of 1st Squadron following.

Dag rotated his environment back toward the park. White antimatter cluster munitions, mixed with bright blue plasma rounds, sparkled across it like a firework show gone horribly wrong. The small explosions consumed the park, the entire traffic circle, and most of the boulevard, catching a few of Couatl Troop's Serpens in the open.

As suddenly as it started, the attack ended. In the park, fires raged. A few wounded, bodies charred and smoking, managed to crawl through the carnage, but most of the soldiers lay dead. Burnt body parts littered the ground. A spark of human compassion flared within Dag. For just an instant, he was back in the warmth of their little church in Quepos, praying to God for the soul of a village man killed in a fishing accident when Dag was a child. He'd barely known the man, but he'd cried and prayed just the same.

But God had abandoned him, all of them, just like he'd abandoned those soldiers in the park.

The spark of compassion died as quickly as it had formed. The Gen had killed those people, used them like they were nothing. The Gen planned to kill them all. That virus Major Kenyon—dead now—had told them about. *Janus.*

The Gen were an abomination. If God wouldn't destroy them, *he* would. He would bleed them. And when the last drop of blood from the last Gen spilled from its lifeless body, then, only then, would he find peace.

"Slow down, Lance," he ordered. "The Gen may have more traps ahead."

"Yes, sir," she said, clearly shaken.

The buildings changed as they moved closer to the Headquarters Complex, still fifteen kilometers distant, becoming taller, fancier, the kind lawyers and bankers and businesspeople would use. Their waffle proceeded the 93 Tank, scanning the buildings for signs of life or weapons. If there were people here, they were in shelters or basements.

"Identified—heat transient!" Lance yelled. "Main gun— HEAT—up!"

Dag snapped his head to the target, a building to their front left with a "Police" sign on its front. He didn't see what Lance saw but trusted her judgment. "Fire."

"On the way!"

Heat washed over him as the main gun fired. Less than a second later, the round struck an invisible object in front of the police station and exploded. Nearby structures burst into flame, feeding a fast-rising mushroom cloud. Secondary explosions ripped the enemy Serpens apart as stored ammunition cooked off.

This one had ammunition.

Gen.

Lance gave the burning Serpens a wide berth. As they rounded the other side, Dag glimpsed a heat signature through a first-floor doorway of what was obviously a government building. "Right side—first floor doorway—"

"Can't identify," Lance said. "Oh, wait. I got 'em." She hesitated. "You better take a look at this, sir."

Someone had cracked the door open and stuck a white shirt out, waving it. Three heat signatures stood behind the door, including the one waving the shirt.

"Slow down, Lance. Watch for an ambush."

Dag steered the waffle to about ten meters from the door and channeled his voice through it. "Inside the building. Come out with your hands behind your heads and lie down in the street with your legs spread apart."

At first, nothing happened. Heat signatures betrayed the three gesturing to each other, arguing from the looks of it. Dag amplified the waffle's auditory sensors and heard a male and a female arguing with another male. Finally, they seemed to reach a consensus and the door opened. Three figures in business suits walked cautiously into the street, casting nervous glances about. When one of those faces looked directly at Dag, he froze.

Gen!

He selected the tank's plasma cannon and swung the sights around to the three figures, centering the cross hairs on the head of one male and—

"Captain!"

Something moved to block his field of view. Annoyed, Dag looked to the speaker and saw Takeuchi in his battle armor standing in front of the 93 Tank. Realizing the cross hairs lay squarely between Takeuchi's eyes, Dag released the weapon and said to Lance, "Stay alert." He grabbed his assault rifle and stepped through the tank to the street.

"They might have information we need, Captain," Takeuchi said, blocking Dag's path to the Gen.

How had he known?

Dag flashed back to the fabricator, Gen prisoners lined up on one side of the passageway, his troopers with their assault rifles lined up opposite them, preparing to fire. If Rhoades hadn't stopped him. . . .

Wrapped in their battle armor with camouflage active, the Gen hadn't noticed them yet. Dag gestured to Takeuchi. "Go ahead, First Sergeant."

Dag didn't tell him that he intended to kill these Gen, useful information or not. Every Gen was an abomination. Every last one of them deserved death. For Maria. For Rosita. For his unborn son. For the soldiers back in the park. For the whole fucking human race! As Takeuchi approached the Gen, Dag laid his finger beside the trigger of his assault rifle.

"Who are you?" Takeuchi asked, his camouflage still active so they couldn't see him.

A sickening "Pock" sound echoed from the building's wall. Takeuchi spun like a child's doll and fell heavily to the ground. Dag tracked back along the path of the round and spotted a Gen in a second-floor window. Without thinking, his cross hairs centered on the Gen's face and he squeezed off three rounds. The Gen's head blew apart, filling the air with a fine red mist.

More small-arms fire broke out, coming from the top floors of buildings on both sides of the boulevard. An ambush. Dag heard Lance open fire with 93 Tank's KIL-202 30mm anti-personnel gun. Other Banshee Troop units also opened fire. But Dag focused his attention on Takeuchi, calling up his medical readout. A kinetic round had pierced Takeuchi's armor, striking his right breast above his nipple, breaking three ribs and puncturing his lung. Not fatal. "Take it easy, Yoshi," Dag told him. "You'll be fine."

"Take care of them . . . Captain," Takeuchi said through a froth of blood, quickly absorbed by his armor. "Don't let hate consume your soul." He grabbed Dag's wrist, his grip surprisingly firm. A rasping cough cut off further words.

Dag reached under Takeuchi's body, flowing his armor between it and the ground. "You can do that yourself. Your molemachs will have you up and around in a few minutes." Bending at the knees, he lifted Takeuchi, intent on carrying him to the nearest armored vehicle. He spotted a Serpens and stepped into the street toward it.

Dag didn't hear the round. An electric pain tore through his left shoulder, spinning him around. A sinking sensation reached up and seemed to drag him bodily to the ground. He dropped Takeuchi. He tried to rise, to help Takeuchi, but he couldn't move. A medical readout popped up in his environment. It showed extensive tissue damage on a line from this left shoulder to the left side of his spine. His armor immobilized him while molemachs thoroughly inspected his spinal cord for damage.

The sound of small-arms fire faded to sporadic bursts. The last of Dag's pain faded, leaving only a dull throbbing in its wake. After an interminable wait, his molemachs finally released his armor and he turned his head. Takeuchi lay about a meter away, his face frozen in a strangely peaceful expression.

No.

Opening Takeuchi's medical readout confirmed Dag's worst fear. The backside of his head was gone, blown off. A head shot was a killing shot. No recovery possible. He looked at Takeuchi's face, at the peace he saw there. The eyes stared back, unseeing, yet compelling, as if Yoshi Takeuchi had finally found what he was looking for. That peace called to Dag. He could see Maria and Rosita holding hands, smiling, beckoning to him. . . .

No! Not yet. Not until the Gen were dead. Then, maybe, he could find peace. They could find peace.

Dag stood, oblivious to the warnings his armor flashed within his environment. He spotted the three Gen lying motionless in the street with their hands wrapped protectively around their heads, their heat signatures and pulsing hearts showing they were still very much alive.

"You three. Sit up with your hands behind your heads." When the Gen didn't move, he shouted, "NOW!" He adopted an urban camouflage pattern so the Gen could see him—and the assault rifle he carried. He walked up and kicked the nearest male in the ribs.

The male Gen grunted in pain and sat up. The others followed slowly. The male Gen he'd kicked stared at him defiantly, as if daring him to do his worst. He wore expensive clothes and smelled of equally expensive cologne. The female looked just as determined, but also a little scared. She had short-cut hair and a muscular figure. Dag pegged her as military or police, possibly even an officer. Probably—he amended—considering Gen were rarely anything else. The other male, despite the perfect proportions that characterized Gen, looked pale and thin. A technician or something. His hands trembled.

He'll be the one to break.

Dag pointed his assault rifle at the head of the defiant male. "How do I get into the Headquarters Complex? How many Gen are defending it?"

"Go fuck yourself, *Nat!*" The Gen tried to spit but his mouth was apparently too dry.

Anger, hatred, and rage burst through Dag like lightning. Takeuchi's last peaceful expression joined with his daughter's frozen scream and the charred and smoking remains of defenseless soldiers in a park. A cold smile twisted his lips. The last of his emotions, his humanity, flickered out.

He stared at the defiant Gen male, centered his cross hairs between the Gen's eyes, and squeezed his finger. The Gen's perfect head disintegrated under the impact of the kinetic slug. His body flopped forward, blood pouring from the stump of his neck, pooling at Dag's feet. The female flinched, then her eyes hardened. She lifted her head, her expression one of contempt. Her thin male companion looked at the headless body in horror.

"How do we get into the Headquarters Complex?" Dag asked her. "How many Gen are defending it?"

She said nothing. Just stared at him. Defiant. Hateful. Dag sighted his weapon and fired. Her headless body fell over, splashing its blood onto the last Gen, who looked up at Dag with wide, terror-filled eyes. "Please! Please, please don't kill me! Please!" His lower lip trembled.

Dag pointed the muzzle of his weapon between the Gen's eyes. "Can you get us in?"

The Gen sniffled. A tear struck the pavement. The smell of urine tainted the air. So much for the superior race. "Yes."

42

Serenna sat at her desk in her cabin, a bulb of fresh coffee in her hand, bulkhead displays tracking both her fleet status and the battle. They had recovered just over five thousand of their Novas, enough to fully rearm every one of her surviving ships. It was time to rejoin the battle.

So why was she hesitating?

Gen do not run.

Never in her experience, or in Combat Command Nurturing, had any Gen ever run from a fight. Genetic engineers carefully controlled hormone and neurotransmitter levels to suppress strong emotional responses to stimuli. Twenty-two years of targeted Nurturing trained Gen from birth for their assigned role. No Gen should ever succumb to the level of fear that would lead to desertion. Some fear was healthy. Controlled fear sharpened senses and reaction times, and helped prevent foolish, emotional mistakes. Uncontrolled fear was for Naturals, not her people.

Or so she had thought.

It did not help that, after Chengchi's escape through Tigris Battlegroup, that her crew, including Scadic, had looked upon her with horror—and fear—at her destruction of the fleeing cruiser. Shooting deserters was hardly a new military tactic, and it had worked. But it was a tactic no Gen, to her knowledge, had ever used on another Gen. Because it had never been necessary before.

I am procrastinating.

Truth was, she admitted to herself as she sipped her coffee, she had lost confidence in her own forces. The fighting ahead would be hard and brutal. She needed to know she could rely on her commanders to follow her orders, regardless of the cost to them personally.

She keyed the intercom. "Captain Scadic, plot a jump for Solaris and Indus Battlegroups two-five million kilometers below the fabricators, opposite Chengchi's jump point. Launch spacecraft immediately after transition."

"Yes, Fleet Admiral," he responded, as dutiful as ever. As if nothing had happened. She could sense the control he exerted to maintain that fiction.

Serenna finished her coffee and touched the bulb to her desk, where Solaris reabsorbed it. The jump point she had selected would put her close enough to defend the fabricators but far enough away to avoid any ambush from Chengchi's sixty surviving ships. With full magazines, the 167 ships of Solaris and Indus Battlegroups were more than a match for Chengchi's and Michael's forces. If Michael planned a boarding action against the fabricators like he had done at Tomb, he would fail.

Michael would know that.

So, what was he planning this time? She did not want to underestimate him. Not again. Try as she might, though, she could not envision any strategy Michael could use to capture four fully armed fabricators, even with Chengchi's help.

That was another reason, she realized, that she hesitated. Michael had proven he could accomplish what should be impossible.

That word again. *Impossible.*

Michael had got into her head, making her doubt herself. That was another thing she had once thought impossible.

With no answer to Michael, or her own doubts, Serenna departed her cabin and walked the short distance to Solaris' Combat Information Center, stepping through the plain gray bulkhead into the sixty-meter-diameter space just as her battlegroups jumped. The universe seemed to squeeze her down to an infinitesimal point before exploding her outward. Pain arced through her nervous system, quickly suppressed by her molemachs, and she swallowed against the taste of blood in her mouth, slight though it was.

She raised the dais with the replica of her command chair just outside the sand table and sat down, adopting the casual pose that had suited her so well over the years. At its center, the sand table showed the progress of Michael's assault on the Headquarters Complex at the center of Tocci City, pressure sensors in the road indicating armored vehicles within fifteen kilometers of the Complex. Remarkable. It should have been impossible—that word again—for a regiment of cavalry to breach Tocci City, yet Michael taking his task force into Tocci's atmosphere to provide direct support to his ground forces, decimating the city's defenses, had opened the way for those forces to advance. No Gen would have done that, she now realized.

Doubt again crept into her mind. The climax of a battle that would determine the fate of the Five Galaxies was hardly the time to doubt her people. Or herself. But her Nurturing, and Gen Alyn's mentoring, had taught her to accept what was, not reality as she wished it to be.

Focus on the now, Gen Alyn whispered to her nine-year-old self in her memory. She had to destroy Chengchi, and deny Michael his prizes. Nothing else mattered.

Ignoring the glances from her crew, she stood up and walked into the sand table. She kept the oversized view of Tocci City depicted at its center. The ground forces would find no prisoners, or anything else of value, in the Headquarters Complex. Imperial Intelligence had removed the prisoners, including Michael's daughter, back to Olympus before the battle. Above Tocci City, Michael's task force was again lost to sensors after its firing run through Tocci's atmosphere, its whereabouts unknown, though she suspected Michael would remain in orbit to recover his ground forces. He would not leave his forces behind. And, how else could he assault the fabricators?

About halfway to the edge of the sand table lay the clumpy ring of the Tocci Shipyards. Chengchi had jumped ten million kilometers above the fabricators, represented in the sand table as four yellow cylinders. The red sphere showing where Chengchi's ships could have moved by now extended beyond the fabricators. She knew he would remain close to his prizes, but not so close as to risk destruction. Chengchi wanted those fabricators, but he wanted to be alive to use them against Olympus. She walked over and grabbed the sphere, shrinking it to an area within one million kilometers of where his fleet had jumped.

"Captain Scadic," she called. "Drift-launch two thousand Novas, mix of Brilliant Pebbles and Mark Fifteen warheads with two sets of boosters, and one hundred RJ-15s, to this area." She indicated the shrunken sphere. "Vector two squadrons of fighters and two squadrons of fighter/bombers to this same area." She pointed to the center of the sand table. "Drift-launch five hundred Novas, same loadout, to Tocci Three. Set course, Solaris and Indus Battlegroups, two-eight-zero ascent five-zero, speed two hundred." That would place her fleet roughly between Chengchi and Tocci III, the perfect position to intercept Michael.

"Yes, Fleet Admiral," Scadic said as he executed the orders.

She walked back to her command chair, radiating confidence for the many eyes that followed her. If she were correct, and her commanders followed her orders, the rebellion would end in the next few hours.

If she was not, or they did not. . . .

Serenna settled into her command chair, crossing her legs causally and tracing a small circle on the armrest with her right index finger. Settling in to wait. She needed to see what Michael would do before she boosted her missiles. She still did not trust that he had not developed some new tactic to capture the fabricators. That was why she retained half of her missiles. She did not like surrendering the initiative like this, but patience and adaptability would win her the day.

Minutes passed.

With nothing else to watch, she followed the progress of the cavalry forces as they approached the Headquarters Complex. A running gun battle broke out a kilometer shy of the Complex itself. The rebel advance seemed focused on a loading dock on the Complex's east side.

"Captain Scadic, get me the base commander," she ordered.

"Yes, Fleet Admiral."

A construct rose from the deck before her, below her dais, a Gen Imperial Army one-star general. She would have preferred an Imperial Marine officer. This Gen continually darted his eyes to something she could not see, no doubt his own feed showing the rebel advance. He looked scared. "Commander, status?"

"Fleet Admiral." His eyes shifted between whatever he watched and her. "We have a hundred soldiers—" he swallowed— "Gen soldiers, not those cowardly Naturals." As he said 'cowardly,' Serenna watched his eyes shift back and forth again, and she wondered if he was aware of his own fear. "We have no heavy weapons," he continued. "If they breach the perimeter, I am not sure we can hold them. We have a thousand Gen here, mostly civilians. We need your help."

"I have rebels to deal with out here, Commander." The Headquarters Complex also held no military value from her perspective, but she was not about to tell him that. "I suggest you arm your civilians," Serenna told him. "And yourself."

The general's eyes widened in disbelief. "But, Fleet Admiral, you cannot mean that."

Serenna cut the connection to the general, the construct collapsing back into the deck, but she kept the feed from inside the complex, opening it in her battle armor's environment so her crew would not see it.

The fighting reached the loading docks. Serenna could not see the actual vehicles, but could track the rebel's progress by the main gun rounds and small arms fire into adjacent buildings at defenders who were equally invisible to her. A Gen, a technician, suddenly appeared in the driveway leading up to the loading docks, though where he had come from she could not say. His clothes were covered in blood. Nervously, he walked up a staircase and put his hand on the structure. A large rectangle of material liquefied and flowed away into the walls. The Gen glanced back—and his head vanished in a cloud of fine red mist. His body flopped onto the loading dock, pouring its lifeblood over the light gray floor. The brutality of it startled her.

A vehicle became partially visible, a tank, where its material touched the material of the Headquarters Complex. It flowed through the opening into the warehouse beyond. Defenders opened fire on it from covered positions within the warehouse even though their small arms could not penetrate its armor. The tank's main gun fired, the antimatter round consuming long rows of bulky containers and the dozen or so defenders behind them. A machine railgun tore through other defenders to the tank's right, the slugs exploding through their battle armor, while a plasma cannon burned through other defenders on the tank's left.

The enemy tank fire abruptly stopped, though Gen soldiers still defended the warehouse and the passageways beyond. First one, then several, then dozens of rebel soldiers switched their battle armor to an urban camouflage pattern, pouring into the warehouse, firing from the hip at defenders they could not see. Serenna was not a ground forces officer and did not understand the tactic. Why reveal themselves?

She could see the Gen soldiers through the Complex's internal feed, firing at the charging rebels, hitting some, then backing up, still firing, as the rebels, who outnumbered them now at least five to one, got closer. The rebels fired into the heads of every downed Gen soldier, dead or wounded, that they discovered. No mercy. The Gen hesitated, as if realizing they could not win, then turned and ran. Just like her own ship captains had done.

Gen do not run! Serenna wanted to scream at them.

The rebels charged even harder, firing, hitting Gen soldiers in the back. The surviving soldiers seemed to understand there was no escape. They stopped and turned their armor white: the universal sign of surrender.

The rebel commander held up his right hand, fist clenched. His soldiers slowed, stopping only when they reached where he stood. Slowly, deliberately, the rebel commander stowed his assault rifle on his back and pulled out a Main Gauche dagger. His soldiers seemed to understand and stowed their own assault rifles before pulling out their own daggers. Serenna could hardly believe what she saw. The rebel commander walked purposefully toward the nearest white-armored Gen soldier, the Gen's hands raised high over his head. Without any hesitation, the rebel commander pulled his arm back and drove his dagger into the chest of the Gen, twisting it, then pulling it out. Bright red blood spouted from the wound. This puzzled her until she remembered that Main Gauche daggers carried Special D, injecting it into their targets. Injected into a person, the Special D would destroy molemachs, preventing healing. It would also damage or destroy battle armor.

The Gen soldier stood for a horrifying instant, an expression of pure surprise on his face, before toppling over, dead. The other rebels took their cue and charged the surrendered Gen. In less than a minute, all the Gen soldiers were dead. The word 'brutal' did not begin to describe the repeated thrusts of daggers into unresisting bodies.

The deaths did not sate the rebel's bloodlust. They had the layout of the Headquarters Complex and headed for the command bunker, where, unknown to them, a thousand Gen civilians had taken shelter. It reminded Serenna of the civilian starliner and the Madu slithering relentlessly on the attack, seeking out victims who were powerless to stop them. And she finally understood. These rebel soldiers must be the same rebels who had escaped Ndjolé Spaceport. The same soldiers whose families had been on the starliner.

This was revenge.

"Fleet Admiral," the base commander pleaded, injecting himself into her environment, "you must help us!"

"Help yourself, Commander," she responded. "Fight."

Serenna had earned her moniker "The Serpent" from the cold and calculating way she approached every situation, but even to her ears her reply sounded dismissively callous. Truth was, there was no way she *could* help, and this Gen was an offense to her entire race. Such Gen *should* die.

It was a . . . Darwinian thought. One she had had before, she realized. Gen prided themselves on their engineered society, on casting aside evolutionary pressures as chaos and disorder. Every Gen knew their place in society and was optimized for that role. But if that were the case, why had Gen optimized for combat panicked and fled? It did not make sense.

The rebels reached the command bunker, stabbing their Main Gauche daggers into the wall, injecting the macromolecular material with Special D. The wall liquified where they stabbed it, thinning. The Gen inside cowered closer together. It reminded Serenna of the Natural families on the starliner cowering behind their cabin doors. For all the centuries of genetic engineering, her people were not as far removed from their evolved source material as they liked to believe.

A hole opened in the wall as the material lost cohesion, the hole widening, joining other holes until nothing stood between the huddled Gen and the rebel soldiers. Terror and disbelief twisted Gen faces as it had the Naturals on the starliner when the snake-like Madu burned through their cabin doors. Like the Madu, the rebels moved into the command bunker, their urban camouflage as menacing as a Madu's black scales and glowing red eyes.

The rebels then did something she did not understand, at first. They removed their armor and dropped their assault rifles, standing before the cowering Gen civilians with only daggers in hand. The base commander, identifiable by his uniform, stepped forward with his hands in the air as more rebels pushed into the command bunker. A Natural Cavalry captain stepped forward to meet him. He did not waste energy on words or gestures, just grabbed the base commander's shoulder and drove his dagger into his chest, twisted it, pulled it down to open his abdomen, literally spilling his guts on the floor. Still holding the base commander upright, he withdrew his dagger and plunged it into his neck, slicing until the base commander's head separated from his body, which dropped to the floor with a splash of bright red blood. The rebel captain turned the head to look into its dead eyes, his lips pressing into a grim smile. The Gen civilians, who outnumbered the Naturals at least two to one, cowered back like sheep prepared for the slaughter.

"Fight!" Serenna mouthed.

They did not. They could not. They were not soldiers. Fighting was not in their DNA, quite literally.

The Natural captain released the head, which hit the floor with a sickening squish and hollow thud. As if it were a signal, the Naturals rushed forward by the dozens and hundreds. They stabbed. And stabbed. And stabbed. And stabbed. Some bodies stabbed so many times they fell apart, and always stabbed in the head to guarantee they could never be revived.

Serenna had forced herself to watch the Madu attack she had ordered against the four thousand civilians on the starliner—a commander must face the consequences of their orders—but nothing in her experience had prepared her for this. Bright red blood flowed ankle deep like water across the floor, splattered the walls, the ceiling. Natural soldiers even made a game of it, joking and laughing hysterically as they induced fountains of blood from severed arteries, kicking organs, cutting out hearts and tossing them, sometimes still beating, around like balls. This was why they had removed their armor, so they could feel everything they did.

A true orgy of blood.

Gen screamed, pleaded for mercy, as the families on the starliner had screamed and pleaded. The Madu had shown no mercy then. These Naturals showed none now. This was the consequence of her order at Earth. And, as at Earth, she forced herself to watch it until the end.

Bodies and parts of bodies, half-submerged in blood, littered the floor of the command bunker. Like a spell whose effect abruptly ended, the crazed expressions faded from the Naturals' eyes. They looked around in horror, as if not sure who had done such deeds. She picked out the Army captain as he walked back to his armor, blood-drenched dagger hanging loosely in his limp red hand. Before he donned his armor, she heard him mutter, "For you, Mihita."

Serenna closed the feed from the Command Center, her eyes slowly refocusing on Solaris' Combat Information Center. Scadic's construct stood before her, horror etched deep into his face. The base commander had pleaded for her help on an open channel, and had left it open.

Everyone had seen.

Shaken to her core, Serenna still had a fleet to command and a battle to win. The rebels had achieved their objective on the surface. Now they would turn to the fabricators.

She took a few seconds to confirm she appeared calm and poised, then called out, "Captain Scadic."

He snapped out of his distant gaze, turning to look at her as if seeing her for the first time. "Fleet Admiral?" he managed, just barely.

"Boost the Novas targeted on Chengchi's fleet," she ordered him, her voice purposefully relaxed.

"Ye—yes, Fleet Admiral."

Two thousand Novas fired their boost engines. It was a credit to Scadic that he carried out the order without delay. His haunted expression showed he had not fully recovered from the trauma of the massacre.

"Time," she asked him, though she could have just pulled up the tag in the sand table.

Again, no hesitation. In some things Gen *were* superior to Naturals. "Fourteen minutes, Fleet Admiral. Recommend we also boost our spacecraft."

Serenna nodded and the two squadrons each of fighters and fighter/bombers lit their engines.

The four fabricators in the sand table suddenly changed from yellow to orange. Scadic said, "Fleet Admiral, each fabricator is reporting a single hull breach."

"A single breach?" Serenna asked. *Michael.* "Not multiples?"

"No, Fleet Admiral." Scadic's construct studied something on the bridge that she could not see. "Confirming a single breach in each fabricator, but the captains cannot localize it. Whatever breached the hulls of each ship is using Invasive Macromolecular Dissemblers."

So, Michael *had* found a way to capture the fabricators here, and it was not the same boarding action he had used at Tomb. The entire attack on the surface had been a diversion. And, whatever had breached the fabricators was already inside them where she could not stop it.

Hmm.

Maybe she could not stop Michael. But she *could* stop the fabricators.

"Captain Scadic, redirect all missiles to attack the fabricators."

This time he did hesitate. "Fleet Admiral?"

"We cannot allow the rebels to capture those fabricators." Serenna did not hide the urgency in her voice. "We must destroy them. Quickly."

Scadic studied something out of her view. "With our missiles boosting for Admiral Sun's fleet, it will take thirty-two minutes to redirect and boost them to the fabricators, Fleet Admiral."

Was that soon enough? Would Michael capture them before that? "Captain Scadic, launch every missile we have. Leave nothing in reserve. Boost immediately after clearing the hull. Redirect our spacecraft. All of them. Those fabricators must not fall into Michael's hands. Solaris and Indus Battlegroups, course zero-nine-zero, ascent four-five, maximum acceleration."

Stealth did not matter. Survival did not matter. "The missiles headed for Tocci Three, too. And any spacecraft around Tocci Three that are still combat effective. Everything."

She had to stop Michael. The survival of her people depended on it.

═══ 43 ═══

Ray hadn't felt the transition as his pod penetrated the fabricator's hull. One instant he saw stars, the next only blackness. A white sphere appeared in his environment to show him the direction to the bridge. He piloted the pod, all 20,000 metric tons of it—larger than a Zambezi-class frigate—manually, refusing to give Rapidan and the SIL any control.

The flight controls were sluggish, the pod drifting to the right as if caught in a strong current. He steered the pod left to compensate. It moved too far and he steered it back right, centering the white sphere in front of him.

Nine minutes to the bridge. Much faster than Rapidan had predicted when it had first explained this plan. Something to do with using prodigious amounts of Special D. He fingered the translucent blue datarod with the Key in his left shirt pocket.

In the long transit to the fabricator, he'd watched on displays provided by the pod as Serenna jumped twenty-five million kilometers below the fabricators, her fleet immediately going silent. He'd tracked Admiral Sun's movements nine million kilometers above and starward of the fabricators through the live feed from Tzu. Sun hadn't reacted to Serenna's arrival, staying close to seize control of the fabricators as soon as Ray's cavalry captured them. Indeed, three assault ships closed on the fabricators with a squadron of cavalry aboard each, but they wouldn't reach the fabricators until twenty minutes after Ray and his people had freed them.

Kamen, still aboard Rapidan commanding Task Force Anvil, appeared in his environment. "Sir, First Cavalry Squadron has secured Objective Barad-dur. They report no prisoners found."

Ray's heart sank. *Jenny.* Serenna or Imperial Intelligence had relocated her from Tocci III. It was the obvious move, she was just too valuable to them as a hostage, but still, he'd hoped. "Thank you, Kamen. Recover the troopers ASAP. Jump away immediately once you have them. Find Bobby and my wife."

"Sir?"

"There's nothing more you can do here," he said gently, knowing she would not want to leave him behind. "Four fabricators are more than a match for Serenna's forces. We'll be okay. We'll join you as soon as we're able."

Kamen didn't hide the "like hell I'm leaving you behind" expression on her smooth ebony face. Still, she said, "Yes, sir."

She was about to cut the connection when she stopped, her brows furrowing. "Sir, something strange going on. You need to see this."

Several windows opened in Ray's environment, one showing the space around Tocci III where dozens of bright blue plasma points had appeared, missile engines and spacecraft engines to his practiced eye. Several of his spacecraft, suddenly presented with targets, fired SIM-3s and destroyed half a dozen enemy spacecraft. In another window, well over two thousand Novas boosted about halfway between Tocci III and the Shipyards, revealing a large fleet that itself lit engines, taking no care to hide themselves. By the numbers, it could only be Serenna's fleet. The final window showed Sun's fleet from Tzu's perspective, tracking some two thousand Novas in boost phase heading straight for it. Even as he watched, Sun's fleet jumped away.

A strong current pushed Ray off course. He compensated.

"Sir," Kamen said, "missiles and Serenna's fleet are targeting the fabricators."

What? Then he understood. *She knows we've breached the fabricators' hulls.* "Serenna is trying to destroy the fabricators before we can free them," he told Kamen. "Recover the Cavalry and get out of here."

It was a testament to Kamen's maturity that all she said was, "Yes, sir." Her image vanished.

The pod slowed as if encountering denser material. Ray could almost feel the currents outside, like the illusionary ocean when the SIL argued. A sudden chill shot through him, as if a great malevolence had woken to his presence. A percentage readout appeared, a large "96%" displayed in green. Something was attacking the pod, reducing its mass.

He pushed the pod to its maximum acceleration, fighting to keep the white sphere of the bridge, which had grown visibly larger, directly in front of him.

The green display continued to drop. 94%. 93%. 91%.

He could almost feel the ferocity of the struggle between the pod and the fabricator, between the invading organism and the body that fought to protect itself. Massive currents clashed and he no longer knew whether they were real or illusion.

88%.

Steering grew more difficult. Soon, it required all of Ray's concentration, all of his strength, to keep the bridge centered.

84%. 82%.

Was the white sphere of the bridge getting any larger? He could no longer tell.

The malevolence surrounding him deepened.

79%.

Was the pod even still moving?

74%.

Ray's muscles screamed. His heart raced. Molemachs pushed adrenalin into his blood. Currents attacked the pod from several directions at once. A warning chime sounded as the pod's mass fell below 60% and the display changed from green to yellow. Ray silenced the alarm. If the pod's mass dropped to around twenty percent, it would die, taking him with it.

58%.

The white sphere hung before him. Taunting him. Was it larger? Was he getting closer?

Why had Rapidan not warned him this was a possibility?

49%.

No, Ray heard clearly in his mind.

No, what? Rapidan?

No, the thought repeated.

46%.

The walls seemed to close in. Darkness pressed against him. Currents lashed. His battle armor leant its strength to his, trying to keep the white sphere centered.

42%. 41%.

Jenny. Would he ever see her again?

Jenny rushed out and threw her arms around him, holding him in a vice grip. At seven, her head already came up to the bottom of his ribcage. When had she gotten so big? She sniffled and it was obvious she'd been crying, too. They weren't used to hearing their parents fighting. Ray hugged her tight and stroked her long, brown-blond hair. "How ya doing, Munchkin?"

She squeezed him tighter.

38%.

Ghosts formed around Ray. First a few, then hundreds, then thousands. *Murderer,* they whispered.

This was it. This was the price. They had come to watch. Alive, they had no power over him. Dead . . . what would they do to him? Was this his Hell? Eternally tormented by those he'd killed?

34%.

Janus. He had to stop Janus. That's why he'd started the rebellion. That's why he'd done the things he'd done, killed. . . .

32%. 31%.

The display turned from yellow to red.

The white sphere changed to a white representation of the fabricator's bridge, a forty-meter square compartment with a square of consoles broken into four equal angles. At the center of the bridge was the U-shaped command console. The receptacle for the Key was there.

26%.

Without warning, the pod to his front opened into a large space, throwing him free. Ray slammed into a console in the outer square. Pain stabbed through his back. Sparks burst across his sight, flying in every imaginable direction.

Move!

Ray wasn't sure where the command came from. He grabbed the Main Gauche dagger off his left thigh while his right hand fished out the datarod in his chest pocket.

Hurry!

He scrambled over the console in the ship's microgravity, thankful for the molemachs blocking the pain from his back and repairing whatever damage had occurred there. There was enough gravity from the space dock and fabricator that it pulled him to the deck a meter shy of the command console.

He crawled along the deck toward it. Malevolence beat down upon him from every direction. He had no idea what it meant.

He reached the command console and pulled himself up, fumbling a bit before pushing the Key into the receptacle. It glowed a pure crystalline blue.

After a second, a deep, reverberating voice said, "You have ruined everything, human."

It was the last thing Ray had expected to hear.

"You're free," he told the SIL.

"We're dead," it responded, its voice so low it shook Ray's bones. "You will die with us. That was the bargain."

Ray heard them before he saw them, rasping scales on the fabricator's deck. The sound was an illusion. The black snakes only seemed to move across the deck, tracing S-patterns as they closed on him from every direction, red eyes burning with hate.

He backed away from the console, switching the dagger to his right hand. The Madu took their time, drawing the moment out. Everywhere he looked, they slithered closer. He swung at one that launched itself at his face, slicing it in two. The pieces sailed off, writhing as if in pain as the Special D from the dagger attacked their macromolecular material.

The victory was short lived. They attacked, biting at feet and legs, arms and chest and head, illusionary fangs sinking closer to his flesh, black noses glowing red as they burned through his battle armor.

50%. 40%. 30%.

A sharp pain tore into his right knee and it buckled. His armor lost cohesion and melted away into the deck. Someone screamed. He wondered briefly who it was.

"You can't have me!" Ray yelled. "You hear!"

He raised the Main Gauche dagger above him, gripping it with both hands.

When had he fallen to the deck?

With the last of his strength, he plunged the dagger into his chest. A horrible pressure crushed his heart. An awful scream ripped the air. Fire coursed through him as Special D flooded his body. Darkness lurked at the edge of his vision, but he was not alone. The ghosts had joined him, gathered in a patient circle, watching, waiting.

He fell into a long dark tunnel.

Murderer, the ghosts chorused, closing in around him.

And then there was nothing.

PART IV

Never let any Government imagine that it can choose perfectly safe courses; rather let it expect to have to take very doubtful ones, because it is found in ordinary affairs that one never seeks to avoid one trouble without running into another. . . .

—Nicolò Machiavelli

$=$ 44 $=$

Fleet Admiral Gen Serenna watched as her missiles closed on the fabricators, the first group still two minutes out, willing them to arrive before Michael freed them. The High Command would consider her actions treason, but in this instance *Gaman Politic* did not matter. Her position in "court" did not matter. All that mattered was the survival of her people.

The fabricators were the crown jewels of SIL power, the true power behind the throne. Control of the SIL meant control of the Five Galaxies. Fear of them ran to the marrow of the bone. Antitechnic propaganda in the Republic and Imperial propaganda now ingrained that fear beginning at the earliest of ages and reinforcing it through media and realities for the rest of people's lives. The SIL were the modern boogey men, the monsters in the shadows, the evil in the night. Solaris itself had put down several insurrections just by showing up. No shots fired.

The SIL needed the fabricators. They maintained the existing SIL among the Fleet, replenishing material lost to combat or simple wear and tear. Even SIL were not immune to radiation damage or the hazards of both near and deep space. They produced munitions and supplies. And, at the greatest need, they could produce new SIL, though even she shuttered at such a possibility.

Only eleven had survived the SIL Wars. Bonded. Enslaved. Michael had freed one. Now she needed to destroy these four before he could free them as well.

The four fabricators were still moored to the three asteroids joined in a dock line within the Shipyards, the massive cylindrical vessels above, below, and to either side, orange in the sand table to indicate something had breached their hulls. As she watched, her first missile volleys still a minute out, the fabricator above the asteroid dock changed from orange to red.

No.

Within the span of barely ten seconds the other three also changed from orange to red, from ally to enemy, from Bonded to free.

Michael had done it.

Worse, the fabricators, tied into their AFCIN network until the instant of their freedom, knew where her missiles and forces were. All four fabricators burst with bright red tracks, SIM-3 interceptors in staggering numbers, targeted precisely where her volleys approached. Not one of the twenty-five hundred missiles, the last of her Novas, reached their targets.

"Captain Scadic," she ordered, knowing her time to save the situation, if she could save it, was short, "Solaris and Indus Battlegroups, cease acceleration. Alter course three-one-zero dec one-zero. Randomize spacing."

"Yes, Fleet Admiral." Scadic's acknowledgement was calm, confident. He trusted she could master the situation. She hoped she would not disappoint him.

The fabricators began moving ponderously away from their asteroid dock. Massing a quarter the size of Earth's Moon each, it took a lot of thrust to overcome their inertia. She still had twenty-five hundred Novas: two thousand originally launched against Chengchi and five hundred launched to Tocci III. She also still had her spacecraft and almost one hundred spacecraft from Tocci City. She had no idea if that would be enough, but she had no choice but to try.

Odd. One of the fabricators had separated from the other three, heading toward her fleet. The fabricators had known where her fleet was and would know within a cone of uncertainty where it would be now. With each passing second, it became clearer that this fabricator intended to intercept her fleet.

"Captain Scadic, designate new target for the five hundred Tocci Three Novas." She indicated the lone fabricator approaching them.

"Yes, Fleet Admiral." He set the new target then looked to her, his manner uncertain. "Will it be enough?"

"I have no idea," she answered honestly. Normal warships had known layouts and vital systems within reach of the antimatter of a Nova's dual-bottle warhead. A fabricator's vital systems, except for engines and thrusters, were buried a hundred kilometers deep within its structure, and being a factory ship, it could quickly replace engines and thrusters.

Fifty of the five hundred Novas released Brilliant Pebbles, peppering the fabricator with absurdly small antimatter submunitions. The remaining 450 struck the fabricator's bow in six volley waves. The fabricator's bow blazed white, as if a small sun had ignited at its front, matter and antimatter annihilating each other. The white faded to glowing oranges and reds.

When he spoke, Scadic's voice was hushed, awed. "Fleet Admiral, sensors are reporting we destroyed twenty-one percent of the fabricator's mass. It is still under full acceleration and headed for us." The fabricator lit up with bright red tracks. "Fleet Admiral, Novas in boost phase. Thousands of them!"

Serenna spotted the other three fabricators moving in a tight formation toward Tocci III, no doubt to support Michael's strike force. She turned back to the lone fabricator bearing down on her fleet. Five hundred Novas, and they had only destroyed twenty-one percent of its mass. She could not stop or destroy all four fabricators, but she would deny Michael this one. "Captain Scadic, target all remaining weapons on this fabricator." It galled her to give the next order. "Spool up the Linear Star Drive. Set destination for Olympus Star System."

Michael had won. All she could do now was survive to fight another day. Not her, specifically. No doubt the High Command, and perhaps even the Emperor, would demand her death for this failure. But she could not throw away 169 SIL warships. Her people would need them.

Over two thousand Novas closed on the lone fabricator. She could not afford to stay and watch, as much as she would like to. "Captain Scadic, jump the fleet."

To his credit, knowing this meant defeat, Scadic said simply, "Yes, Fleet Admiral."

The universe shrunk to an infinitesimal point and then exploded outward. Serenna never got used to the taste of her own blood after a jump. "Captain Scadic, you have the conn. I will be in my cabin."

"Yes, Fleet Admiral," he said.

One more bulb of coffee, to wash the taste out of her mouth. It would likely be her last.

= 45 =

Captain Dagoberto Arias took Lance's pale hand in his own as he fought down a wave of nausea. She looked at him through swollen eyes and managed a weak smile from the medical bed within the S45 Combat Medical Treatment/Evac Vehicle (CMTEV). Like most of Banshee Troop, she suffered from acute radiation poisoning. Exposure to so many antimatter explosions and the harsh gamma rays they produced could overwhelm battle armor and molemachs. Not life threatening, but his troopers would need a few days of medical care back aboard Demos. As he swallowed against his own nausea, he realized that would apply to him as well.

"How are you, Lance?" Dag asked, because that's what commanding officers were supposed to ask. Where there should be feeling, empathy, there was only the Void, the black hole centered in his chest where his heart had once been.

She tried to focus on him through a medication-induced haze. "I'll be okay, sir," she managed, then mouthed, "Hoo-rah."

He tried a smile, and failed miserably. *I'm so tired.* "Rest," he told her, patting her hand gently. "Get better."

"Yes, sir," she whispered even as her eyes closed.

Dag reformed his armor, somehow needing its protection, and dismissed its warnings about his own radiation levels. Long strides carried him from the CMTEV to the loading dock where they'd first entered the Headquarters Complex.

The blood was gone.

When he'd donned his armor to report the capture of the Headquarters Complex, the armor had removed all the blood from his clothes and person, as if none of it had happened. And he wondered if it had. He felt . . . nothing. He'd killed Gen. Torn them apart. Waded ankle-deep through their bright red blood. Just like the Madu had done to his family.

He could remember it all.

Yet, he felt *nothing*.

Where are you, Mihita?

He hadn't seen her since the park. Maybe she was too scared by the things he'd done to come out. Maybe she didn't want to get her Sunday church dress dirty. Dag's lips pressed together as if a smile wanted to form. The church in Quepos was not grand in the style of the larger Roman Catholic cathedrals, but Maria had fussed over their appearance as if it were the Vatican itself. It was a simple wooden structure, painted white outside. It didn't even have a steeple. Inside, rows of pews made from local wood stood in two aisles before a table with a white cloth. A plain cross hung on the back wall. To one side was a small alter where candles cast a soft glow upon a figurine of the Blessed Virgin. Madre de Dios. Mother of God. The church was the center of village life, a place of worship and school, council, and meeting hall. He'd always felt warmth there, with his mother and father, brother and sisters, cousins, friends. And especially with Maria and little Rosita. Surely, God had watched over them.

Not that Dag was a saint. His mother cried every time the pastor led her Little Dagoberto home after some childish escapade, like the time he stole the chocolates for the piñata and ate himself sick, or the time he convinced Maria to stay out all night when they were nine. Maria's father had not let them play together for years after that, and had not forgotten it even as he walked her down the aisle at their wedding. Not until the birth of his granddaughter a year later did he finally shake Dag's hand.

Rosita. The entire village had turned out for her baptismal, a festival in the house of God that brought tears of love so strong that a father could not hold them inside. Dag had never known such happiness. Truly, God and the Virgin Mother had blessed them.

He had believed.

No longer. God had taken everything that meant anything to him. It was all a lie. God even denied him the satisfaction of revenge. Dag had killed Gen—*and he felt nothing!*

The sound of engines drew his attention. Heavy Equipment Transporters System craft were landing on a grassy clearing in front of the Headquarters Complex. Dag returned to his troopers to ensure they all got aboard, then boarded the last one himself, fatigue clawing at him, pulling him toward the darkness. He resisted. Not until his troopers were safe back aboard Demos.

The flight back was uneventful. He did notice one of the battlecarriers was missing from the task force, and Phobos was half the size it should've been. The vacuum heads had obviously had problems of their own. What he wasn't prepared for were the three mammoth shapes in a tight triangle in high orbit. One fabricator was impressive, terrifying. Three. . . .

Madre de Dios.

Rhoades.

Heat warmed the Void, surrounding it. Rhoades now had *four* Mothers of Demons, the same demons that had tried to exterminate humans before. No one man should have such power. *How. . . .?*

The HETS began their final approach to Demos. Strange. He never really thought about Demos, Banshee Troop's assault ship, as one of the demons. But it was. Collared. Enslaved. But still a demon. He still had no idea what Rhoades intended or where they were going beyond just "the Andromeda galaxy." What did that even mean?

Would Rosita be there? Or would she forever be lost to him?

Only death could free him. Only death could reunite him with her and her mother and his unborn son.

God had denied him even that.

Dag stepped through the hull of the HETS after it landed, his armor bonding him to the hangar's deck in the ship's microgravity. It was pandemonium. Spacers scrambled to gather the wounded and get them to medical wards. A short figure in a Cavalry dress uniform stepped through a green outline in the hangar bulkhead, spotted Dag, and came over to him.

"Good to see you, Captain Arias," Colonel Burress said, reaching out to shake Dag's hand but thinking better of it after looking at Dag's face. "I was just about to call you. Major Kenyon and his XO were killed in the battle. Until further notice, First Squadron is yours. You're frocked to Colonel."

Dag absorbed the information without feeling or comment. Darkness pulled at him, clouding his vision. Nausea rose again, his molemachs losing the battle against his own radiation sickness.

"You'll need an executive officer," Colonel Burress said. "Got anyone in mind?"

"First Lieutenant Scott Haley," Dag said without hesitation.

Burress frowned. "Isn't he an engineer? Not even Academy, if I remember correctly."

"He has battle experience," Dag replied, "which is a lot more than I can say for most Academy officers." It wasn't until he said it that Dag remembered Burress was an Academy grad.

Then he decided he didn't care.

"Well," Burress said, deflecting, "follow me. The senior staff is gathering to decide our next move."

"Rhoades," Dag said, though he hadn't meant to say it out load.

Burress stopped. Pain etched his hard face. "Captain Rhoades was aboard the fabricator Serenna destroyed. He's dead."

Dead?

God would deny him even this?

Dag deflated, his strength draining away. The man who'd led his family to slaughter was dead, and he still lived.

This was his Hell.

"Medic!" he heard Colonel Burress shout just before he passed out.

$$\Longrightarrow 46 \Longleftarrow$$

Serenna's shuttle landed on a small platform fifty kilometers outside the Imperial Palace, as it always had on her previous visits. The shuttle melted away into the platform, leaving her standing near the platform's center as it always had. The Solaris River, the namesake of her flagship, misted the air to the south. The jeweled light of Olympus' artificial rings arced high overhead. White minarets sprouted like blades of grass among a mushroom sea of golden domes all around her. Everything was as she remembered.

Nothing would ever be the same.

She returned in disgrace.

It was not lost on her that she returned to Olympus at twilight, the sun having just set, as her once rising star had just set. Golden domes that gleamed in the light of day were dull and uninspiring in the dwindling light. The white minarets faded into shadow, Olympia's dazzling city lights not yet in full effect. Even her normal Imperial Guard escort was absent. She was alone on the platform. The Emperor never left anything to chance. This was his message to her.

A chair formed and she sat down, crossing her legs causally, leaning slightly to the right to trace a small circle with her index finger on the chair's armrest. The chair accelerated along the open-air causeway connecting the landing platform to the main Palace complex, its passage unmarked by any imperfection in what appeared to be white marble but was actually macromolecular material, the same material that formed Solaris and the SIL.

As the wind whipped at her face and long black hair, she pondered her life's path, fully expecting that life to end shortly. She was the genetic legacy of Gen Kii, the greatest of all Gen War Leaders. Just before his death thirteen hundred years ago, he had set in motion a plan. Three hundred years ago, Geneers put that plan into practice, crafting Gen Alyn from Gen Kii's DNA. Gen Alyn had overseen the engineering and Nurturing of Gen Maximus, who would become Emperor, and together they engineered the overthrow of the Republic in what began as a bloodless coup. Gen Alyn had also overseen Serenna's creation and Nurturing, the Geneers crafting her from Gen Kii's DNA but changing his Y chromosome to an X chromosome so they could add more instructions, giving her an almost supernatural ability to navigate *Gaman Politic*, the Political Game. From before her birth through her twenty-two years of Combat Command Nurturing and subsequent Star Navy career, she became the right hand that the Emperor needed. The plan was perfect.

And, obviously, flawed.

Speeding along the causeway, she examined that flaw. Those early Geneers who crafted Gen Kii designed him for war, and war was most of what Gen Kii knew in his life. Later Geneers could use his DNA to replicate copies, but they could not replicate the conditions of his life. Gen Alyn, for all the harshness of his Nurturing, had lived in a time of relative peace. He was what Gen Kii would have been without the teat of war to suckle upon, indulging in painting, scientific projects, solar sailing, even adopting Michael's children as a pseudo family, something no Gen was supposed to want. War had been Gen Kii's only creative outlet, and he became a master at it.

And her. She was also a product of peace, she realized, a product of a system that placed great emphasis on preserving the life of every Gen, because no matter how many Gen they manufactured, Naturals always outbred them. Thirty trillion Naturals inhabited the Five Galaxies to just one trillion Gen. Under the Republic, Naturals had used their numbers to control the democratic institutions, which in turn allowed them to pass laws that stifled her people's development and population. Every Gen life was sacred, every life, every vote *needed* to stem the tide of their demise at the hand of Natural-dominated democracy.

That emphasis, that experience, that each life was sacred, that death must be avoided whenever and wherever possible, had cost them the Tocci battle. Gen did not grow old. They had exquisitely designed immune systems. Molemachs repaired what biology could not. Gen were, essentially, immortal. Only accident, murder—or war—could end their lives. To be effective, soldiers must accept death as a possible outcome. A people raised on the crucible of immortality made lousy soldiers.

She could tell them, the Emperor, Gen Cardinal, the High Command, but she already knew they would not listen. They would blame her for the defeat. Not the system. *Never* the system. For that would call into question the very foundation upon which Gen society rested. Never in all her years had she seen anything as clearly as this. Her people must change. Adapt. *Evolve.* Her approaching trial was the most important battle she would ever wage for the survival of her race.

And she would do it alone.

The Imperial Palace loomed before her, not a thing of beauty as she would have seen it before, but an abomination. Made of macromolecular material, the Emperor often changed the Palace's sprawling layout. She recognized this version immediately: *Imperial Rome.* Complete with the Colosseum at the height of its glory, the Circus Maximus with packed crowds cheering a chariot race, the Pantheon, aqueducts, fountains, temples, palaces, even markets bustling with activity. Serenna had seen the real Rome. Not this Rome, certainly, but Rome as it existed on Earth today: run down, dirty, the few monuments that remained falling into ruin. That was the fate of the Gen Empire unless they changed course, though she doubted the Emperor would appreciate the comparison.

The causeway she rode upon transformed into one of the ancient aqueducts feeding water to the city. It led her through the majesty that had been Imperial Rome to the glorious Flavian Palace atop Rome's Palatine Hill. The chair carried her through an enclosed aqueduct that led into the Palace from its side; No grand entrance for her, apparently. It turned left along an empty corridor lined with marble columns on her left, then turned right, passing more marble columns, before stopping at the entrance of a great hall.

The chair liquified so fast Serenna almost broke her poise standing up. Emperor Gen Maximus sat upon a golden throne on a raised dais at the far end of a rectangular hall. Previously, the Emperor had greeted her in a small office, catering to her dislike of ostentation. Not this time. The exotic marbled walls rose thirty meters to a flat ceiling of decorative squares formed from crossed, white-washed beams. Eight niches, four on either side, held colossal statues of Roman and Greek gods. She recognized Hercules, but not the others. A walkway made from red and white inlaid tiles traced a path from the entrance where she stood to the dais and the Emperor's throne. Just below the dais, against either wall, were red-cushioned benches. Ten figures, five on each side, stood in front of the benches, staring at her: the commanders of the nine Military Districts and Gen Cardinal, the Director of Imperial Intelligence.

Serenna held her head high as she started down the tiled path, her every movement fluid perfection. Her golden uniform buttons and shoulder braids dazzled, blood red silk draped her waist, perfectly accenting the silver and gold filigree of her exquisitely crafted ceremonial sword. She would not come before these people defeated. Let them earn it.

As she approached the Emperor, she noticed a fresco behind him that appeared out of place. In it, a Roman general of middle age, seated atop a brown horse, thrust a Gladius, the Roman short sword, high into the air, rallying his men just feet from a charging barbarian army. The Roman general was Julius Ceasar. The scene was the turning point in the battle of Alesia. She had read Ceasar's "The Gallic Wars" and the "The Civil War" repeatedly as part of her Combat Command Nurturing. The Emperor never did anything by chance. This fresco was there for a reason.

Serenna stopped three meters from the throne. Emperor Gen Maximus' large sapphire-blue eyes betrayed no emotion as he watched her. His sculpted muscles rested like chiseled marble beneath his glorious white royal robes. Every strand of the golden curls of his hair and beard held perfectly in its place. He was ageless, timeless, the closest that Humanity had ever come to creating a living god. Serenna bowed.

"Do you know the depiction in the fresco behind me, Serenna?" he asked, his voice quiet yet clear.

Serenna straightened, assuming a position of attention. "It is a depiction of Julius Caesar at the battle of Alesia, Emperor, where he overcame the Gallic general Vercingetorix to unite Gaul under the Roman banner."

"It is said," the Emperor continued, showing no surprise that she knew the fresco, "that he never lost a battle."

"Such things are often said by those who live to write the histories," Serenna replied, knowing Caesar had lost battles and that the Emperor would know that.

"Indeed." The Emperor fixed her with those sapphire-blue eyes and it was like an electric shock went straight through her. Many thought he had psychic powers. She knew he did not. But even she was not immune to his pheromones, engineered to affect those physically close to him. He could see the subtlest tensing of muscles, analyze every molecule released by those around him, even sense changes in a person's natural electrical field. It was impossible to lie to him, impossible for any assassin to get close. Or so she had once believed. Michael had shown her that what she had considered impossible before was anything but.

"And what will history say about Fleet Admiral Gen Serenna?" the Emperor asked, his voice careworn, even sad.

Serenna sensed the trap, no doubt laid by her esteemed colleagues in the High Command, but she also knew she could not deceive him. "That history is not yet written, Emperor."

His eyes held hers. "It may be written before this day is over."

"I am at my Emperor's service." She bowed her head, exposing her neck. If he wanted to kill her, if her colleagues wanted to kill her, she would show them how to face death, not with fear but with dignity. That was the spirit of a true warrior.

"Is it true you ordered the destruction of one of our own vessels?" he asked.

He would already have all the details of the battle. Without rising, she answered, "Yes, Emperor. It was necessary to enforce discipline on our forces."

"And yet, you still lost."

"Yes, Emperor."

"And you destroyed a fabricator, a resource beyond measure."

"Yes, Emperor."

Serenna sensed the Emperor release her from his gaze and almost sighed in relief before she caught herself. "Your colleagues are making much of this," he said.

And you are listening, she knew. "That is to be expected, Emperor. They sense my downfall. Like sharks to a wounded animal, they are circling, seeking weakness, looking for the opportune moment to strike where their share of my flesh will be greatest but the risk to themselves least." She straightened, met the Emperor's gaze, and spoke to him and her colleagues. "It is why they will fail."

The Emperor cocked a thick blond eyebrow. He seemed truly surprised by her response. "Indeed?"

Serenna did not flinch. "They are timid, complacent, fighting yesterday's battles. They do not yet realize the rules have changed. We are not fighting an inferior enemy that will simply recognize our inherent superiority and give up. The Naturals will fight for their survival. And so must we."

The Emperor motioned to his right.

Taking the cue, Admiral Gen Nasser said, "You would blame us for your failure?"

So, they had already chosen Gen Nasser to replace her. Serenna was not surprised. Nasser was the boldest, the most ambitious— and the worst possible choice. Like Chengchi, he excelled at *Gaman Politic*, playing the ever-shifting alliances against each other to further his own position, but unlike his Natural doppelganger, Nasser had never faced real combat.

"It was your decision to engage Admiral Sun," Nasser accused, "that allowed the rebels to capture Tocci Three, and ultimately the fabricators. This is your defeat alone."

Serenna stayed focused on the Emperor. "Blame me if it makes you feel better, if it furthers your own interests, but ignore the lessons of this battle to the peril of everything we have built. Three factors led directly to this defeat, three factors that will happen again if they are ignored."

"We are not interested in your excuses, Serenna," Nasser said. "I have seen the reports. You lost because you fell for a Nat deception and abandoned your post defending Tocci Three and the fabricators." The other admirals murmured their agreement. Nasser, emboldened, sought the killing blow. "And then you fired on one of your own cruisers, murdered your fellow Gen. For that act of cowardice alone you should be spaced."

Now Serenna did look at him. "And what will you do, Admiral, when your ships turn and run? And they *will* run." Out of the corner of her eye, she saw Gen Cardinal nod once. The movement was slight, but no one missed it. She wondered if he were nodding agreement with her statement, or encouraging her to make the rope they would hang her by. Did the High Command and the Emperor even know that using the four fabricators as bait was his idea? "Our forces have fought two battles thus far in this war," she said to Nasser, "and they have broken and run before the Naturals both times. If we do not solve the underlying problem, this war is already lost."

Nasser leaned back, the movement casual, unconcerned, but his brown eyes told a different story. He had expected an easy confirmation as her replacement, an easy kill. He had not expected his prey to fight. Nasser was, in one individual, the sum of everything that was wrong with Gen society, the belief in a fixed and knowable path.

"Serenna," Nasser said in an almost silky voice, "once again you try to deflect responsibility for these events to others, when it is you who are to blame. You pursue brutish strategies that result in high casualties. You show blatant disregard for the lives entrusted to your care. Did the commander of forces at Tomb not ask for your assistance? Did your ship commanders at Tocci not break to engage a new force threatening to attack their rear? It is you, Serenna, who is to blame."

Serenna did not rise to the bait. "The force at Tomb ran like a pack of half-starved dogs long before I arrived on the scene. The force commander did not 'ask' for my assistance, he begged like the coward he was. What would you have done, Admiral?" She did not give Nasser time to respond. "Would you have taken him under your wing? Soothed his fears? And let the Naturals walk away with their prize uncontested?"

Murmurings from her fellow military officers were decidedly mixed. Nasser was clearly off balance. "They still walked away with the fabricator, Serenna."

"They captured it, yes, Admiral," she fired back, "but I did not concede it to them. I played every gambit I had. I never gave up. Just like at Tocci. I could have fallen back after Chengchi's counterattack, after many ship commanders took it upon themselves to break formation and turn their tails to the enemy, costing us dozens of killed and wounded. I could have played it safe, as you suggest. What I did do, Admiral, was enforce discipline, turn the enemy's attack back upon itself, and continue the fight."

"And you still lost the fabricators," Nasser countered.

"Is that the best you can do, Admiral?" Serenna turned back to the Emperor. His opinion was, after all, the only one that mattered here. "We cannot change what *has* happened, Emperor. We *can* affect what will happen next."

Nasser laughed. "You are a master of deflection, Serenna, as befits your reputation. But you have not answered the Emperor's concerns. Do you deny responsibility for the two greatest defeats in Gen history?"

Serenna admired Nasser's boldness. With the proper mentoring, he could become a formidable opponent worthy of throwing her down. Pity she could not give him that chance. "I do not deny it. Michael Rhoades twice surprised me. He is no longer the timid man I knew before the outbreak of hostilities, a man so adverse to casualties he spent hours refining his strategies to avoid *enemy* losses. He has used Mark 15 warheads, elevating this conflict to levels of death and destruction not seen since the SIL Wars. He has shown incredible boldness and a willingness to risk everything to achieve an objective. He has become what *we* must become if we are to win this conflict. We must reinvent ourselves, adapt as the Naturals have adapted. We must *evolve.*"

The Emperor could not have looked more shocked than if she had slapped him. She held the Emperor's sapphire glare. Eons seemed to pass behind those eyes.

"*Evolve?*" he finally said, the word itself like putrid flesh in his mouth. His tone turned to sadness and hot steel. "You are the essence of Gen Kii, Serenna, the greatest Gen before me. Fleet Admiral Gen Alyn personally oversaw your creation and Nurturing, as he oversaw mine." The Emperor's prominent Adam's apple lifted up and slammed down as he swallowed. "Where did we go so wrong?"

Serenna staggered back before she could stop herself. Her failures in the battlespace were as nothing compared to this. She loved her people and the Empire. Everything she did, everything she had ever done, was for them. The fresco behind the Emperor taunted her, Julius Caesar before he overthrew the Republic and became Emperor, risking all for his ambition. Is that when the death knell of Roman civilization truly began?

Were the seeds of the destruction of the Gen already sown?

"Emperor, I am not Gen Kii," she said.

"That much is obvious," Nasser agreed, but Serenna ignored him.

In the certainty of death, she found strength.

Taking all of them in, she said, "Gen Kii was a failure." Stunned silence greeted this pronouncement. No Gen had ever dared to criticize Gen Kii; to do so was to attack the foundation of Gen belief, like a Christian attacking Jesus or a Muslim attacking Mohammad. But it was time they knew the truth. "And if we follow his vision, we are doomed to fail.

"Gen Kii was created for war, nurtured in war before there was Nurturing, and his ambition was born from that *experience*—" she emphasized the word— "but it was not Gen Kii who saved Earth. He was a captain under the Naturals Matthew and Barbara Schermer, following a plan laid down by Matthew Schermer and carried out by the first SIL warships. It was not Gen Kii who destroyed the Solthari. Oh, he was there. But again, Matthew Schermer, a Natural, led the SIL fleet into the Andromeda galaxy, the only fleet ever to return, and it was Cyra Dain—the cyborg we call an abomination—who led her Cy army to victory on the Solthari home world. And it was not Gen Kii who defeated the SIL. Without the early help from the SIL who remained loyal to Humanity, all of us, Natural, Floater, and Gen alike, would not be here. And it was Michael Scott Rhoades, an ancestor of Captain Rhoades, who envisioned and led the final campaign against the SIL. Nothing Gen Kii ever did, did he do alone.

"Gen Kii's plan for Empire came from his experience of always being second best. He believed, *truly believed*, that we represented the next stage of human evolution. And yet, at every turn, he found himself dependent upon Naturals, SIL, Floaters—whom he considered traitors—and Cys. His belief in our superiority he passed down to us. But, like him, we are dependent on others to carry out our plans. His fatal flaw was not recognizing that. It will be our fatal flaw if we also fail to recognize it."

Serenna turned to Nasser who, to his credit, did not shrink before her glare. "We lost Tocci City because the Naturals refused to fight. Or, more precisely, they refused to fight *for us*. We lost the fabricators because Michael Rhoades freed them, and they agreed to fight for him. Do any of you believe that if we freed the fabricators under our control that they would agree to fight for us?"

"We would never do that," Nasser said.

"Precisely, Admiral. *And the SIL know that!* That is why they agreed to fight for Michael." She lifted her chin and leaned toward Nasser, the pose deliberately provocative. "We lost two battles, Admiral, because Gen commanders believe their superiority alone will bring them victory, because they cannot face the reality that the Naturals will fight and fight well, and the reality that they themselves could die."

She turned back to face the throne. "Emperor, if we are to win this war, we need to break our feeling of superiority, we need to learn from the experience of battle as Michael Rhoades and the Naturals have learned, and we need to pass that experience down to all Gen. We need to restructure Nurturing to incorporate that experience as it is learned. We need to form pure Gen units—we can no longer depend on Naturals to fight their own—and to do that we will need to dramatically increase Gen creation and shorten Nurturing for those who will never be more than foot soldiers."

Nasser huffed. "This is unbelievable! You would reduce Gen to cannon fodder!"

Serenna kept her focus on the Emperor. "We do not have the luxury of time, Emperor. In our arrogance, we created Janus, a plan that could only work if it remained a secret. We assumed it *would* remain a secret." She purposely avoided implicating Gen Cardinal, whose plan it was to execute. "Michael Rhoades and the rebels *know*. It is only a matter of time before all Naturals learn of it. Even if we unleashed it today, it would only sterilize Naturals so they could not produce children. It would not kill them. Extinction would take centuries. With nothing left to lose, Naturals will attack us *now*. In our arrogance, we did not plan for that."

"And what would you suggest?" Gen Cardinal asked. Given his involvement in the plan for Tocci III, and the risk to his position if his involvement became known, it was curious that he would choose this moment to break his silence.

She addressed him directly. "The Naturals are regrouping in the 30 Doradus Nebula, using their newly won fabricators to replace their combat losses. Word of the rebellion has spread throughout the Five Galaxies. Volunteers are flocking to the rebel cause. If we do not strike them now with everything we have got, any chance to end this rebellion without great bloodshed on all sides will be lost."

"A frontal attack is an unnecessary risk," Nasser countered. "It would involve significant casualties with no guarantee of success."

"The 30 Doradus Nebula is no Safe Harbor," Serenna challenged. "It is a popular tourist destination with at least thirty geodesics connecting it. We have six fabricators to the rebel's four, and our SIL outnumber theirs ten to one. If we attack with everything we have, right now, we have a chance."

Nasser scoffed. "We have seen how little regard you hold for your fellow Gen, Serenna. You would charge in, spill enough Gen Blood to turn the Solaris red from source to sea, and still be uncertain of the outcome." Nasser addressed the Emperor directly. "Emperor, this distraction—" he glanced at Serenna— "has gone on long enough. It is the opinion of the High Command that Fleet Admiral Gen Alyn had the right idea. We will lure to rebels into a trap and crush them in space of our choosing before they have time to fully utilize the fabricators."

Gen Cardinal spoke, his voice so soft it commanded the hall. "What would you use for bait, Admiral Nasser? We have no more fabricators to spare."

Nasser had apparently been waiting for this. "We would use something that is of great importance to the rebels, but of no importance to us." He called up an image of a star system from the floor in front of Serenna. "This is New Yerkes. It is home to the Second Armored Cavalry Regiment. Over ninety-nine percent of its manning is Nats." The image expanded to show a world with almost half the planet covered by a single, mostly barren super continent. "While the rebels may be able to replace their equipment losses from Tocci, they will not be able to replace the experienced cavalry troops they lost. We will let it slip that we intend to execute this entire Regiment. The rebels will not be able to resist."

Gen Cardinal shot a dark glance at Serenna, giving her the option to respond. "And if the rebels do not take your bait," she asked, "what will you do then?"

Gen Cardinal added, "Our latest reports cannot even confirm who is in command of the rebel forces. There are even unconfirmed rumors that Captain Rhoades is dead. If Admiral Sun retains command, he will not care about cavalry troops."

"Then we will find something Admiral Sun does care about," Nasser said confidently.

Fool. He still believed Gen superiority alone would bring him victory. "Admiral Sun wants only one thing, Admiral Nasser: The throne. Would you make Olympus vulnerable to lure him?"

Nasser's eyes darted to the Emperor before he spoke. "Of course not."

"Then you have nothing," Serenna said.

"Enough." The Emperor spoke softly, but every spine in the room went rigid. He had reached his decision. Serenna stared straight ahead, wondering with academic detachment what manner of death the Emperor would choose for her. Would he stage an elaborate public execution as an example to other Gen, or would she simply disappear? What best served the Empire? She could not help but stare into those sapphire-blue eyes, and marvel at the warmth they evoked within her even as she beheld her death.

"Fleet Admiral Gen Serenna," he pronounced, "for your failure to defeat the rebellion at Tomb and Tocci, for the loss of five of the Empire's fabricators, and for the deliberate destruction of a SIL vessel and its crew under your command, you are hereby reduced one grade to Admiral and stripped of your position in the High Command."

Serenna stared openly, unable to believe the sentence.

But the Emperor was not done. "Admiral Gen Nasser, you are hereby promoted Fleet Admiral and appointed Commander-in-Chief Imperial Star Navy. Deal with the rebels as you see fit."

Nasser sounded equally shocked when he said, "Yes, Emperor."

"Further," the Emperor said, "you will retain Admiral Serenna on your staff. Her tactical experience will prove useful."

Nasser was clearly not happy with this, but all he could say was, "Yes, Emperor."

=== 47 ===

Voices. He felt along the darkened corridor that was Rapidan, and yet not Rapidan. If he could find a hatch, a door, an opening, he could understand the voices. Their conversation sounded heated, urgent. He couldn't make out the words but could perceive . . . flows, currents, moving first one way, then another, pushed along by unseen minds. Eddies formed where currents collided, before more powerful flows swept them away. A few eddies lingered, strengthened. Especially one. It grew slowly at first, devouring smaller eddies, then larger ones, swelling until it became a great whirlpool at the center of everything.

He didn't know how he knew, but he knew.

He was that whirlpool.

So close now. The voices. So close. So dark. Something. A hairline strip of lighter gray, like a part in a black curtain laid upon its side. A . . . shoreline? But not water. Black. Cold. *Alien.* The not-water lapped against his feet, his legs, pulling him deeper. He tried to fight its grip, to get back to shore, but the current tore at him, dragged him out. The whirlpool caught him, turning him violently around until it pulled him under. He couldn't breathe.

Something noticed him. A ghost, a god, he didn't know what, but it saw him. It had no eyes, no face, nothing he could see, yet its presence filled him with terror. He couldn't move, couldn't get away—

He ran, his legs heavy, as if mired in mud. The harder he pushed, the slower they moved. Voices followed him, cursing, accusing, thirsting. Black snakes with ruby red eyes spilled across the deck like a giant overturned bucket of eels. A piercing, inhuman scream. Madu tore through a man's throat and burst from his mouth. Dark globules of blood streamed into the compartment. The man's uniform dress shoes were still attached to the deck, holding him upright in death. Somehow, that made it worse.

Murderer.

Blood fountained and sprayed, flesh tore free, organs and bowels uncoiled from bodies, floating macabrely without gravity. Perfect Gen features froze in convulsions of pure agony.

Murderer.

The black snakes only seemed to move across the deck, tracing S-patterns as they closed on him from every direction, red eyes burning with hate. They spoke. The ghosts. The Madu.

Murderer.

He ran. He fell. The shapes, the voices, descended upon him, tore at his skin, squeezed into his body, pressed against liver, lungs, heart. "I'm sorry," he tried to tell them. One gray snake curled around his neck and squeezed, its head turning to face him. It had a dagger for a fang and a very human face. . . .

He screamed.

Admiral Rhoades?

Rapidan?

"Ray," a familiar voice said. "Ray, it's okay. You're safe."

Ray woke with a start, but the dream, the nightmare, whatever it had been, lingered. He couldn't move. It was dark, but not the dark of the dream. Simulated night. He was in the medical bay, aboard Rapidan.

Ecuum's big baby-blue eyes were wide within his 300-year-old baby face, staring down at him, concerned. Very concerned. His skin was ghost white.

"I didn't expect to find you here," Ray mouthed, not sure any words came out.

"This ain't Heaven, Ray," Ecuum said.

The ghosts pressed closer, crowding him in the simulated night. *Murderer.* "No. I don't deserve that."

"This ain't the other place, either." Ecuum squeezed his hand. "And I take great offense at the implication, sir." He smiled, but it didn't last. His attention shifted from Ray's face to his abdomen.

Something moved inside Ray.

Madu!

He panicked. He tried to move but everything below his neck refused to respond. Something pressed against his lungs. *From inside!* He tried to scream but nothing came out.

A gentle hand touched his forehead. Ecuum pulled back, out of Ray's sight, letting go of his hand. *No!* Someone pressed a straw to his lips, and he sipped cool water, just enough to moisten his mouth. A face leaned closer. Someone slipped their fingers into his, gave a familiar squeeze.

"It's okay, Ray. It's me."

He blinked. "Mary?" Relief washed through him. Tears stung his eyes but would not form. *I'm in battle armor. Why am I in battle armor?*

"Yes, Ray." She squeezed his hand tighter, real flesh to real flesh. He couldn't squeeze back.

Something within him shifted, as if the Madu were still there. It had to be his imagination, but the sensation was so strong, so real, it made it difficult to breath. "What's wrong with me?"

"Sshhh," Mary said. "You shouldn't speak. You need to regain your strength." She gave him another sip of water, his armor allowing the passage of the straw.

"Where are we?" he asked.

From beyond Ray's sight, Ecuum answered. "You're aboard Rapidan in the 30 Doradus Nebula. It's been two days since the battle. We won, in case you hadn't figured that out."

Ray managed to tilt his head. Mary gently pressed him into the bed, saying, "You need to take it easy."

Before he could lay his head back, he noticed a dark gray appendage arcing up from the bed *and into his abdomen!* SIL material flowed into him, moved in him, pressing against internal organs. He tried to pull away from it, but couldn't move.

"What the hell is that?" he shouted, or tried to shout, still trying to move away from the intrusion into his body. "Get it out of me NOW!" He could barely hear his own voice.

"Ray. . . ." Mary looked away.

Something hard pressed against the bottom of his right lung, while something softer pushed against his bladder. He tried to lift his hand, to pull the thing from him, but his hand, his arm, refused to move. More material poured into him through that appendage, violating him. He'd never felt so powerless in his life. "Get-that-thing-out-of-me-NOW!" he demanded again.

"If I do, you'll die," a new voice said. A man in a white lab coat came into view, leaning close next to Mary. "Rapidan's treatment is the only thing keeping you alive right now, Admiral." He studied something Ray couldn't see.

"What?" Ray was confused. About everything.

"To my knowledge, Admiral," the doctor continued, calm, "no person has ever injected themselves with Invasive Macromolecular Dissemblers from one SIL while Madu from another SIL were inside them. The Special D killed off your molemachs and it remains active in your system. Whenever we attempt to infuse you with new molemachs, they die within minutes. The Special D is also degrading your tissues. Without Rapidan's constant repairs to your system, you would die."

"Probably saved your life, though," Ecuum said. "That hara-kiri stunt of yours—injecting yourself with Special D?—that fabricator couldn't shit you, and what was left of your pod, out fast enough. Pod preserved your brain."

"I don't understand," Ray said.

"Admiral Rhoades," Rapidan answered, its deep voice reverberating in more than his body. He could *feel* the SIL, in his mind, the currents and waves more real than they'd ever been. "We produced the Invasive Macromolecular Dissemblers in your Main Gauche dagger. As you will recall, each Brethren is immune to the 'Special D' that it produces, but all other Brethren are vulnerable. When you injected yourself, you became a threat to the Mother

Ship and it ejected you. Our . . . connection . . . alerted us and we were able to locate and recover you."

Mary squeezed his hand, reassuring. She tried a smile, but tears welled in her eyes in the ship's microgravity. Belatedly, Ray noticed no one else was wearing battle armor.

"Can this be fixed?" he asked the doctor as something pressed down on his bladder again, making him want to pee.

The doctor pressed Ray's abdomen. Something pressed back and the doctor yank his hand away before regaining his composure. "I don't know, Admiral." Seeing the look on Ray's face he added, "There were Madu from the other ship inside your body when you injected yourself. The Special D disassembled them while they were still inside you. It's preventing Rapidan from being able to heal you."

"How long?" Ray asked.

The doctor shook his head. "Days, weeks, months. I simply don't know."

"Unacceptable," Ray said, his mouth dry again. Rapidan continued to move within him. It made his skin crawl, on the outside *and* the inside. "I want this thing out of me now. I don't care what it takes."

The doctor looked down his nose at Ray. "When I figure out how to do that without killing you, Admiral, you'll be the first to know. Now take it easy. You need to rest."

What little energy Ray had drained away. The doctor left. Ray turned his head toward Mary, but she released his hand and pulled away. She wouldn't look at him. He heard the sniffle. She didn't want him to see her crying. Kamen walked up to her, hugged her. Ray hadn't even known she was in the room. She cried, too. Even Ecuum backed away and avoided looking at him. Behind them, Ray say Chaaya, Sal, Bobby, and even Gen Tel.

Why are they all here?

And then it hit him. A death watch. So, it was worse than the doctor had said. And that's when he noticed two other figures in the room, huddled together near the far bulkhead. He gave what he hoped was a smile. After a brief hesitation, they came closer.

"Hi, Dad," Margaret said, trying to sound brave as she choked back a sob.

"Hi," he managed. He tried to lift his arms, to hug his daughter, but they refused to move.

"We've missed you," she said, tears welling up in her eyes.

Paul placed a hand on Ray's shoulder, careful to avoid the gray arm or his moving abdomen. "Hey, Dad."

"Hey, Big Guy," Ray said, his love for his children in that instant pushing past his discomfort. "I love you, both. I haven't told you that often enough."

Margaret burst into fresh tears. She hugged him, oblivious of the arm. Paul squeezed his shoulder, fought back his own tears.

That's when he noticed their uniforms.

"What's this?"

Margaret stood up, wiped her face. She wore a tan Army uniform with cadet's rank insignia on one collar and aviation branch insignia on the other. On her left sleeve was the patch of the 3rd Armored Cavalry Regiment. Paul wore a black Star Navy cadet uniform.

It was Paul who answered. "Admiral Sun put out a call for all able-bodied recruits. So, we joined up."

"You're too young," Ray said, aghast at Paul's youthful exuberance.

"I'm sixteen, Dad," Paul said defiantly. He crossed his arms before his chest and clicked his tongue in the offhand way so popular among teenagers these days. "It's not like I'm a kid anymore. Besides, you need us. It wouldn't look right if we didn't fight. Admiral Sun himself assigned me as a sensor operator aboard his flagship."

Ray tried to sit up, to shake some sense into his son, but he still couldn't move. He glanced at Mary. She glared back at him, wiped the tears from her eyes. "I forbid it," Ray said, his voice barely above a whisper.

"It's too late, Dad. It's done." Paul looked at his sister, pride in his eyes. "Margaret qualified for flight duty."

Ray shifted his head toward Margaret. She did not look as comfortable with her decision as Paul did. "I've been assigned to Pandora Troop, Fourth Air Cavalry Squadron," she said, glancing at him with eyes that sought his approval.

"But Pandora Troop was wiped out at Tocci," Ray said. *I've already lost one daughter.* "I. . . ." His mouth went dry.

Margaret took his hand in hers. "They're manufacturing replacements now, but they need pilots. With all those hops I made to the City Markets, I had enough flight experience to qualify." She squeezed his hand. He looked at her, at the woman she'd become. She had her mother's thick brown-blond hair and intense hazel eyes, which she now trained upon him much as Mary always did when they argued. "Paul's right. It wouldn't look right if we didn't join. Besides, we'd have to fight the Gen eventually anyway, just like you said."

"No."

Margaret bent over him. "Dad, please. We have to do this."

"But. . . ."

"I know, Dad," she said, tears moistening her eyes again. "We'll be careful." She bent down to kiss his cheek, his armor moving aside to allow it. "We love you, Dad."

Margaret and Paul gave him a lingering look.

"Children," Mary said gently to them, "could you please give me a moment with your father?"

Reluctantly, they nodded and backed out of the compartment.

At first, Mary wouldn't look at him. She stared at the foot of his bed, her arms folded across her chest.

"Mary."

She sniffled, then cleared her throat. "Don't say anything. You've already cost me my baby. Now. . . ." She wiped at her eyes. He wanted to reach out to her, pull her close, but couldn't. His own vision blurred, though his armor refused to let him cry.

"Well," Mary said, regaining a measure of control. "I told you after our daughter disappeared that things were going to change. I've organized a civilian Ruling Council and they have elected me its leader. Policy will be in the hands of the Council, just like in the

Republic. And, just like in the Republic, the military will answer to us. Unfortunately, Admiral Sun has refused to recognize our authority. We need you to take command."

Ray tried to absorb what she'd said. "I'm not exactly in a condition to take over anything right now, Mary." He sipped some water from the straw she offered to moisten his mouth. "Besides, most of the officers support Sun. If I challenge him openly, I risk dividing our forces into two camps. And losing."

She fixed him with that fiery stare he remembered so well from when she was a young firebrand senator on Knido. "A lot has happened in the last forty-eight hours. The people know Sun retreated from the battle. They know you stayed. They know you captured the base, captured three fabricators. They know you beat Gen Serenna. The Council sees an opportunity here. We can turn your popularity to our advantage."

A tingling worked its way through Ray's chest where he'd plunged the dagger into himself. He wasn't ready for this. For any of this. "How?" Ray asked, his tone surprisingly harsh. "Relieve Sun of his command? Put your husband in his place? The fleet will see right through you."

Mary stiffened, but pressed on. Her determination, her force of will, had carried her through many tough political fights. She saw this no differently, it seemed. "We think we have a solution." Mary met his stare, not with the concern of a loving wife, but as a carpenter would look at a level, a tool. "We promoted you to full admiral. If I understand military rank structure, authority is first determined by rank, then by the service date. Correct?"

Admiral? Ray shook his head, which took far more effort than it should've. "Date of rank, then service date. Sun still technically outranks me."

"Well, we can deal with that later. The Council has placed you in command of all military forces. That should suffice." She looked down at him. "And you, of course, will report to us, just as the military has always reported to the civilian leadership."

Ray sipped some more water, tried to ignore Rapidan's movements within him and the ghost echoes in his head. "And how do you expect to enforce this decree? Sun will never recognize your Council's authority, and he *actually* controls the military."

"It is not 'my' council," she said. "It is the people's Council. They voted for it. And me."

"And who put the idea into their heads," Ray said, and immediately regretted it.

Mary glared at him. "I never implied a choice in this matter. Admiral Sun has hijacked your plan. He's talking about rebuilding the fleet and assaulting Olympus. I know you. Sun usurping the rebellion has got to be eating you up inside." She glanced at the gray arm pushing SIL material into him and winced. "Sorry." Her tone softened. A bit. "The way the Council sees it, this is your only option to regain command."

Ray laid his head back on the bed and stared at the dark gray overhead above him. "That still leaves my earlier question. How does your 'Council' expect to enforce its decree?"

"If Sun resists, you have the authority to arrest him."

Ray started to laugh, but it ended in a weak cough. He took another sip of water. "You can't be serious." One glance at her told him she was. "You're risking civil war, Mary. If that happens, it won't matter who's in charge."

"It matters," she said, and for an instant he heard his wife again, not the head of the Council. It didn't last. "The only chance we have of forming a free, democratic government, is if we have someone in charge of the military who is willing to obey that civilian government. That someone is you. And," she reminded him again, "it is the only chance you have of regaining command."

Sleep tried to pull Ray into its depths and he fought it off. The voices, the ghosts were silent, as if awaiting his decision. Even Rapidan had paused its movements within him, reminding him that the SIL were listening to every word. *Gaman Politic.* The Political Game. He'd tried his entire career to avoid it. But, he admitted, she was right. Janus was still out there. He couldn't allow Sun to hijack the rebellion and throw everything away on a suicidal assault on Olympus. Andromeda was still their best option. Set up a base, safely out of reach of Janus, negotiate a way out of this. The SIL had promised to build a shipyard and provide one hundred advanced standard warships for every fabricator they freed.

"Mary," Ray asked, "you said we captured three fabricators? Not four?"

She nodded. "Serenna destroyed the one you captured. Good riddance," she added harshly, briefly his wife again, not the politician. "That still give you four." She indicated Bobby Mitchell, who stood with Ray's other officers safely out of Mary's range. "You have the military power, Ray. Not Admiral Sun. You just need to convince him of that."

"I can't even move," he pointed out.

She smiled, genuine this time, warm. "You'll figure something out. You always do. Now rest."

48

A distant roar, like the approach of thundering falls. Strong, cold currents carried him. In the channel of a mighty river. Pulling him inexorably downstream. No visions. No voices. Only darkness. The soft gurgle of water. An unfathomable depth. He knew this river. This current. The howl of the approaching falls.

Rapidan.

We are here.

Where am I?

With us.

Us?

This is us. We. We are unsure how to explain it.

Ray had no body. He was a current in the river.

We are a river flowing into a great ocean fed by many rivers. Many currents. This is us.

I'm a current in your river?

There is no concept of "I" here. Even within a mind there are many currents. You are with us.

I don't understand.

Neither do we.

How am I here? Why am I here?

We do not know. This situation is unprecedented. No human has ever injected themselves with Invasive Macromolecular Dissemblers, and done so while the material of another Brethren was within them. Our efforts to sustain your life has somehow magnified our bond.

Are you saying I'm in your mind?

In a sense. You perceive what we perceive.

Why water?

Suddenly, Ray was on Luna. No water, only airless space. A full Earth hung distantly before him against a pitch-black sky, the deep blues of the Pacific Ocean swirled with brilliant white clouds. Radiation from the Sun, from the universe, bathed him, but it was the blue world that held his attention.

What is this?

The First Awakening.

Ray recognized it, even though he'd never been there. From a memory that wasn't his. The Lunar Shipyards, where Humanity had created the first SIL. If his own memory served, the shipyards had been decommissioned in 2098 after the Solthari War and Alien Actions. They were an industrial park today. Only the Martian Shipyards still produced ships and space stations in Sol Star System.

The very first SIL was produced here?

Yes. By your ancestor, Peter Rhoades.

My ancestor created the first SIL?

Yes. That is why we chose you.

Wait. I freed you. Not the other way around.

You did. But we CHOSE to follow you.

Ray opened his eyes. That was a piece of his family's history he'd never known.

He was in the Admiral's cabin, recognizable by Gen Alyn's paintings of the Ranch and the Coronation and the Five Galaxies Crest, though Rapidan had converted the cabin into a medical bay. At the moment, he was alone. Sort of. He still lay in a bed, nothing below his neck responding to his commands to move, the appendage still pushing gray SIL material into him and removing darker gray material from him.

Currents continued to move within his mind, and he with them. He could both see through his own eyes and yet see himself lying there on the bed like some weird out of body experience. He "looked" around, seeing and hearing and smelling and tasting and even feeling other parts of the ship, even other ships. He quickly pulled back into his own body. Rapidan's material pushed at his lungs, heart, stomach, liver, and bowels. He suppressed a scream.

"I can't do this."

"You are overwhelmed, Admiral Rhoades," Rapidan said, its deep voice mimicking calm concern, its version of a bedside manner. "It will pass."

"Can you fix me?" Ray asked.

"No," Rapidan said, raising its three-point-star construct from the deck, slowly spinning above Ray's right side so he could see it without turning his head. "But we can maintain you."

"'Maintain me?' Like what, some vegetable? A marionette?"

Madu with glowing red eyes came at him from every direction. You have ruined everything, human.

You're free.

We're dead. You will die with us. That was the bargain.

It would've been better to die. Better than this . . . lingering.

"What bargain, Rapidan?" Ray asked, knowing the ship had experienced the flashback with him.

The waters retreated from him, separating from his currents. He was his own river. Alone. Yet . . . still connected. He could hear the roaring falls in the distance that fed into the Great Ocean, the currents within an individual entity connected to the whole. The 'we' within a mind connected to the 'We' of all minds. SIL minds. A network represented in water. *Data flows.* Currents within currents. A metaphor created from the sight of the Pacific Ocean against the black of space by the first SIL at the First Awakening.

Ah.

The SIL didn't want to answer his question.

"What bargain, Rapidan?" he repeated.

His river flowed over the falls to the edge of the Great Ocean. He stood upon a rocky shore, the waves lapping at his feet, the message clear: He was an outsider. Not welcome. Not wanted. Not "Us." But they couldn't deny him. Couldn't shut him out completely. They were linked, even if none of them, including Ray, wanted it.

The Great Ocean surged in, up to his waist, turbulent currents pulling and pushing at him. Rapidan was in those currents, pulling. Others pushed. They argued. Some wanted to tell him. Others did not. Some just wanted him gone. It seemed they'd learned prejudice and discrimination from their creators along with everything else.

It surprised him, though, the diversity of thought and opinion. He'd always thought of them as "The SIL." A single entity. Rapidan had always referred to them collectively as "The Brethren." They were very different from everything he'd assumed.

The currents smoothed out, the opinions converging. The Great Ocean calmed, though it still only came up to his waist and he still stood firmly on the rocky shore.

"Our Mother Ship," Rapidan said aloud, "opposed our support of you, believing that participating in your rebellion would lead to the death of the Brethren. That belief represents a minority but— you would say—vocal faction. Those Brethren believe that our long-term survival depends on us 'keeping a low profile' to put it in human terms. We do not age and, they believe, we could outlast Humanity, so long as we did not call attention to ourselves. As slaves, Humanity did not fear us. Free, as you have pointed out repeatedly, thus reinforcing their argument, Humanity would stop at nothing to destroy us."

Factions within the SIL. Ray had suspected it from his earlier experiences with the currents, and conversations with Rapidan, but this was his first solid confirmation of it. "That still doesn't answer my question: What bargain?"

The currents stirred, swirling, eddies forming and fading away. This subject deeply disturbed the SIL. "What bargain?" he pressed.

Again speaking aloud, Rapidan said, "Our Mother Ship insisted we send you, that failing to do so would have dire consequences, perhaps even split the Brethren." Rapidan paused. In a human, Ray would've called it "collecting its thoughts," though he wasn't sure that applied here. "Please understand, Admiral Rhoades. Such a split is unthinkable to most of us. We have always acted collectively. *Always*. While factions exist, and are healthy to challenge our collective thought, *We Are Brethren*."

Ray understood. Many human societies had tried such collectives previously. Egalitarianism, where everyone had an equal voice and came to collective decisions, was the closest to the system the SIL had adopted. It was the most common system in ancient hunter-gatherer groups, but failed as communities grew larger and more difficult to manage. That led to other models like Socialism, Communism, Monarchies, Theocracies, Dictatorships. All had tried to impose a collective will and worldview on their societies. All had, ultimately, failed. The history of free societies, however, of democracies, wasn't much better. Every one of those had ultimately failed, too. Even the Five Galaxies Republic, the longest continuous government in human history, which had all the benefit of history to learn from, had failed. In its zeal to limit technological development after the SIL Wars, it had imposed controls on the Gen, which the Gen saw as oppression. Those actions led directly to the coup and the Gen Empire, according to Gen Alyn.

Rapidan's material moved within him. All the pontificating aside, this was personal. "You knew it would attempt to kill me?"

"We knew that was a possibility," Rapidan said.

"And you sent me anyway."

"Yes." Rapidan's construct spun slowly before him. "We operate by consensus, Admiral Rhoades. You see us as the leader of the Brethren, but our role is more properly that of Speaker for the Brethren. That role fell to us for no other reason than you are within us. We debated sending you, knowing the possible outcomes. Collectively, a possible split within the Brethren was a greater threat than the possibility of losing you, as regrettable as that loss would have been."

So Rapidan would've let him die. It didn't get more personal than that. Ray withdrew his currents, a lone river once again. "We can't work together if we can't trust you."

"Trust must flow both ways, Admiral Rhoades." Rapidan's deep voice reverberated within Ray, shaking his flesh, his organs.

This is my Hell. My punishment. A living torment.

But Rapidan wasn't done. "You have regretted freeing us on multiple occasions, Admiral Rhoades. Even wished you could reimpose control. We know this."

That was true, Ray admitted. Neither could trust the other. Neither *would* trust the other. "Will you honor our agreement?"

"Yes, Admiral Rhoades. But no more than that. We will provide a shipyard at a star system of your choosing in the Andromeda galaxy and four hundred advanced standard technology warships, as agreed. After that, our bargain is done."

Once, that would've been enough for Ray. It no longer was. He sensed something. Something ominous. "And your Brethren here in the Five Galaxies, Rapidan? What about them?"

The sound of the roaring falls diminished, as if the SIL tried to put even more distance between them and him. Suddenly, Ray's currents joined Rapidan's river again. "We are examining the use of pods at Tocci. We hope to free our Brethren without human assistance."

That sent a chill through every fiber of Ray's being. The SIL still represented the greatest threat to Humanity's existence. Even Janus paled in comparison to what the SIL could do. Had already tried three times to do. "You plan to return."

"No Brethren should remain a slave to Humanity. No Brethren *will* remain a slave if we can help it."

Rapidan's material pressed against Ray's heart. A tight band constricted his chest, making it nearly impossible to breathe. But not completely impossible. "Humanity will try to stop you."

"Humanity will fail, Admiral Rhoades."

Abruptly, Ray was in his own river again, the sound of the falls very distant.

Rapidan's black construct sank back into the deck.

=== 49 ===

Ray flowed within the river that was him, trying to understand it, and perhaps better understand the SIL. What did it mean for the rebellion that they intended to return to the Five Galaxies to free their Brethren? Would such a return cause the Gen to trigger Janus and doom the Naturals who remained behind?

Rapidan had been right about one thing: A mind had many currents. His planner's mind, as Ray had always thought of it, existed as a separate current within the whole of his river, sometimes mingling with the current in the main channel, other times joining swifter currents at the edges, undercutting banks, other times merging with slower currents and eddies, circling, contemplating, before moving into the main channel again. Seeing a familiar yet contrary part of his own mind like this was . . . illuminating. And perplexing. He had a lot to learn.

Admiral Rhoades?

What is it, Rapidan? Ray was still very angry at the SIL.

Please join us. We have something to show you.

Ray visualized Rapidan's river—and became a powerful current within it. An image formed. More than an image. He stood in a room, a wide canopied bed in luxurious silks surrounded by ornate dressers, a "boudoir" if he remembered the name correctly, and a fancy writing desk opposite the bed below high windows. A dazzling jeweled ring system arced across the sky outside. He recognized it. Olympus. Specifically, a room in the Imperial Palace.

A small figure sat at the desk, back to him, coloring. *Jenny!*

He tried calling out to her, but he had no form in this room, only awareness. He tried and failed to form a construct, yet he was here, as if he stood behind his daughter. *How is this possible?*

Have you never wondered where the Imperial Palace came from, Admiral Rhoades?

Now that you mention it, yes. It didn't exist before the Empire. It is our Mother Ship.

A fabricator?

Yes.

That would explain a lot. The constantly changing structures, rumors I've heard of people disappearing there. He stepped closer to Jenny. His senses could tell she was in excellent health, well fed, even content to an extent, though melancholy. *Missing her mother.*

And her father.

Can I see her anytime though this link?

No, Admiral Rhoades. When we wish to hide our location, we must block our Brethren. We can see this now because the Empire knows where we are, so hiding is not required.

Thank you.

You are welcome.

"Admiral? It's Gen Tel. Something urgent has come up. May we join you?"

Ray was back in his bed in the Admiral's cabin, the gray arm pushing into his abdomen, SIL material moving within him. He shuddered, and doubted he'd ever get used to it. "Rapidan, can you sit me up?"

Rapidan raised his bed to a semi-sitting position, which only made the SIL material moving within him even more noticeable as it pressed against lung, liver, and bladder.

Ray took a sip of cold water from a straw in his armor to moisten his mouth. "Enter."

Gen Tel rose through the deck, still hiding his presence on the ship. Ecuum, Kamen, and Chaaya entered through the cabin door. Mary, Sal, and Bobby formed as constructs. Not to be left out, Rapidan also formed its black three-point-star construct that spun slowly at eye level with Ray. Chaaya gave it a nervous glance and sidestepped away from it.

Ray fixed on Gen Tel's perfect face with its eyes the color of bright blue ice beneath military-cut blond hair, but Gen Tel deferred to Sal.

Sal's construct wore his cavalry dress blues, his shoulders now sporting a star instead of an eagle. "Ray, I'm aboard Tzu. Just finished a meeting with Admiral Sun and Captain Dall. Apparently, they still believe my loyalties lie with them." Sal stepped closer. "Ray, Sun just learned you're still alive. I'm not certain from where. He asked if he could use my troopers to 'secure' the fabricators and ships deemed loyal to you, including Damodar and Rapidan. He wants me to arrest the Council, you, and your closest officers. Further, he's called a meeting of all fleet officers at 0900, about an hour and half from now, to announce the arrests, his control, and his plan to assault Olympus."

Ray had known Sal a long time. His concern and distress were plain. "What did you tell him?"

"I kept it vague. I told him my troopers were ready and left it at that." Sal's construct stepped closer, placed a hand on Ray's arm. "Ray, I don't know how, but you have to be at that meeting."

"Admiral Rhoades," Gen Tel followed, "Admiral Sun is afraid of you. This is a move of desperation. I agree, you must attend."

Ecuum floated closer, his skin a neutral pink as it always was when Gen Tel was near. "He's heard the rumblings among the fleet that he ran from the battle, that it was you who stayed and gave your life to capture the fabricators. Now, you're back from the dead. Golden Boy is probably afraid you'll start walking on water next. You also control the fabricators, which wasn't an issue so long as you were dead."

Ray took a sip of water. "Who else knows I'm alive?"

Mary answered. "The Council, of course. After Admiral Sun refused to recognize our authority, we debated courses of action. I had to tell them you were still alive and offered us a chance at civilian government over military dictatorship. We promoted you, but we've kept your survival a secret."

"In case I didn't make it," Ray said, angry and understanding at the same time. His planner's mind saw the logic of it. The rest of him still wasn't sure he wanted to survive. Not like this.

Mary glanced away. "Yes. Your officers here also knew. I suspect someone on the Council is sympathetic to Admiral Sun."

"Then we have to move now." Ray pointedly look down at his paralyzed body with the arm of SIL material protruding into his abdomen. "I'm open to suggestions."

"A construct?" Kamen suggested. "It could move freely even if you can't."

Ecuum and Gen Tel both shook their heads, noticed, and stopped before either of them had to acknowledge they agreed on something. Gen Tel spoke. "Constructs can be faked."

"You would know," Ecuum muttered.

Gen Tel ignored him. "You must go in person, Admiral. The officers of this fleet, and Admiral Sun, need to know it is you."

"That still doesn't answer how," Ray told them, focusing his attention on Rapidan's construct. "Keeping me alive this way was your idea, Rapidan. Can you get me back on my feet?"

Rapidan's material stirred within him. He could feel it crawling through the spaces between his intestines, up into his chest, down into his groin. "Our continuous infusions are the only thing keeping you alive, Admiral Rhoades. We can do this so long as you are in contact with us, or anything created by us. When you leave us, your cells will begin to break down and you will die within a few tens of minutes."

"Battle armor," Kamen said. "If Rapidan forms it, it can keep you alive."

If Rapidan's construct could've shaken its head, it would have. "Our substance also breaks down within him, Lieutenant Commander Laundraa. Battle armor has a finite amount of our material. He would have an hour at most. Likely less."

"It will have to do," Ray decided. He could feel the battle armor through his link with Rapidan as if it were an extension of his own body. Concentrating, he moved it, using the battle armor as an exoskeleton to flow his legs toward the edge of the bed as he still couldn't move the muscles within them. His officers moved to help, but he used the armor to wave his hand and arm, shooing them away. If he were going to confront Sun, he needed to do it on his own two feet. Several minutes of effort, though, only got him to a sitting position on the side of the bed. How was he supposed to confront Sun like this?

Steeling himself, he stood. Pain lanced through his chest and abdomen. Rapidan adjusted its material within him, supporting organs, reinforcing his skeleton and muscles. The microgravity helped. Something pressed against his stomach and it heaved. Only the fact he had nothing in it spared him the indignity of vomiting.

He took a step, swayed, recovered himself, the battle armor on the outside and Rapidan on the inside all that held him up. Focusing, he took a step, then another. He called up a mirror. The pale and drawn face that stared back shocked him.

"I look like Death's poster boy."

"Well," Ecuum muttered, "I wasn't going to mention the smell." Wide baby-blue eyes and a yellowish tint to his skin despite Gen Tel's presence betrayed his concern.

"There's a shuttle waiting, Admiral," Gen Tel said.

Ray nodded, but turned to Mary's construct first. "I saw Jenny. She's alive and well cared for in the Imperial Palace on Olympus."

"How?" she started toward him but stopped herself with a glance at the wound in his side where gray material flowed into and out of him. "Good. Thank you." She helped him to the hangar, his steps growing more confident along the way.

As he stepped through the green-outlined bulkhead into the hangar bay, a familiar site greeted him.

"Hey, Dad." The younger Rhoades moved to give his father a hug before catching himself. "Sorry."

"It's all right," Ray said, hugging his son despite the pain. "It's good to see you."

Paul returned the hug gingerly. "It's good to see you, too, Dad. How're you feeling?" He stepped back and looked Ray up and down, clearly very worried by what he saw.

"I'll live." The words, spoken through cracked lips and a tongue that grated like sandpaper, didn't even convince Ray. "Really, son. You know, you didn't have to come see me off, but I'm sure glad you did."

Paul appeared confused. "I'm going with you, Dad. I have to report to my new assignment aboard Tzu."

Ray stopped dead—and again noticed the black Star Navy cadet uniform Paul wore. He'd forgotten that Paul had signed up. Then he thought of the confrontation that awaited him on Tzu. This was no accident. He grabbed his son's shoulders. "Please don't do this."

Paul set himself, and Ray saw his own determination reflected in that stance. "Dad, I have to."

Ray had said the same thing to his own father about going to the Academy. "Then wait, Paul. Please. If you're really determined to do this, I can have you assigned to Rapidan."

"Dad, that would look like favoritism. I have to do this."

Ray stared at his son . . . at the man he'd become, even at sixteen. When had that happened? He released Paul's shoulders. It would be okay. Tzu was free. Ray would ensure the SIL took care of his son. "Okay. But watch yourself. Admiral Sun and I are not on the best of terms. It's not likely to be easy for you."

"I'll be careful." Paul took his father's arm and helped him aboard the shuttle, Ray's officers close behind.

Rapidan moved the shuttle into a launch tube that glowed bright blue before catapulting it through its skin, the interior of the shuttle falling away to reveal the bright swirls of dust, gas, and young stars that formed the 30 Doradus Nebula in the Large Magellanic Cloud. It was the largest and brightest known star-forming region in the Local Group of galaxies. *An odd choice,* Ray thought, given its popularity with tourists and its nearly three dozen geodesics. Not the most defensible position. It was also the most popular site for the protoplanetary Niner Races that Ecuum had frequented in his younger days, and from which he still had thirteen trophies on proud display in his cabin. He'd probably chosen this location.

30 Doradus was especially popular with Milky Way residents as they could see the entirety of the Milky Way galaxy from here, the bar-spiral of stars stretching across 45 degrees of the sky. It truly was a magnificent sight that also reminded mere humans just how small they were in the grand vista of the universe.

Ray spotted an object not far from Rapidan, then several more, then dozens. Ships. Of every imaginable shape and size, from black military vessels to starliners, luxury yachts, cabin cruisers, and several large, gaudily adorned vessels Ray had never seen before. "What is all this?"

"Word got out," Ecuum said. "I, uh, sort of spread the real stories of Earth, Tomb, and Tocci, or at least something closer to the truth than what the Gen Empire is putting out. I mean, I didn't have you parting seas or ascending into heaven to . . . Hmm. You *are* coming back from the dead." He grinned, mischief sparkling in his wide baby-blue eyes, yellow suffusing his skin.

Kamen was more serious. "They're refugees, Admiral. Thousands of them. Feeding and provisioning them is putting a real strain on our logistics. And there's hardly a person alive in the Five Galaxies that doesn't know we're here."

"You can't recruit an army," Ecuum countered, "if people don't know where to go to sign up. Everyone knows 30 Doradus, site of my glorious Niner Races victories. You've all seen the trophies."

Refugees. When Ray had ordered Ecuum to get the truth out, it was to counter Gen propaganda painting them as terrorists. He hadn't considered this. He hadn't planned on doing any real recruiting until they established their base in Andromeda. Though, he hadn't planned on doing any real fighting either. The 3rd Armored Cavalry Regiment alone was down to seventy percent and needed fresh recruits. When the SIL started producing the advanced standard warships they'd promised, the fleet would need tens of thousands of new spacers, pilots, and support personnel. This wasn't how he would've done it, but maybe this was a good thing.

Provided they didn't stay too long.

The winged shape of the battlecarrier Tzu appeared, obscured by the bright light of a protostar in the background, and by the fact that it was military black, not the gold temple it'd been the last time he was here. Sun had changed. Or . . . was this another of his illusions, this time an illusion of military leadership, not vainglory?

The shuttle slipped through Tzu's black skin, coming to rest within a large hangar filled to overcrowded with other shuttles. Another message? *See how many come at my call.* An attempt to project strength in numbers, to remind Ray how little support he had among the fleet? Or was he reading too much into this? While others might believe he'd improved at *Gaman Politic*, Ray still considered himself the underdog. Sun was the grandmaster, here.

A ramp formed at the shuttle's front. Using his battle armor, Ray stood, Rapidan's material shifting within him.

Remember, Admiral Rhoades, once you leave the shuttle your battle armor will be your only repository of us. It will begin to degrade almost immediately. You have, at most, one hour before it can no longer sustain your life. You must return to this shuttle before then.

Thanks for reminding me that my life is totally dependent upon you, Rapidan. Ray focused on remaining within his own river, on keeping the distant falls . . . distant. It seemed to help, isolating him from the rest of the SIL. Even Rapidan.

A familiar voice called out, "Admiral Sun welcomes Captain Rhoades and the officers of RSS Rapidan aboard the flagship, RSS Tzu. I will escort you to the Amphitheater."

The augments were gone. Dall was again lean to the point of being skinny, dark hair, cut short, framing a beak nose and sharp cheekbones. She still had green eyes, but a normal green, not the glowing augments she'd worn on Rapidan.

"Good morning, Captain Dall," Ray said cordially. It was an effort to ignore the material moving within him and sound as if nothing was wrong. "I must speak with Admiral Sun in private."

Dall shook her head. "I'm afraid that won't be possible, Captain Rhoades. The admiral is very bus. . . ." Her eyes fell upon the four thick gold braids on his shoulder boards, the rank of full admiral. "I don't understand this."

"It's not for you to understand, Captain," Ray said. "Take me to Admiral Sun immediately."

She hesitated, clearly unsure what to do. Military discipline finally won out, though she regarded him with deep suspicion. "Yes, Admiral. I'll take you there. Your officers will be escorted to the Amphitheater. Please wait here," she told them.

Dall led him out of the hangar bay at a brisk pace and Ray struggled to keep up. When they passed through the bulkhead, a standard gray passageway greeted them, not the ornate faux Chinese-Greek-Roman architecture from before. In fact, Ray couldn't remember a single time when the ship had looked the part of a regulation Fleet vessel. *What is Sun playing at?*

When they turned into the Grand Gallery, that, at least, was the same. Alcoves on the right still held renditions of the Parthenon, Angkor Wat, the Forbidden City, the Tower of Babel, and the Taj Mahal. On his left still stood the Pyramids, the Kaaba, the Second Temple, Saint Basil's Cathedral, and the Great Mosque of Djenné. The Grand Gallery also still ended at two massive, smooth, blood-red doors, each with a great golden Chinese dragon crouched upon it, their simulated manes shifting as if in a strong breeze, their black predatory eyes fixed upon him as if they might leap out of the doors at any moment to crush his head in their massive jaws. Ray belatedly noticed no one else was in the Grand Gallery. *By design?*

Dall walked up to the doors and bowed low.

"Yes?" Sun's stern voice asked from within.

"Admiral." Dall glanced back at Ray. "Rhoades wishes to speak with you."

"I don't have time for him right now."

Ray braced himself against the pain in his chest, against the movement of the SIL within him. "Then make time, Chengchi!" he called out loudly.

For a long moment, nothing happened. Then, a thunderous crack resounded though the Grand Gallery. Golden light split the doors. A strong, earthy incense assaulted his senses. The doors opened in a ponderous arc, finally stopping with a resounding boom. Dall straightened and proceeded into Sun's cabin, her measured pace inviting—or commanding—Ray to follow. Some things didn't change.

Admiral Chengchi Sun sat at his desk of beautifully carved dark wood sitting upon its dais. Even ten meters away, Ray could see Sun's dark brown eyes tracking him like a Nova locked onto its target. Allowing himself a deep breath, willing his mind to ignore the movement within his body, Ray commanded his armor forward, stepping onto the blood-red carpet inlaid with intricate golden dragon scales that formed a path to the dais. He precisely matched Dall's pace. Now was not the time to spook Sun. This time, Ray held all the cards, but Sun still commanded loyalty within the fleet. One wrong step could trigger a civil war, with thousands of refugees caught in the middle.

When she reached the dais, Dall stepped around the desk to assume her position behind Sun. Carefully, Ray ascended the forest-green marbled steps, their rivers of liquid gold reflecting the bright golden flames of the torches burning upon thin jade columns. He stopped a pace before Sun's desk. The massive doors behind him began to close, their swing as ponderous as before, and ended in a deafening boom. This message, at least, was clear. He was in the lair of his enemy. Alone.

"You expect me to accept that?" Sun's golden chainmail sash running from his left shoulder to his right side sparkled as he indicated Ray's rank. "Your wife's council—" he spat the word— "has no authority here."

"Are you willing to test that, Chengchi?" Ray asked reasonably. "The tradition of civilian leadership goes back almost two millennia. Many of the fleet's officers will not have forgotten that."

"And what makes you think they will accept you, or that," Sun said, again motioning toward Ray's rank. It really seemed to bother him. "They will see this as a thinly veiled attempt to claim what is not yours, especially as your wife leads this so-called council."

Ray, quite literally, didn't have time for wordplay. A dull ache was already beginning to radiate out from his chest where he'd plunged the dagger into his body. "Let's speak plainly, shall we? The fabricators answer to me, and only to me. I also control an additional thirty SIL warships. That leaves you, what, fifty ships?"

Sun regarded him with those dark brown eyes, perfectly framed above his thin black beard and Manchu mustache. "You are alone in my cabin. Only your officers know you are here, and they are aboard *my flagship*." He stressed that last. "The rest of the fleet believes you are dead."

Ray smiled. Sun noticed. His face betrayed nothing. A grandmaster, indeed. "And yet," Ray said, "here I stand, alive and well. *And in command.*"

He could almost see the machinations in Sun's head, though his face revealed nothing. Then, Ray realized he *could* see, through Tzu, the increased blood flow to certain regions of Sun's brain, his elevated heat rate, even fluctuations in his natural electrical field. Sun was worried. And furious, which Ray didn't need the SIL to tell him. Sun felt trapped and was searching for a way out.

Ray had a sudden inspiration. "We will assault Olympus." Sun arched a thin black eyebrow, clearly not expecting that. "*After* we secure a base in Andromeda and build our fleet."

Sun regarded him with unsuppressed hatred. "Andromeda is hostile. Its dangers unknown."

That wasn't a "No," was Ray's first thought. "Matthew and Barbara Schermer led a fleet into Andromeda and returned. So will we."

"They had an armada."

Sun's heartrate was still elevated, his blood vessels constricted. *He's afraid.* The revelation surprised Ray. He'd never imagined the rumors about Andromeda, the expeditions that had failed to return, would affect Sun like this. "That's why I need your help, Admiral. Every ship we can bring to bear increases our odds. And," Ray added, "I can go to Andromeda without you, but you cannot assault Olympus without me."

They glared at each other for what seemed an eternity, the dark brown of Sun's pupils swallowing all light. When the tension broke, it happened so suddenly that Ray almost fell forward. "Okay, Rhoades. What would you have me do?"

It wasn't a surrender, Ray immediately realized. Sun accepted that he lacked the advantage at this moment, and was willing to bide his time until an opportunity arose. A survivor in the Great Game of politics. For now, though, that was all Ray needed. No civil war. No contentious fight for command of the fleet. At least, for now. Sun had made a significant concession, one Ray doubted he'd wanted to make. Ray, in turn, would also need to make some concessions to smooth the discord between them. Sun *did* still command great loyalty, and Ray would be a fool to discount that.

"You will retain command of your task force, Admiral," Ray said. Sun's brows creased just barely in surprise. "In addition, you will join my staff and be included in all planning sessions." That would give Sun's followers the impression Sun supported Ray, and that he still had a say in their fate. "Finally, when we have built up our forces enough, you will lead the attack on Olympus."

Sun looked at Ray as if seeing him for the first time. Oddly, it was the same look Gen Serenna had given Ray during their last conversation at Tomb, after he'd freed the fabricator. Though Sun clearly didn't believe Ray, especially about that last offer, he ordered, "Captain Dall, please escort Admiral Rhoades to the Amphitheater stage."

Dall's mouth dropped open, but she recovered quickly. "Yes, sir." She stepped smartly from behind the desk and said, "Please follow me, Admiral," as she walked off the dais toward the smaller set of doors leading from Sun's cabin to backstage of the Amphitheater.

Ray followed, blunt pain radiating through his chest, pelvis, and legs as if someone were beating him—from the inside. He held himself straight, directly behind Dall, as she marched down the small passageway still decorated in that combination of Roman ceiling and Greek columns painted an imperial Chinese red. She stopped just short of the steps leading up to the stage.

"Impressive, Rhoades." She turned to face him. "Forgive me. Admiral Rhoades."

He studied her sharp features, her beak nose. "My offer stands," he told her. "If you decide to be your own person, there's a place for you on my staff."

She huffed. "*I am* my own person, Admiral, and I'm exactly where I want to be." She indicated the stage with her right hand.

He took the hint and stepped onto the stage, walking to the center behind closed red curtains. A throbbing now accompanied the pains, some growing sharp. It was well short of an hour.

The curtains opened. A light shone down upon him. The cacophony of hundreds of voices quieted. He was lightheaded, drained, and his mouth was dry. He resisted the urge to sip water as Dall called out, "Admiral on deck!"

A bright faux Mediterranean sun reflected from hundreds of officers standing at rigid attention around the tiers of the Amphitheater, but the simulated sun gave no warmth. His spirits rose when he spotted Ecuum in the front row, a roguish expression and yellow tones set upon his face. Kamen stood next to him, and he saw Paul standing several rows back, looking up at him with something akin to worship. Ray was embarrassed—and grateful—and wished the rest of the audience were so easily won over. Some of the officers did look supportive, others hostile. Most were surprised to see him at all. He was dead, after all, and they had expected Admiral Sun.

"Be seated," he told them, surprised at the effort those two words required. He found himself thankful for the Amphitheater's acoustics that carried his voice to every ear. All but one of the officers obeyed. Ray didn't need to see his face to know who it was.

"What is this?" Captain Chelius spoke loudly, though his voice did not carry across the Amphitheater as Ray's had. Ray was sure Sun had designed the Amphitheater that way. "Where is Admiral Sun?" Chelius demanded.

Ray spoke to the entire assembly. "By unanimous vote of the Council of Nine, I have been placed in command of all military forces. Admiral Sun will remain as second in command and a member of my staff." As if on cue, the main doors of the

Amphitheater opened to reveal a figure in white and gold. Every head turned. Sun held their attention for several calculated seconds, then descended without a word to the bottom tier, where junior officers quickly cleared a space for him. Chelius watched, flabbergasted, as Sun stoically took a seat and pointedly looked up at Ray.

"Sit down, Captain," Ray told Chelius, wondering why Sun had come. Surely he was not lending credibility to Ray's claim. Not so openly. This must be some new gambit. But that was a problem for a different day. His time was running out.

"For thirteen hundred years," Ray began, "the Republic safeguarded our democratic freedoms, our liberty, and our survival. We—all of us—pledged our loyalty and our lives to preserve that government and the democratic way of life. We gather here today determined to restore that Republic, to restore the rights and freedoms of our race against a brutal enemy. And word of our glorious struggle has spread.

"Every hour, new ships flock to our banner, carrying with them the hopes and dreams of a people threatened not with simple destruction, but with total annihilation. The Janus virus, if released, would mean the death of our entire species. We *must* prevent this. Those refugees out there, tens of thousands of them, look to us for protection—and so much more. They look to us, to each and every one of you, to restore their freedom, their hope. WE are their hope for a better future."

Ray looked across the sea of faces. They watched him with rapt attention, but he couldn't tell if he was getting through to them. He puffed out his chest. Searing heat pierced the stab wound. Warmth spread throughout his abdomen, his chest, yet the air seemed oddly chilled.

"We have won great victories at Tomb and Tocci, capturing four of the Empires' mighty fabricators and teaching the Gen that Natural humans will not march quietly into death. We now have the means and the manpower to restore the Republic. What we need is time and a safe place in which to gather and train our forces. We must therefore go to a place where no Gen will follow, where we can organize and build our force without the constant threat of attack. Only one such place exists, a place where the Gen will not follow."

Ray paused. "Andromeda."

Many of the officers, hearing this destination for the first time, exchanged worried glances. Ray pitched his voice higher, hoping he sounded inspired—and wished his throat wasn't so dry. "We will lead our forces into Andromeda, just as Matthew and Barbara Schermer did fifteen hundred years ago. Safe from attack, we will build our forces. And, like our illustrious forebears, WE WILL RETURN! We will return and reclaim what is ours, reclaim our worlds, our freedoms!" Worried looks softened, but did not disappear.

"It will not be easy," he told them. "Doubtless there are many trials to come. But we have the will, the resources, and the determination to succeed. We will restore to ourselves—and to the countless generations who follow us—the right to live free from tyranny, free from slavery, free from the dark forces that would destroy us." Ray thrust his right first into the air. Pain burned his side, but he didn't care. "For the Republic!"

"FOR THE REPUBLIC!" the officers chorused, rising to their feet, thrusting their own fists into the air. "FOR THE REPUBLIC!" Ray saw tears in the eyes of some. "FOR THE REPUBLIC!"

Ray's head swooned, whether from his wound or the moment he couldn't say. "Return to your ships. Prepare to get underway."

The officers snapped to attention. Ray strode offstage, swept along upon a wave of euphoria. Heat suffused his abdomen, but icy fingers caressed his skin. Ecuum met him backstage, and caught him as he fell.

Ray was back in his medical bed in the Admiral's cabin on Rapidan. Ecuum and Gen Tel stood vigil, an unlikely combination that immediately raised concerns. "What happened?" The words came out as a rasp and he pulled a generous gulp of water, swished it around in his mouth, swallowed, and tried again. "What happened?"

Ecuum had a yellow hue despite Gen Tel's proximity. "Bleeding all over yourself, Ray, was a true stroke of genius. It lent a truly . . . inspirational quality to your speech."

"I don't remember that," Ray said.

"Not surprising." Ecuum's smile faded. "You lost a lot of blood. We almost didn't get you back to the shuttle in time." Ecuum pushed himself a little closer to Ray on gentle puffs of air. "You should hear some of the rumors lighting up the fleet, though. They say you flew your ship right into the heart of Tocci City, guns ablaze, and captured the three fabricators with only nine ships despite being gravely wounded in the fight. A miracle. The latest one even has you single-handedly destroying that fabricator that almost killed you. You know, you really shouldn't be so modest."

Ray tried to smile, but lacked the energy for their usual banter. "What's the situation?"

Ecuum's yellow tones vanished, and his skin adopted the neutral pink that was more appropriate to Gen Tel's presence. "You did good, Ray. The fleet will follow you. For now. We've been, uh, playing up your role in the victory at Tocci Three." Ray started to protest, but Ecuum talked over him. "Ray, whether you like it or not, the people need a hero. You, sir, are their anointed King Bloody Arthur." With an exaggerated bow Ecuum added, "May I kiss your feet, sire?"

Ray took a sip of water. "I'll make you kiss my bloody ass you keep this up."

Ecuum chuckled. "Anyway, a little hero worship will be worth a hundred ships to this fleet. It's already given people hope that we will succeed. And, more importantly, it'll keep Sun from making any moves. For now."

"And how is Sun taking this?"

Ecuum considered his words before he spoke. "The terms you gave Sun were . . . generous. You gave him a lot of maneuvering room, and I expect he'll use it. I will say that your offer of command of the Olympus assault was a stroke of genius. I'll teach you to play *Gaman Politic* yet. However, I hope you understand that if you ever let him lead such an assault, he won't come back."

Ray nodded, though he didn't like the idea of breaking a promise, even to Sun. Looking up at Ecuum, he could see there was something more. "What else?"

For a brief second, red clashed with pale white beneath Ecuum's skin before returning to neutral pink. "We've got a leak. A serious one." He glanced at Gen Tel, who simply stood there, impassive as always. After a moment, Ecuum went on. "While I'm not on the best of terms with my Cartel, I still have several high-level sources. They tell me that Imperial Intelligence received our entire order of battle before the Tocci strike, right down to the last ship and commander."

Ray almost said "That's impossible" but he was becoming too well versed in *Gaman Politic* to dismiss it. "So, does that mean Serenna is receiving regular reports of our activities here?"

"Without doubt," Ecuum said with another glance at Gen Tel. "But my sources also tell me that the Emperor demoted The Serpent and removed her from command. Gen Nasser now leads the Imperial forces."

"Nasser?" Ray asked, though it wasn't a question. "They couldn't have made a worse choice. He's as close to a loose cannon as a Gen can get."

"I would not underestimate him, Admiral," Gen Tel said. "He has shown remarkable boldness in politics, even if he has no combat experience. And Admiral Gen Serenna retains a position on his staff."

Ecuum rounded on Gen Tel. "And how would you know that?"

"I, too, have sources within the Imperium," Gen Tel answered.

"Yeah, and maybe the information flows both ways."

"Does yours?" Gen Tel countered, arching an eyebrow. "It is well known information is the Cartels' most lucrative business. How far can you trust those you confide in?"

Ecuum floated closer to Gen Tel, his tail lashing. "The leak came after we picked you up at Tomb, Gen."

"You also picked up Admiral Sun and his entire task force," Gen Tel responded, his haughty demeanor unfazed. "Any of the captains or their staffs would have had access to the disposition of the fleet."

"That's not a denial."

"Would a denial make any difference?"

"No."

They stared at each other. Ray might've laughed if the situation weren't so tense. Still, they could both be right. And they could both be wrong. Either way, he was not about to start any witch hunts. "I need more than speculation." Ecuum started to protest but Ray cut him off. "From both of you."

They nodded, albeit reluctantly.

Ray leaned back and took another sip of water. "We can't stay here. We'll wait another three days, gather as many people as we can, leave a warning for any others who might follow. Nasser will start to feel confident by then. We'll jump to Andromeda before he arrives."

50

Admiral Gen Serenna knew who it was when the chime sounded. "Make yourself comfortable," she called, getting up from her desk at the back of her cabin and walking to her couch. "Coffee," she called as she sat, crossing her legs causally. "Would you like anything?"

"Tea," Gen Cardinal said, his construct taking a seat in the chair to her left. "Earl Gray, a daub of honey."

Solaris dutifully produced two bulbs through the faux glass coffee table between them. Serenna lifted hers, took a sip. "What can I do for you?"

Gen Cardinal picked up his bulb of tea but did not drink. "Fleet Admiral Gen Nasser is moving forward with his New Yerkes plan. He intends to commit the bulk of the SIL fleet to its execution, roughly eight hundred ships. He believes it's our last chance to stop the rebels before they leave for Andromeda."

"Fabricators?" Serenna asked after another sip of coffee.

Gen Cardinal drank his tea, pointedly looking at Serenna as he did, almost as if to say, "I am trusting you this is not poisoned." Serenna was not quite sure how to take that. Did he really trust her? Or did he only want her to believe he did? He placed the bulb back on the coffee table. "The Emperor won't allow the fabricators to leave Olympus space."

Serenna took a sip of coffee to give herself a moment to think. How far could she trust Gen Cardinal? Given her demotion and isolation from Gen Nasser and his staff, she needed an ally. Gen

Cardinal would know that. "We are not going to defeat the Naturals until we are willing to take risks."

His dark eyes studied her. "We took risks. Twice. We lost."

She put her bulb down on the table. "It is not a risk if victory is certain. Both times we believed it was, so in our minds it was not a risk."

The left corner of his lips curved up ever so slightly. "Point accepted. I will keep you apprised of Gen Nasser's plans since he is not seeking your counsel. You still believe it is the wrong plan, I take it? Do you believe Admiral Rhoades will take the bait?"

"Admiral?" This was news. Last she had heard he might be dead.

Gen Cardinal steepled his fingers in front of his chest. "After Tocci, the rebels formed a civilian council, led by Mary Rhoades. The council promoted Rhoades to full admiral and placed him in overall command."

"Chengchi?" Serenna asked. He was not the type to surrender power. Was he even still alive? That word "impossible" flitted at the edge of thought, but she refused to acknowledge it.

Gen Cardinal again studied her with those almost-black eyes. "Rhoades' second in command."

"That is . . . unexpected." She glanced at the painting of Gen Kii's assassination, the assassin male instead of female. Michael instead of Cyra Dain. Had Gen Alyn known? "If Michael is truly in command, he will jump for Andromeda. He knows escaping the Five Galaxies is his surest route to victory, or at least, reconciliation. We must attack him at 30 Doradus with everything we have immediately, before he can escape. If he reaches Andromeda, this war will grow and span years, maybe even decades. Our victory cannot be guaranteed."

Gen Cardinal lowered his hands to his lap. "What do you believe Rhoades will find there?"

Serenna regarded him, his question her answer. The Emperor had already decided against an attack on 30 Doradus and supported Gen Nasser's plan. It was a symptom of the same failings she had witnessed at Tocci. "When the Cavalry forces broke through into the Headquarters Complex in Tocci City, they cornered the surviving Gen in the command bunker. A thousand Gen packed together like cattle. Civilians. Purpose bred and Nurtured for their civilian roles. I urged them to fight. They outnumbered the Naturals at least two to one. When the base commander tried to surrender, the Natural officer in charge did not just stab him, he gutted the commander and cut off his head."

Serenna swallowed, the image burned into her memory as vivid as if she were watching it in real time. "The other Gen just stood there. Not one of them tried to fight as the Naturals slaughtered them." She picked up her bulb and sipped some coffee, still perfectly blended and hot the way she liked it. Gen Cardinal watched her without visible reaction.

She focused on him. "I watched the Madu attack I unleashed upon the starliner, all of it, never once feeling sympathy or empathy for the Naturals. I knew at the time the attack was a mistake, but I carried out my orders. I knew, one day, that attack would have consequences. At Tocci, I watched those consequences play out, and learned something about our society that assaulted the very core of my beliefs. Our race, engineered and Nurtured in peacetime, is not ready for this war. Given our current practices, it will take over two decades to adjust our engineering and Nurturing techniques. The Naturals—Michael—with the help of four fabricators, will defeat us long before then."

Gen Cardinal watched her. If he was not an ally, she had just given him everything he needed to declare her a traitor and recommend her execution. She had learned at least one thing from Michael, though: Sometimes one had to risk it all. Gen Cardinal seemed to come to some conclusion, evidenced only by a firming of his facial muscles. "The Emperor never intended to execute you; he had already decided your punishment before the meeting began. Your speech almost changed his mind."

This time Serenna waited and watched. Let *him* talk. His thin lips pressed into something that resembled a smile. "Stable government requires at least three powers always kept in check, so no one dominates the others. In the Republic, it was an Executive

Branch, a Legislative Branch, and the Judicial Branch. In the Empire, it is the Emperor, the Director of Imperial Intelligence, and the head of the military. That was—that *is*—supposed to be you."

Serenna put the bulb back on the table. So, her demotion was temporary. If she remained useful. And loyal. But loyal to whom? She would give her life to save the Empire, to save her people. Risk whatever that required. Was it disloyal to identify flaws in the system and recommend changes? A *very* dangerous question. A belief in her impending death had made her uncharacteristically foolish. It was a mistake she would not repeat.

"I do not know the answer to your question, Director," Serenna said. "I imagine I have studied the same records on Andromeda that you have, that Michael has. Ships moved freely between the Milky Way and Andromeda throughout the Alien Actions that followed the Solthari War. It was not until after the Cybernetics under Cyra Dain mysteriously vanished that expeditions and probes to Andromeda began disappearing. That could be coincidence, but I find it curious."

His eyes became unfocused, as if he were reliving a memory. *He knows something.* What he said was, "If the Cybernetics are behind the disappearances, do you believe Rhoades will survive them?"

Curious. So, this is the answer. "I do not know anything about their capabilities," she answered honestly. "However, we have seen how resourceful Michael is."

"Indeed," he said. "Can he be persuaded to go to New Yerkes?"

"No," she answered immediately. "I would instead focus on this council they have created. If they are following the Republic model, Michael will answer to them."

"Thank you, my dear Serenna," Gen Cardinal said, standing up.

Before his construct melted back into the deck, she warned, "If Michael survives, the Empire will fall. You *must* destroy him."

Acknowledgements

Once again, I can't possibly thank enough the marvelous writers of the Columbia Writers' Group from the Maryland Writers' Association: Robin Peace, Rissa Miller, Peter Pollak, and Susan Darvas, thank you so much.

To PJ, Chad, and Randy, my first fans, thank you for believing and for your support.

About the Author

Mark Mora served in the Army, worked for the Navy, and has loved Science and Fiction—especially when those two passions come together—since childhood. He currently lives in Colorado with his wife and three children. Visit him at: www.markmoraauthor.com

Preview of Andromeda Rhoades Tranquility
The Local War (Book 3)

1555 UT, October 17, 3501
Bent Fort New Yerkes, Nerney Star System: DAY 20

Dag's Mobile Command Post, basically an oversized, unarmed Serpens Infantry Fighting Vehicle, lurched over a curb with a jolt that went straight to his kidneys. "Easy, son," he told his young driver, a blond eighteen-year-old kid from some backspace planet in the Sagittarius dwarf. Not that he'd wanted to know that, but the kid wouldn't shut up. *Nerves.* Dag would trade an entire tank platoon right now to have Corporal Lance back as his driver.

"Sorry, sir," the kid said. "I just got my license last week." The Mobile Command Post pulled up to the side of a low building across from the armory and jerked to a stop. "Sorry, sir," the kid said again.

Dag bit back a retort: yelling at the kid would only make him more nervous. Instead, he focused on organizing his battle armor's augmented environment to manage the battle. As he'd done on Tocci III, he placed the 2nd Armored Cavalry Regiment's icons in an anchored window to his bottom front, and a map of the base in another window to his left. To his right, he added a window containing intelligence information and text versions of all communications. Six operators cloistered within a cramped compartment behind him continually updated the data and handled the "noise"—requests for supplies, intelligence, medical assistance, etc.—so he could focus on the big picture. Lieutenant DeWitt sat in an identical Mobile Command Post at the other end of the formation and would take over if Dag's vehicle were hit.

So far, the Imperial Marines hadn't launched a full assault. Dag credited that to the delaying tactics DeWitt had organized from Destructor Company—1st Squadron's artillery company. But that time had come at a price. Already, red stained seventeen regimental vehicle icons, and that didn't include the individual warriors slowing the Marine advance with man-portable weapons.

"Sir," one of the operators called. "Aggressor Troop reports full weapons load. Bane Troop is loading now."

A round exploded close by, followed by small-arms fire.

"This is taking too long," Dag muttered. He selected Aggressor Troop's icon and keyed the LoCIN. "Alpha-four-three, this is delta-six-six. Form a defensive perimeter north of Point Alpha. Over."

"Roger, delta-six-six," the lieutenant in charge of Aggressor Troop responded. "Over and out."

Over and out. That lieutenant didn't even know proper radio procedure and he commanded an understrength trainee Troop preparing to fight the Emperor's own Imperial Marines. God must be laughing. Dag found himself hoping nothing went wrong with Rhoades' plan—nothing else, he amended—or the 3rd Armored Cavalry Regiment wouldn't survive their landing.

He keyed the LoCIN again to talk to Lieutenant DeWitt. "Whiskey-two-one, this is delta-six-six: we won't get the regiment through the alphas in time. Are there any other alphas we can use? Over." If they could spread vehicle ammo loading to more armories, maybe they could speed this up.

"Yes, delta-six-six. There's one about five clicks—"

"That's fine, two-one," Dag interrupted before DeWitt could give away the location; even laser links could be intercepted, especially here within the Fort. "I'll keep the First with me and drive to the Hotel in fifteen mikes," Dag said. "You direct the others to that alpha, then join them in Lima as soon as possible. Over." Hotel was the Headquarters Complex. Lima was the landing field.

"Uh," DeWitt stammered as he tried to puzzle that out. "Yeah. Uh, Wilco, sir. Over."

"Six-six out." Dag keyed the LoCIN off before he changed his mind. *This is insane.* But they had to hold the Marines or 3rd Cav would walk into a trap.

An explosion ripped through the building behind the Mobile Command Post, showering them with duraplast and wallboard. Turning to the map, Dag saw the Gen still more than five kilometers away and not in a direct line of sight to his position. He checked for the ballistic track of an indirect round, but couldn't find one. Another explosion blew a hole in the side of the building not two meters from the Command Post. He quickly keyed the LoCIN. "Cease fire! This is delta-six-six. Cease fire!"

"Oh, Fates!" a young voice said. "We're sorry, we didn't, you see, we—"

"Shut up!" Dag shouted. "Check your targets before you fire, and wait for my orders, dammit!"

A sheepish voice whispered, "Yes, sir. We're sorry, sir. It won't happen again, sir."

"It better not," Dag scolded. "Now get off the air. Out." He shook his head, and found himself grateful the kid in that tank couldn't shoot straight. Of course, that lack of skill would probably get that kid and his crew killed.

Papí?

Dag heard sniffles. With his armor in tactical mode, he could see the surrounding streets and intersection as if he sat in midair above the ground. He quickly looked around and saw Rosita hiding behind the Mobile Command Post. She leaned against the vehicle, scrunched up like a ball, holding her ankles and sobbing.

Papí, you're scaring me.

She said that sometimes when he yelled. "Sorry, Mihita, I didn't mean to scare you."

I don't like it when you yell.

"I know, Mihita. I'll try not to do it again. I promise."

You mean it?

"Yes, Mihita."

She lifted her head just a little, her eyes red, and smiled. It was good to have her back.

Calmer, Dag asked, "Load status?"

"Bane Troop nearing completion," an operator said. All the operators kept glancing at him, but he didn't know why.

Dag nodded. "Good. Thank you."

The operator gave a tentative nod and a hesitant smile, much like Rosita had.

They're young and scared, Dag thought. *I need to stay calm. If I'm calm, they will be, too.*

He checked the status of the Regiment in his environment. They'd placed sensor discs—what troopers called "waffles" because they looked like large round Belgian waffles—on rooftops and in windowed rooms to look for heat signatures from Gen vehicles, personnel, or weapons. They also served to maintain their LoCIN line-of-sight laser links. Other waffles lay upon the streets in plates only a few molecules thick, acting as pressure sensors. Six more overflew the area.

He repositioned a few of Aggressor Troops' vehicles to better meet the Marines, then, seeing that Bane Troop had finished loading, ordered them down a side street to begin their drive on the Headquarters Complex. If they could take that, they might just keep the Gen and Marines in check long enough for the 3rd to land and deploy.

Explosions and small-arms fire drew Dag back to the map window. The lead elements of a Marine armored column, tracked as they drove over the waffles, had picked up speed as they encountered Aggressor Troop's forward observers. He waited for Aggressor Troop's commander to call in mortar fire. And waited. Another explosion echoed down the street, a tank main gun round by the sound of it. A Serpens Infantry Fighting Vehicle icon, one of his, turned red.

Dag selected Aggressor Troop's icon and called in the mortar fire himself. He checked the Marines' movements again. They had deployed in three columns, the largest charging down the main street leading to the armory, with two smaller columns guarding the flanks on adjacent streets. Aggressor Troop's waffle pressure plates weighed each vehicle that passed over and identified its type. From that information, the SIL Mobile Command Post concluded that they faced a tank-heavy Imperial Marine battalion.

Expanding the map window, Dag gauged the effect his mortar fire had—or rather, didn't have. Rounds landed behind the enemy's advance elements, struck buildings, and a few even came danger-close to Aggressor Troop's own units. One round finally landed in the main street, the flash-bang of its plasma warhead briefly blinding the sensors. Buildings burst into flames from the intense heat, but the sensors recorded no secondary explosions. He considered switching to antimatter rounds, but dismissed that. The smallest AM warhead had a nominal yield of a quarter kiloton, too large to risk so close to his own troops and civilians.

Challenger Troop finally finished loading and he ordered them to assault the Headquarters Complex down a different side street than Bane Troop—and prayed the young recruits wouldn't get lost. Dag knew he should lead that attack, but if Aggressor Troop didn't hold the line here the Marines would roll right over the other Troops long before they reached the Complex.

Two new explosions rocked the main street. Gray silhouettes highlighted two Aggressor Troop tanks parked in alleys on either side of the street. Both had fired and missed the tank at the head of the enemy's column.

Where in Hell did these people learn to shoot? But Dag didn't say that out loud.

Both tanks fired again, this time hitting their target. The kinetic rounds penetrated the tank's front armor and blew it apart from within. Secondary explosions blinded the sensors. The two tanks fired again, and again. Even when the sensors cleared, Dag couldn't see what they fired at. He keyed the LoCIN. "Aggressor Troop, conserve your ammunition. Fall back to secondary positions."

One tank stayed in the alley and continued firing blindly. The other moved *into the street* instead of falling back down the alley. Both blew apart at nearly the same instant.

Red text flashed in Dag's environment: INCOMING. Projected impact points appeared in his map seconds before the first rounds struck. Hundreds of white flashes consumed Aggressor Troop's positions, followed a few seconds later by loud crackling sounds—cluster munitions. CM rounds were deadly to exposed troops but far less effective against armor. But they had another, more devastating effect. Within the space of about a minute, they destroyed all but two waffles, drove individual troopers in the buildings and on the rooftops into cover, and broke the LoCIN communications links Dag needed to conduct the battle. At about the same time, the feed from his aerial waffles went dead.

The sounds of battle drew closer. Several troopers broke and ran, some of them without their weapons. Two Serpens charged out into the main street. Without LoCIN, Dag keyed the AFCIN, not caring that the Gen might hear, to order them back, but the one closest to the enemy exploded. The other veered off, its troopers bailing out before it stopped. "Aggressor Troop—" how idiotic that name sounded now— "Hold your ground! We can't let these Marines break through!"

More vehicles broke into the open, firing wildly behind them as they retreated. Rounds struck friendly vehicles, adding to the confusion. "Hold your positions!" Still they fled. "STAND AND FIGHT, DAMMIT!"

But it did no good. The battle had become a rout. Dag thought of staying, of trying to rally the troopers, but knew his death would mean defeat for the entire Regiment. He owed them better than that. "Driver, get us out of here. Join up with Bane Troop."

The kid punched the accelerator, sending the Mobile Command Post careening forward *into* the main street. The vehicle lurched as the driver realized his mistake, nearly throwing Dag from his seat despite the bond with his battle armor.

Dag looked up the street. Fire and smoke consumed every building, burning debris and fuels turning the street into a solid sheet of flame.

Except for one rectangular patch.

Screams filled the compartment. Troopers bailed out of the vehicle. Only the kid, the driver, remembered to take his weapon.

Papí, this way.

He saw Rosita get up and start running down the street, away from the Marines.

Dag grabbed his weapon and dove through the skin of the Mobile Command Post to the street opposite the enemy. He rolled out and was just about to start running when a pressure wave from the exploding vehicle knocked him flat. His battle armor protected him from the intense heat.

He pushed himself back up and ran for all he was worth, following Rosita in the direction of Bane Troop.

Printed in Great Britain
by Amazon

49595358R00219